THE GUIDAL
UNEARTHING SECRETS

BY ROXY ELOISE

CONTENTS

DEDICATION

This book is dedicated to all the people who brought my debut to life. It's for the readers whose words encourage me to keep going. And it's for those who keep my dream alive. Without you, I would still be living in my imagination, escaping reality.

I would also like to give a special mention to Nicole Bible, my WBFL! This book wouldn't be what it is without you. Also to Jack for enabling me to write for endless hours without needing to move. And finally to my parents for always being supportive and encouraging me on my journey.

ACKNOWLEDGEMENT

I really need to thank all the people involved in bringing this book to publication. I especially couldn't have done it without my beta readers. Thank you to you all. I don't know all of your names, but for those I do, I would like to give a special mention to: Nicole Bible, Louisa Norvall, Joely Marshall, Ronin Wing, Kee Nethery, and Yaren Nisa. All of you have had an input in the final draft, and I'm so glad I listened to your feedback.

I would like to say a big thank you to Haileybury Turnford for inviting me back to motivate your students. My passion for writing ignited in your school over a decade ago, and I love returning to encourage current students to write. Fingers crossed, I'll get to read the books of budding authors who walk the same corridors I used to.

Lastly, I'd like to thank Entrada Publishing for believing in The Guidal and giving it a home.

If you're enjoying The Guidal Series and you'd like to show your support, please leave a review. Thank you.

CHAPTER ONE

AN UNEXPECTED GUEST

When I opened my wardrobe, piercing-blue eyes greeted me, sending a sudden raspy inhale down my throat. My clenched fist reacted, throwing itself out on impulse.

"*Tayo*," I grunted on my exhale.

His large black pupils gawked at my knuckles hovering an inch away from his nose. He slowly lowered my fist, telling me to '*relax*' in his mind. When he grabbed the door to lever himself out, I shoved him back and closed him in the dark, waiting on the other side with my feet crossed. After some noisy clambering, the mirrored door slid open again, and a dishevelled Tayo emerged.

"Ow." He rubbed the back of his head, his jet-black hair looking even messier than normal.

"What are you doing here, Tayo?" I folded my arms.

"You wouldn't respond to my messages; what else was I supposed to do?"

"Get the hint?"

Tayo's shoulders slunk. "Roar, I'm sorry."

"I know. You've said—every day for two weeks."

"I added a 'really' to the message every day." He twisted his lip into a timid smile.

"Yeah, I got that, thanks. Day two: I'm really sorry. Day three: I'm really, really sorry. The stupid message is a page long now." I took my Slate out from my pocket and threw it onto the bed. "Tayo, you were going to match me in Unity. That's an arranged marriage—you understand that?"

Tayo's gaze dropped to the floor panels.

"Well, do you?" I demanded an answer, not willing to accept his silence as an attempted apology. "At least the Unity assessment tries to find a partner 'science' considers compatible. You—*you* were just going to marry me off with some random boy. That was not your decision to make, and the only reason you didn't was down to chance. *Chance*, Tayo. Not from having second thoughts—*chance*."

"Roar, I was doing it for you." He found the courage to look at me again. "How else were you going to be assigned this room? How else were you going to have access to the tunnel in the wardrobe?"

"I should've been allowed to make that decision."

"Are you telling me you haven't missed me?" Tayo crept forward, tidying up his wayward hair. His sides were freshly tapered, but the top remained unkempt. "Not even a little bit?"

I backed away, moving to the centre of the room. "Whether I've missed you or not is beside the point."

"Please forgive me, Roar." He tilted his head to the side, flicking his jet-black fringe out from his entreating eyes.

When he tried to come closer, I sidestepped around him, easily avoiding his attempt to block me. I ducked under his outstretched arm and swirled behind him.

He spun on the spot quickly, trying harder to capture me. "Please, Roar."

Trying to keep a straight face, I evaded him, and we continued this dance for a while until Tayo yielded. He knew he was never going to catch me unless I wanted him to. So, he huffed and retreated to my comfy super-sized bed. After discarding his black leather jacket, he propped a few pillows against the display screen and slumped himself into them, sitting with his legs outstretched. My eyes were drawn to his tattoo sleeve, over the bold black ink embodying his masculinity. Realising I was staring, I threw my gaze down onto my white socks.

Tayo found something by my pillow and held it up. "You haven't been pining for me, no?" He lightly flapped a creased piece of paper.

"That's a drawing of me."

"Yeah, but one I drew for your birthday."

"So?"

"Come on, Roar." He dropped his arm inertly. "How long are you going to be mad at me?"

Shrugging, I turned away, blocking out the sorrowful expression on his face. I took a sweep of the room, the desk, the door, the corner sofa, and the platform steps around the bed, all the way until I lifted my eyes to check on him again. Every movement, from fiddling with the paper in his hands to sweeping the hair from his eyes, tempted me to move closer to him. He caught my eye, and I averted my gaze.

"I know something about your Unity assessment that I think you'll want to know." He crossed his legs at the ankles.

I brushed nothing off my navy jacket and answered without looking at him. "What do you know?"

"Come and sit down, and I'll tell you." He moved my Slate onto the floating bedside table, creating a space beside him.

"Fine, but that doesn't mean I want to sit with you, it just mea—"

"Shut up and come sit down."

I narrowed my eyes whilst hating myself for wanting to sit there. Then I perched at the foot of the mattress, resting my feet on the platform steps. Tayo arched his perfect eyebrows, having no intention of speaking until I shuffled in a little farther, sitting with my legs crossed like a child in front of an instructor.

"Go on, then." I folded my arms tightly across my chest.

"Your best friend, Pipila"—he smirked, knowing full well we were not even friends—"didn't match in Unity. Out of curiosity, I checked her results after checking yours. She didn't have a match."

"She and Ryker both cheated and ended up matching with each other."

"You can't cheat the test, Roar. Changing your answers doesn't do anything. There's a lot more to that assessment than just answering questions."

"So how did they match?"

"Boulderfell picks the families he wants his biological children to marry into. I've told you before, he is a bloody weirdo."

"You know what?" My brow furrowed as I pulled on my lip. "It's so obvious those two don't get on. They're always arguing."

"Now you know why." He relaxed deeper into the pillows, turning on his side a little.

"Well, that explains why she's trying to end the betrothal to Ryker. If she manages a high score, she'll be leaving with Pax."

"You never told me how Pax was ending your betrothal. What's he getting a high score in?"

"The machines we use for training. A first-place spot on the scoreboards gets you an invitation to enrol at the *Boulderfell Institute for Fell Agents.*"

"I know that place. They use the same software as here. The company I work for does their systems, too. Maximum Security, right?"

"Yeah, in Avalon of Second City."

"You know"—Tayo stopped fiddling with the drawing in his hands to fix his round eyes on me—"Fell agents dedicate their lives to Boulderfell. They actually pledge a vow of celibacy and swear never to take a husband or wife. They can't have children, and once they're an agent, they can't leave. They fully commit themselves to protecting—"

"Okay, please stop."

"What's the matter?" Tayo's charming face suddenly grew deep with creases as he fixed me with a stare.

"Pax is putting himself through all that just to get away from me. He doesn't even want to be an Enforcer, so there's no chance he wants to be a Fell agent." The lump building in my throat thickened, and I swallowed it. "He is doing it because of me."

Tayo lifted his arm and waved me over, raising his eyebrows questioningly. I pulled my fists into my stomach, leaning away and deciding whether to move. Did I forgive him? Should I forgive him?

My eyes skidded down his outstretched arm and across his chest, taking in the defined muscles under his black T-shirt. I could almost feel my head resting on him, his strong arms wrapped around my shoulders. Shaking my head to silence my thoughts, I followed a longing and crawled into his arms, allowing my body to relax deeply against him. I couldn't help but imagine what his skin would feel like under his T-shirt. I wanted to run my hand over his chest, feeling the heat radiating from his body.

Glancing over his lean waist and long legs, I remembered him in his Juvie overalls. Not so long ago, touching Tayo in this way was an off-limits fantasy, figments of my perverse imagination. I rubbed my fingers together, fighting with the temptation to lift his top. My fingers started to fiddle with the hem on his T-shirt, inching it closer and closer to his bare stomach. When my little finger grazed the hot skin above his boxers, my senses awakened, becoming totally absorbed by it. I kept subtly stroking my knuckle over the small soft area, all whilst pretending it was unintentional.

Tayo held me tighter, resting his chin on my head. "Pax is leaving because he's a coward."

"Practising magic is punishable by death, which means I'm a death sentence for him."

"It's not something you chose." A hint of annoyance coloured his tone. "He abandoned you when you were scared and needed him the most."

"I know." I sighed at the memory. "But he has his own issues. He sees rule-breaking as the reason he is here. If his parents had kept to the rules, he'd be living in the city, happily being raised by them."

"You're all spoiled little brats here. He hasn't got it so bad."

I stopped playing with the hem of his T-shirt and kept my little finger still, trying to pay attention. "I know what I would rather..." My mind wandered on to my parents. If they were still alive, I would definitely choose them. "And anyway, sounds like you were a spoiled brat growing up, too."

"I was. I don't deny that. With two parents on Band A, earning four Worths per hour each, I had everything I could possibly want." His voice was deep, and I honed in on the way it resonated through his chest. I imagined the words leaving his lips, seeing the way his tongue moved between them. "They were annoyingly strict, but still, I'd always do as I pleased. They made me a recoiling spring. If they hadn't pushed so hard, I wouldn't have resisted so hard."

"It's strict here, too, you know?" I tilted my head back to see his mouth. The last time I saw him, we had our first kiss. If I kept my lips within reach, maybe he would do it again.

"Yeah, but it's different here." Tayo covered my eyes with both hands and pushed my head back onto his chest, holding my forehead down with interlaced fingers. "You're all made to feel like princes and princesses ruling over a kingdom. You're raised to believe you are better than us out in the city. That pathetic marching display you put on every week is so transparent."

My attempt to instigate more had fallen flat, and stiffness was setting into my neck and shoulders. Surely, he wouldn't embrace me like this if he only saw me as a friend. But why wasn't he trying anything? Starting to feel something solid building inside my chest, I took my little finger off his skin.

"Do you want to know something else about the test?" He let go of my forehead.

I chewed my fingernail, unable to fathom why he didn't want to kiss me. "What?"

"You had a real close second match."

"*Who*?" I sat up, taking the opportunity to get off him.

Tayo grimaced and shook his head. "Ryker."

"Oh, shut up. You're winding me up."

"I'm really not."

"Ryker Boulderfell?" My head dropped forward, sharp pains streaking through my stiff neck. "The sarky, antagonistic slimeball?"

"The very one."

"What the hell does that say about me?" I hid my face in my hands. *Ryker Boulderfell? There's no way.*

He cupped both my cheeks and lifted my head, looking me in the eyes. "My little Roar has a dark side."

"I don't have a dark side." I frowned but my words lost their oomph, becoming distracted by his warm hold on my face. I froze, looking between each of his dazzling blue eyes. My gaze dropped to his lips, but he let go of my cheeks, a weird sympathetic expression sweeping his face.

"I best get going." His mouth twisted in an unconvincing smile.

"What?" I felt my chest crunch as if suddenly stamped on. "Why?"

"I'm at work in the morning. Becoming a Juvie only suspended my employment. I didn't lose my job."

My head shook as words failed me. "Okay." I crawled backwards off the bed, rushing to open the wardrobe.

He lifted the panel in the wardrobe floor and paused, his eyes squinting lightly. "Do you want to see me tomorrow?"

I nodded quickly, a little wave elevating my chest. "Do you want to see me?"

His lips lifted into a real smile crinkling his bright eyes. "Yes." He kept my gaze as he climbed down the ladder, his cheeks softly blushing. I let the panel go and gave a relieved sigh, rubbing the tension from my neck. Something was definitely up, but he still wanted to see me. That had to be a good sign. I had so much I wanted to tell him. He was the only person who knew I was Puracordis, and now I had something even better to share with him.

But it would have to wait.

CHAPTER TWO
UNDISCLOSED SOURCE

The next day, I kept my Slate close to hand, constantly checking for notifications. After finding a blank home screen once again, I shoved it into my combat pocket, grateful to be heading into the classroom for an hour of history. The special chairs called augreals offered great escapism, fully immersing the user in a virtual reality world. I climbed up into the augreal next to Silliah, placed on my headset, and waited for Sir Praeter to recline our chairs.

The soft leather took my weight as the augreal tilted backwards. My eyes grew heavier until I could no longer keep them open, and then the darkness behind my eyelids filled with a sheet of white. When my new eyes adjusted to the brightness, a heavy fog obscured my vision. I coughed, feeling it stick to the back of my throat, the ashy smell of burning seeping into my lungs. Screaming and shouting assaulted my ears as bodies created havoc around me.

I hopped backwards, narrowly avoiding the squealing fire engine tearing up the old tarmac road. A long, blocky building, unlike anything we had in our city, was engulfed in flames. Crowds were throwing bottles at it whilst riot police flailed their little black poles. Old money littered the ground like autumn leaves, nobody bothering to collect it.

"Twenty-first century," shouted Silliah over the sirens, emerging from the chaos and hooking my arm. "London, I think."

She looked exactly the same but no longer wore her Navy uniform, now sporting high-waisted jeans with a white crop top. I checked my outfit, pleased my vest didn't reveal my midriff and also appreciative of the flat white trainers. We escaped the haze and sat on the curb, watching the burning building from a distance.

"Humans do not always get it right the first time." A voice resounded from the smoke-infested heavens. It was slightly robotic, like Soami the digital assistant, but with a formal tone. "We make mistakes and learn our lessons from them. The devastation you are witnessing came as a result of poor decision-making. The collapse of the old-world currency caused major upheaval, eventually calling for a new system: the Worths system."

Our surroundings disintegrated until we were watching a room of suited officials in a conference, all sitting behind microphones. My classmates lined the aisles on either side. We were also trussed up in old Seioh-Jennson-style suits.

The female voice continued from the domed ceiling, "Spearheaded by the late Seioh John Boulderfell, the world's richest families formulated a collective of new-world leaders, each responsible for rebuilding a section of the world. Deprivation, homelessness, disease, famine, and poverty became a thing of the past." Images of the old world flashed before us: starving people with prominent rib cages, sick children crowded in hospital beds, and beggars in torn, dirty clothing. "With each leader allocated the rule of seven cities, our human race began to thrive." We were taken into an empty, white space until we plummeted towards a city. My hair flew off my shoulders whilst my clothes flapped furiously and my stomach kept rolling. "Time is the most valuable commodity"—the voice surrounded me, coming from everywhere and nowhere— "so precious you are unable to buy more. Thus, time became the new currency, an intelligent and equitable system providing resources based on the number of hours spent working. Seioh Borgon Boulderfell and his board of trustees oversee the project and have been the governing body for the pilot country Venair since 2060."

Our freefall slowed, and we landed lightly on our feet outside the institute, our clothes morphing into our Navy uniforms. Silliah had time to grin at me before the voice came back. "Vencen, the capital city of Venair: home to the world's first institute for underprivileged children. Given a secure and safe upbringing, as well as a sense of purpose, these children are raised to be well-rounded individuals who serve the people of Vencen."

The ground disappeared from beneath our boots, and we hovered above another city, considerably larger than Vencen. The infrastructure was the same, still circular, with the side roads and streets all in uniform quarters, meeting with four main roadways drawn like a cross through the city. "Avalon of Second City: a place where these children become integral members of society, keeping the whole of Venair safe." We were above a glass building, domed and circular, the words 'Boulderfell Institute for Fell Agents' written digitally above the door.

Before I'd managed a good look, the class was soaring over another city, this one full of skyscrapers and large buildings. I looked around for Silliah, seeing her taking full advantage of her avatar by corkscrewing through the air with her arms wide open. Other Navies began copying her until fear of missing out made me join in. The exhilarating rush of wind made my eyes water, and a laugh bubbled up from deep inside me. Becoming dizzy, I brought my avatar to a halt, standing myself upright. "Faden of Third City," said the female narrator, "where business predominates and its economic impact extends worldwide."

Another city replaced this one, and our avatars were lowered to the ground.

"Gotta love history," said Silliah, her long walnut-brown fringe swept back from the flight.

Around us, elderly people were swimming whilst some were reading eBooks under parasols. Others played handheld computer consoles and digital board games. "Celestine of Fourth City," said the narrator, "a retirement city where elderly members of society reap the rewards of their lifetime commitment to Venair. This is a city where Worths allocation is disbanded and residents live freely, enjoying their time recreationally."

Soon, the swimming pool glitched, being replaced by a science laboratory. AI robots served the scientists, bringing them refreshments. "Gabbro of Fifth City," said the voice from nowhere. "It is here where advancements in technology are taken in leaps and bounds. With a population rich in innovative thinkers, it is the hub of all invention."

The science lab dissolved, and now Kalmayans roamed streets of simple houses. Orange and brown clothing hung on washing lines as children played and adults cooked on fires. Every individual from young to old had shaved hair and black facial tattoos. "Larimar of Sixth City," came the formal female voice, "the city where the old-world monarchy is still honoured. Home to the Kalmayans, it is located at the world's most famous prehistoric monument, Stonehenge. To show their gratitude for Seioh Boulderfell's generosity, they gifted the city of Vencen with a glass fountain, crafted and erected by the people of Larimar."

As quickly as the others, this city vanished and made way for a colourful city, modern in design. Bright flashing lights spiralled over the dancing crowd as loud music thumped through into my brain. A man in a tie-dye T-shirt ambled past me, his pupils large and his jaw rolling. "And finally," said the narrator from the sky, "Helidor of Seventh City: a place for the adventurous and inquisitive. Here alone, the controlled distribution of mind-altering substances allows its residents and visitors to experience induced euphoria. However, an intensive rehabilitation program is required before leaving the city."

After the narrator finished explaining the history of the schooling system and how it hadn't changed since the eighteenth century, we returned to our real bodies in the classroom. Sir Praeter dismissed the class, and Silliah linked my arm, leading us to the Food Hall for dinner.

"History is my favourite lesson," she said, leaving the Khakidemy. "I wish more of our lessons were on augreals."

"Yeah, history has to be my favourite too." I felt in my pocket for my Slate. "I had no idea the cities weren't all the same."

"I didn't either. Helidor of Seventh city looked fun. It was like a holiday destination. I mean, I wouldn't take drugs I don't think, but the festivals and dancing looked amazing."

All the way there, I kept checking my Slate for any messages from Tayo. When nothing came through whilst I scoffed my dinner, I rushed to my room and perched on the end of my bed, waiting. He'd asked if I wanted to see him, but he hadn't messaged me at all. At least when we weren't talking I would get an apology message from him daily. My fingers were starting to feel clammy around my smooth glass handset, so I threw it over by the pillows. I rested my head on my knees and tried to think of *anything* else.

My Slate buzzed, and I dived onto my belly.

'*Are you back from dinner?*'

'*Yes!*' I typed but urgently deleted it. Tayo would've seen I'd started typing, so I quickly wrote another response: '*Yeah. Just having a shower.*'

'*Alright. I'll see you in an hour.*'

An hour? Dammit. I should've said I'd just gotten out of the shower. *Idiot.* Giving a huff, I dragged myself into the ensuite and switched on the rainfall shower, sitting down in front of a row of jets. I had a lot of time to kill.

I wondered if Tayo would kiss me tonight. He had kissed me on his visit two weeks ago. What if he'd changed his mind? What if it was because I wasn't a good kisser? The thoughts returned the streaking pain in my neck. To take my mind off everything, I tried using magic to manipulate the water. I could use my mind to move objects and couldn't think why water would be any different. After imagining what I wanted the water to do, I tried to get it to pour harder. Nothing happened and I sighed. Surely, he still liked me in that way…right? *Shut up.*

When I exited the ensuite, my heart jumped into my throat. A black silhouette closed my wardrobe, but it only took me a second to register his lean frame, his jet-black messy hair, and his black leather jacket with the fabric hood, collar, and cuffs. My shoulders hunched as my bare feet wriggled against the floor panels.

"Roar." His bright-blue eyes smiled, a cheekiness beaming in them. He came straight over and engulfed my frame in a strong embrace, making me stumble and catch my balance by grabbing him tight. The cold leather cooled my warm cheeks, and his woody aftershave made me inhale long and slow. Tayo didn't stop walking me backwards until I'd circled around and touched the platform steps.

"God, I've missed you so much, you know that?" he mumbled into my neck.

A shiver threatened to trickle my spine as his breath fanned down my back. "It's been one day."

He stepped back and started removing his jacket and trainers. "I mean the last two weeks, not being able to see you, not being able to speak to you. I've seen you every day for nearly a whole year. I really missed that."

Missed 'that' as a friend? Unsure, I stopped watching him undress and lowered myself onto the bed, inspecting the strands of cotton weaving through my navy duvet. "Where have you been, anyway?" In my periphery, I saw him going around to the other side of the bed. "Why'd it take two weeks to come see me?"

"Oh yeah." Tayo sat by my side, leaving a gap between us. He wore a pair of those black combat-like trousers he loved so much, with the drop-crotch and baggy knees. "So," he said, sitting against the display screen, legs outstretched, "I was granted early release the morning after you tried to convince Poynter your birthmark wasn't real. I had no idea how it went and didn't know if you were safe or not, so I spoke to him about it when we left together. You did manage to convince him it wasn't real, so that was good, but then he told me something about hunting the 'Guidal.'"

"Yeah, we had the same conversation." My eyes kept flicking to the space between our bodies. "The Guidal is supposed to summon the darkness or some nonsense."

"Also something about devil or imposter or…I don't know. He's eight—making sense of anything he said was difficult. Well, anyway, that's where I've been. I arranged to stay with him. It's not easy to stay in Larimar of Sixth City because the Kalmayans are really paranoid and careful with who they allow in, but they've been watching me break Curfew since I was a kid and gave me permission to stay."

"They've been watching you break Curfew?" I repeated, unable to help my body angling towards him.

"It's alright. I've known about them watching me. They're breaking Curfew, too, so I knew I didn't have to worry."

"We do random night patrols, you know? To catch Curfew breakers."

"I do know," he said in a way that cemented me in the friend zone. "I've been breaking Curfew since I was six, and I upgrade the software that creates your schedules. I know more about this place than you do."

A puff of air escaped my lips. "Alright. Next stop: Arrogant Central. I think I'll let you get off there."

"*Let* me? I'm not your Juvie anymore, Roar."

"I could still *make* you get off." The gap between us felt huge. I couldn't help but think it was intentional. Feeling weird, I pushed him towards the edge of the bed with my foot.

Tayo grabbed my ankle to stop me. "Don't."

"Go on. This is your stop." I took no notice and pushed him again with my other heel. When he tried to take hold of that foot, I hooked my ankle around his neck, pulled his head towards me, wrapped the duvet over his face, and shoved him down the platform steps.

After a second of flailing, he crawled back onto the bed with his tongue in his cheek. "Aurora." He allowed the silence to reprimand me, planting himself firmly on the mattress before continuing, "You sleep, you know? And I have a way into your bedroom whenever I want."

The hollow look on his red face made my gut tighten. "That's just creepy," I mumbled, playing with my hands, desperately searching for a reset button.

"Do that again, and I'll put an ankle trap on you while you're asleep. Then I'll get my own back for all the times you used it to control me."

I nodded, feeling myself crumbling. *What did I just do?*

"That really hurt." He rubbed his lower back, getting comfortable against the pillows again.

"I'm sorry." My calves ached from beneath me, but the weight of silence held me there. I blinked at my lap. *I'm so stupid. I have to ruin everything.* Why couldn't I control myself, even when it really mattered?

"Hey, it's alright." Tayo's brow lifted. "It's fine." He held up his arm, inviting me in.

I crawled over, face-planting his chest. He rubbed my back, and I felt the tension leaving my shoulder blades. Relief poured over me as I inhaled his delicious, spicy scent. *Was this a friendly hug? Shut up, Aurora.*

Tayo spoke on a long inhale, "I best go."

"No." The word slipped out as I sat up. "Tayo, please, don't do that again. You were my best friend, but now you're feeling like a stranger. I'm so confused."

His forehead creased with worry. "You're still my best friend."

Friend... I swallowed and fiddled with the buttoned cuff on my pyjama shirt. Maybe it was better if he did go. I needed to build some defences before I fell for him too hard.

"Roar?" He touched my cheek and aligned his eyes to mine.

"Go on. You should go."

I didn't expect him to smirk, and now I was even more confused.

"What is this? Reverse psychology?" He stroked his knuckle along my jaw. The gentle tickle spread to my heart, and I pushed my cheek into his hand. "Hmm?" he hummed, patting my knee. "Why are you being weird?"

"Why are *you* being weird with me? Always rushing off suddenly."

Tayo sighed and linked his fingers, bringing his arms over to hug his bent knees. His eyes held steady on his legs, and my chest started to constrict, waiting to hear what was on his mind.

"I just want to do this right, you know?" He looked at me again. "We lead very different lives, and I just want to make sure you understand I'm not your Juvie anymore. That relationship, that dynamic is all we've ever known. It's killing me not"—he held his hands out, palms to the ceiling and gestured them at me—"but I need to know you see us as equal first."

"Of course we're equal. Does that mean I'm not friend-zoned?"

He scoffed in his throat and threw me a quizzical look. "What? You're not in the friend zone. Did my kiss last time not make that clear?"

"It wasn't last time."

His eyebrows rose, and he paused. Then he climbed onto his knees, running a hand behind my neck. "Does this make it clear?" Tayo pressed his lips to mine. My heart swelled, releasing warmth as it waned, washing through my legs and out through my toes. Brightness shone behind my eyelids, and I knew my skin expressed my innermost feelings. I curled my toes, controlling urges rising from their depths. When he pulled back, I tasted his kiss, reliving it, wanting him again. He sat back, leaning on both hands, one leg bent, the other stretched out beside me. His cheeks were the nice kind of pink, and my heart inflated once more. *Should I kiss him again? No, stop it. But maybe I didn't have to be a thirty-year-old virgin? Stop it.*

His lips held a tiny smile as his eyes roved over my glowing skin. It slowly faded, and Tayo met my gaze, his smile strengthening. "Clear?"

I nodded, still tasting my lips. "If you're staying, I've got a secret I want to tell you." I readjusted to sit cross-legged. "But I'm not allowed to tell you how I know it."

"Nanny Kimly."

"No. I'm not allowed to tell you how I know it."

"Nanny Kimly," he repeated in the same tone.

"Tayo—"

"I'm not going to tell anybody about her. Just tell me your secret."

"Everybody can do magic. It's called conjuring." I could feel my face brightening at his reaction, but then it dropped after seeing his mouth twist.

"I'm pretty sure I can't," he said, dropping onto his elbows. "I think I'd know if I was Puracordis."

"No, that's the thing, Tayo, we are all Puracordis. The reason you can't conjure is because of a pollutant in the water supply."

"Are you sure?" Tayo said sceptically. "Sounds like your Nanny Kimly is a bit of a conspiracy theorist."

I huffed, my head falling forward, catching my cheeks and resting my elbows on my knees. "I knew I should've waited until I could prove it to you."

"Prove it how?"

"Err, um, I'm waiting…"

"You're waiting for Nanny Kimly to?"

"*Tayo.*" I patted his shin beside me.

"Look, Roar"—he ducked his head to look me in the eyes, his messy fringe falling over his brows—"I know Nanny Kimly has told you not to tell anyone, but I was in the room when she saw you use magic. I know she knows about Puracordis, because otherwise, you'd be on death row. She's protecting you; she's definitely Puracordis."

"That's what I'm trying to say, Tayo, we are *all* descendants of Puracordis." My legs began to judder underneath me. "We can *all* conjure."

"You're positive?"

"Yes." I threw my knees down, holding them still. "There's a chemical called Cryxstalide in the water supply. It calcifies a part of the brain called the pineal gland and prevents conjuring."

"So why can you do it?"

I shrugged. "The Kalmayans are looking for—"

"The Guidal. You can do magic on the chemical because you're the Guidal?"

I shrugged again. "I guess?"

Tayo sat up from leaning on his elbows and crossed his legs like mine. "What has Nanny Kimly said about it?"

"Tayo." I gave him a desperate look. How many times did I have to tell him I couldn't speak of her?

"Aurora, enough. What do you want me to call her: 'You know who'? What? You can trust me."

"I know. Okay." I straightened up and flicked back my long white hair. "Nanny Kimly knows about Puracordis, but she's told me to never tell anyone."

"I'm not going to tell anyone, Roar, I promise. What does she know about the Guidal?"

"I'm not sure yet. She's told me to sit tight until she knows I'm safe. I told her about the Kalmayans hunting the bearer of my birthmark."

"You are safe. That's what I've been doing for the last two weeks. You can tell Nanny K you're safe. Poynter isn't going to tell anybody about you. You convinced him you're not the Guidal, and he said they would all laugh at him for even thinking you might've been."

"Oh, I feel so bad for him."

"You did what you had to, Roar. Don't feel bad. It was either that or be caught."

"Hmm." I played with the black streak in the front of my hair, inspecting the split ends. Tayo was right. If I hadn't lied to him, I would be in a much worse situation. I just wished my birthmark wasn't on my wrist in such an obvious place. It was lucky an eight-year-old, who could be easily fooled, was the first Kalmayan to see it. Things could've been a lot worse than a young boy feeling stupid.

"You know that huge door down there?" I stopped inspecting my hair to point at the wardrobe behind me. "It's the Puracordis Temple. Apparently, I can open the door, but Nanny Kimly has told me not to go down there just yet."

"Why not? Oh my God, come on, Roar. Should we go now?" Tayo swung his legs off the bed.

"No. You're terrible." I laughed, throwing a pillow at him. "The area is cordoned off, Tayo. Boulderfell *knows* about the temple."

"Nobody is ever around that house. I have a contact lens which allows me to see thermal radiation. I use it to see if the Kalmayans are watching me. They're quiet on their feet, and I'd never see them without it. Boulderfell might know about the temple, but he isn't watching it. And somebody hid all the tunnels, so I don't think he knows about them. If he did, I'm pretty sure this room would be out of bounds." When I nodded, Tayo stood up. "Come on. Should we go? It's literally just down that tunnel. Let me take you."

My skin started to buzz at the idea. But then Nanny Kimly's disappointed face dissipated my high. I propped myself up against the display screen, legs bent, grounding my bare feet on the mattress. "I can't, Tayo. My Nanny Kimly said wait."

"I don't care what your Nanny Kimly says." Tayo climbed back on the bed, straightening my legs and putting his head on my lap.

Butterflies took flight in my stomach, kicking up and swirling around my chest. Overwhelmed that he instigated physical contact with me, I combed my fingers through his long black fringe, pretending it was the most normal thing in the world. "You don't care what anybody says," I said, trying to sound natural. "You always do as you please."

"I might just throw you over my shoulder and take you down there."

Yes, please. I grinned, still feeling the silkiness of his jet-black hair. "If you're allowed to use your man strength against me, then I'm allowed to use my *enforcery* stuff on you."

"That sounds fair. And in that case, a complete waste of effort on my part. Ohhhh, Roar"—Tayo wriggled onto his side, facing me—"*pleeeease.*"

I giggled at his childish tantrum, amazed he felt comfortable enough to be silly.

Tayo sighed and rolled onto his back, staring at the ceiling. "So, is this your parents' old room, then?"

"Yeah, I think it is." I looked around the room as if expecting to see some trace of them. "Nanny Kimly still won't talk to me about them, but it's obviously their old room. It's sad to think they got caught conjuring."

"Just make sure you never do." He furrowed his neat brows.

"I think I'm quite well protected here." I continued to play with his hair, giving it more attention than necessary. "The Kalmayans can't get in, and nobody would ever expect it from an Enforcer. My parents were practising as Enforcers and were discharged for five years before they got caught."

"So, are you saying I can do magic, too?" he asked, turning his gaze on me, his eyebrows now high.

"Yep. I begged Nanny Kimly to show me how. It's got something to do with decalcifying your pineal gland. She said she doesn't want me conjuring but knows I'll just go to the temple without her if she doesn't help me, so she's going to show me soon."

"When you learn to do it, I'll be able to do magic?" His shining blue eyes held unblinkingly on mine.

"Everyone is born with the ability to conjure, so yes. When I decalcify your pineal gland, you'll be able to do magic with me."

"I don't want to get too excited in case it's not true. I can't imagine actually using magic myself." He turned over his hands, analysing them. "Can you do anything else?"

I grinned down at him. "I can."

Tayo threw himself up, spinning to face me. "Oh my God, what? And don't tell me Nanny K said not to."

"Well, I pretty much don't have a birthmark anymore—look. It comes back during the night, but at least it's gone all day. Nanny Kimly said there are ways to make it go permanently, not go-go, just invisible."

"I think your birthmark was a good start. At least that's something that will keep you safe."

I can do this too, I spoke to Tayo, using my mind.

"Holy shit, that's unbelievable. Can you..." Tayo's face dropped. "Can you hear my thoughts?"

"No. Don't worry. You have to *want* to share your thoughts. You're not the one doing the magic, but you are opening your mind, almost like allowing me access."

Like this? Tayo allowed me to hear his thoughts.

Yeah.

I'm going to marry you one day, Roar.

My breath hitched in my throat. We held each other's eyes, not saying a word but allowing our tiny smiles to speak volumes. I felt myself connecting to something deeper than his blue until my heart couldn't take anymore, and I had to break the silence. "You know my skin-glowing thing?"

"Hm." Tayo snapped out of it, too, but his rosy cheeks told me he hadn't moved on.

"It's called showing, and apparently, it has nothing to do with me using magic. As in, I don't conjure anything when it happens. You know, in the tunnel, when my skin glowed and the tunnels appeared. *Nothing* to do with my skin."

"What the hell is that, then?"

"It's basically a greeting to show you are open, trustworthy, and, like, revealing all. You can only do it when you emit a vibration of trustworthiness or a feeling of openness. Basically, if you don't come in peace, you won't be able to do it."

"So why on earth did you do it when you kissed me?"

I shrugged. "I guess…I was opening myself up to you, dropping my guard. I don't know. I definitely came in peace."

Tayo's hearty laughter pealed around the room. "I'm sorry, I'm not laughing at you. That's just funny."

"Shh." I gave the interconnecting door a glance. "Keep your voice down."

"Sorry. What else can you do?" Tayo assumed a cross-legged position.

I looked at my bedside table, trying to remember what I had inside that I could use. I concentrated on the drawer, focusing on it opening, picturing the action in my mind, repeating it again and again. The drawer slid open magically. I felt a draining on my body as if I'd just completed a long session in the Colosseum. Tayo watched the drawer open and shook his head. I lifted my index finger, letting him know I wasn't finished. Then I imagined my bracelet clearly in my mind. The long snake chain, the locking clasp, I pictured it lifting out the drawer. The bracelet mimicked my imagination. As I brought it over to Tayo, I again felt the energy leave my body as though I had transferred my own energy directly into the movement. The chain dangled in mid-air in front of Tayo, bobbing up and down like it was floating in water. With his eyes wide, he opened his hands to receive it. I let go, dropping it into his cupped palms.

Tayo clapped a hand over his mouth. "Shut the—that is *crazy*. Oh, wow, you could have so much fun with that. I remember when you could only rattle things."

"It takes a bit out of me." I yawned, sinking down into the bed and turning on my side. Tayo moved up against the wall and guided my fatigued head onto his chest.

"You, my little Roar, are truly amazing."

CHAPTER THREE

COLD SHOWER

I paced up and down my room, wondering how to do it. Last week, I hurt Tayo once again. He'd been visiting most days, but then I used my *enforcery* stuff whilst playing, performing some basic martial arts on him to win our game. I'd completely ruined everything. He would message me, but he hadn't visited in almost a week, so I had a plan which I hoped would bring him back.

I thought long and hard about what to message him and decided on: '*Guess what?*'

'*What?*' came his prompt reply.

My heart skipped at how fast he'd messaged back. '*Whoa. Keen. Were you waiting for me to text you or something?*'

'*I've been watching you pacing in your room for the last fifteen minutes. I expected a message fourteen minutes ago.*'

I shot a look at the wardrobe door to see if I could see his round piercing-blue eyes peeping through the darkness, but the wardrobe door was closed all the way. Then I checked the ensuite, just in case. When I returned to my bed, I had another message from him on my Slate: '*No. I'm not in there.*'

'*You're creeping me out. Where are you?*'

'*Bored at work. Watching your picoplant live tracking.*'

As if my heart could take anymore, it now danced to a quick beat. He was clearly thinking about me. I wrote back: '*You are a little bit weird.*'

'*I know, but you love it.*'

True… '*Anyway! Guess what?*'

'*Nanny K is coming to see you.*'

'*How the hell did you know that?*' I sent my message just before my bedroom door opened. *Ah.* He must have seen her on her way round. *The little creep.*

"Little Lady." Nanny Kimly gave the room a sweep with her eyes as she approached my bed. She never changed, and even though she was no longer my caregiver, she was still my constant, always the same. She sat in front of me, and I wrapped my arms around her, inhaling her calming scent. I always thought she smelled like earthy flowers with a soothing, motherly essence.

After she felt my grip loosen, she leant back, surveying my face from under her trim red fringe. "How's everything going? Have you been keeping out of trouble?" She tapped a hooked index finger under my chin.

"Yes, Nanny Kimly. I don't go looking for trouble, you know?"

"It just always seems to find you, hmm?"

"Yes." I held a defensive tone. "That guy pushed *me* last year."

"And what about conjuring? Is your mind still set on practising?"

"Yes," I replied, feeling as though I contradicted myself. I didn't go looking for trouble, yet I wanted to practise something illegal. "Don't—"

"I didn't say a word."

"You didn't have to."

"Is Mr. Tessan still visiting you?"

"Okay. I get your point. Maybe I don't go looking for trouble, but *maybe* I don't help myself either. And before you say anything, Pax is leaving."

"I've said all I needed to say on the matter, Little Lady. You should be waiting until you're no longer betrothed, but anyway, that's not why I ask. I know you trust Tayo with your life, and if

26

you're insistent on practising magic, and you two are insistent on seeing each other, then maybe he's the best person to introduce conjuring to first."

A smile began to grow on my face, and I didn't try to hide it.

"I'm not encouraging you—"

"I know, I know. Does that mean you're going to show me how?"

"Yes, Little Lady. But as I said before, you never tell anyone how you know what you know. Do I make myself clear?"

"Yes, Nanny Kimly, but—"

"Tayo already suspects me. I know. He is the *only* exception."

"Okay," I said, feeling lighter.

"Have you had your Mando-sleep?" Nanny Kimly couldn't seem to help herself.

"This is my Mando-sleep." I gave her a nervous grin.

Nanny Kimly frowned, her eyes falling on the Slate beside my pillow. "Then why aren't you asleep?"

"I…er…" I didn't want to lie, but I also didn't want to tell her the truth. Although, in saying that, she probably guessed it was Tayo keeping me up.

"Sleep when I leave, Little Lady." She gave me a stern look.

"Yes, Nanny."

"Right, okay." Nanny Kimly took a long deep breath. On her steady exhale, she made herself comfortable. "Conjuring is highly complex, and it is something you will learn more and more about as you go. There's so much to take in, and it's better learnt in time with practise.

"When you are born, you are born with a branch of magic from the Tree of Conjuring. It is not a physical tree, just a representation to help people understand the science. The branch you are born with determines your abilities. I am an Astralist: the first of the six.

I suspect you, my dear, are an Illusionist: the second branch of the six. Other than cloaking, what else are you able to do?"

"I can speak to people with my mind," I reminded her.

"Oh yes. Very good. That is the ability of an Illusionist. Anything else?"

"I can also move things with my mind."

"True to your branch, telekinesis is the ability of an Illusionist."

"Wait. What are the other four branches?"

"The order of the six is important. The branches are Astralist, Illusionist, Healer, Intuitionist, Summoner, and Elementalist—in that order. My brother, who I believe you've met, is an Illusionist, too."

"Your brother? I didn't even know you had a brother."

"He has been keeping an eye on you when you leave the institute."

"What?" My face screwed up.

"My brother Ikegan disguises himself as a black dog."

"*No*. That's your *brother*?"

"Indeed. He is fascinated to know how you managed to see through his illusion."

"*Nanny Kimly*." I almost lifted off the bed. "I *knew* I saw someone."

"He said you chased him for a while, but then you gave up when you eventually saw his illusion."

"I did! It was so embarrassing. Pax wouldn't stop laughing at me."

"Aha." Nanny Kimly repeated the word that made Pax roll around with laughter. It was what I'd said when I jumped out to catch the person hiding in the flowerbed.

"Yeah, I jumped onto the wall, thinking I caught a Curfew breaker, but then a dog ran out from the tulips. I *knew* I saw a human at first."

"That, Little Lady, is my brother. He keeps an eye on you when you're in the city. What we're wondering, though, is how you saw through his illusion?"

I shrugged.

"I noticed you don't use any incantations, either," she said, sounding more like a question than a statement.

"I don't know any. I just use my emotions and thoughts."

"You're already using extremely advanced conjuring. It's unheard of for beginners to conjure without the use of a verbal aid, but I suspect you are not the average conjurer."

"Do you think I'm that 'Guidal' the Kalmayans are hunting?"

"I do, Aurora." Her face hardened, fine wrinkles appearing around her hazel eyes. "It would appear the Kalmayans have read a prophecy and come up with their own interpretation. The Guidal is foretold to bear the Puracordis symbol of creation, and you are prophesied to return balance, not darkness. The Kalmayans have their own view on conjuring, and they would like to believe it is maleficium, as do the rest of the indoctrinated."

"Tayo says I'm safe, Nanny Kimly. He stayed with them last month."

"I'm aware of Tayo's whereabouts, and he is correct...for now."

"So you don't need to worry about me...for now," I said, concerned that if she did worry, she would impose restrictions on me 'for my safety'.

Nanny Kimly nodded. She fidgeted with the thin silver buttons on the side split of her black tunic. "Okay." Her eyes focused on me. "Are you seeing Mr. Tessan tonight?"

"Hmm, probably." *If my plan works.*

"Okay, get Mr. Tessan to set a delay on your door."

"A delay?"

"Yes, so when the access button is pushed, you have some *time*."

"Oh."

"Practise cloaking him. If you are caught together in this room, you are both going to Maximum Security, you understand?"

"Yes." The word brought with it a wave of anxiety breaking in the pit of my stomach.

"Right. Tell Tayo not to eat or drink anything else today. After six to eight hours of fasting, Cryxstalide is usually low enough to conjure with incantations. Healers are able to cleanse the body of Cryxstalide with the incantation *Spella Tair*. And I suspect eventually you'll be able to perform it. Powerful conjurers can perform magic from the branch either side of them by using an advanced technique called branching out. That's why the order is important. Since you are an Illusionist, you'll be able to branch out to both Astralist and Healer, so I imagine you'll be able to cleanse blood soon enough."

"*Spella Tair?*"

"Yes. Beginners usually need to be holding on to the other person."

At that moment, a fuzzy feeling curled around my body. It was almost like pins and needles but less prickly and more *furry?*

Then, I felt it.

My whole body pulsated with the strength of a thousand suns. From my head to the tips of my toes, I could feel the power accumulating inside each and every cell. As the energy grew, I felt my senses sharpen. My body seemed to come alive, throbbing with power and vitality. A surge of strength coursed through my veins, ready to unleash the full force of my being. For the first time in my life, my blood was free from Cryxstalide.

"Erm, Nanny Kimly…" I showed her my hands glowing bright green, releasing a thin luminescent smoke. As I turned my hands inwards, the green light met in the middle and grew brighter still.

Nanny Kimly gave a reassuring smile. "Conjuring in the mind doesn't come with any visual magic, but certain spells have a colour depending on which branch they belong. Those, Little Lady, are the hands of a Healer. You're branching out already."

"I don't like it." I closed my hands, extinguishing the green smoke.

"With practise, you'll be able to control it, and you'll be able to say incantations without them working unless you want them to. Don't worry about telling Tayo not to eat. Since you're branching out to Healer already, you can use *Spella Tair* to cleanse his blood. His pineal gland will still be crystallised, though, and it'll need to be cleared of buildup. To do that, all you have to do is draw the Puracordis symbol of creation on him."

"My birthmark?"

"Yes, Little Lady. It's one of the reasons you've been able to conjure on Cryxstalide. Puracordis symbols hold the magic within them, and your birthmark has the power to decalcify the pineal gland. Your birthmark has been protecting your brain from the chemical your whole life."

I pulled up my navy jacket sleeve to inspect my birthmark. "I've got a magic symbol on my wrist and you never thought to tell me?"

"It is a long-forgotten science, one I didn't want you practising. Once I expected you'd discovered Puracordis, I waited until you felt safe to tell me, if ever the time came. I didn't know the Kalmayans knew about the symbol. If I'd known, I would've done things differently. I would've made sure your birthmark wasn't on display."

"Where's this prophecy you were talking about? I want to see it."

"It's down in the temple. Go later with Tayo."

"Yes!"

"Those shiny black stones on Tayo's bracelet are what block his picoplant. It's called hematite. Get Tayo to give you one of them so you are untraceable down there. You can open the temple door with *Mandus Erdullian.*"

"*Mandus Erdullian?*" I repeated quietly, trying desperately to not open any doors in my room.

"Yes. It's an incantation all Puracordis can use to open that particular door. Maybe it would be nice if you show Tayo how to open it." Nanny Kimly got to her feet.

"I will. Thank you, Nanny Kimly. I love you so much."

"I love you, too. Now get some sleep."

"Don't go."

"You need to sleep. You may be breaking the law conjuring, but you still follow the rules here, okay?"

"Okay, fine," I grumbled.

"Have fun down there tonight, and be careful." She lowered her head, walking out of my door.

I instantly spun onto my belly, crossing my ankles in the air and reaching for my Slate to continue with the rest of my plan.

'*I'm sorry I hurt you. Will you forgive me? I'll let you take me to the temple...*'

'*You're so transparent. Nanny K blatantly gave you permission to go.*'

I grimaced and messaged back: '*Alright. She did. But I am sorry. And I miss you.*'

'*No enforcery stuff.*'

'*Promise.*'

'*See you tonight, gorgeous.*'

Yes! Turning on my back, I hugged my Slate to my chest. *Mandus Erdullian*, I thought, keeping the words fresh in my mind. *Mandus Erdullian.* Then, I changed into a pair of my charcoal-grey pyjamas, threw my Navy uniform over the back of the desk chair, and crawled under the duvet, curling up. Tayo on my mind, conjuring on my mind, the Puracordis Temple on my mind, the Guidal on my—*enough*. I told my mind to be quiet.

"Soami, lights off."

"Sleep well, Miss Aviary," Soami's mellow voice filled the darkness.

Waiting to see Tayo that day seemed to take longer than Pax's climb to the fourteenth position on the Flexon Pro leaderboard. For anyone who cares, he scored one hundred and ninety.

As nineteen-thirty hours neared, the familiar butterflies collected in my belly. I put the Parkour Games platform up on my display screen, choosing *Sovereign Skill's* last playback as a distraction. I did want to learn a thing or two, but my attention kept falling on the wardrobe. My ears pricked at a tapping from behind the mirrored door. Switching off my display screen, I rose from the bed, waiting patiently.

Then I started fidgeting from foot to foot.

Then I couldn't help myself and went to slide open the wardrobe door myself.

"Whoa. Hey, beautiful." He took an unintentional step back. "Keen." He quoted my text message from earlier.

I stood like a lemon, holding my hands behind my back and twisting from side to side. I hurt him last time. Did his visit mean I'd been forgiven? Tayo's eyes studied me for a moment before he lifted me up by my thighs, wrapping my legs around his waist. My butterflies flapped in a frenzied swarm, and I gazed into his playful eyes as he laid me down on my back. He climbed onto the bed, crawling over me, his lips hovering close enough to reach if I lifted. I could already taste his kisses, feel the warmth of his tenderness. The anticipation made me ball his T-shirt in my fists, controlling the urge to undress him. But then he flicked his eyebrows and slid off me, removing his trainers before getting comfy against the display screen.

I released my breath slowly, defusing the desire burning inside me. I turned on my elbow and shook my head, pretending to scold him with my eyes. He shrugged one shoulder, giving me a charming smile. His tattoos showed just under his jacket sleeve, and I recognised the gold and silver watch on his wrist. He'd worn it the day he was released from being my Juvie. *My Juvie…*

He was my Juvie. I could do this. Climbing to my knees, I straddled his lap, my whole body starting to jitter at my boldness. I could see in his eyes it was what he intended all along. He held on to the back of my neck, his delicate touch tickling and sending a nervous flutter down my tummy. He didn't ease me to his lips, waiting for me to lean in instead. I met his parted mouth, and a powerful rush elevated my chest, thrilled I'd taken charge. I didn't have to always wait for him. I could have control.

This time as we kissed, he allowed his tongue to brush against mine. It was as if two forbidden parts of us had merged, and their forbidden touch ignited a fire within me. I could feel the heat spreading through my body, making me crave more and more of his touch. I knew I was breaking the rules, but I didn't want him to stop.

Thoroughly losing myself in his deep kiss, I was on my back, Tayo leaning over me. I pulled his jacket off his arms and slid his T-shirt over his head. I'd seen him topless many times as a Juvie, but having him on top of me half-naked was entirely different. My eyes soaked him in, unable to stay off his tattoo sleeve. He kissed my neck, and my breathing grew heavier as I considered the question on my lips.

"Tayo," I whispered breathlessly, "do you have any protection?"

He held still. "I'm on male contraception."

My body pulsed at the thought in my head. "I was thinking… maybe I don't have to be a thirty-year-old virgin?"

He moaned airily through clenched teeth. "I've wanted you for such a long time, and I'm going to regret saying this." Tayo sat up, the pained expression on his face making me want to crawl into a hole. "Really, *really* regret it—but not like this, Roar."

"What do you want—candles and classical music or something?" I quipped, leaning on my elbows and shuffling out from under him.

"No, Roar, you cheeky cow. I want you to be my girlfriend first and not betrothed to another guy. When Pax leaves, if you *want* me to, I can stop you from matching in Unity again, and then maybe you'll be my girlfriend?"

His reasoning eased the tightness in my gut. "Well, you're going to have to ask me again nearer the time, aren't you?"

He leaned over me and gently sucked my bottom lip, sending a rush of blood to my cheeks. "There was a time when you wouldn't come anywhere near me," he said quietly, his deep notes carrying under his breath.

"I remember." My heart raced thinking about him as my Juvie. "You were a complete jackass."

"And now look." Tayo stood from the bed, lifting me into his arms. He trod back towards the ensuite, and I tried to read his face. He checked to make sure his path was clear. "I'm taking you for a cold shower. You need calming down."

"Oh no, I'm not having a cold shower." I reached for the ensuite archway, but my fingers couldn't keep their grip.

A topless Tayo lowered my feet to the floor. Standing alone in the ensuite with him reminded me he really shouldn't have been in my room.

"Can I?" Tayo gathered my vest in his hands.

I nodded, unable to stop myself from smiling. *Yes, please.*

When he lifted the vest up over my head, goosebumps flecked my skin, and I shook the shiver out of my spine. Tayo smiled at my reaction, clearly enjoying the effect he was having on me. My stomach lurched inwards as his fingers pinched around my trouser button. Once my navy combats fell to the floor, I became aware of my exposed body, and it began quivering all over.

"Are you nervous?" Tayo stopped and attentively searched my face.

I responded with a decidedly intentional head shake.

His subtle smile returned, and he circled around behind me. He blew on the back of my neck, sending a thrilling wave through my skin. Before my visible shiver had dispersed, Tayo unhooked my bra. He tucked his thumbs into my underwear and lowered them to my ankles, kissing my hip where the waistband had indented my skin. Getting back on his feet, he opened the shower doors for me to step in. The water wasn't cold, but I was shivering.

The stream flattened our hair to our heads, and water dripped from our chins. He really was beautiful, but the water made him completely captivating. I swept his soaked fringe from his eyes, exposing the full intensity of his gaze. His attention pierced the cascading stream, penetrating deep into my gaze as if I were the only girl he'd ever laid eyes on.

When he leaned down, his wet kisses felt better than I could've imagined. Something about the moisture made me want to kiss him deeper, explore him further. Unable to satisfy my thirst for him, my toes wriggled against the shower floor, but as if reading my mind, he stepped between my legs, pushing my feet apart. His lips left mine, moving to my neck, my collar bone, my chest, above my belly button, below my belly button, travelling down as he lowered onto his knees. The rolling sound of the shower intensified all my senses. I closed my eyes, immersing myself in the hypnotic noise, the sensation of Tayo's lips on my thigh, his hands slipping on my wet skin. Feeling his tongue, I dizzily fell back into the wall, where he steadied me and pulled me closer. *Oh...*

CHAPTER FOUR
WHAT ARE THOSE

Tayo wrapped me securely in a towel and held me tight. I didn't want him to let me go, overwhelmed by a new feeling, a strange sense of gratitude.

When I left the ensuite, Tayo was on the bed sliding a black hematite stone on my dainty rope bracelet, a bracelet Silliah gave me for my birthday last year. She thought I'd lost mine, so she bought me an exact replica, but without the engraved stones. Truth is, I'd actually given my old one back to Tayo. He'd had it since he was a child, anyway, and it felt more his than mine. Plus, it was how he broke Curfew safely.

I soaked up his every movement as I watched him from the ensuite archway. His messy fringe fell over one eye as he concentrated on my bracelet, his strong hands moving capably. Even the sound of the stones sliding across the rope had me transfixed by the way he worked, knowing exactly what to do. The confidence in his movements made me study him even closer, from his black socks to his broad back tapering down to his lean waist, even the vein in the side of his neck. I couldn't help but wonder what it must've been like to have that kind of confidence. "Look at you being one step ahead. Nanny Kimly told me to ask for one of those stones."

He spoke without breaking his attention on the bracelet. "Oh, I don't need dear old Nanny K to tell me how to look after you."

"What is wrong with you?" I laughed, dragging my eyes off him and pulling my boots on. "Why have you got such a problem with my Nanny Kimly?"

"It's not just her; it's this whole place. I can't stand it."

"This is my home, Tayo, and I'm one of those 'Youngens' you hate so much."

"Tut." He dismissed the conversation. "Come here."

Tayo was quite justified in his hatred for Enforcers. The night my parents died (the same night Tayo tried to save me as a child), my bracelet broke and Tayo caught hold of it. In doing so, he blocked his picoplant, and the Enforcer was unable to retrieve Tayo's information. As Tayo was being escorted to the institute, he pocketed the bracelet, unblocking his picoplant, ready for my Nanny Kimly to scan. The Enforcer who failed to identify Tayo was embarrassed and punished Tayo by tasering him repeatedly on the way home. As a result, Tayo was left with small electrical scars on his back as a constant reminder.

When I joined him at the end of the bed, he wrapped my golden bracelet around my picoplant wrist twice. Then he leant over and kissed my cheek. "I really care about you, Roar."

Heat flushed through me, and I could feel I was about to show. I thought for a second about stifling it, but realising I didn't need to in front of Tayo. I allowed it to shine through.

"You are so beautiful." He reached over to touch my glowing cheek.

I wriggled and held my wrist against his. "We've got matching bracelets."

"We do." Tayo didn't seem quite as impressed as I was. "So, can we go now?"

"One second, I need to decalcify your pineal gland."

I crossed over to the far side of the room, near the laundry chute, and took a pen from my desk drawer. I hadn't used a pen in so long, and I hoped this one still worked. Returning back to the platform steps, I reached for his hand, pausing before I took it. They were the same hands I'd watched working moments ago. I turned them over, running my thumb along the length of his finger down to his nail. His fingers were so much wider than mine. After stroking his neat white nails, I blinked, realising I'd become engrossed.

"We're going to have matching birthmarks now, too," I said effusively, hoping he hadn't noticed I'd been weird.

"Is that all you have to do?"

"Pretty much." My voice fluctuated, and I coughed. "It's a magical symbol which holds the power within it. That's apparently how I've been able to conjure on Cryxstalide. It keeps my pineal gland from calcifying. But I am weakened by the chemical when it's in my bloodstream. That's why conjuring was so hard for me before. When I cleansed my blood, I could feel how powerful..." I subsided. "It's not nice, actually."

"You're not going to hurt anybody, baby. I'm telling you, it's not maleficium. That is just to deter people from trusting Puracordis. For some reason, the power-hungry don't want us using it. I suspect either they can't do it, for whatever reason, or there's no reason to have people in positions of power when we can all conjure. I bet we are self-sustaining."

I kept switching between each of his captivating eyes, aware of a softness glowing in my chest. I averted my gaze, staring at my knees. The feeling was pleasant but strong, making me wonder if it was a good thing. What if something happened and it all went wrong like Pax and me? Could I handle that much pain again? My eyes regained focus on my pyjama bottoms, and I forced myself to look back up at him. "There are six different branches of magic, and we are all born with one."

"That's so cool," he said, a sparkle brightening his blue eyes. "Come-on-come-on-come-on. Let's go." He bounced on his seat and slapped his thighs.

"Come here, then." I smiled, taking his wrist and drawing my birthmark in black ink. It didn't look as good as if Tayo had drawn it. My hand control wasn't great, and the drawing was childish, which was silly, really, since my birthmark was so simple to draw. It was basically a number eight but the bottom was open; one line swirled inside the body of the eight and the other curved downwards. Around the outer bend, I had a number of tiny dots.

Tayo pulled his arm away before I could finish. "You don't need to draw that on me."

"Er...yes, I do." I held out a flat hand.

He fidgeted, keeping his wrist out of reach. "No, you don't."

"What's the matter with you?" My lips lifted, realising that Tayo could be awkward sometimes, too.

"You don't need to draw it on me...because I already have it on me." Tayo turned over his left wrist to show me his tattoo sleeve. "I had it tattooed on me a few years ago. It was to remind me why I was doing what I was doing."

I inspected Tayo's tattoos and saw it hidden amongst all the other drawings. He had disguised it quite well, making the birthmark difficult to make out, but I could see it now he'd pointed it out.

"You had my birthmark tattooed on you?" I asked, a little burst of something in my chest making me giggle.

"Don't laugh."

"I'm not laughing. Actually, I am laughing. Have you got 'my little Roar' tattooed on you somewhere as well?" I began twisting his arm around, inspecting his sleeve.

"No." Tayo tried pulling his arm away from me.

"Are you going to?"

"Stop it." Tayo managed to get his tattoo sleeve away from my prying eyes. "I still can't use magic, though, Roar. I've had this on me for over two years, and I don't feel any different." He opened his hands up to the ceiling as if he were feeling for raindrops.

"*Spella Tair.*" The words rolled off my tongue eloquently. I didn't mean to say it weirdly, and I gave Tayo a crooked smile.

His mouth opened as though he was about to say something, but then he caught sight of the mystical green smoke swirling from my palms. Watching it being absorbed into his bare arms, he whistled on an inward breath. "Oh-ho, I feel that. Whoa." He rotated his hands up and down; visibly, they appeared no different.

"What can you feel?" I wondered if it was the same thing I'd experienced earlier.

"Err..." He rubbed his fingers against his thumbs. "It's not something I've felt before."

"I know, right? It's a bit like pins and needles, isn't it?"

"Yeah, but...softer?" He squinted one eye.

"Furry?"

"Yeah." Tayo laughed. "What did you do?"

"I cleansed your blood of Cryxstalide. After six to eight hours of fasting, Cryxstalide is usually low enough to conjure, but it can be cleansed with a spell."

"Are you telling me, all the times I skipped breakfast, I could've found out I was Puracordis on my own?"

"I guess so, if you went without drinking anything, too. Your pineal gland hasn't been calcified since you had that tattoo. Although, Nanny Kimly did say beginners need to use incantations. But the question is, do you come in peace?" I encouraged him to show.

"How do you do it?"

"I don't know. Kiss me."

Tayo crinkled his nose. "Really?"

"What are you cringing for? Just kiss me."

Hmm...well...that didn't work.

"I knew that wasn't going to work." He readjusted, bringing one knee on the bed so his trainer hung over the edge. "It was too forced."

"I don't know. It worked for me."

"Yeah, but you didn't show just now either."

"Yeah, I suppose so. Anyway, forget about it for now. I'll ask Nanny Kimly how to do it."

I headed over to the wardrobe, and Tayo joined me, lifting up the plain white panel. We both stared down a ladder leading to darkness.

"After you." Tayo held the panel for me.

My boot hovered over the dark entrance as I wondered about the potentially dangerous adventure up ahead. Leaving my bedroom where I was safe, venturing out to a temple that Boulderfell knew about, and learning about a practice which was punishable by death—it all made my body still.

"It's okay," Tayo whispered from beside me.

I lifted my gaze, seeing confidence in his eyes. It gave me the push I needed to pierce the darkness with my foot, sitting on the edge with my legs dangling. Thoughts of using magic coaxed my boot on the ladder. This was the first time I'd ever done anything like this in my life, the first time I was going anywhere other than for a walk in the city. I swept my leg through the darkness, kicking it up and detecting a subtle breeze. It stirred a reaction in me which made me look up at Tayo. He held my head against his knees, bending over to kiss me. I wouldn't have wanted to share this adventure with anyone else. He stroked my hair back, and then I placed my other boot on the ladder.

"Do you not have any lighter footwear?" Tayo observed my clunky black boots.

I shook my head.

"What are you," he said, still analysing my feet, "like a size five?"

"Yeah," I said, weirded out by his accurate guess.

"I'll get you something for next time."

"I can order my own shoes."

"Yeah, but are you going to?" He knew I was useless with the internet.

I shrugged. No was the answer. "Stop killing my buzz. Can we just go?"

"Go on." Tayo softened his eyes.

I began my descent under the wardrobe, and Tayo, after closing the wardrobe door, followed down after me. The self-closing hinge lowered the panel above our heads. Delving deeper into the black, a cold air immersed my body, lifting the tiny hairs on my neck.

CHAPTER FIVE

ANIMAL INSTINCTS

Standing at the bottom of the ladder in my charcoal-grey pyjamas and leather boots, I waited for Tayo's feet to reach the ground. We walked quietly side by side, not touching but close enough for me to smell his woody aftershave. We headed down a long tunnel which didn't appear to have an end. Even though the walls were curved, the tunnel was still large enough for Tayo to walk upright, and the small rectangular lights gave me a clear view of him. Seeing him in all black was still novel for me. It suited him and gave him an enigmatic edge. But I still preferred him in claret.

My eyes drifted to his hands, which were resting by his sides. They looked inviting, making me want to feel the comforting touch of his skin against mine, but I forced myself to look away.

His hands looked soft.

I tipped my head forward and peered through the black streak in my hair at his fingers. There was something about Tayo's hands that drew me in. Perhaps because he was good with them, knowing exactly what to do. Or maybe it was the way they looked: distinctly male, quite unlike my own. Aware I fixated again, I tucked my hair behind my ear, catching an amused smile on Tayo's lips. I shoved my fists into my pyjama bottom pockets and trained my eyes forward. I had to get a grip.

Straightening up, I took my hands out of my pockets and tried to figure out how I normally carried them.

"If you want to hold my hand, Roar, you can just ask."

My fists wanted to dive straight back into my pockets, but I locked my elbows and kept them by my sides. "What makes you think I want to hold your hand?"

"You just do..." Tayo brushed his fingertips along my palm, leaving an electric trace of his touch right to the tips of my fingers.

I clenched my fist to quell the tingle, and I rubbed my palm against my side, attempting to neutralise the charge. He opened his hand, inviting me to entwine our fingers. I considered ignoring it, but an inexplicable force drew mine to his, and the warmth of his affection flooded my cheeks.

As I continued to navigate the pipe-like tunnel, I wanted to forget about his hand in mine, but I couldn't help remembering he was my off-limits, former Juvie. "Sometimes"—my mouth moved before my brain had time to think—"I remember what it was like when you were my Juvie, and...well, I never thought I would ever feel this way about you."

"Winding you up was my favourite pastime." Tayo smirked as he stared straight ahead.

"I know," I said, giving his hand a sharp squeeze. "I hated you one minute and would warm to you the next."

"Until you wanted to kiss me," he sang, swinging my arm.

I stopped our arms dead. "I did not."

"Ohh you so did. On your birthday, you spent the whole time in the Food Hall staring at me."

"I said I would punch you in the mouth if you kissed me."

"You were never going to punch me. I could've kissed you that day."

'*That day*' we were playing in his cell when I told him I could put him down on his back. He said he preferred me on my back because he liked to be the one on top. Well, the idea of Tayo being on top of me made me see him differently, and I completely melted. For the first time, I saw him as a male and not an idiot Juvie.

"Oh yeah?" I stalled, trying to think of my answer. "If you could've kissed me, then why didn't you? You know I would've punched you."

"I didn't want to kiss you as a Juvie."

"I was betrothed to Pax, and at that point, I didn't know there was a way for him to leave. I wouldn't have kissed you."

"You would have."

"Tayo," I whined, staring at my boots.

"How long do you think it took to mosaic these walls?" He reached up and ran his fingers along the top of the tunnel.

"It's not real. It's an illusion. When we first stepped down, I saw what the tunnel really looked like. It's just concrete."

"You can see that?" Tayo let go of my hand to feel the small square tiles on the walls.

"Mm-hm."

"It feels real."

"Well, it's definitely magic."

"Talking about magic." Tayo linked our hands again and started walking. "It's around here somewhere." He trod carefully, holding his other hand out in front of him, almost as if he were blindfolded and about to walk into something. "There." He looked at me with widened eyes. "Can you feel that?"

I could feel a resistance in the air. "What is that?"

"Kinda feels like you're stepping through a spider's web, doesn't it?"

"Yeah. What is that?"

"Well, at first I didn't know, but then I realised this tunnel should be miles long, meaning it should take us ages to reach the temple, but…" He pointed.

"The end of the tunnel." I caught sight of the adjoining pipe Tayo and I stood in last year when we snuck out together.

"Yeah. It's like a teleportation barrier or something."

"That's so cool." I started to feel the very magical nature of our adventure. "Do you want to open the door?"

"Can I?"

"You can."

Tayo's mouth fell open. His blue eyes glistened, reminding me how much of his life he'd dedicated to this moment. If it weren't for him, we wouldn't be on this magical journey. Tayo casually hooked his arm around my shoulder, leading me into the other tunnel. It amazed me how confident he was in making physical contact with me when I worried so much about coming on too strong. Was it his experience? Or my lack of experience? How many girls had Tayo actually been with?

We approached the temple door in silence, transfixed by its enormity. A golden tree trunk held the centre as intricate carvings masqueraded as leaves, reaching out and embracing the curved frame. My eyes wandered over the detailed engravings, trying to take in all of the different images and stories that were depicted. We stood mesmerised by the craftsmanship of the door. It was clear that a lot of time and effort had gone into creating such a stunning piece of art.

"Wait a minute," I said as my brain made a sudden connection. "Show me your tattoo."

"No. And yes, it's the carvings on the door." He kept his arm securely around my shoulder. "I drew them into a tattoo."

"That's pretty cool."

"Oh. I thought you were going to take the piss."

"No. I actually like your sleeve. And I like that you have my birthmark on you. I was only teasing you earlier." I stroked Tayo's tattoos, trying to inspect them whilst still being trapped in his arm.

"What's this? That's not supposed to be me, is it?" I ran my fingers over a girl pressing a finger to her lips.

"It's not you, but it kinda symbolises you."

"Why am I shushing?"

"It's not you."

"Why is *she* shushing?"

"Because I suspected you were Puracordis."

"Why are my eyes so light?"

"It's not you," he repeated for the third time. "I lightened the iris to make her look mysterious—also why she's wearing a hood. So, how do we get in?"

I unwrapped his arm from around my shoulder and placed his hand on the trunk of the tree. "Just say *Mandus Erdullian*."

"Manda what?"

"*Mandus...Erdullian*."

"What the hell kind of language is that?"

"I don't know. Can you just say the words already before I accidentally open the door?"

"Say it one more time."

I turned my head to see him.

"*Mandus Erdullian*," he said with a wink.

I expected some kind of clicking of locks, but the door didn't make a sound. We blinked at each other for a few, waiting for the door to do something, before Tayo decided to give it a push. The tree trunk split in half, and the right-hand door cracked open.

"You don't think this has been open the whole time, do you?" Tayo used his foot to nudge the door ajar.

"No, it hasn't. I tried pushing it last time."

"I've gotta say, I was expecting a little more from the first time I used magic. No glowing skin, no smoky green hands—you've disappointed me, magic door."

"I wish my first time was as discreet."

"Oh, baby." He put his arm around me and kissed the side of my head.

The first time I used magic, I showed after my first kiss with Pax, and he freaked the fuck out. He actually threw himself off me and said, 'Ergh.'

"Whoa." Tayo slipped off me and walked through the door with his head back. "It's quite deceptive from the outside. I didn't expect it to be so big in here."

We entered a grand entrance hall with architecture full of arches, domes, and coves, giving the room an endless feel. In front of us was a wide staircase divided into two paths leading up to a balcony that encircled the room. Tipping my head back, I saw the ceiling was a work of art in itself, with intricate designs and patterns that seemed to stretch on forever. It was supported by a curved alley of white marble columns, each one perfectly sculpted and polished.

"This is the room from my dream," I whispered under my breath, drawn away from Tayo and inspecting a golden skirt around a marble column. The same picture carvings from the door were on it, and I spotted the symbol of creation amongst the array of spirals, eyes, hands, stars, moons, and animals.

"What dream?" Tayo came to look at the pillar with me.

"The dream I told you about last year with that book. Do you remember? The one that taught me how to cloak."

"I remember." He turned around to see the rest of the entrance hall. "Is this all real? Not an illusion?"

"Oh yes, it's real."

We walked together to the centre of the room. The floor's glass-like stone almost perfectly cast back our own reflections.

"For an empty room"—Tayo gazed around at all the extravagant décor—"it sure is busy. I don't know where to look."

"I quite like it. The institute is so *white* and samey; this is refreshing."

"Mmm, it's a bit..." He looked up at the golden balcony. "It's a bit *shiny.*"

Something caught my attention through an archway to my right, and at the same time, Tayo spotted something of interest to his left. We split up in opposite directions.

"I wouldn't touch anything until we know what it does," I called over my shoulder to Tayo as he entered an identical archway on the opposite end of the room.

"Alright," he replied without a backwards glance.

I passed under a golden archway into an octagonal room. This room carried the exact same theme as the entrance hall, but the floor was a glossy red. I followed the white-quartz walkway from my dream, tracing the golden trim with my eyes. After stepping onto an octagonal plinth, I paused.

There it was: the big leather book from my dream, the one that taught me how to cloak.

It was a deep brown, with a layered cover holding a bronze embellishment of my birthmark. I reached out to open the hard-backed book when the brilliant, pure sound of violins made me snatch my hand back. The sweet song played through my soul, feeling like it glided along my heart strings, vibrating my chest, and releasing a deep warmth. At the same time, a plethora of yellow orbs crowded the room. I watched them all dance around to the song's passionate melody. But as abruptly as it started, it stopped. The sophisticated song ended, and the yellow celebratory orbs disappeared.

Electrified, I spun to acknowledge Tayo. He came creeping out of the archway at the far end, only making eye contact with me briefly.

"*Tayo*...what did you do?" I called across the grand entrance hall to him.

"Nothing."

"What did you do?" I marched his way. "What did you touch?"

Tayo gave a small shrug and hung his head.

"Show me," I said, trying so-so-so hard not to smile.

Tayo took me into another octagonal room smaller than the one I'd just come from. Engraved on the stone floor was a perfectly symmetrical tree with six branches reaching out towards the edges of the room. Each branch held an exquisite golden ornament with a pierced-metal design.

"I didn't *touch* anything; I just stood on this." He tapped his foot on a glass circle set in the floor where the roots of the tree would be. His trainer disappeared under a mysterious ultraviolet mist.

I wafted my boot through it, feeling nothing, no resistance, no magic, no nothing. "What happened to not touching anything until we knew what it did?"

"I didn't *touch* it."

"No, you just thought you would stand on a peculiar, portal-looking thing without knowing what it did."

"Should I stand on it again?" Tayo jogged his eyebrows.

I pouted at him for a second before I returned his grin. "Yeah, go on, then."

Tayo stepped onto the glass-esque panel, and the mysterious mist swirled around his trainers. Then a bright yellow light burst up the trunk of the tree and veered off to the right, down the fourth branch. Upon reaching the ornament, the richly crafted device began to open, and the components revolved like an old-fashioned carousel. At the same time, the wealth of translucent orbs appeared, and the beautiful song from earlier commenced.

Tayo gave me a look as if to ask if his inquisitive behaviour was worthwhile. I almost smiled before I turned away, ignoring his seek for validation, and I reached out towards a yellow orb. The light source appeared to have a mind of its own, and it swerved my touch.

I held out a flat hand, and another came to rest weightlessly in my palm. As I tried to touch the resident, it sped off and disappeared amongst its peers.

Tayo came off the base, returning the room back to normal. The spinning ornament closed up, the orbs vanished, and the music stopped.

"What is this?" Tayo looked over all the other ornaments set around the branches.

"I'm not certain, but I think I have an idea. Nanny Kimly said we are all born with a branch of magic from the Tree of Conjuring. I think that just told you what you are."

"What does it say I am?" Tayo asked without breathing.

"That beam of light followed down the fourth branch. So, if the order is Astralist, Illusionist, Healer, Intuitionist, Summoner, then Elementalist, I think that means you're an Intuitionist."

Tayo clamped down on his bottom lip with pearly white teeth. His deep-blue eyes shimmered. "That is seriously cool. It sounds like I'm going to know a lot of stuff. I already have a photographic memory; I'll be a walking encyclopaedia."

"You have a photographic memory?"

"I do."

"You've never said anything about that."

"It's not exactly a conversation starter, is it? Hi, nice to meet you. I'm Tayo. I have an eidetic memory."

"Alright, but I've known you for a year. I thought you might've been able to slip it in somewhere."

"I just did."

"Whatever." I shook my head, giving him a dismissive look. He could have told me sooner.

"Hey, don't look at me like that." Tayo came and stroked the edge of my jaw, leaning down to me. As tempting as his lips were, I pretended to meet his mouth but turned my head away. "Hey," he repeated in a significantly deeper tone. "Kiss me." The strength of his voice made me want him even more, but I liked that he wanted me too. With four fingers on my chin, he eased my face to him again. When he leant in, I leant back. He paused inches from my lips, and then his frown turned into a dark smile.

I responded to his look with a tilted head and raised eyebrows before taking a tread backwards. He tried to grab my pyjama shirt, but I swooped my body, backing out of the room to allow myself more space to move.

My insides jolted at Tayo's sudden movement. I wasn't expecting him to take the bait so quickly. He usually knew how futile it was trying to capture me. With a surprising determination, he came at me. Where was this misplaced confidence coming from?

"I'm warning you." I giggled, grabbing hold of a pillar and propelling myself around it back the way I came.

But somehow, Tayo's fingers snagged my shirt. My heart thumped at the narrow escape. Knowing I needed to up my game, I swung my arms into a type of cartwheel, engaging my hips and thrusting my body into a back handspring. My hands met the smooth ground three times until I landed a few metres away from him. The surprise display had the desired effect, leaving Tayo stunned, watching.

"You know that just makes me want to kiss you more, right?" He pointed to his feet. "Come here."

My heart thrummed, persuading me to go get what I wanted, but I took one small step away from him. Tayo showing this level of desire for me was too irresistible.

"Please?" His eyebrows lifted.

My grin spread at his request, and I made my way to him. The chase might be over, but I wasn't quite ready to give in. I stood out of reach, lifting my knee towards my chest, shifting my weight onto my supporting leg. Then I steadily extended my boot up to his face. Gauging the distance, I led straight into a controlled wheel kick.

I twisted my body creating momentum to spin 360 with my heel brushing so close to his nose he would have felt the wind. I say 'would have' because I didn't make it that far.

Tayo caught my leg in mid-air. "No *enforcery* stuff."

"Are you using magic?" I fell forwards onto my hands.

Tayo snorted in the back of his throat. "No. You're just being really predictable."

Predictable? I'm not predictable. Tayo hugged me around my belly and lifted me up until my feet left the floor. The blood rushed to my head, but I still had the presence of mind to think. With Tayo's centre of gravity leaning back, all I needed to do was hook my legs around his calves and pull forwards, putting him on his back.

Tayo's jaw snapped shut as he hit the ground. I spun to straddle him, hovering my mouth seductively close to his.

Tayo licked his lips briefly. "Seriously, Aurora? Again? How many times do I have to ask you not to use your *enforcery* stuff on me?"

"Sorry." I immediately stopped the game and sat up. "You're not mad, are you?"

"No, I'm not mad. I bit my tongue." He opened his mouth, showing me diluted blood swirling down onto his lip. "You don't need to win, Roar. We can just play. This isn't an equal battle between us. You've been raised to be a weapon, so you'll always win. I'd just like to be able to muck about with you without getting hurt."

"I'm so sorry." I leant over to kiss him, a building pressure causing pain in my chest.

Tayo turned his head away from my kiss and guided me off him. "Come on, it's getting late. Let's go see what branch you are and head back."

No, no, no. He was being weird with me. "If you're not mad, then why aren't you kissing me?"

Tayo held out a helping hand and pulled me to my feet. He cupped my jaw and pressed his lips to my forehead. Relieved he wasn't mad, I took his wrists and lowered them, attempting to plant a strong kiss on his lips.

"Because you don't deserve it." He turned his mouth away, doing the exact same thing I'd done to him earlier. Tayo knew I wasn't going to walk with him, not until I knew we were okay, so instead of waiting, he picked me up over his shoulder and carried me into the tree room. He placed me down on the strange smoky panel, and we waited for the room to burst into action...

"I told you, you must be using magic," I said after nothing happened.

"How can I be using magic? I don't know any."

"I didn't know any either, but I still used it. I made those tunnels appear in the pipe last year, and I have no idea how I did that."

"You said that was advanced magic."

"That's what Nanny Kimly said. She said it was unheard of for beginners to conjure without the use of an incantation."

Tayo shrugged. "I have no idea. Come on, let's go. Talk to Nanny K tomorrow if you can, and we'll try again another time."

"Can we go see that book in there first?" I pointed through to the other octagonal room. I needed more time with him to figure out if he was being weird with me or not.

"Is that the book from your dream?"

"Yeah."

Tayo looked at his watch. "Alright, quickly, though. It's gone ten, and we're both up at five."

Was that really the reason? "Do you not have Mando-sleep out in the city?"

Tayo made the same snorting noise as earlier. "No."

"Why? It's proven that our consciousness fluctuates throughout the day. Without Mando-sleep, the risk of accidents is higher and productivity lower. Are you not tired?"

"Yeah, but I guess we just train ourselves to get through it. We haven't got a choice."

That could've been the reason. Should I just ask him if we were really okay? We passed through the large entrance hall and entered the room with the mahogany lectern. The first time I came into this room, I was so entranced by the book that I didn't notice the other objects around the room. Tayo immediately set out for a black grand piano to our right.

He stroked the keys and rubbed his thumb and fingers together. "Why is there no dust down here?"

"Magic, I guess? The air feels cleaner down here too."

"Yeah, I thought that."

I watched him admiring the piano, trying to establish if he was really interested in it or just trying to get away from me. "Can you play?" I asked, drying my palms on my pyjama bottoms.

"You think I was raised in a home without a piano?" He didn't bother to look at me.

He's definitely being weird. "You can be such a twat sometimes. Can you play or not?"

"Yes. I can play." He gazed down at the keys, precisely touching a few of them.

Watching his hands, I was reminded of how good he made me feel. I didn't want to lose him, and I needed to make this right. "Is there anything you can't do?"

He flicked his jet-black fringe from his eyes, looking over at me. "I can't do backflips across a room, perform some high-ass ninja kicks, or juggle burning torches."

"I bet you can juggle, though, can't you?"

"Shit." He scrunched his nose. "Yeah."

Feeling like he was being a little normal, I tested him. "Play something for me, please? I've never heard anyone play an instrument before."

"Tomorrow. Grab the book and let's go upstai—I was going to say upstairs but there are no stairs. You know what I mean. Back up there."

"Please?" A lump formed in my throat. I wasn't even sure if I was asking about the piano anymore.

"Tomorrow." He yawned, stretching his arms back. "Come on."

Slouching, I dragged my feet to collect the large leather book. When it didn't lift, a spark of hope ignited within me. "Well, I can't, apparently."

"It's stuck?"

"Yeah."

"*Ohggh.*" Tayo slumped down onto the piano stool.

With more time to make this right, I ignored his restlessness and opened the sturdy leather book. It didn't release a flash of light like it did in my dream, so I fanned through its many pages filled with handwritten text, symbols, and illustrations.

"I think this is a grimoire," I said to a daydreaming Tayo.

His eyes sharpened on me. "A grimoire?"

"That woke you up." I laughed.

Tayo looked over my shoulder, and I paid attention to where he placed himself. There was a gap between our bodies. He flicked through the edges of the book, turning to a random page and landing on one introducing the Intuitionist branch of conjuring.

"You are definitely using magic, Tayo. How else did you do that?"

"Coincidence?"

"Or *intuition*?"

He put his arm around my neck, placing his hand over my mouth. I smiled beneath it, feeling his body press against my back.

Tayo began to read from the book. "The Intuitionist, whose magic has the visual indicator of yellow, is born of the fourth branch from the Tree of Conjuring."

I licked Tayo's hand still over my mouth, and he stopped reading to wipe my saliva down my face. He wrapped his arm loosely around my throat. After wiping my wet cheek across his tattoo, I rested my chin on his arm, a light fluttering in my heart telling me everything was fine.

He continued to read. "Intuitionists are born with an exceptionally strong extrasensory perception and do not need to depend on incantations to rely on their natural instincts."

"So, basically you're an animal," I quipped. "I told you, you were using magic. I wasn't being *predictable*."

Tayo pretended to catch on to a scent and started sniffing all over my face, neck, and shoulders. I giggled at the tickling from his nose, and he began walking me backwards out of the room.

"Yeah," he said between sniffs, "and right now I'm smelling your pheromones, and you definitely need a cold shower."

Mmmm. I actually couldn't think of anything better. But then I remembered something Nanny Kimly said. "Wait-wait-wait."

"No."

"Tayo—"

"No."

"But there's supposed to be a prophec—"

"No."

"I think it's in the bo—"

"*Mandus Erdullian.*"

CHAPTER SIX

THE MORNING AFTER

After I re-dried my hair and dressed back into my charcoal-grey pyjamas, I set the mood lighting around the edge of the ceiling to purple, and we cosied up in bed. My head rested on his bare chest. Tayo's fingers caressed the small of my back.

Tayo had never stayed over, but it was late now, and I was becoming hopeful that tonight would be the night. Our relationship had grown more intimate, and even though I'd messed up again earlier, he didn't rush off home. I leant up on one elbow, placing my hand on his chest. "Will you stay?"

His mouth quirked, and he gave a subtle nod. A huge smile grew on my lips, and something immense overwhelmed me to the point my head felt a little dizzy. I placed a kiss on his smooth chest, humming with a sigh. We were fine.

Lifting my head, a glint of metal on the bedside table grabbed my attention. I gasped, causing Tayo to instantly let go of my back as if I were burning hot.

"*Nooo.*"

"What?" Tayo glanced over his shoulder in the direction of my eyeline.

I held an unsteady hand over my mouth. "Pax knows you're in here."

"Huh? How?"

Sitting on top of my Slate was my Promises Ring, a ring I gave back to Pax after he implied I needed to heal my broken heart and get over him. I reached over to the floating bedside table, picking up the plain platinum band. "He must've come in here when we were in the shower."

Tayo's mouth thinned. "We were quiet in there. You sure he knows?"

"Your jacket and T-shirt were on the floor. He knows. I think he's reminding me we're still betrothed."

"Well, that's a dick move. He's the one who's leaving you."

I lay motionless. Pax knew about Tayo. He knew we were in the shower together. I was breaking the law by being intimate with him, I was breaking the law by having him in my room, and I was breaking the law by being Puracordis. How much could Pax handle? Where was the line? When was enough...enough?

"Come here." Tayo slid up against the display screen and pulled my arm, guiding me onto his lap. I crossed my arms against my chest and burrowed into his neck. I didn't know what to do about it. With his arms hugged strongly around me, my eyes began to close, the security he provided stilling my running mind.

A bright flash then a black dagger. Another bright flash and blood.

"Roar, it's Midnight," Tayo whispered, waking me up. "Happy New Year."

"Happy New Year." I sat up, forgetting where I was. Waking up to the sound of his smooth voice was new and rejuvenating. "Were you watching me sleep?"

"No." Tayo coughed.

I laughed. "You blatantly were."

"Shh." Tayo kissed me to keep me from speaking.

It didn't work, and I whispered in his mouth, "I think somebody's falling in love."

"Stop," Tayo whispered back to me, "or I'll take you for a cold shower again."

"Oh, no, please don't." My sarcasm was received, and he lifted me up.

※

The automatic lights turned on, and I prised my eyes open. The events of the night before began igniting in my head. I sat bolt upright, slapping Tayo across the back.

"Hurry up. *Get out.* Anyone can be letting themselves in any minute."

"Ow." He laughed, calm as you like. "The doors are locked, numpty."

"Go!"

"Alright, alright, I'm going. Good morning to you, too, baby girl."

"You have to be gone before the alarm, Tayo."

"Okay, you grumpy head." He planted one on me, gathered his things, and entered the wardrobe. "Message me, yeah?"

I nodded quickly, needing him to leave. After watching him go, I turned to my surroundings, checking for any incriminating evidence. About a week's worth of towels was strewn across the floor. I gathered them up and threw them down the laundry chute. Spotting Tayo's gold and silver watch on the bedside table, I shoved it into the drawer. The Promises Ring…I had no idea what to do with it. I assumed Pax would talk to me about it this morning. Perhaps I'd give it back to him when he did.

Today, when I put on a clean jacket, the small screen on my left arm displayed the institute logo. The bevelled ring with a sharp 'X' underneath began spinning on the spot so fast it became a blur, and then it morphed into the number *two*. The small screen declared to the world I was officially a Second-year.

Grabbing Silliah's birthday present from my desk, I headed to her room. En route, a hypnotic rumbling sounded from behind me, and I checked over my shoulder. A Navy girl followed a few paces back with a large black storage trunk in tow. She wore her new slim-fitted jacket, her shiny black boots, and her pristine navy combats. The wheels of her trunk ran over the joins in the white floor panels, and that rumbling was the familiar sound of a First-year finding their new room. She would've advanced from Mustard Quartz this morning. I watched her, wondering if I looked that young and naive on my first day. I could remember it like it was yesterday; I pretty much spent the whole day in bed after being insulted by (now frenemy) Pipila Darlington for having white hair.

Reaching room 189, I pressed the ice-blue access button. Silliah was already sitting up in bed, but she wasn't alone. Settled on the bed with her was Brindan, Pax's best friend.

"What's with you always getting in there first to say happy birthday?" I tore into Brindan. Last year, he and Silliah raced to my bedroom to try and wish me happy birthday first—Brindan managed to beat Silliah to the post.

"It's not my fault you girls take so long to get ready." He flicked an eyebrow at me.

I decided to ignore Brindan, and I squeezed myself between them both, giving Silliah a long hug. "Happy birthday, Silliah."

"Thanks, Aurora." She gave an awkward giggle because I didn't get to say it to her first.

I backed up and shuffled into Brindan, trying to push him off the bed to take his spot. He reacted by twisting my arm behind my back and applying force until I stopped. With one arm taken hostage, I gave Silliah her gift with my free hand. Her lips lifted at my failed attempt to take Brindan's seat, and then she sat up straighter so we could all fit on the single bed together. Brindan and I silently compromised and sat diagonally side by side.

Silliah started to open my gift, tearing the wrapping paper halfway. "No way." She looked up at me, her hands poised over her gift. "How on earth did you get this?"

"Meh. I have my ways." The answer was Tayo helped me last year when he was my Juvie, but I thought I ought to keep that to myself.

"It's a signed first edition." Her big green eyes blinked at me through her strong glasses.

"It is. I remember the first time you read it and how badly you wished a letter would arrive for you when you turned eleven."

"I wanted it to be real so badly." She grinned before looking back down at her gift. "This book is well over a hundred years old. Only five hundred copies were printed, and three hundred of those went to libraries. This is incredible. Thank you so much, Aurora."

"You're welcome, Silliah."

"Way to trump everyone's presents there, Aurora." Brindan pouted at the book.

"Shut up, Brindan. She's my best friend."

"Brindan, I told you. I love your gift. It's amazing." Silliah straightened her leg underneath the duvet to nudge him.

"Hey," I said, turning to see his freckled face. "I didn't get anything from you on my birthday."

"Well, maybe you should be nicer to me."

"I *am* nice to you."

"I said *nicer*." He patted my cheek.

"Oh, whatever." I pivoted back to face Silliah. "What did numpty here get you, anyway?"

Silliah gestured towards the laundry chute behind me. I'd walked past her gift on my way in. God knows how I didn't see it.

"Is that…" I forced my eyes away, bringing them back to Silliah.

"The Davoren Sisters' bookcase? Yes." Silliah nodded, a genuine smile brightening her whole face.

"Whoa. Okay, Brindan, I'll give you that. I was just about to take the piss at whatever you got her, but that's actually amazing."

But Brindan only scowled at me for swearing.

"I know. How amazing is that?" Silliah's eyes flitted to Brindan. "It's from Pax and Brindan."

Brindan suddenly sat up straight, my swearing no longer his main concern. "It was my idea."

"I know, you've said, but Pax arranged for it to be brought to my room."

Silliah was one of the few people I knew who read actual books. The rest of the modern world read eBooks on our Fellcorp Slates or tablets. Actually, most of the population didn't read; they used augreals to have the storytelling experience. Along with the narration came visuals, and the 'reader' would become a character in the story, following in the centre of the action. But not Silliah; she loved all the really old books, the interaction of turning pages, the feel of the ancient paper. She was obsessed.

Last year, Pax's Juvies left after two and a half years of intentional imprisonment. The young girls didn't want to be taken into care and would get caught on purpose just to avoid becoming Young Enforcers. As Juvies, they weren't allowed to use electronic devices, so they used real books to study instead. Silliah's gift from the boys was the young girls' old white bookcase.

"And all I got from Pax was a peppermint hot chocolate." I stared at Silliah's thoughtful gift.

"Have you...spoken to him?" Silliah asked.

"No." My stomach rolled, reminding me of the imminent conversation Pax was going to have with me soon. I grasped the Promises Ring inside my pocket. He didn't have the right to comment on Tayo being in my room. Pax was the one leaving me. If he thought I should've waited until he actually left, he could go love himself. If it hurt...good. Now he knew how it felt. Not that I was doing it to hurt Pax, because I wasn't. I didn't mean to like

Tayo; he was my best friend, and the only person who knew me and accepted me unequivocally.

"Still mad at him?" Silliah always could read me like a book. Brindan's bluish-green eyes dropped to his linked hands.

"Wouldn't you be, Silliah? Sorry, Brindan, I know he's your best friend."

"You don't have to apologise," said Brindan. "He is sorry, and he does really like you, you know?"

"I know," I said. "Just not enough." Nobody knew the real reason why Pax wanted to leave. They thought his parents breaking the law and conceiving him whilst being enlisted at the institute caused him to fear history could repeat itself. They thought he liked me too much and didn't trust himself. In actuality, I was breaking the law by being Puracordis and was a potential death sentence to him. Little did he know, we were all Puracordis.

Rubbing my neck, I brought the conversation to an end. "Anyway, happy birthday, Silliah. I'll see you at breakfast."

"Unity assessments first." She gave an apprehensive, toothy grin.

"Of course. Alright, see you after. Good luck."

I walked to the Food Hall with tension weighing on my skin. My fingers clenched and unclenched around the Promises Ring in my pocket. I knew he would probably be at our table waiting for me. I took a deep breath and passed under the Food Hall archway.

My body jerked, not expecting what I'd stumbled into, and I glanced back at the exit. Being the first day of Unity, it meant the only people likely to be at breakfast were Musties and betrothed couples. The only betrothed couple I knew out of my group of friends was frenemies Ryker and Pipila…who were currently sitting at a table with my betrothed, Pax.

Knowing it was too late to turn back, I kept stepping one foot in front of the other, weaving my way between the rows of white tables. Most were empty and still set in their default table of four.

However, Ryker, Pipila, and Pax had theirs programmed to make a long bench ready for twelve, waiting for the rest of our group to complete their Unity assessments. I eyed the tables in Claret Quartz where I would have sat early last year before I was betrothed, but it would be so weird if I sat there now. Besides, betrothed or not, Ryker would probably make a big scene until I joined his table in Navy Quartz.

I swallowed, lowering down onto my chair next to Pax.

"Good morning, sunshine," Ryker greeted me in his usual sarky overtone. I felt his beetle-black eyes watching me closely.

"Morning," I returned, feeling rigid and unnatural.

"So, what you saying about Unity?"

"I'm not saying anything."

"Wouldn't expect anything less from you, you little ray."

I double-tapped the table, bringing up the breakfast menu. When Pipila began talking, I zoned out and chose a breakfast I could scoff down quickly. But just as I rose to retrieve my food from the meal dispenser, Pax spoke out the side of his mouth, "Have trouble sleeping last night?"

I froze mid-way off my seat, the already-tense muscles in my stomach twisting together. Was he really doing this in front of these guys? My head rotated slowly to see him.

"Three showers," he responded without an invite.

I lifted myself up fully and leant over into his ear. "Go to hell, Pax." Then I left the table quickly. How could he do that with Pipila and Ryker sitting right there?

When I returned from the meal dispenser with my plain toast, three girls with matching blue hair ribbons loitered around our table.

"Are we allowed to sit here now, Ryker?" asked a short girl, standing behind Ryker, resting her hands on his shoulders.

"Yes, Crys, now you're a Navy. Just couldn't have it look like we were running a kids' club over here, that's all. Take a seat."

The three girls didn't take a seat. They kept on their feet, watching me sit down next to Pax. Then Crys flicked her salon-wavy blonde hair over her shoulder and scurried around the tables. "Thank you, Ryker." She giggled from behind me. "Come on, sit, Maylene, sit, Roebeka." Her arm slipped in beside my ear and wrapped around Pax's neck. "Hey, Pax." She pushed her cheek up against his.

Pax touched her forearm lightly. "Hey, Crystal. Finally old enough to sit at your big brother's table, eh?"

She's Ryker's sister?

"Yes. I'm so excited to be in Navy. I finally get to be with you all."

Her arms stayed around Pax's shoulders for an annoyingly long time before she removed herself from him and sat down beside him. The other two girls remained on Ryker's side, sitting opposite their friend. I shuffled in my seat, blocking her from my peripheral vision. I recognised the one she called Maylene. She was the tall blonde girl who boldly turned to gawp at me before leaving the Food Hall last year. They were the three girls gossiping about me and spreading rumours that I cheated on Pax. It was completely untrue, and I had an unnerving feeling about this lot.

"Ooh, look," Crystal squawked at Pax. "I've got a *one* on my arm now, too." She stroked the number four on Pax's arm. I licked my teeth and inhaled through my nose. I had no claim over Pax anymore, and it shouldn't bother me, but I had the impression this idiot was trying to wind me up.

"Yes, Crystal, you do," Pax replied, a slight smile playing in his voice.

"Oh, look at your ring." She held on to Pax's hand, running a finger along his platinum Promises Ring.

This should not be bothering me. This should not be bothering me. This should not—

"But, where's yours, Aurora?" Crystal leant forward to see me past Pax. She maintained an exaggerated coy expression as she met with my equally fake simper.

"It's right here." I pulled the ring out of my pocket and slid it on my finger. "I forgot to put it back on after my showers."

Pax watched me put my ring on and looked up to meet my eyes. I gave him a sarcastic smile and stood. Before I did something I regretted, I gave my tray to a Juvie on duty and left the hall.

"Aurora," Pax called after me down the corridor.

For God's sake. "I'm not having this conversation with you, Pax," I said before he could start. I knew he wanted to speak to me about Tayo, but I needed to calm myself down first, in case I said something I couldn't take back.

"Alright, whatever." He continued up the corridor towards me, one hand in his trouser pocket. "But we are still on duty together. We're taking the First-years' Juvies to clean their old Mustard rooms."

"Whatever."

I spun round and walked a few paces ahead, keeping my arms in and weaving left and right between Navies busy completing their duties. I stormed my way into Claret Quartz, and after checking my Slate for my Juvie's cell number, I soon arrived outside J-227.

The cell was identical to Tayo's old one, and I hadn't been in one since he left back in November. In my mind, I still expected to see him sitting on the bed in the back corner. I stared absently at the ensuite doorway, somewhere we used to hide sometimes, somewhere we almost had our first kiss. My eyes sharpened on the small white wardrobe on my right. That was how I first knew he had been granted early release. The doors were open and the rail empty, his clean sets of claret overalls no longer in there…then the worn white plimsolls by the bed. *My Juvie.*

"Errrr…are you alright?" A stroppy voice jerked me from my memories.

A freckly teenage girl leant up against the wall, one leg stretched out, the other bent with her plimsoll on the mattress. She sat twirling her curly brown hair around her finger.

"Get up." I jerked my head back once.

"No. I'm not moving until—*ouch!*"

I'd twisted her elbow in a lock, making her follow the pain until she was on her feet. "I said get up." I scanned her picoplant to check her details. I did not envy the First-year allocated this Juvie. I thought Tayo was bad. "Right, Mimsy, you address me as ma'am, you do not talk to me like you know me, and we are not—and never will be—friends. Do you understand?"

"Suits me fine." She quickly added, "ma'am," at the end after catching my eyes.

Checking back down at her details, I gave a weak laugh. "You are going to want to be careful around your allocated chaperone, Mimsy. I don't expect Crystal will be as tolerant as I am."

"I ain't scared of nobody."

I sucked air in through my teeth, remembering that when Ryker beat up Tayo in the Food Hall last year it was considered 'correctional protocol'. I'd learnt that Juvies had no real protection, and this girl was soon to be left unsupervised with a Boulderfell. "Alright, what is it?" I put my Slate away. "What's with the attitude?"

"I want to be a Young Enforcer, but nobody is listening to me." She stuck out her hip and folded her arms.

"Right." I thought about what she said. "You're fourteen?"

"Yes, ma'am." She unfolded her arms and blinked a few times.

"Okay, Mimsy. You come with me and clean the room you're supposed to, and after, I'll go talk to somebody about it. Agreed?"

"Yes…ma'am."

It was sorted. Stroppy teenager tamed, Pax and I spent the next two hours ignoring each other, sitting on foldable chairs in the Mustard residential corridors. I was okay, though; I had Tayo preoccupying me on my Slate.

He wrote: *'I'm thinking I might need a shower later...'*

'Oh, yeah?' I replied.

'Hmm.'

'Have fun on your own.'

'As if I'd be on my own.' He sent a smirking face. *'See you at seven-thirty?'*

'I'm busy tonight.'

'Busy breathing into my ear.'

After checking the Mustard rooms had been cleaned to an acceptable standard, we slotted the chairs back onto the cleaning trolley, put the trolley back into the storage cupboard, and escorted the Juvies back to their cells. Now, all I needed to do was keep my end of the deal with Mimsy and pay a visit to Seioh Jennson, the head of the institute.

As I approached the office, my footsteps slowed considerably. I couldn't believe I was voluntarily going to speak to him. If I was smart, I would've just left it and let Crystal pick up the pieces. Yet, here I was, fist poised over Seioh Jennson's office door. I closed my eyes, listening, waiting, and deliberating. I couldn't hear a thing, but I saw his cold, impassive face in my mind's eye. Before I convinced myself to turn around, I banged my knuckles on the door.

"Come in."

I took a few breaths to steady my heartbeat and then pushed the access button. "Good morning, Seioh."

"Good morning, Miss Aviary," he spoke without taking his barren blue eyes off his touchscreen computer. He rested his elbow on his weird wooden desk, staring at his screen and leaving me standing in silence.

Whilst waiting, I took another long inhale, trying to release my breath quietly. The last time I had been in Jennson's office was

November last year when I lost my temper with an idiot called Nickel, who pushed me after I beat his score on the Flexon Pro, taking his place on the Colosseum scoreboard. I visited Jennson to pre-empt my punishment for lashing out, but, of course, he didn't allow me to control the situation and instead waited until the next day to punish me. I wasn't on my own, though. I had a joint punishment with Nickel.

We were told to take turns and keep the Flexon Pro running continuously for four hours straight. Lady Joanne Maxhin, the head of the Khakidemy, was asked to supervise us, and I spent the whole time watching a grown man struggling to keep on his feet. The Flexon Pro was a reflex-training machine which kept you spinning on the spot, and Nickel could not cope with his dizziness. In the end, I kept the machine going for as long as I could, just to give Nickel a rest. He would have to jump on for a second, intentionally fail, and then allow me to get back on. I watched a grown man projectile vomit that day, too.

Still standing in front of Jennson, waiting, I took yet another deep breath and concentrated on not starting my sentence with 'erm'. Finally, once he allowed me to sit, I sank down on the black leather wheelie chair and cooled my clammy palms on the chrome arms. "Er-ahhhmmmmm—"

"Stop." Jennson put up his hand and closed his eyes. If it wasn't for a faint pained but amused expression, I would have thought I'd already irritated him, but I swore he tried to fight a rare smile. When he opened his eyes, he had composed himself and successfully rid his face of any traces of happiness. "Miss Aviary, it's not difficult. Just use your brain before you open your mouth."

"Yes, Seioh." I rubbed my lips together. Did he not think I'd already given that a go? I took a moment and tried again. "A Juvie wants to be enrolled here for training, Seioh."

"That wasn't so hard." He repositioned his monitor to type on it. "What's the Juvie's cell allocation?"

"Erm...oh." I covered my mouth. Jennson's unwavering stare told me I'd irritated him that time, and I urgently pulled out my Slate to double-check her cell number. "J-227, Seioh."

After a minute of tapping on his computer, Seioh Jennson ended my enquiry. "Mimsy Jackson will be fifteen when she completes her sentence. She does not meet the requirements to be enrolled."

"She's too old?"

"Yes, Miss Aviary."

"By how much?"

Seioh Jennson ignored my question and simply dismissed me with a hand gesture.

"Oookay. Thank you, Seioh."

"We can't accept every child who wants to be enrolled here, Aurora. We would be inundated with them."

"Yes, Seioh."

Hmmm. Chewing my cheek, I left Jennson's office and headed straight to Claret Quartz to give Mimsy the bad news. Whilst walking the suffocating red-panelled corridors, I wondered how to approach it. Abrupt? Sympathetic? Open with a joke? Thank God she wasn't my Juvie. I wouldn't have to put up with her for much longer. My only hope was that she'd take my advice from earlier and curb her attitude with Crystal.

I stood outside cell J-227 readying myself. *Okay, I'm sorry but— no. Mimsy, you're too old—no. Oh, I don't know.* I quit procrastinating and forced myself into the cell.

Mimsy sat up straight. "Ma'am," she said, blinking with a vulnerable innocence. Maybe there was hope for her after all.

"Hi, Mimsy. Look, I've spoken to the person in charge—"

"Seioh Jennson."

"Yes...Seioh Jennson, and unfortunately, you're too old to be enrolled here."

"I'm not too old." She stood up in front of me, her former self returning in a flash. "I'm fourteen."

"You'll be fifteen after you've completed your sentence."

Mimsy pulled a face, thinking about it. "I'm released in June. I would've been fifteen for a few days."

"Oh…" No wonder Jennson dismissed me without answering my question. "I've done all I can, Mimsy. I'm sorry."

"That's bullsh—"

"*Mimsy*," I snapped. "We can't accept every child who wants to be enrolled here. There has to be an inquiry into your biological parents, how you're treated, and if you're being neglected. Even if you were released earlier, it all takes time. The chances of you being enrolled here were slim to none. Now, I will leave you with one word of advice, okay? *Obey*. That's all I'm saying."

The rest of my day was spent obsessing over the time, willing for the moment I got to see Tayo. I didn't know what Christmas Eve felt like because we didn't celebrate Christmas in the institute, but I imagined it felt a lot like this. The longer I waited on the edge of the bed, the more my belly swirled. As nineteen-thirty hours neared, I listened intently for movement inside my wardrobe. My foot jogging escalated with every passing minute.

"My little Roar." Tayo climbed out of the wardrobe.

I couldn't contain the smile spreading across my face as I rose up, switching my weight from foot to foot. He tilted his head back, calling me to him, his smile withheld in pressed lips but shining in his crinkled eyes. My heels never touched the floor as I went to him. He hoisted me up, and I buried into his neck.

"How's your day been?" he said, his mouth on my shoulder.

"Mmm," I mumbled into his skin before being lowered to the floor. "Better." I watched him take off his leather jacket and fold it over the desk chair. "Yours?"

"Better."

A little flame flickered in my chest, warming my entire being. I backed up to the bed, fighting the compulsion to touch him, undress him, take him straight into the ensuite. He kicked off his black trainers and unclasped a silver watch, placing it beside my Slate on the bedside table. Hopefully, that meant his mind was in the same place as mine, and he didn't want it to get wet in the shower. His black T-shirt drew my eyes to his wide biceps and down to his lean waist. I took a long inhale and a quick exhale, controlling my urges. Tayo noticed my breathing, and he quirked an eyebrow. "You okay?"

I nodded quickly and threw myself against the display screen, making it look like my intentions were to stay on the bed. Tayo adjusted the pillows and joined me. *Say something, Aurora. You're being awkward.*

"Erm...Aurora." He scratched his eyebrow. His eyes were on the mattress, but then they shifted to my hand.

"Oh, shi—" I saw what he saw. "I...it was...some stupid girl was trying to wind me up today. Sorry, I don't really know why I put it on." I took the Promises Ring off and hid it in my drawer, out of sight.

"Roar, it's alright. Don't apologise for that. You're in a really unnatural situation thanks to that Boulderfell guy. People aren't usually forced into marriages, but if they are, they certainly can't get out of them. Because of Boulderfell's paranoia, he has given an out for the talented ones. It's really damaging for the one left behind. You still like him. You don't need to hide the ring."

"No. I don't want to wear it."

"Alright, that's your choice, but do not feel bad for the way you're feeling." He opened his hand for mine and stroked his thumb over my knuckles.

My mind wandered on to Pax. The happy memories we once shared all seemed to be tarnished with a deep-rooted hatred. There was a time I thought Pax would come around to the idea of me being Puracordis, but that was soon lost after Silliah told me he'd found a way of leaving the institute. I think Lady Merla Liddicott, our relationship coach, lost hope, too, because she put our monthly counselling sessions on a break. The sooner he left, the better. Perhaps then I could start mending my heart once I no longer had to see his face every day, acting as a painful reminder.

CHAPTER SEVEN

JACKASS

A pair of delicate warm lips pressed against mine, stirring me from my peaceful sleep.

"Bye, baby," Tayo whispered. "Don't work too hard today."

"I won't," I replied without opening my eyes. "See you tonight?"

"You will."

I sucked my bottom lip, savouring the aftertaste of his goodbye kiss, and I waited for the sound of the wardrobe closing. I had ten minutes before the alarm and had something I wanted to do first.

"That was the sound of the door *opening*," said an amused Tayo.

Every cell in my body jerked, and my hands slid up to my chest.

"Don't stop on my account," he said in a contained laugh.

"Leave." I squeezed my eyes tightly, my stomach clenching.

"Think of me."

I opened one eye, double-checking that *was* the sound of the wardrobe door closing, and my pulse steadied. Smiling, I pulled Tayo's pillow over my face. The sexy scent of his aftershave met my nose, and I inhaled it.

Ten minutes later, the alarm rang, and I reached over, stroking the sheets where Tayo would have been. I twisted to roll onto his side of the bed. But my foot didn't move comfortably. I sat up rigid and swiped the duvet off my legs.

Nooooooo. No, no, no.

I grabbed my Slate. *'TAYO, YOU NEED TO TAKE THIS OFF ME, RIGHT NOW!'*

'Yeah, I don't think so. Did I not warn you what would happen if you used your enforcery stuff on me again?'

'But I've got the Boulderfell Show of Force Display today.'

'Have fun.'

I sat with the arch of my hand covering my eyes, digesting the fact I had an ankle trap clamped around my leg. It was the day of the Unity results, which meant a busier day than normal. I couldn't do it with a weighted trap, not without attracting a lot of attention.

'Please, Tayo. I'm begging you.'

'Are you going to stop using your enforcery stuff on me?'

'Yes, I promise.'

I waited for a response whilst listening for movement inside my wardrobe. As the minutes ticked by, I kept my screen active, waiting for Tayo's typing bubbles.

'Are you coming back?' I sent him another message.

More minutes crawled by and still nothing. Hauling my leg out of bed, I stood in my room, testing how capable I was to walk and march. The brushed-metal ankle trap hidden beneath my pyjama bottoms wasn't too heavy, but I certainly couldn't walk normally, and marching…well, that was out of the question for my left leg. As I practised, tapping at the interconnecting door sent my foot slamming to the ground.

"Erm, come in?" I stood like a plank.

"You…alright?" Pax gave me a strong look.

"I'm good," I replied, my whole body seizing up. He hadn't yet spoken to me about Tayo, and I had a feeling this was why he was here.

"Are you sure?" His amber eyes read the room, my body, my face.

"I'm good. What do you want?"

"I was just checking if you knew about the Unity pre-meeting this morning."

"Yeah. I do. Fanks."

"Do you want to head down together?"

"Um, no. I don't need babysitting, Pax."

"Alright." He sighed dejectedly and shut the door behind him.

I sheltered my head in my hands, taking a few breaths and trying to rebalance myself. His kindness only reminded me that he didn't accept me. He was making it so much harder, and I wished he would leave the institute already.

Tayo hadn't responded and was taking too long to come back. I couldn't hide out in my room all morning, so to avoid anyone noticing I couldn't walk normally, I decided to skip breakfast and took a solitary shuffle to the Auditorium. Nearing the end of my residential corridor, Calix Bane, a fellow Second-year, turned in. This blue-eyed boy was my Boulderfell Show of Force Display partner when we were in Mustard. He headed my way, so I crouched down, pretending my boot laces had come undone.

"Aurora." He greeted me with a nod.

"Calix." My neck arched up uncomfortably to see him.

He stopped in front of me, so I finished fumbling with my lace and stood up. "Whoa, you've grown," I said when my head still tilted back to look at him.

"You've grown too." He smirked, looking me up and down.

"I remember when we used to be the same height."

He raised an eyebrow. "We were like…twelve."

Past his shoulder, I glimpsed a group of First-year girls stopped a short way down the corridor. They all whipped their necks forward as I met with their eyes. "Who's your entourage?"

"I have no idea." He combed his fingers through his blond swept-back hair. "They definitely were following me, though, weren't they?"

"Yep." I held an inward breath and a fake smile.

"Seioh Jennson's office down here?" He glanced over the room numbers close by.

"You don't know where Seioh Jennson's office is?"

"I know it's your second home, but no. I've never needed to see him before."

"Last-minute alteration to your schedule today?" I imitated Soami, the digital assistant.

"Yeah."

"What did you do?"

He gave a small shrug, but a watery look in his eyes told me he was worried. "Nothing, as far as I know."

"Well, it's not down this corridor. It's the next one along."

"What, back this way?" He pointed in the direction I headed.

Clart. No. That means he will want to walk with me. "Nah. It's quicker that way," I lied. I'll just have to deal with that one later when I sit next to him during the Unity results. I couldn't have him realising I couldn't walk properly.

"Alright, cheers. See you later, Aurora." He set off down the corridor. The First-year girls giggled as they tiptoed past me.

I arrived at a dark Auditorium with empty rows of tiered seating. I could just about see what was in front of me, and I was glad I only needed to make it to the second row. I followed the seats along, feeling them with my leg, and I placed myself in the last chair.

I waited alone.

Behind me, a low humming and an occasional clicking noise made me peer into the dark. I squinted at the darkness making phoney shapes at me. A scraping by the stage made my neck twist sharply towards the front. Light seeped in through the front door, followed by a stretched shadow, and soon after, a suit-adorned Seioh Jennson. I held my breath. What was I doing sitting in the dark on my own? It was a question I didn't have an answer for. Hopefully he wouldn't notice me. *Please don't start talking to yourself. This could get extremely awkward.*

"Do you not feel like standing to attention today, Miss Aviary?" Jennson spoke with his back to me.

"Oh!" I jumped to my feet, hands behind my back, chin up. "Sorry, Seioh, I didn't…"

"You didn't think I saw you sitting over there in the dark?" He adjusted the lights, brightening the entire room. "You can sit."

I opened and closed my mouth like a goldfish, but when words failed me, I perched on the edge of my seat.

"I see you learnt your lesson from last year."

"Yes, Seioh."

Last year, I didn't read my welcome pack and arrived late to the Unity pre-meeting. I entered the Auditorium in front of a room full of waiting Navies. (This was the reason why Pax felt the need to remind me this morning.) For turning up late, Seioh Jennson banned me from taking part in the Show of Force Display. The conceited fool thought that this was why I sat in the Auditorium early today.

"Would you like to know how to turn on the lights?" Jennson still addressed the wall, tinkering with the light panel.

"I saw you do it, Seioh," I lied, severely hoping he wasn't going to ask me to the front. I had a weighted ankle trap keeping my leg prisoner, and I was sure my odd walk would not go unnoticed.

Seioh Jennson didn't reply. He kept busy, walking this way and that way, checking the room for imperfections. Was it me or did the air suddenly feel heavier? I could almost feel it weighing down my shoulders.

I twiddled my thumbs. "Do you…have a family outside in the city, Seioh?"

"You do not need to fill the silence, Miss Aviary; it's fine."

"Yes, Seioh." *Phew.* I settled back in my chair.

"And I am not permitted to take a family in my line of work."

Satisfied with his quality check, Seioh Jennson left the Auditorium. I sat for a while, thinking about how Jennson must've been considered a Fell agent. According to Tayo, they weren't allowed to have a family either. I was sitting alone, wondering if all staff at the institute were under the same obligations, when soon enough, Navies began swarming in, taking their seats. Ryker was the first from my group to arrive, and he headed my way, walking down the aisle behind me.

"Oi. Why didn't you come to breakfast?" He rested one hand and one takeaway cup on my shoulders.

I waited for a second to see if Ryker was trying to deliberately burn me with his hot drink, but when the cup remained lukewarm on my shoulder, I answered his question, "The Food Hall is open all day today."

"Hmm," he gave a high-pitched squeak as if approving my answer.

He kept his hand (and cup) on my shoulders but didn't say anything else. I checked to see what he was up to and saw he watched Pax coming over with Brindan and Silliah; they, too, walked down the row behind me.

Ryker straightened up, greeting Brindan and then Pax with a fist bump. "Ready to hear the same speech for the fourth year in a row?"

"I wasn't listening last year," said Pax. "I was too busy watching this one." He tapped my head.

"Let me just throw up in my mouth," said Ryker, giving Brindan a nudge. "Actually, I think we were all watching 'this one.'" Ryker crossed his arms and legs animatedly, crossing them, uncrossing them, and crossing them again.

The boys laughed along with him. He was imitating me last year when I wore a creased uniform and attempted to hide it from Jennson. The three boys turned for the fourth row, still laughing, and Silliah, smiling, joined me on the second row by climbing over the seats.

"Why didn't you come to breakfast?" She heaved herself over and gave me a hug.

"I thought we would be going after the meeting."

"But the Show of Force rehearsals are after. I did message you."

"It's alright, I'll grab something quickly." I searched for something to change the subject and spotted Pipila in the fourth row, nursing a rather sore split lip. "What happened to Pipila?"

Silliah leant into me until her forehead almost touched mine. "You can't tell anyone"— she waited for my nod before continuing— "but apparently, Ryker can get a bit heavy-handed."

"Really?" I couldn't stop my face from screwing up.

"Well, yeah, apparently. That's what Brindan said. Pax doesn't like the way he tries to hurt you som—"

"Oh, I don't need Pax to protect me."

"Exactly, that's what he says."

"Stop whispering." Ryker threw his empty takeaway cup at us. It bounced off my shoulder and landed on Silliah's lap, spraying us both with specks of cold coffee.

See what I mean? I heard Silliah's thought in her head. At the same time, she gave me a bold stare with a slanted mouth.

"Or what?" I picked up the khaki-green cup and threw it back at him.

Ryker caught it one-handed. I prepared myself for it to be flung at us again, but Pax intervened and told Ryker to let us speak. Then Hilly, Tyga, Hyas, and Shola (aka the Fanciable Four) joined our row, and Hilly took the attention by removing Silliah's glasses. "I'm so excited for you," she squealed, squishing Silliah's cheeks.

"What do you think, Aurora?" Silliah asked, showing me her face without her glasses.

"It's going to be weird seeing you without them," I said, trying to get accustomed to Silliah's unfamiliar face. "When's your surgery?"

"It's been moved from Monday to this evening." She smiled nervously.

A collective silence ended our chat, and the Auditorium stood to attention.

"At ease." Seioh Jennson cleared his throat and waited for the ruffling of uniforms to cease. "Good morning, Navies. For a select few of you, matching in Unity is the greatest perquisite you'll receive as a Young Enforcer. The advancement in technology has allowed us to locate a spouse with such close affinity that the connection you both share is far deeper than any you could have discovered on your own. The time you spend with each other is significantly greater than any civilian engagement, leading to a stronger understanding of each other and a deeper bond."

The whole time Seioh Jennson spoke, I couldn't stop thinking about how I was going to leave the Auditorium without anyone noticing I walked funny. My eyes stayed focused on my ankle trap hidden beneath my combat trousers. After Jennson went on to brief us regarding today's agenda, he finished with a, "*Serve, Honour, Protect, and Defend*," and vacated the room.

Everyone started piling out of their seats. I stood up carefully and began shuffling my feet. But I quickly realised we were all shuffling our feet, and the slow-moving crowd meant my ankle trap was going unnoticed. This shroud covered me all the way to the EU Changing Facility in Claret Quartz.

We entered the busy, dimly lit room where Navies were stepping onto plinths surrounded by blue lights. A contraption unfolded their polished navy-blue suits around them. Despite there being over four hundred Navies needing to suit up, the one-way system meant the operation was efficiently handled. We would enter through one door, suit up, and then leave using the exit at the far end of the room.

I dragged my heavy foot up onto a large circular plinth, waiting for the machine to lower from the ceiling and unfold an EU around my body. After grabbing hold of the chunky white taser gun ejected from the wall, I joined up with the others, and we headed for the exit. The suit's mobility assist meant I couldn't feel my ankle trap, and I began to think today wasn't going to be so bad.

"Aurora, what quarter have you been issued?" Silliah asked as we headed to the Claret reception.

"Navy. You?"

"Yes! *Navy*," she sang, holding out a high-five. I met her armoured glove with mine and they clanked together. "I bet you have front formation, though, don't you?"

"Yeah. Why?" I replied. "What have you got?"

"Back."

"Oh, right."

"What about you guys?" Silliah asked the Fanciable Four.

"Khaki Quartz, back," moaned Hilly, throwing her armoured arms down by her sides.

"Khaki, back, too," said Shola.

"We've got Claret Quartz, back," answered Tyga and Hyas together. "See you later."

The twins turned to join the assembly of approximately one hundred Navies standing in the road. Silliah and I parted from the others and joined our formations in Navy. I found my place next to Pax, and without acknowledging him, I waited for the rehearsal to begin. A constant buzzing hummed overhead, and a dozen cameras flecked the blue sky like dead pixels on a display screen.

From my position, I could see the two Mustard children (specially chosen to lead the display) in the Navy reception being prepared by Sir Hiroki, the martial arts instructor, and Seioh

Jennson. Since Boulderfell's children were forbidden from being out in the city with their faces on show, they had to wait inside until they had their helmets on. The young boy and girl were going to be given special child-size Fell agent uniforms. Then they would lead Boulderfell and the brigade into the institute whilst completing a choreographed martial arts routine in their jet-black suits.

"Hey, beautiful," said a sudden voice in my helmet.

My heart recognised its smooth tone, but I checked down at my computer anyway, reading '*unknown*'. Setting myself to private, I replied, "Go away, Tayo."

Without warning, my foot welded with the ground, and with it, my computer flashed with the words 'MOBILITY ASSIST DISABLED' in bright-red letters.

"No-no-no, Tayo. I'm sorry." I was *not* sorry and would love to throw him off the bed all over again. "Tayo?"

The rehearsal display began, and I used all the strength I had to lift my left leg. With the weight of the ankle trap, I could only extend it a short way. My right leg lifted into a full march, and it was safe to assume I looked ridiculous. Tayo's laughter rang in my ears.

He can see me?

"Where are you?" I examined the forming crowd of civilians but suspected the tiny drone cameras above our heads.

"Over here by the wind tree."

My tinted visor helped keep the low sun's glare out of my eyes, and I spotted him leaning up against a wind turbine tree, one hand tucked into his trouser pocket, the other holding his Slate. The black leather jacket he always wore was zipped up at a slant across his body, and he'd pulled the fabric collar up, protecting his neck from the bitter wind.

"Tayo, I look ridiculous. This is too obvious."

"What are you doing?" Pax interrupted, noticing my unusual march.

I switched to his ID to reply, "I've got a cramp." I changed back to private. "Tayo, you need to disable this trap right now. You are going to get us both caught."

Still giggling to himself, he said, "Punch Pax in the arm, and I'll disable the trap."

"No! Are you crazy? It won't hurt him, anyway. I'll just be punching his EU."

"I know. Punch him in the arm, and I will disable the trap."

"Tayo." I tried to keep my voice straight and hide any amusement.

"Do it."

"*Grrrr.*" I swung my fist across my body, clashing my knuckles against Pax's solid, plastic-like armour.

"*Are you alright?*" Pax reacted, referring to my mental state.

I closed my eyes. "Sorry. It was an accident."

When my knee nearly hit my chin, I knew Tayo had finally come to his senses and disabled the trap. Turning smoothly in my formation, I continued with a perfect march, keeping the rhythm with everyone else. That was until Pax kicked the back of my heel to trip me up. With my mobility assist still disabled, I almost fell to the floor, but the flailing of my arms regained my balance.

"*Do you mind?*" I shouted at Pax.

"Sorry. It was an accident."

All the while, Tayo clutched on to his stomach, thoroughly amused by what he had orchestrated. I forced a pout, trying to stop my lips curving into a smile. "You're not funny, Tayo."

"No, you are." Tayo composed himself. "Okay, baby, I will leave the ankle trap deactivated. Come and see me at lunch, and— providing you don't strop—I'll take it off. Do we have a deal?"

"Nooo. That's not fair. How am I supposed to get back at you for putting the trap on me?"

"Oh, I'm not stupid. That's precisely why I've stipulated you don't strop. Now, do we have a deal?"

"Fiiiine."

"Good girl."

"Ergh. You're disgusting, Tayo."

"Okay, Navies," Lady Joanne Maxhin's voice infiltrated my helmet.

"That I also know," Tayo said quickly. "See you later, gorgeous."

"Hm."

"There was a slight disruption in Navy, front formation," continued Lady Maxhin. "Can we take it from the top? Everyone back to their starting positions. Aurora, Paxton, out. Get back in the institute and suit down. Roman Gavardo, Silliah Van de Waal, step in. Can we get two stand-ins for Navy, back, please?"

"Seriously, Aurora?" said Pax, storming past me and leaving the formation.

"You kicked me back."

"You punched me *first*."

I followed a safe distance behind Pax as we took the walk of shame back into the institute. Lady Maxhin looked down her pointy nose at a tablet. Her short black hair tousled in the icy breeze as she watched all four formations using the aerial cameras. She didn't bother to look up from her intel when we passed her. In the Navy reception, however, we weren't so lucky. We caught Seioh Jennson's attention, and his eyes followed us.

He had no idea who we were because the tinted visors concealed our identities, but I'd bet Worths on it that he suspected us. After excusing himself from Sir Hiroki and the two Musties, he called after us, "Hold it, you two, get back here."

I held my breath and turned on my heel. Pax and I stood to attention.

"Suit down," demanded Jennson.

Pax and I attended to the computers on our sleeves to release the EU. The components expanded and retracted into themselves until they came to rest by our feet in neat little carry cases.

"Of course it's you two." Jennson looked off to the side, his jaw set. "I am getting *sick* of seeing both of your faces, especially yours, Aurora. Take the EUs back, go and eat lunch, and then remain in your bedrooms until dinner. I do not want to see either of you for the rest of the day. Am I understood?"

"Yes, Seioh," we muttered.

"Get out of my sight." He dismissed us with a flick of the hand. We immediately moped away to the EU Changing Facility.

"I hope you're pleased with yourself," Pax said once we were out of Jennson's earshot. "I get that you're mad at me, Aurora, but you don't have to hit me."

"You didn't have to hit me back."

"We're not watching the results now. I hope you realise that."

"You don't like Unity, anyway. Unity ruined your life, remember? What do you care?"

"Oh, less and less."

After dropping off the suits, we exited out of the Claret Quartz doors together, but then I turned one way and he turned the other. I took the Mustard corridor to get to the Food Hall, Pax used the Navy. We didn't interact at all. I ate my lunch at my own table, and we didn't speak a word.

'*Tayo, you bastard. You got me and Pax kicked out the display,*' I texted Tayo whilst eating my lunch.

'*I heard her. I'm sorry, Roar. I didn't realise the institute was THAT strict.*'

'*Well, now you know.*'

'*Sorry, baby.*'

'*Guess what, though…*'

'*What?*' he responded promptly.

'I'm banished to my bedroom all day. Do you need a shower?'

'Obviously. When?'

'Now?'

I gulped my lunch, gave my tray to a heavily ankle-trapped Juvie, and hurried to room 432. My feet couldn't move quickly enough. I was like a puppy being told to heel, desperately controlling the urge to run. When I pressed the round access button, the ice-blue light made a silhouette of the institute logo, and the door slid open. Initially, I thought Tayo was yet to arrive, but when I opened the wardrobe door, he sheepishly appeared around the ensuite archway behind me.

"Sorry, Roar," he said with a meek smile, lowering his head forward between slightly raised shoulders.

Something about his submissiveness made my spine straighten. "You have a lot of making up to do." I used my eyes to indicate the ensuite.

Tayo bit his bottom lip and cocked his head to the side. His gripping look made me wilt, bringing my ego back into check. Coming to take my hand, he led me to the bed and said, "Be quiet."

"Here?" My eyes darted to the door.

Tayo pulled his Slate out from his back pocket. "Locked."

With everything swirling, I nodded, watching him unbutton my navy combats. Knowing what was coming, I scrunched the sheets into my fists. He kissed the exposed skin above my underwear, and my hips started to rock. I cupped his head and guided him to my lips.

"I want more, Tayo," I said breathlessly.

"I know." He took my wrists and moved them down by my sides, leaving slow kisses around my ear.

Unable to keep my hands where he left them, I pulled his black leather jacket off his arms. He put my hands back by my sides and sat up to remove his T-shirt. I became riveted by his body. The way he leant over me, his strong shoulders, his smooth neck, it all mesmerised me into stillness. Kissing my chest, he unzipped my navy jacket and lowered my combats to my ankles.

Realising he was ignoring my request for more, I guided him onto his back, moving to sit across his lap. He watched me carefully as I unbuttoned his trousers. His arms were above him, supporting under his head, and he appeared relaxed, enjoying me fumbling around clueless. When I hovered in place, he shook his head ever so slightly. It made me nervous, but I took no notice, slowly lowering onto him. I could feel it was right, and a tingling enlivened my body.

Before I had achieved what I wanted, Tayo lifted his knees, shifting me out of position. He shook his head again. "I said no."

"Oh, *Tayo*. How are you so controlled?"

"Because I really care about you, that's how. Now, come on, let me calm you down."

"Can I...calm you down?" I circled my finger around his belly button.

"You are too cute." He lifted onto his elbow, kissed me, and turned me over. "Be quiet, you're going to enjoy it more lying down."

෴

Tayo lay propped on his elbow across the foot of the bed, and he rubbed my leg where the ankle trap had been. "So, did I make up for earlier?"

"Mmm, yes." I smiled to myself, sinking down the display screen. Although, no longer being a virgin would've been better.

"My mum had a right go at me when I told her what I'd done... with the ankle trap. She's not spoken to me like that since I was in school."

"So your mum knows you're a dickhead, too?"

He breathed air out of his nose and rubbed his eye with the heel of his hand. "Hm. I told her that I really liked you, and I didn't know what else to do."

"You told your mum about me?"

"Don't let it go to your head." He stopped rubbing his eye and looked at me like something was on his mind. "This is going to sound really pathetic on my part"—he dropped his eyes on the mattress—"but I'm just worried by how much you can overpower me with your training. You've hurt me so many times, and it worries me. I would never hurt you."

"I know you wouldn't." I crawled to put my head by his chest. "I'm sorry. Self-control has never really been my strong suit. But I honestly don't mean to hurt you. I am really sorry."

"It's okay. I'm sorry, too. But you know that's the only reason why I don't want you to use it on me, right? You hurt me a lot as a Juvie—I know I probably deserved most of it—but I don't want us to be like that. I'm not a Juvie anymore, and you don't need to dominate over me like before."

I nodded, staring at his black T-shirt. I'd never really heard Tayo be straight with me. Usually, he would leave, and I wouldn't see him for a while. I much preferred him being open with me... even if I did feel a little guilty. I still loved the idea of him being my Juvie.

Tayo mindfully stroked my hair. He followed my hairline and tucked loose strands behind my ear. My eyes closed at his soothing touch, and I released the sensual shiver.

"You weren't kidding when you said it was strict here," he said, still repeating the same tranquilising strokes. "In school, I would've maybe had some Band Merits taken off me."

"What did you do last time when your mum had a go at you?"

"A teacher took some Band Merits off me, so I made it look like her house was haunted." He snorted in his throat. "I made the lights flicker and left messages on her display screen and shit."

"You're such a little hacker." A big lazy smile grew on my face whilst I absorbed myself in his fingers on my scalp. "What are Band Merits?"

"They're basically points determining how well indoctrinated we are. Listen, obey, and regurgitate what they teach, and then we will be awarded Band Merits. They're counted and added to the results of the Worths exam to allocate our Band."

"What if you didn't go to school to receive Band Merits, then what?" I thought about the Davoren Sisters, Pax's Juvies from last year. Maigen studied really hard to take the Worths exam so her sister could live at home with her mum and not be a Young Enforcer.

"You'll never be awarded Band A, that's for sure. You wouldn't have enough Merits. Based on the Worths exam alone, you'll get Band C at a push, but most likely Band D. All you spoiled brats are awarded Band A automatically, aren't you?"

"Yeah. But not until we advance into Navy. Then it's four Worths an hour every day until we're discharged. But instructors can take Worths off us whenever they want."

"Yeah, same with Band Merits. I needed a hell of a lot of self-control to get me through school and land me Band A. I knew I would never meet you otherwise."

I fought back a smile. Tayo spent his whole life planning to meet me. I stopped suppressing my smile and let it show, until something dawned on me. "Do you even like what you do?"

Tayo shrugged, thinking about his answer. "I like technology and knowing how it works, but I'd rather be in Gabbro of Sixth City, developing new technology rather than creating automated systems."

"Can't you leave Fellcorp and get a job you like?"

"I won't leave until you're discharged."

"Why not?" I rolled onto my back to see his face.

"Because I will lose my ability to look after you. When you're my girlfriend, I'll need to keep you from matching in Unity again, and I'll need to keep this room vacant so you can still use the tunnel. Plus, I'll be able to allocate you a new room of your choice, too. There's a lot I'll be unable to do if I leave."

"You're working a job you don't enjoy because of me?"

"Not because of you." He pecked my lips lightly, holding my cheek. "Because I *want* to. Besides, I like knowing the agenda for this place. It helps me break Curfew safely."

"Oh." I turned my face into his chest again, stifling a yawn.

"Aww, is my bubba tired?" Tayo stroked the white hair away from my eyes. "Do you need your nap?"

"*Hey.* I don't need a *nap.*"

"Do you want your Mando-sleep?" he asked in a less patronising way.

I readjusted myself, turning around, putting my head level with his, and backing up against him. "With you." I pulled his arm around my waist.

"Let me just double-check the doors." He reached for his Slate from the floating bedside table. "I'll receive a notification if anyone pushes your access button, and it should wake us up."

"Take these off." I tugged at his black trousers.

"Take this off." He did the same to my vest. He tucked me under his arm, and I hooked my leg over his knees.

"Soami, lights off," I instructed the digital assistant.

"Sleep well, Miss Aviary," replied Soami.

"Hey, Soami, what about me?" Tayo asked the ceiling.

"Sleep well."

"She doesn't know my name because my picoplant is blocked." He laughed. "Soami, call me Seioh."

"Tut, Tayo." I covered his mouth with my hand. "Soami, call him Jackass."

"Sleep well, Jackass," responded Soami.

"You little cow," he mumbled under my hand.

"Shh."

CHAPTER EIGHT

THE LAST STRAW

"Aurora, baby, wake up," came his urgent whisper. Then a flurry of quick kisses before Tayo said, "That's Pax knocking at the—"

Tap, tap, tap.

Tayo pulled the duvet up to cover my topless torso, and then he backed up to climb into the wardrobe. I remained still, waiting for the mirrored door to close and giving him a second to unlock the door.

"Come in," I called out.

"Oh, sorry, sweetheart," Pax spoke from the interconnecting door, throwing a flood of light across my face. "I didn't mean to wake you."

I squinted through the garish rays. "It's fine. What do you want?"

"Have you heard the news?"

"I've been asleep, Pax. What news?"

"Ryker messaged me. Silliah and Brindan matched in Unity."

"No." I attempted to sit up but then remembered I wasn't wearing my pyjama shirt. I lowered back onto my elbows. "Do you think they're happy?"

"Oh, I'm sure they are." Pax invited himself in and leant against the edge of the sofa. "Well, I know Brindan will be."

I pulled the duvet under my chin. "He likes Silliah?"

"Yeah, I'm sure they both like each other."

"She's never said anything to me."

"You shouldn't really share that type of thing. The institute chooses who you're allowed to be in a relationship with, so it's best kept quiet in case they end up matching with someone else."

"Are we allowed to go see them?"

"I wouldn't think so." He gave a short head shake. His light-brown eyebrows lowered, forming wrinkles between his eyes. "Seioh Jennson said to stay in our rooms. He cleared my schedule. I suspect yours will be the same, but we will be allowed to see them at dinner. They'll be coming out of the meeting with Lady Merla Liddicott about now."

"Silliah has eye surgery tonight; she won't be at dinner. I'm going to message her."

"Alright," he said, scratching his head. "Just…maybe don't go see—"

"You can go now, Pax."

"Aurora—"

"I'll be in her new room, Pax. I won't see Jennson."

Pax huffed quietly, pushed off the arm of the sofa, and turned into his room. I waited for a few seconds before leaping off the bed to let Tayo back in.

"Your friends matched, huh?" He climbed up the ladder, crawling back into my bedroom.

"Yeah, my best friend and his best friend. Do you think you'll be able to allocate them a Unity room opposite or close by?"

"Hmm." Tayo looked towards the ceiling. It didn't take long before his piercing-blue eyes were back on mine. "No. It's too late. The rooms have been allocated and will already be printed in their welcome packs."

"Can't we pretend there was an error?"

"It doesn't work like that, gorgeous." He picked up my vest from the platform steps and passed it to me.

"That's creased; I need a clean one."

"No, you don't." He took the vest off me and slipped it over my head. "You're not going anywhere."

"I've got to go see Silliah." I giggled, trying to prevent the vest from being pulled down my body.

Tayo twisted it into a knot and eased me to his mouth. "No, you've got to see me." He pressed his parted lips against mine, kissing me slowly and teasing me with his tongue.

Distracted by the pleasant tingling in places, I almost forgot what I was meaning to do, but remembering, I pulled back. "I know what you're doing."

"I don't know what you're talking about." He pulled at the vest, inching me towards him again.

"I'll only be a little while." I fought against his strength.

When he met resistance, he leant into me. He kissed my cheek and my neck, slowly circling around to my ear with each deliberate kiss. "What if I gave you something you *really* wanted?"

The gentle tickle from his breath and his titillating voice froze my limbs. "What…are…are you…are you serious?"

"No, you jittering mess." He let go of the vest. "Would you really not go and see Silliah just to have sex?"

"No." I tried to sound casual, but my voice fluctuated. "No," I tried again. "I would still go see her. I was just asking."

"Mmm-hmm."

"Oh, shut up." I threw my creased vest at him. I knew I hadn't been convincing, and my cheeks were burning, so I entered the ensuite to calm down and change my underwear.

When I finally re-entered the bedroom, Tayo was fully dressed and sitting on the bed. Something about seeing him in his jacket made me want to stay. My stomach was reacting like he'd just arrived.

Ignoring the feeling, I searched around him, feeling under the pillows, under the duvet, all around, looking for my Slate.

"Are we going to practise conjuring tonight?" He retrieved my Slate from under his legs.

"Yeah, but I haven't seen Nanny Kimly today to ask about that smoky panel."

"Don't worry. We can have a proper look through the grimoire to see if it can tell us about the tree room."

"Okay," I said slowly, lowering onto the platform steps around my bed to message Silliah: '*I heard the news. I'm coming to see you. What's your new room number?*'

'*440. I'm only a few doors down! Are you coming now?*'

'*Yes. Just getting dressed. See you soon.*'

"Did you…?" I spun to read Tayo's expression. "Silliah was allocated a Unity room four doors down."

"Nothing to do with me."

He looked earnest enough. "Maybe my Nanny Kimly." I shrugged. "What are you going to do whilst I'm gone?"

"Is there any point in me going home and coming back again?"

"I won't be too long. Silliah has laser eye surgery. Under an hour, I'd say."

"Probably not much point in me going home, then. I'll just sit down in the tunnel and wait for you."

"Are you sure?" An image of Tayo sitting in a concrete tunnel for an hour lingered in my mind.

"Yeah, it's fine. I usually sit down there waiting for you to eat dinner. Don't worry about me."

"Okay." I picked myself up to finish getting ready. "As long as you're sure."

"Where are your knickers you changed out of? In there?" He pointed through the wall into the ensuite.

"Yes." I laughed, taken off guard. "Don't be gross, Tayo."

After seeing Tayo off down the tunnel, I left for Silliah's room. The residential corridor had Navies and Juvies on a late housekeeping round. It was usually done during the morning, but the Show of Force Display had disrupted everyone's schedules. I quickly messaged Tayo to warn him. He was down in the tunnel, but I wasn't sure how likely he was to re-enter the room without me.

'Tayo, there's a late housekeeping round. Don't go in the room.'

'I am aware, baby. And don't worry; I never enter the room without checking a picoplant tracker first.'

Aw. Reassured by Tayo's answer, I pressed the access button to room 440. I entered a room exactly like mine: a double wardrobe to the right, an ensuite at the back, and Brindan's interconnecting door on my left. The wall-length display screen behind Silliah showed the same tropical fish tank that played when I moved into my Unity room last year.

"Hey," I greeted Silliah, edging gingerly into her room.

Silliah leapt up from the bed and swung her arms around me. "Hey!" She squeezed me tight, took my hand, and pulled me to the bed.

"So…?" I tried to read her expression. "You're happy?"

With dancing green eyes, she gave a notably strong nod. "So, so happy," she whispered, using her chin to point at the open adjoining door. Brindan's in there.

Unable to talk to Silliah openly, I got up to congratulate Brindan. Silliah and I would have to wait until later for our girly chat. I knocked on the wall before poking my head into Brindan's room.

"Hey, you." Brindan left his paperwork on the desk and hooked me into a one-armed hug.

"Congratulations," I said, my cheek pressing on his chest, hearing his quick heartbeat.

"Thank you." He kissed the top of my head, then let go.

Silliah snuck in from behind me and wrapped her arm around Brindan's waist. He rested his arm around her shoulders, and I couldn't help but smile.

"So, you're both happy?" I confirmed, although the answer became perfectly clear.

Smiling from ear to ear, they both gave shy nods.

"Do you want to sit in here?" Brindan invited us to stay. Without needing to answer, Silliah and I made ourselves comfortable on his bed. "What the hell happened to you and Pax today?" he asked, sitting on his corner sofa and resting his feet up on the white coffee table.

"I punched Pax in the arm, he kicked me back, then Lady Maxhin chucked us out."

"You two are *terrible.*" Silliah chuckled, shaking her head at Brindan.

"Everyone was talking about your TPG video loop last year because of how playful you both are," said Brindan before a frown swept in. "But how come you didn't watch the results?"

"Seioh Jennson caught us in the reception," I said, the memory still able to fill my body with something palpable. "He saw it was us two, then put us on a restricted schedule for the day. I'm not actually supposed to be out of my bedroom."

"What?" Silliah gasped, her once glinting green eyes reflecting distress. "No, Aurora, you need to get out quickly—" She broke off when the door to her room opened.

"*Nooo,*" I mouthed to Silliah. I pressed my eyes closed with stiff fingers and stood to attention. I didn't need to see the visitor to know who'd just arrived. Letting my hands drop to my sides, I reopened my eyes. He didn't look at me. My fingers linked themselves behind my back.

"At ease." Seioh Jennson relieved us from our rigid stances.

I lowered down on the bed, bringing my hands on my lap and keeping my eyes on my knees.

"Good afternoon, Miss Van de Waal."

"Good afternoon, Seioh."

"Subsequent to your match with Mr. Haywards, we assumed you would prefer your surgery to be brought forward so you could have a Promises Ceremony recording without your glasses. Are you still happy to go ahead with the procedure?"

"Yes, Seioh."

"Very good. Shortly, you will be escorted to Vencen Hospital. You are required to be chaperoned by two Enforcers. Do you have any objections to Mr. Haywards being one of your chaperones?"

"No, Seioh."

"Mr. Haywards, do you consent?"

"Yes, Seioh." Brindan nodded firmly.

Seioh Jennson attended to his Slate before continuing, "Unfortunately, Miss Aviary and Mr. Fortis are not permitted to leave their bedrooms today and are therefore unavailable for the duty. Would you like to choose a second chaperone, or shall I assign someone myself?"

"Is Ryker available?" Silliah gave a validating nod to Brindan.

"Yes, and he has already consented. I will see you both at Claret reception in fifteen minutes. Miss Aviary, go and wait in my office."

"Yes...Seioh." The look on Brindan's face cemented what I already knew. I was in a *lot* of trouble.

The last time Jennson asked me to wait in his office, I was fuming about Na-Nutta (the Navy receptionist) making up lies about me. I had my anger riling me up and didn't care what happened to me. This time, I didn't have the energy to pace the office. I sat quietly in the seating area, keeping unusually still.

'*Tayo, I got caught. I'm in trouble.*' I realised I should probably message Tayo so he could go home.

He messaged back: '*Are you alright?*'

'*I think it's bad this time.*'

'*You're going to be fine, baby.*'

'*I don't know. Maybe you should go?*'

'*I'll be here for you when you get back, whatever the time.*'

'*Are you sure?*'

'*Yes, darling.*'

Jennson entered his office, and I stood to attention, linking my sweaty hands behind my back, chin up, and heels touching. Seioh Jennson didn't acknowledge me standing in front of the black leather sofa, and he sat down at his computer. He didn't have any ankle traps or Juvie overalls or even a Mustard uniform. When he cleared his throat, I waited to be told to sit.

But Jennson continued working on his computer.

I slouched, suffering from an achy back and having to loosen the stance. It was bad this time, but how far was Jennson prepared to go to teach me a lesson? Endlessly lapping the institute until I passed out like last time? By making me wear a Mustard uniform as a Second-year? I doubted it would go unnoticed this time. That was probably worse than the weighted traps.

Unable to bear the images tormenting me, I pulled my attention back into the room and checked on Jennson, needing to hear what was in his head. *Come on, let me in. I need to know what you're thinking.* His upright posture, the old-fashioned suit, the sharp greying haircut—it all painted a picture which gave me a dreadful feeling. He still tapped away as though I wasn't in the room. When no voice entered my mind, my eyes glazed again as I saw myself locked in the Juvie cells.

A sudden surge of impatience rattled through my nerves when I realised I was still just standing to attention. I involuntarily huffed to release the agitated energy.

Austere eyes caught me in a flash. I straightened up and turned my head to face forwards. Once I was back in my rigid stance, Jennson continued to work on his computer. My mind troubled me more than the pain in my body. It plagued me with images of my punishment. It convinced me my time of avoiding Juvie overalls had come to an end.

Realising Jennson was living in my head rent-free, and his intentions for leaving me standing there were probably so my mind punished me, just like when I was eight and left to sit in a chair all day, I fought back, trying to focus on anything else. But if I wasn't in my head, numbness became the overwhelming force as it set in my feet. I wriggled my toes to feel them and encourage blood circulation. Discreetly, I shifted my weight from foot to foot, and soon enough, my weight shifting developed into an agitated leg judder. Hours had to have passed.

After constantly refraining myself from rubbing my eyes and countless stifled yawns, the sharp ache forming in my spine became my new oppressor. I arched my back to relieve the building strain. A grumbling in my stomach told me dinner time loomed, and the noise from passers-by out in the corridor confirmed it. I had, undoubtedly, been standing on the spot for *hours*.

Seioh Jennson kicked back from his desk and left the room.

"*Uuuuuuugh.*" I slumped down on the sofa in a heavy heap.

'*He's making me stand to attention forever!*' I messaged Tayo.

He replied: '*I'm relaxing on your comfy king bed.*'

'*I wish I was with you. I'm not sure how much more of this I can take.*'

'*Don't let him win.*'

'*I'm trying. I'm pleased you're not still down in the tunnel, but be careful.*'

'*Both doors are locked, and I have a picoplant tracker on. I'm safe, gorgeous.*'

'*Okay. Where is Jennson?*'

'*In Claret Quartz.*'

'*Oh no.*'

'*Stop worrying. You've got this.*'

I put down my Slate. Doom suffocated my body like toxic fumes. Air would not pass freely into my lungs. Before I had swallowed enough oxygen, the office door opened, and I stood to attention.

"At ease," instructed Seioh Jennson *finally*.

He placed a bowl of Juvie food on the black coffee table in front of me. I felt sick already, but now I had a feeling I was going to be forced to eat the gross grey goo. I had only eaten this clart once before, and it was vile. I had to chance my luck and decided to leave it.

"Eat," ordered Jennson, quickly catching on.

It was not worth further punishment, so I took up the cold slop and scooped a level spoonful. The slimy gruel stuck to the roof of my mouth. I peeled it off with my tongue, swallowing hard to try and ingest the horrible stuff. Preparing myself, I took another mouthful. My stomach churned, rejecting the lump worming its way down my throat. It didn't really have a smell, and it tasted like flour, no salt or sugar—just a bland, lumpy turd in a slime sack.

When I eventually put down an empty bowl, Jennson took it and vacated the room.

'*Tayo, I'm not sure I'm coming back until late tonight.*'

'*Okay. Are you still just standing there?*'

'*Sitting now. Just ate Juvie goo.*' I sent the message with a sick face.

'*I spent ten months eating that crap. Are you feeling any better?*'

'*I guess. I just want this over with. I think this has been my punishment.*'

'*Yeah. Knowing Jennson, he probably allowed you to punish yourself. Just stay strong. I'm thinking about you.*'

The door opened once again, and Jennson entered holding two khaki-green takeaway cups. He placed one down in front of me and returned to his desk. Feeling like it was a set-up, I hesitantly leant over to pick up the cup. After sipping it cautiously, a smooth molten liquid with a zingy aftertaste delighted my taste buds. Surprisingly, Jennson had brought me a peppermint hot chocolate. There were only three people who knew I didn't drink tea or coffee: my Nanny Kimly, Lady Merla Liddicott, and Pax—and now, somehow, Jennson.

With my legs crossed at my ankles, I took shallow sips and savoured the decadent, chocolatey treat. I held on to that cup with both hands until every last drop was regretfully gone. Well, actually, I never put the cup back down. I kept hold of it, scratching in lines with my thumbnail until every last inch was indented…and then I ran over them all again.

And again.

It must've been getting late, but Jennson still hammered away at his projection keyboard. I passed the time by trying to count every book on Jennson's full-length bookcase. On the top shelf alone, I counted two hundred and thirty-four books. There had to be way over sixteen hundred on that wall, and I wondered if Jennson even had time to read one.

Just as I completed an open-mouthed exhale after my deep yawn, Seioh Jennson folded down his touchscreen monitor.

"Miss Aviary, come and take a seat." He gestured to the leather wheelie chair in front of his desk.

The request made my stomach clench. I took my cup-comforter with me and sat on the edge of the chair.

Jennson observed me impassively. I tried keeping eye contact but couldn't for longer than a few seconds before my eyes skidded away. With every passing second, the muscles in my face felt heavier, and I was certain I looked terrified no matter how severely I fought against the drawing feeling.

Seioh gave a short forceful sigh. "Miss Aviary, I am seriously concerned by your total disregard for rules and your inability to follow the simplest of instructions. My orders were clear, were they not?"

"Yes, Seioh," I said quietly, fingers tensing around my cup.

"Then can you please explain to me why you were unable to follow them?"

I remained silent at the assumed rhetorical question, but Seioh Jennson raised his eyebrows.

"W-w-why I was unable to-to-to follow your instructions?" I tried buying time for my brain to engage.

"Yes, Miss Aviary."

Think, think, think. "I...erm...I...don't know, Seioh."

"You don't know?"

"No, Seioh."

"You show a complete lack of respect for your superiors, and quite frankly, your impudence has no place here in the institute. You leave me with no choice but to issue you with a dishonourable discharge and a sentence of thirty years imprisonment."

The blood drained from my face in a hot flush, leaving my head spinning. Nausea unsettled my stomach, and the thought of Juvie goo returning almost made me heave. "Seioh, I only wanted to see Silliah after she united."

"Mr. Haywards is Paxton's best friend, but I did not see Paxton in there flagrantly disobeying orders."

"Seioh, I'm sorry." I shook my head.

"You are not sorry, Miss Aviary. You are just sorry you were caught."

I was unable to hide the quaver in my voice. "No, Seioh. I am sorry. I swear to you."

"Miss Aviary, I have exhausted all punitive measures on you. I have never been witness to such callous disregard for the Institute's Code of Conduct, a gross inability to follow orders, and a sheer lack of self-control such as yours."

My heart pounded painfully in my throat and tears began to swell.

"It is therefore regretful to—"

"Seioh, I promise I will never get into trouble again. I will prove it to you. Please give me one more chance." Repentant tears already dripped off my chin.

"Aurora, if I thought for one sec—"

"*Seioh, I will prove it to you,*" I growled through gritted teeth, trembling from head to toe and crushing the cardboard cup in my fist. "I will *prove* it to you. *Please* let me prove it to you." I tried to hold his gaze through the watery sheet over my eyes. "Seioh… please."

But begging had never worked before.

Jennson leant back in his chair and steepled his index fingers. "You are going to prove to me you can follow orders?"

"Yes, Seioh. I promise." Something huge and weighty quite literally fled my body.

"Then follow this direct order: return to your room and remain there until further notice. You do not leave for *any* reason, and you will eat Juvie food to act as a reminder of your narrowly avoided diet. Are my instructions clear?"

"Yes, Seioh." I snivelled, my empty heart no longer in overdrive.

"This is your last chance, Aurora. Disobey me again and you will see yourself in Maximum Security."

"Yes, Seioh."

"You are dismissed."

I turned for the door. "Thank you, Seioh."

"Mm-hm. I hope for your sake I do not see your face for the next twenty-four hours."

"You won't, Seioh."

CHAPTER NINE
THE AWAKENING

When I exited Jennson's office, two black Fell agents stealthily flanked the doorway. The smell of stale tasers emanated from their guns as I felt their eyes burrow into my temples. The severity of what I just narrowly avoided came soaring in like a strong kick to the chest. They stood there, ready for my arrest.

The corridor began spinning, and I held on to the wall. *I was almost arrested; I wouldn't have seen my Nanny Kimly ever again.* A crushing in my throat blocked my airways. I dropped my cup and grasped my neck with tingling fingers. My throat closed up. I couldn't breathe. Sharp pains stabbed my heart. I pushed a fist into my chest and slid down to the floor.

The world was spinning.

I was suffocating.

A blazing heat overwhelmed my body.

Is this what it felt like to die?

My abnormal behaviour alerted a Fell agent, and they turned into Seioh Jennson's office. A pair of polished black shoes walked into view. "Aurora, do as I say," said Seioh Jennson.

The crushing worsened.

I really was going to die in this corridor right at Jennson's feet.

"I can't breathe," I wheezed, trying to alert Jennson of my impending death.

"Aurora, you are having a panic attack." Jennson knelt down on the floor with me. "Aurora, look at me. You are having a panic attack."

I couldn't see him. A black wall closed in on my blurry vision. "Help me. I can't breathe."

The sweat pushing through my pores prompted Jennson to unzip my navy jacket, and I ripped it off my shoulders.

"Aurora, relax. This will pass. I want you to breathe in with me." Jennson took an audible inhale. He released the breath when I didn't cooperate, and he said again, "Breathe in with me, Aurora."

I tried to inhale, but no air reached my lungs.

My body began shaking violently.

"I am here with you. You are safe. I promise you, you are not dying." Jennson settled down on both knees and tried to keep his eyes locked on mine. "Breathe in for four seconds, Aurora. One, two—do it with me."

"I can't." I panted, my whole body shaking like a plucked string.

"I know you feel like you can't, but I'm telling you, you can. Now, breathe in. One, two, three, four. That's it. And out. One, two..." He exhaled with me. "And again. One, two, three, four. Keep doing it. This will pass."

Air moved through my constricted airways. The swollen feeling around my lungs seemed to be fading. I took another desperate breath.

"See, it's working, isn't it? Can you feel it working?"

I nodded.

"Good. Keep doing it. Slow your breathing right down."

"I think I'm having a heart attack."

"You're not having a heart attack. You're having a panic attack. It will pass. Why don't you drink tea or coffee?"

I'm dying, and he's asking me why I don't drink tea or coffee.

"Hm?" he hummed for an answer.

"I don't like them."

"Have you tried them?" Jennson continued with the odd interrogation.

"No."

"How do you know you don't like them?"

"I-guess-I-don't," I answered quickly, more concerned about the world spinning. My stomach rolled over as the doors zoomed past me again and again.

Jennson followed my eyeline down the empty corridor. "Are you okay sitting on the floor in the corridor, or would you like to get into my office?"

"I'm too dizzy." I closed my eyes and rested my head against the wall to stop it from swaying.

"Okay. You can stay on the floor if you want. Would you like me to call for someone to sit with you?"

"No." I opened my eyes and checked the corridor again.

Jennson moved to sit by my side. He leant against the wall, undid his silky red tie, and unfastened the top button of his white shirt. It seemed he was taking up the job of supervising me at this pathetic hour. "It's past twenty-three hundred hours, so nobody will see you, but are you sure you wouldn't be more comfortable on my sofa?"

"I don't want to."

"Okay, floor in the corridor it is." Jennson's breath sounded almost like a laugh. He settled in, bringing his elbows onto his knees. "Can you breathe now?"

"Yes."

"Does a panic attack take away your ability to say Seioh?" he said casually.

"No, Seioh."

"Oh, just checking. Of all the people to sit with you through a panic attack, huh?"

I checked up and down the empty corridor again. "I don't want anyone to see me."

"There's nothing to be embarrassed about, Aurora. What you are experiencing is perfectly normal. But just know, you're not going anywhere tonight. The institute is still your home."

"My chest is really tight." I kneaded at the sore area above my heart.

"I know. You will feel better soon. Just keep working on your breathing."

I watched him for a minute, sitting there, shoes flat on the floor, knees bent, hands together, gaze anchored centre, sitting there like this was the most normal thing in the world. "I'm not the first person you've seen having a panic attack, am I, Seioh?"

"In my line of work? No, Aurora."

"What are you exactly?"

"I'm the head of the institute, but you already knew that, so what is it you're really asking me?"

"Are you a Fell agent?"

"No, Miss Aviary."

"But you take the same vows as a Fell agent?"

"I do, yes."

"Why?" I burped.

"Why what?"

"Oh…nothing." I swallowed, my tongue sticking to my dry mouth. "How did you even become the head of the institute?"

"I was approached by Seioh Boulderfell. He wanted to spend less time here and offered me the position."

"Were you…a Young Enforcer?" I asked, putting the pieces together.

"I was."

"So, you really don't have any family in the city."

"No, Miss Aviary, I do not." He almost laughed. "Do you not think before you speak, Aurora?" It sounded like a genuine question and not a condescending remark.

"Sorry, Seioh."

"How are you feeling now?"

"Much better, but this is the last time I'm going to see anything other than my bedroom walls for a while, so I'm taking full advantage."

Seioh Jennson didn't react to my cheek as I expected. His eyes were on his shiny black shoes, and he rotated his heel side to side, looking for marks. "Were Miss Van de Waal and Mr. Haywards pleased with the results of Unity?"

"Yes, they were, Seioh."

"Good." He ended his shoe inspection to look at me. "Perhaps next time you are told to remain in your bedroom, you should ask for them to come and join you in your room?"

"Yes, Seioh." The feeling of dying had worn off, but a prong of guilt stabbed me. "I meant what I said earlier, Seioh. I am going to stay out of trouble."

"Well, that's advisable because—not to induce another panic attack—you are on your final warning."

"I know, Seioh." I pulled away from the wall. "Well, I think I'm about ready to begin my solitary confinement."

"Enough," he warned, the reaction I expected a few moments earlier. "Good night, Miss Aviary."

"Good night, Seioh," I returned, facing in the direction of my room. "Thank you."

"Take your cup."

I swooped down and picked up my seen-better-days takeaway cup. Jennson remained on the floor as I walked away, his head tilted up against the wall, his eyes closed. He took a deep inhale, gave an even deeper exhale, slid up to his feet, brushed down his suit trousers, and re-entered his office. I didn't notice when the Fell agents left, but they were no longer flanking the doorway.

When I returned to my bedroom, Tayo was still making use of my luxury super-sized bed. He used his Slate to lock the door behind me and waved me to him. I threw my navy jacket on the floor, collapsed forward onto the mattress, and crawled between his legs into his consoling arms.

"I have had the weirdest evening ever," I mumbled into his bicep. Every jittering fibre in my body absorbed his calmness, becoming still under the pressure of his hug. He was my safety, and he felt like home.

"From what I could see, you just spent the last hour standing in a corridor with Jennson."

I listened to the deep hum of his voice reverberating through his chest, feeling the way it soaked into my ears and washed over my mind before I answered, "I was sitting. *We* were sitting…on the floor…talking, not long after he'd arranged for me to be arrested and issued me with a dishonourable discharge."

"What?" Tayo slanted over to see my face. "That comes with a thirty-year prison sentence, doesn't it?"

"Yep."

"What the fuck?"

"It's okay. I literally *begged* him to change his mind and then had a panic attack outside in the corridor."

"Whoa, Roar." Tayo pressed his lips to my head. "What the hell." He squeezed me tighter. "Are you alright?"

"Yeah. I've never been so scared in my life."

He exhaled, the heat of his breath fanning over my face. "So, what now?"

"I'm banished to the confines of my bedroom again, but this time, I'm staying in here. I'm never breaking a rule ever again."

"Except for having your illegal boyfriend in your bed, doing illegal things to you, and practising illegal magic?"

"Boyfriend?" was the only word I decided to comment on from that sentence.

"Well, not just yet, but it won't be long, and then what?"

"I'm just going to try and stay in Jennson's good books, I suppose. I'm obviously not going to stop seeing you, I'm never going to stop practising magic, and I'm certainly not going to stop having cold showers."

"That's what I like to hear. At least you weren't scared straight."

"It was a bit of a reality check, though."

"We're safe in here, baby. Both doors are locked, and I'll be in the wardrobe within seconds. You're allowed to have the door locked to everyone except staff, anyway, and how often do they come into your room?"

"It's only ever Jennson or Nanny Kimly."

"Well, you don't need to worry about Nanny K. How often does Jennson come in?"

"Hardly ever."

"Exactly. If we're down in the temple, we will get a notification that he entered. We will know to come back up. He'll think you're not in your room and should leave, and if he ever asks, just say you were at Silliah's."

"But I'm not allowed to leave my room at the moment, though."

"Alright," he said, still sounding unfazed. "So we don't go down to the temple until you are. Here, pass me your Slate." I reached into my trouser pocket and handed it over. He tipped it back and forth. "Aren't you supposed to be issued with the newer models by now?"

"Yeah, I should've collected it from Khaki reception today, but I was locked in here all day. I don't know when I'll get mine now."

"Hmm. Okay." Tayo continued with my old handset. With my head on his chest, I tried to watch what he was doing, but I didn't understand any of it. "Well"—he handed it back—"I've installed a picoplant live tracker, anyway. It won't be transferred over to your new Slate when you get it, but it doesn't matter; I'll just install it again. But for now, you can see anyone who's hanging around your bedroom."

"Thank you, Tayo. How do you always have everything under control?"

"I'm just good with technology. It makes life easy when you know how."

"I'm so useless with anything like that."

"You've been raised to be a machine, not build them."

"Hmm." I turned on my back and stretched my stiffened muscles. "I'm going to take a quick shower."

He unhooked his legs from around me and allowed me to get up. "Do you want me to come in with you?" He also sat up.

My mouth pulled at the corner.

"I meant the ensuite." He destroyed the image in my head.

"Ohh." I stuck out my bottom lip.

"What are you like? It's so late."

"Do you have to go to work tomorrow?"

"I don't *have* to do anything. If I go in, it's because I want to."

"Right…?" was my way of asking if he intended to go in or not.

"Duvet day?" was his way of saying he didn't.

I grinned. "Then what does it matter how late it is?" I tugged at his boxer shorts.

"Come on." He took my hand and led me into the ensuite.

⁂

After what felt like five minutes of sleep, the automatic lights turned on. I twisted over and buried my head under Tayo's side.

"Good morning, Miss Aviary," greeted Soami.

"Oh, let me guess: last-minute alteration to my schedule today?"

"Yes, Miss Aviary."

"It's three in the morning," grumbled Tayo, squinting at his Slate. "Oh, shit. It looks like Jennson's on his way round."

"What?" I sat bolt upright.

"Urgh," moaned Tayo, giving me my pyjamas, stepping into his trousers, grabbing his T-shirt, kissing my head, and closing the wardrobe door behind him.

After getting dressed, I scanned the room for any remnants of Tayo. There were a few towels, but I wouldn't have time to collect them, so I lay back down trying to act natural and waiting for my bedroom door to open.

"Good morning, Miss Aviary."

"Good *morning*, Seioh." I exaggerated the 'morning' since it was still the middle of the night, and I pulled myself up to a lazy stand to attention.

"The state of your room..." said Jennson, his squinted blue eyes skimming across the floor.

"It's just towels and clothes." I shrugged, still maintaining my weak stand.

"The laundry chute is right there..." He pointed with his eyes and a tepid finger.

I held my shoulders up to my ears.

Jennson blinked and shook his head. "At ease."

I slumped down on the bed, throwing myself on my back and covering my eyes with my arm.

"How are you feeling today, Miss Aviary?"

"Drained."

"Well, you have one hour to train in the Colosseum and thirty minutes to eat breakfast in the Food Hall before I want you back in here for the rest of the day."

"Train?" I dragged my arm off my eyes.

"Yes, Miss Aviary. Get dressed."

I couldn't help but groan. "How are you even awake?"

"You have the rest of the day to recuperate. Get up."

"Yes, Seioh."

An annoyingly equable Jennson waited for me to get dressed and then escorted me towards Khaki Quartz. In the corridors, only one set of twin lights was on in every ten. Not even the coloured tube lighting was on, and it felt rather unnatural to walk down—I mean jog, if you were with Jennson.

Before we entered the Khakidemy, we stopped by the Khaki reception first. Dull-green tube lighting illuminated the white surfaces, but the holographic projection on the rear wall was switched off.

"Nice to see you've returned back to the institute, Mason." Jennson greeted a broad-shouldered man with a short-back-and-sides haircut similar to his own.

"Thank you, Seioh." Mason stood up behind the large curved reception desk. "I must say, a year spent out in the city was extremely peculiar. For the first time in my life, I experienced a huge lack of purpose."

"I can only imagine. As Young Enforcers, you grow up in an important role. Purpose is all you've ever known. Did enrolling to be a Fell agent never interest you after being honourably discharged?"

"I couldn't decide. I love this place too much. Coming back was my first choice; being a Fell agent my second."

"Well, the next daytime receptionist position to become available will be yours. Could I get a new handset, please, Mason?"

"Ah, yes. Is that for Miss Aviary?" He glanced over at me with keen round eyes. "She's the last on my list."

"Yes. She has been undertaking disciplinary action." Jennson spoke as if I weren't in the room. "So, Mr. Fortis received his Slate yesterday?"

"Yes, Seioh. I have it recorded here at nineteen-thirty hours."

The goody-two-shoes had received his Slate at dinnertime just as he was meant to.

"Miss Aviary," called Jennson. I had somehow drifted farther and farther away from the reception desk. "Come and put your wrist here."

Unable to look Mason in the eyes, I held my picoplant over my new Slate, allowing the transferring process to begin. Everything from my old Slate would now be moved to my new one.

"All done, Aurora. Here you are." Mason placed a small box on the screen and pushed the handset to me. "Your old Slate, please?"

He prised it from my grip until it slipped from my fingers. I followed it with my eyes, aware just how much…Tayo was on there. But then I sighed after Mason threw it into a huge recycling bin filled with old handsets.

"Could you inform me when Miss Aviary leaves the Khakidemy, please, Mason?" Jennson placed a hand on my shoulder.

"Yes, Seioh, of course."

"Off you go, Aurora. You have one hour."

"Yes, Seioh." And with my cheeks still burning, I took the west-side door.

The lights in the changing room were already on, and I wrinkled my nose at the stale sweat odour. I'd never heard my own footsteps walking to my locker before. Passing row after row of towering lockers, I felt as if I shouldn't be in the room, as if I were somewhere out of bounds, somewhere I definitely wasn't supposed to be. Getting undressed without the cover of a crowd made my neck hair bristle. I shuddered out the unsettled energy and slipped on my workout clothes, leaving the changing room whilst still putting on my fingerless gloves.

The lights in the Colosseum were already on, but I much preferred the smell, which somehow made me feel strong and limitless. I wandered between the dormant machines, having no crowds to wade through or queues to stand in. Choosing a machine that made me feel a little less exposed in this huge, empty room, I stepped up to a four-metre-wide cylinder with a glossy black exterior. A toxic-looking red liquid streaked through the black mirror like drops of blood through water. Inside the cylinder, the floor became equally as perilous as it sparked and spat with red electrical discharge, popping and bubbling around my feet. This machine was called Floorslava.

Five red flashes indicated a countdown, and I grabbed the lit hand and foot moulds. The red moulds plummeted as the walls revolved downwards, giving endless vertical climbs. I planned my moves three steps ahead, keeping myself planted on the walls and my feet safely off the treacherous floor. Even though reaching took more effort than normal, I still trained hard. I wasn't leaving my room for the next twenty-four hours, so I owed it to myself. I reached, I climbed, and I lunged, again and again, always planning ahead. It didn't get faster like the Flexon Pro, and it was a true test of stamina, strength, and forward thinking.

Dripping with sweat, I ended my session with one last go on the Flexon Pro, managing around my usual one hundred and sixty mark, and then I returned to the changing room. Keeping my back towards the wall, I removed my soggy khaki vest, peeled off my stretchy black trousers, and threw them down the laundry chute whilst continually checking over my shoulder.

After a brisk shower, I left for the Food Hall, calling out to Mason on my way past. I settled on a table in Claret Quartz, ordered a large portion of toast, stuffed what I could into my cargo pockets for Tayo, and then I wandered back to my prison cell—sorry, I mean bedroom.

Tayo wasn't in my room when I arrived, which was just as well because only moments passed before Jennson came in behind me. He carried a blue housekeeping caddy stocked with dusters, chemicals, and cloths.

"At ease." He handed me the caddy. "Here you are. You can clean your own room today. I will be checking, so ensure it is done properly."

"Yes, Seioh."

"Did you train hard?"

"Yes, Seioh."

"Good. Now rest up. Juvie food will arrive at both eleven hundred hours and nineteen hundred hours. You may want to get an early night; your wake-up call will be at zero three hundred hours again. When the alarm sounds this morning, Soami will inform your friends of your 'solitary confinement', and they will be prohibited from seeing you. I strongly advise you not to encourage them otherwise.

"Now, tomorrow, the Unity celebration is mandatory, so your 'solitary confinement' will end at nineteen hundred hours for you to appear at the dinner-dance. Sunday, your schedule will be as normal. You do not leave your room from now until I collect you at zero three hundred hours. Are my instructions clear?"

"Yes, Seioh."

"Good. I will be checking up on you throughout the day." He gave one final look around the room. "Clean." He nodded to the caddy in my hand before leaving.

Tayo must've been aware of Jennson's presence because he resurfaced only seconds later. A sweet, woody fragrance carried with him, and I abandoned the caddy, my belly giving a light swirl. "You smell nice." I stood shuffling my feet, admiring his usual drop-crotch trousers and black jacket.

"I went home to freshen up and change my clothes." He took off his jacket and threw it down into the tunnel. It was part of the new exit strategy he'd devised after having too many visitors recently. He needed minimal baggage for a swift exit into the tunnel. I watched him, his movements, the way his hair fell over his eye, his black tattoo sleeve, his neck, his hands.

"I also ate breakfast and grabbed us some food for the day." He held up his backpack.

I blinked as if overcoming a spell. "Won't be needing these now." I dug into my cargo pockets for the cold toast.

"No," he snorted, taking the toast from me. "I couldn't have my little Roar eating Juvie crap...or cold toast now, could I?" He climbed halfway down the ladder, discarding the toast into the tunnel. Coming back up, he headed towards me. I smiled at the wriggling in my belly, frozen to the spot and curling my toes.

"I don't know about you"—he hugged his arms around my thighs and lifted me up—"but I'm shattered." He gave a big yawn as he carried me to the bed. "Take this off." He tugged at my jacket.

"Take this off." I did the same to his black T-shirt.

He removed my vest, took off his top, and tucked me under his arm. I relished in his hot bare skin for a minute before I fell asleep to the calming sound of his heartbeat.

A flash of light. Blood. Another flash. Blood pooled on the white mirror.

The brightness of the room woke me up a few hours later. We must have been so incredibly tired that we didn't even ask Soami to turn the lights out before we drifted off. I quietly moved my head to check on Tayo still sound asleep. He looked so peaceful, almost angelic, and I just wanted to kiss his beautiful lips. I lay there taking in every perfect detail. What was my life like before him? I couldn't remember it. I didn't want to remember it. I didn't want to remember a time when I didn't get to wake up to his touch, his face, his voice. *Kiss him. Just do it. He would kiss you without hesitation.*

"Are you watching me sleep?" Tayo mumbled with his eyes closed.

I lost my breath and held a hand to my chest. "Ohh. You made me jump."

"I think someone's falling in love." He opened his eyes, giving me a look that stole my heart.

"With you?" I said, gazing into his sleepy eyes. "No way."

"You're besotted."

My cheeks were warming up, and I knew he would be able to tell. "No, I'm not."

Am I?

"Besotted," he repeated with a slow blink.

"I think you'll find you're the one who's besotted. You are the one sleeping in *my* bed every night."

"Nah, I think I'm just suffering from Stockholm Syndro—" Tayo choked on his laughter before he could finish his sentence.

"Stockholm Syndrome? Isn't that when a hostage has feelings for their captor?"

"I'm joking."

"I didn't kidnap you. You had yourself caught on purpose."

"It was a joke—chill."

"It's not funny."

He gave a subtle eye roll with a soft smile. I stared into his charming blue eyes, allowing them to calm whatever unsettled energy permeated me. They were a deep ocean blue, and confidence rocked clearly in them. It made my lips lift in a natural smile, and I exhaled. Feeling something immense flourishing inside my soul, my lips dropped. I threw my legs off the bed and found myself by the desk.

"What's up?" Tayo propped himself up on one elbow.

"Nothing. I've got to clean my room."

"Roar." He gave me time to turn around, but I kept my back to him. "Roar?"

"I'm fine. I've just got stuff to do."

I heard him sigh, and I tensed, wanting to turn around but dealing with something new. The last time I felt that sensation was with Pax, moments before he discarded me.

Tayo's hands slid down my arms and around my waist. His body pressed fully against my back, and my eyes closed. The tightness in my chest unfurled as a small hum rolled in my throat.

His lips pressed on my neck, tickling through his gentle whisper, "I'll make sure that this time, when you fall, you won't hit the ground."

Something hot and sweet flushed my chest, and my lips stretched. I wasn't the best with poetic speech, but I was pretty sure I understood that. Pretending to be interested in the housekeeping caddy, I lifted up a bottle. "What do I do, just put some of this on a cloth and wipe?"

"Whoa, no, Roar." He took the bottle from my hands. "That's bleach. It's for the toilet."

"Oh…"

"Take this"—he held out a yellow duster—"and *I'll* go clean the bathroom."

I took the cloth with my mind and circled it around his head.

"Nice." Tayo winked, plucking the cloth from the air. He placed it in my hand and kissed my cheek. "Dust. We'll play after."

"Do you want me to cleanse your blood first?"

He paused. "Why not?" he said with a mild shrug. "But I know what you're doing."

"It worked, though, didn't it?" I held my hand up for him to touch, and he lined his fingers up against mine. "*Spella Tair.*"

A smoky green substance leaked from my palm, twisting through the air and washing over Tayo's body.

"Gotta love that feeling." He held out his arms, watching the green smoke. "Look after this for me." He removed his gold and silver watch and slid it over my wrist, closing the adjustable clasp until it was a secure fit. Then he cupped my cheeks and said, "Now let's get the cleaning over and done with so we can play."

With Tayo no longer a distraction, I equipped my fluffy yellow cloth and began wiping over the desk. I realised dusting the bedroom wasn't going to be as bad as I thought. Everything was flush to the walls except the floating bedside tables. There were no doorframes or ledges. Tayo definitely had the raw deal.

"Done," I chirped, poking my head round into the ensuite.

Tayo stopped scrubbing the inside of the toilet and raised his eyebrows at me. "If your *cleaning* is of the same standard as your *checking*, then you're not done."

"What does that mean?"

"I had ten months of you checking my rooms to know what you deem 'done'. Before you were my chaperone, I cleaned your old Mustard room, and if Jennson is going to check like that Youngen did, then you are most definitely not done."

"I've finished, alright."

"Mm-hm. Did you dust the platform steps around your bed?"

"Oh, I hate you." I spun out of the ensuite and picked up my duster again.

Not long after, Tayo appeared around the archway with his Slate in hand. "I think Jennson is on his way round."

I watched the stationary white dot on Tayo's tracker. "Why? He's in his office."

"I don't know. I was cleaning, not really thinking about anything, and then a picture of Jennson flashed into my mind. It was so clear that I've got a feeling it was magic."

"Tayo"—I laughed—"the same happened to me. It's normal. We are on edge. Of course we're going to think about him."

"It might be normal for you, but that is not normal for me. Mine was magic; I'm sure of it."

"Alright, get in the wardrobe if you're so sure."

Tayo turned the picoplant live tracker round to show me Jennson leaving his office. "I told you."

"Fuck. Get out. Take your watch. Where's my vest?"

"Here." Tayo launched me my top and put on his own. "I've cleaned the bathroom. You just need to clean the sink. Dust the laundry chute handle, your trunk, and the sofa." Then he disappeared under the wardrobe.

The door opened behind me, and I stood to attention.

"At ease." Jennson thrust a pile of fresh linen sheets into my arms. "Change your bed. Have you finished cleaning your room?" He began pacing around, running a finger across the back of the sofa.

"No, Seioh."

"In here?" He entered the ensuite.

I threw the sheets onto the bed and hurried in behind him. "I only have to clean the sink, Seioh."

Jennson parted the doors to the corner shower and inspected for watermarks. He checked the tiles for soap and even the plug hole for hair.

"An extremely good Juvie standard, Aurora, I must say."

"Thank you, Seioh."

"Why did you leave the sink?"

"To wash my hands after, Seioh."

Without so much as deigning to respond, he re-entered the bedroom. I subserviently followed behind him.

"And what have you left to do in here?" He swiped a finger across the bedside table and wiped it on the sleeve of his black suit, checking for dust.

"The sofa, my trunk, and the laundry chute."

"I see no method to your work. Why would you dust the coffee table but not the sofa?"

I shrugged.

"Well, if it works for you, Miss Aviary. Your food will be arriving shortly—ah." He broke off when my bedroom door opened. A teenage Juvie entered and set a bowl down on the coffee table. He bowed his head to Jennson before vacating the room. "Enjoy your lunch, Miss Aviary."

I curled my lip but quickly corrected my expression when Jennson flashed me a look.

"Thank you, Seioh."

"Finish your room." He walked out of my door.

Tayo climbed back up the ladder. "I told you it was magic," he boasted before he'd even made it to the top.

"Alright, you were right. Happy now?"

"A 'thank you' would have sufficed," he said in an uneven tempo, one that started slow but sped up towards the end.

"Thank you, Tayo." I opened my arms, feeling weird about my defensiveness.

He stepped in, stroking both hands over my hair and holding on to the back of my neck. "I took some photos of the grimoire whilst I was down there. Do you want to play?"

"Yes! Oh. I have to change my bed first."

"I'll do it. Go tip the Juvie crap down the toilet. We can eat lunch, then practise."

After Tayo changed the bed like a professional and I quickly finished the dusting, we sat cross-legged on the bed, eating our lunches. I was surprised to see Tayo had brought me a sweet potato and quinoa salad.

"This is what I would usually pick in the Food Hall," I mumbled with my mouth full.

"I know. You're quite habitual with your food, aren't you? Avocado toast for breakfast, salad for lunch, and casserole for dinner."

"You pay *waaaay* too much attention."

"I didn't really have much to do with my time on dinner duty other than watch you eat. Have you had these before?" He held up a thick paper bag with overlapping triangles covering it.

"No. What are they?"

"Tortilla chips. Do you like crisps?" He pinched the sides of the bag open and tipped it forwards for me to try.

"That"—I tried talking through the dryness—"is like cardboard. People don't actually eat those, do they?"

"These are my favourite." Tayo happily crunched down on one.

"They are sharp and stale at the same time."

"I actually like the texture." Tayo threw another one into his mouth. "Do you have your new Slate yet?"

"Yes, and whatever this is." I tossed him the small box Mason gave me.

"Finally!" Tayo instantly recognised the small box. "Oh, thank God. The institute has finally entered the twenty-second century."

"What is it?"

"An earpiece. It's transparent and fits perfectly inside the ear, so it's impossible for someone to tell it's even there unless they look for it." Tayo eagerly unpeeled the packaging and removed the tiny device, placing it in his ear. He discarded his salad to attend to my new Slate, connecting the earpiece.

"What do I need one of those for?"

"Sound..."

"For...?" I lost interest and stuck some sweet potato with my fork.

"Well, put it this way: I've never needed to type so much on my Slate until I began messaging you."

"Oh," I replied flatly. "You mean voice notes."

"Or video messages?"

"I'd still rather send a text message."

"Well, you can do that, but at least I have an option of how to reply."

"That's if I use it."

"Tut."

I took my last mouthful of food, reclined on my back, and held on to my satisfied stomach. "Thank you, Tayo."

"You're welcome, gorgeous. I'm just pleased I could make your punishment a little less punishing."

"I'm having the best day ever. Is this what it feels like to be a civilian?"

"Erm…I suppose, for some people. Depending on what Band you are, not everyone has to work seven days a week." Tayo began packing the rubbish away into his backpack.

"How come you don't have to go to work unless you want to?"

"Nobody on Band A is overworked. There're loads of us trained to do the same job. Sometimes I turn up and there're so many of us in, I just go home. I can sit there bored, but I'd rather not."

I kicked my plastic container towards him to clear up. "When I'm discharged, I'll have so many Worths I'll never have to work again. We can have duvet days as often as we like."

Tayo got to his knees, and I paid close attention. The thin smile on his lips spread to mine when I worked out what he was doing. He set a swirling in motion inside my belly as he crawled over me. I flattened out across the mattress, unable to keep my hips still as he kissed my neck and shoulders. "On those duvet days," he said softly, "you'll be wearing considerably fewer clothes."

"We could be wearing fewer clothes now. We don't have to wait."

For a brief second, he paused, staring into my eyes before I saw the shield ascend. "We are waiting," he said decidedly, going to sit.

I grabbed his wrist, realising if I played this right, I could probably get what I wanted from him sooner. I would need to catch him in the moment before he switched on that frustratingly controlled head of his. Rolling him over, I straddled his hips, but pre-empting my next move, he held my vest down so I couldn't remove it. I knew he was weak and could be tempted. It would be challenging since his defences were already up, but trying could be fun.

"No." Tayo knew what I was thinking.

"What?" I pushed up on him. Tayo squirmed, driving his lower half into the mattress to make a gap where we touched. I squeezed my thighs around him, rocking my hips and holding his fists by his sides. "What's the matter?" I said, still gyrating against him. "Does someone need a cold shower?"

"You have no idea," he muttered under his breath, taking a final inhale before summoning his willpower and turning on his side.

I slid off him and grinned. "*Spella Tair.*"

"Magic. Right. Of course." Tayo seemed distracted. I think he may have been concentrating on redistributing his blood flow.

"You didn't happen to find a prophecy about the Guidal whilst you were down there, did you?"

His lips twinkled into a smile. "I did."

CHAPTER TEN
A TAYO PERSPECTIVE

Written in, the essence of six, drawn and bestowed upon thee.
Light and shadow together to conserve the land of the free.

Fear would enthral till the one with shine would reign.
The power of this Guidal alone shall remain.
With more than the Puracordis symbol of creation to bear.
Unable to prevent them striving to ensnare.

But the will of nature endeavours to return.
Though it is for the Guidal with balance to discern.
The answer is with the symbol. Creation is the key.
We await the time for Taheke to agree.

Show the tree the six and thus the tree will show the six.
The temple has a secret of its own hidden within its bricks.

"Um…" I paused, my brain needing time to catch up. "I wasn't expecting the prophecy to be so poetic." I gave Tayo his Slate, rested my elbows on my knees, and rubbed my eyes with the heels of my hands.

"From what I can gather from it," said Tayo, scrolling to the start of the prophecy, "the six branches were bestowed on us, but then Taheke feared magic and suppressed it. 'The one with shine' could mean Cryxstalide. It says the power of the Guidal will remain. That's you. You're the only one who can conjure on Cryxstalide. I think you have to work out how to return balance. The answer is with your birthmark. It's the key to everything. You can return magic with it."

"My God, you *are* good, aren't you?" My once-heavy eyes were now wide open.

"I mean, I could be wrong. That's just what I get from it. What's Taheke? I remember the Kalmayan Kid mentioning it."

"Hilly said something about that last year." I thought back to the conversation in the Food Hall when we were all discussing our Juvies. "Poynter said Taheke had no magical blood. I think they shave off their hair to prove they are Taheke."

"All Kalmayans have shaved heads, even the girls. But how does that prove they have no magical blood?"

"Oh, who knows. Your hair would grow back apparently. I have no idea."

"So, the Kalmayans have to 'agree'?" Tayo turned back to his Slate, re-reading the passage. "Probably means to stop hunting Puracordis."

"Yeah, it wouldn't be any good returning magic to the world if they keep hunting us."

"You say 'us'"—Tayo flicked his fringe from his eyes to look at me—"but they are Puracordis, too. It won't be hard to convince them when they can conjure as well."

"Oh my God, yeah. They are Puracordis, too. Oh, the irony."

"Sounds like you've got quite the task."

"Why me?" I rested my cheek in my hand. "I'm not really sure I want it."

"Hey," he said, lowering his eyebrows. "You're going to be alright. And you don't have to do anything if you don't want to."

I straightened my leg, touching his knee with my sock. "I just want to live what normal life I can here, see you, and look forward to our future after this place."

"I want that, too." He closed his Slate, holding my gaze. His eyes switched between each of mine before he pulled his tidy eyebrows together. "Don't worry, okay? If you don't want it, we'll just live our normal life…with maybe the occasional touch of magic."

"I wonder if my mum and dad knew I was the Guidal?"

"Yes. I would say so. Your father risked everything trying to save you that night, even handing you over to me so that you could live out your purpose. I'm pretty sure the Kalmayans almost found you."

I exhaled, crossing my legs and slouching under the pressure. "I wish I could speak to my Nanny Kimly."

"Surely she's allowed to come see you, no?"

"I doubt she would. I'm being punished. She wouldn't disrespect Seioh Jennson like that. I think she's going to be really disappointed with me."

Tayo grimaced. "You only left your room, baby."

"Yeah, but when I was told not to."

"Even still, you didn't do anything *wrong*. You just didn't do as you were told. There's a difference."

My lip pulled upwards. "Is that how you justify it to yourself when you're breaking the law?"

"Yeah, it is actually. So, do you want to practise illegal magic now or after your illegal boyfriend has left your bed?"

"Now, please," I answered in a jovial tone. "What else did you find down there?"

"I found something quite interesting actually." Tayo referred back to his Slate. "There's a section in the book on something called ko-kree. It's where two or more branches merge their magic to conjure something altogether unique and otherwise impossible. The example they give is if a Summoner needs to conjure something that they've never seen, then an Intuitionist can ko-kree with them and help the Summoner acquire the item. Apparently, Summoners can only conjure items that they can picture clearly. So, the Intuitionist, in essence, shares their knowing and helps the Summoner imagine the item."

"That sounds pretty cool, but I'm not a Summoner. So, next!"

"Alright, sarky." He chucked a pillow at me. "I was telling you because if you can branch out already, then we can conjure a memory wisp."

"What do I need to branch out to?"

"An Astralist. They can withdraw their memories into memory wisps. With ko-kree, Astralists can help others withdraw a memory. Do you think you can do it? Branch out already?"

"I don't see why not. I already branch to Healer, but what do we do with the memory once we have it?"

"We can absorb the wisp and watch it. We watch the memory as if it were our own."

I cuddled into the pillow on my lap. "Can you show me that night?"

"What night?"

"The night of my dream, when we were kids."

Tayo's face hardened. "No, Aurora."

"Please. I want to see it."

"No." He gave a short flick of the head.

"Come on, Tayo. I want to see it."

"I said no."

"Why not?"

"I was the last person to see your father before he died, and I was tasered in the back all the way home. I said no. You're not seeing that memory."

"Alright. We need to be in a good mood to conjure, so do you want to relax?"

Tayo got to his feet, heading straight for the ensuite.

"Tayo." A weight plummeted down to my stomach. I leapt off the bed and followed after him. "Tayo." The ensuite door shut in my face. I pressed my forehead against it and closed my eyes. I breathed deeply, deliberating whether to leave him alone, but my fingers lifted to the access button. "Tayo?"

Tayo leant against the sink counter, staring at the floor, his jaw muscles tight.

I stepped to him tentatively. "Tayo, I'm sorry."

He didn't lift his eyes off the floor.

"Tayo?"

"Just give me a minute, Aurora, please?"

"Tayo—"

"*Aurora*," he cut in, freezing my limbs and switching his eyes on me. They weren't as bleak as I was expecting, taken aback by the boundless pain reflecting in his brimming tears.

A battle between my brain and heart broke out. My brain wanted to retreat, but my heart wanted to stay, wanted to make this right, and wanted—*needed*—to stop him from hurting.

I took a step forward. Tayo rolled his head in exasperation. It was enough for me to stop, but not enough for me to retreat. I could reach out and touch him if I dared. I contemplated him, my feet together and my heart in tatters.

Tayo held out one arm and waved me in to him. *Oh.* I could breathe again. He parted his legs so I could stand between them. My forehead dropped onto his shoulder in immense relief. "I'm sorry," I whispered.

Tayo burrowed into my neck. He stroked his lips side to side across my skin before letting the weight of his head rest on my shoulder. After a while he spoke, "When you watch a memory wisp, you feel everything the person felt physically and emotionally. That memory is full of fear and grief, not to mention the worst pain I've ever felt in my life. I don't want you to feel that, okay? Not that memory."

"Okay," I agreed, lifting my head and nodding.

He pulled me into his lips, giving me a single kiss whilst staring into my eyes. "Magic?" He gave a tiny smile.

"What about the memory of when you saw me for the first time?" I asked, raising my eyebrow.

"When I was a Juvie?"

"Yeah. I want to see if you fancied me."

"Of course I fancied you."

"Show me, then." I took his hand and led him into the bedroom.

"Alright…fine. But I'm ending it before that Boulderfell prick punched me in the stomach."

"Okay. I forgot about that."

We both climbed onto the bed and faced each other with our legs crossed. Tayo's messy black fringe covered his eyes as he used his Slate, and I waited for his usual head flick when he raised his eyes to mine.

"So"—Tayo picked up his Slate—"the incantation to begin ko-kree is *Lu-el-ila*. We both say it together to start the collaboration. You put your hands underneath mine, like this." Tayo put his Slate on the bed, turned my hands up to face the ceiling, and placed his open hands on top of mine. "*Ushine Dadinay* is the incantation to conjure a wisp. I think it'll help, especially since I'm so new at conjuring. Then, I'll concentrate on the memory I want to share from start to finish."

"Hushine *Dadinay*?"

"No, Ush-ine. Look." Tayo pushed the Slate forwards to show me the spelling. "Ready?" He placed his hands back on mine and gave a prompting nod.

"*Lu-el-ila.*" We cast the ko-kree spell together.

"Woo." Tayo reacted to the sudden wind rushing our bodies. The magic detected our elation to its breeze and grew even stronger. Tayo and I held each other's tear-swept eyes as our hair tousled over them and our clothes flapped wildly.

"Ready?" Tayo asked over the flapping.

"*Ushine Dadinay,*" we said together.

Our hands absorbed the wind, taking the chaos with it. My outside environment was now calm, but inside my body, it felt as though the wind turned over inside me, running up and down my spine. It was so vigorous I had to stop myself from rocking in my seat.

Tayo closed his eyes, the corners creasing with concentration. I saw a glimmer of purple flicker in his palms. I had a feeling I was supposed to be aiding with this part, so I focused on my positive energy and repeated the incantation in my head. In a bright explosion, the light burst from Tayo's hands and began swirling around and around in a spiral vortex. Tayo sensed the power being released and opened his eyes. The swirling purple mist swelled to the size of a beach ball and then, in the blink of an eye, condensed to the size of an apple.

Tayo lifted the dense deep-purple wisp to eye level, inspecting it closely. It seemed to be floating in his hand and was easily manoeuvred with the slightest sweep. He toyed with it, passing it from hand to hand, running it along the tips of his fingers. Every so often the wisp would display electrical activity like an impulse in the nervous system, and Tayo would ever so slightly flinch.

"Can you feel it when it does that?" I asked, cautious of his reaction.

"Nah."

"No?"

"I just don't like it. Here, take it. It's your turn." Tayo rolled the wisp into my hands. It was incredibly lightweight, and the weird static discharge was the only way of detecting the item. "To watch it, just say *Tri-da Dadinay*."

As the words ran through my mind, the wisp lifted from my hands and forced my eyes closed.

A mumbling from out in the corridor made me still. I hunched on my bed, my white plimsolls placed firmly on the ground and my elbows resting on my knees, supporting my knitted fingers. I kept still, trying to hear what they were saying. The soundproofing of these cells was pretty effective, but I could make out a few words here and there. From what I gathered, the prisoners next door also got themselves caught on purpose. I stopped straining my ears to overhear their drab conversation and waited.

The silence outside made my knuckles squeeze together. *She's coming.* A figure swept past my observer's window, and the cell door slid open. *Come on then, my little Roar, show me what this place has turned you into; show me what I have to work with.*

"Hi, erm…can I…I mean, I need to…tut, just hold out your wrist." Aurora fumbled like an idiot.

I couldn't stop the corner of my lips pulling into a smile. That was not what I expected. She obviously wanted to be nice but tried to be someone she was expected to be. Perhaps they were not all so easily indoctrinated. I ignored the heavy weight plummeting inside my chest.

Okay, I have six months, or longer if I can manage it, to convince you to sneak out of the institute with a Juvie. How tolerant are you? Trying so hard to keep a straight face, I stepped marginally into her personal space. I suppressed my laugh but was caught off-guard by the sudden ripple in my stomach. She was so slender, taller than I imagined, and her angelic white hair suited her. That slim-fitted navy jacket was…erm, accentuating. Taking no notice of my strange feeling, I held my wrist out for Roar to scan. She felt my encroachment and took a small step backwards. *Better than a forceful demand for me to back off.*

Roar stared down at her Slate, and my shoulders tensed, waiting to find out if she remembered anything about me. Being so young when it happened, I highly doubted it, but what if that nanny had reminded her of me?

"You're Band A? Four Worths an hour," Roar blurted after reading my personal information. "What are you doing *here*?"

Good. She appeared too caught up on my Worths Band to notice my name. "Broke Curfew…ma'am." God, I wanted to pluck out my own eyes addressing them as sir and ma'am. *I am not inferior to you, despite what you may have been led to believe.*

"Right. Well, this way, please."

Well, either she didn't pick up on my insincerity, or she decided to ignore it. Either way, that was good news for me.

My eyes opened to see Tayo's gorgeous face staring right back at me. A shockwave of purple gushed from my skin, ruffling Tayo's hair and merging back into the atmosphere.

"*Holy crap.*" I held on to the sides of my face. "That was *incredible*. Seriously, the weirdest experience of my life. It was almost like an augreal but *way* better. I wasn't myself at all. I was you, completely you."

"It's good, then?" he said, holding a note of ribbing in his voice.

"Amazing. Weird as hell, but amazing. I always thought you were a jackass, and that memory wisp confirmed it."

"I never denied it."

"It was so weird seeing that from your perspective. I remember you stepping a bit too close to me, but I wasn't entirely sure if it was intentional." Then I stretched my leg out to kick him for it.

"Ow." He laughed. "I guess I had that coming."

"I gave you butterflies, though." The feeling still lingered in my own tummy.

"No, you didn't."

"*I did*. I felt it. You stepped into me, and I gave you butterflies."

"Nah, I just thought you were hot."

"If you say so." I dipped in my chin. "But how come you felt sad when I first walked in?"

"I dunno." Tayo shrugged and looked away as he spoke. "I guess because you were a Youngen."

"It's not so bad now, though, is it?"

"I'd rather you in my bed. Anyway, it's your turn."

"What do you want to see?" I hugged my knees to my chest.

"Oh, I think you know."

I let go of my legs. "My birthday?"

"Yes. When I almost kissed you in my cell, right up until the end of dinner duty when you wouldn't stop staring at me."

"Do I have to?" I pushed my cool fingers onto my cheeks. He was going to see that I would've kissed him. I intended to hurt him afterwards, but I still wanted him to do it. And then there was that conversation with Silliah on our Slates. She had noticed my newly adopted infatuation, too.

"Yes. You do."

I rubbed my face until it felt sore. Should I let him see it? Being the one branching out to Astralist, I didn't need Tayo's assistance, so I mumbled the incantation, "*Ushine Dadinay*." A pathetic wisp of purple vapour diffused from my palms. "Oh, sorry. I can't. I'm not strong enough."

"Yeah…that's not going to work with me." Tayo stepped one foot onto the platform steps. "Find the enthusiasm for the spell, or I'll go and tell Pax how good you taste."

"I wouldn't. You might make him change his mind."

"Doubtful. The dude's a coward." He stood up and leant his body towards the interconnecting door.

"Alright, sit down," I said in a tight voice. "*Ushine Dadinay.*"

I effortlessly withdrew the memory wisp exploding from my palms in a flash. The purple wisp was brighter in colour than before, and the electrical pulses were more frequent. Tayo extended a flat hand, and I rolled it over.

He winked before absorbing the wisp. "*Tri-da Dadinay.*" His eyes closed, and the purple orb levitated to head height, shrinking down and entering his mind through the space between his eyebrows.

I kept my gaze on his beautiful, peaceful face and waited with a squirming belly. After a short while, the purple shockwave rushed outwards, and his piercing-blue eyes focused directly on mine. He tried to mask his next move with an impassive expression, but I knew he was about to bolt for the interconnecting door, so I threw myself at him and wrestled him down onto his back.

"Give me the memory I asked for, or I will go and say hello to Pax." He didn't try and fight his way out of my hold. He remained perfectly still and allowed his voice to do the persuading.

"I did give you the one you asked for, didn't I?" I ran my buzzing fingers through his hair, focusing on the glossy black strands just so I didn't have to look into his eyes.

"You know full well that wasn't."

"It wasn't?"

"No. That was the time you left me outside my cell with a weighted trap. Give me the memory I asked for..." He held around my jaw and steered my lips to his, brushing his tongue along my parted mouth. I briefly caught his tongue with mine. "Or believe me, I will tell him."

"Alright-alright-alright." I wiped my mouth, trying to take the smile with it. I lifted myself off him and sat back in my spot. "*Ushine Dadinay.*"

"This better be it." Tayo took hold of the new memory wisp. "*Tri-da Dadinay.*"

Before he came back to reality, I gently crossed his legs over each other, and pinned one ankle under my bicep and the other ankle under my knee. I had tangled him up in a leg lock, and it was fair to say he wasn't going anywhere. When he came round, he dropped back onto his elbows. He licked his teeth and tried to look annoyed, but I could see a smile hidden behind his lips.

"That, Aurora, was not what I asked for, but you already knew that, didn't you?"

"It wasn't?" I applied pressure to his ankle tucked under my arm.

"Oow." He followed the pain and arched his back. "Did you like wearing that ankle tr—"

"What memory was it then?"

"A similar situation to this, but when you were trying to make me apologise to you for ducking into my cell in front of that Youngen."

"Sit up and kiss me," I said, enlightening him to the rules of this game.

"Na—ahhhh! Aurora, I'm warning you—"

"Sit up and kiss me."

He laughed silently and shook his head.

"MMMmmmm," he growled at the pain. I'd applied a little pressure to his ankle to act as a bit of encouragement. His cheeks began to glow a rosy red, and he bit down on his knuckle. He could sit up without any pain, but his pride was getting in the way. "Baby, please—MMMmm." He tried to sweet-talk me out of it, but I persuaded him otherwise.

"Sit up…and kiss me."

This time, he still shook his head, but whilst doing so, he pushed himself up onto one hand. When he looked me in the eyes, my heart swooped down into my tummy. Would I be wearing ankle traps in the morning? After an inhale of self-encouragement, he reached to hold onto my neck. He slid his fingers up through my hair and leant in.

An airy laugh burst from his lips. He hung his head, unable to bring himself to do it. He blinked at the mattress for a few as he tried again at swallowing his pride. He held onto my jaw and tilted my head back, his eyes focusing on my neck. "You're using your *enforcery* stuff on me, baby girl." He tightened his grip on my jaw, and I smiled nervously through squished cheeks. My heart raced. We were in a little stalemate, and I loved it.

As his fingers grew firmer around my jaw, so did my lock on his legs. He arched his back before relaxing his hold on me and leaning into my ear. "You, my darling little Roar, are going to regret this." Then, in a determined manner, he brought his lips to mine.

Something fiery ignited between us, and a desire burned deep in my core. Tayo had diminished all pride and was preoccupied with one thing: me. As our mouths loosened, so did my grip on his ankles, and with full mobility, he swept me on my back.

Knowing he didn't have his 'shield' ascended, I unbuttoned his trousers first. This was my chance to get what I wanted. Sliding my hands into his boxers, I made sure he struggled for self-control. He tensed, but it worked, and he guided me up to lift off my vest.

The removal of clothing became frenzied until we were completely skin-on-skin. I gasped as his body weight pressed against me, exactly where I wanted him to be. For the sensitive flesh between my thighs, his skin left a lasting heat. His hand squeezed between our bodies, holding firmly whilst I pushed up against it. When my breathing grew heavier, I pulled his hand away from between my legs, placing *him* there instead.

He gazed earnestly into my eyes. "Are you sure you want to?"

"Yes, Tayo, more than anything."

"But it might hurt a little bit."

"I don't care."

Whispering into my ear, his titillating voice drew my full attention, "Then don't use your *enforcery* stuff on me again." Pushing off the bed, he threw the duvet over my body and disappeared into the ensuite. I laughed airily, surprised at myself for actually thinking he was going to do it after what I'd just done. I rolled my head back and lay still, unable to stop myself from imagining what it would've been like if we'd actually done it.

CHAPTER ELEVEN

I LOVE YOU TWO

"I'm going to miss you tonight, baby girl." Tayo held me tighter and kissed the top of my head. "I've enjoyed the last few days with you. I seriously can't wait for the day you're discharged."

My ear was pressed to his chest, and I lay listening to the bass of his voice, feeling the way it tickled my eardrum. The low humming was soothingly sweet. I wanted to savour my last few moments with him before I needed to return to my dull life of servitude.

"When you're discharged," Tayo said, "I'm going to take you to a beach just outside of Celestine of Fourth City. There's a private sandy cove I found where we can sunbathe and go swimming in the sea. Have you ever laid out in the sun before?"

"No. What is it?"

He gave a short burst of a laugh. "When you...lie out in the sun."

"It sounds boring."

"It's not. There's something really relaxing about it. You don't want to do it for too long, but then you can sit in the shade and watch the ocean. It's one of the most peaceful things you'll ever experience."

"That does sound nice. Will you take me out in the city? I mean before I'm discharged. Take me to your apartment. I really want to see what your life is like outside of here."

"Yeah, I can take you. It's a penthouse. You'll love it. I'll have to time it right so there're no Kalmayans. Not sure how I'll do that, though. Maybe I could just bring you some clothes and hide your face."

"See, now *that* sounds like fun. When can we go?"

He kissed the top of my head. "Soon."

"Soon?"

"Yeah, soon. What time does your party finish tonight?" He released his hold around my shoulders, implying our time together was coming to an end.

"Midnight," I said, not moving, keeping my head firmly on his chest. "You will come back, won't you?"

"Of course."

"If I leave the party any earlier, I'll text you."

"Okay." He pushed himself to sit up, trying to tell me again it was time to leave. I clung to him, pressing my head harder to his chest and hooking my leg higher over his thighs. "Come on, baby," he said with a small laugh. "You've got half an hour."

"Twenty-five minutes with you and five minutes running to the Banquet Hall?" I squeezed him tighter.

"No, five minutes saying bye, ten minutes *walking* to the Banquet Hall, and fifteen minutes being early to make a good impression on Jennson."

"You're right." I huffed, rolling myself onto my back and staring at the ceiling. "I'm sad my solitary confinement is over."

"Back to evenings, it is." He slid to his feet.

I stayed on the bed, but Tayo held his hand out to me.

"And Mando-sleeps if you're not working," I said, taking his hand, playing with the girth of his fingers, and loving how they looked between mine.

He led me to the wardrobe, opened the door, and turned back. His eyebrows furrowed ever so slightly as he stared into my eyes. I held his gaze, getting lost in the deep blue. He cupped the sides of my face and kissed me goodbye. "I love you, Aurora."

My stomach flipped. "I…" Faltering, my skin spoke for me, illuminating with the whitest of lights. It had betrayed me, revealing my deepest feelings. "I…"

"You don't have to say it back."

"I…"

"Have fun tonight."

I nodded faintly, but then falling back to earth, I hummed a flat note. I looked forward to seeing Silliah again but not sitting next to Pax for the next four courses.

"Try and enjoy it?" Tayo lowered his eyes to mine. "Hmm?"

"Mmm." I hummed back even deeper.

Kissing me once more, he reached for the hatch, and I watched him climb down the ladder. The separation already began to poke at my heart. I didn't want him to go. Once the panel closed him out, I looked around the empty room, feeling his absence. It was stupid, really. I'd spent my whole life in a room by myself, but I think I'd gotten a little too used to having constant companionship.

The sentiment made me wander over to my bedside table. I slid open the drawer and stared down at my Promises Ring. It reminded me of the hourglass Pax turned over the day he decided to leave. He left me inside the hourglass, slipping with the sand. I panicked at first, desperately trying to climb up before I suffocated. But when the panic of losing him passed, I surrendered to the fact it was going to hurt. It was only when I was on the other side that I realised I was the one on top; I was on the surface and able to build new foundations with Tayo.

I slammed the drawer shut, leaving the ring exactly where it was. Screw it, screw him, and screw anyone who wanted to comment on our failed relationship.

Leaving my room early for the dinner-dance, I took the elevator to the first floor. I almost stepped round the corner to the Banquet

Hall when a deep, abrasive voice carried down the corridor, stopping my foot in mid-air.

"Joanne doesn't know what she's talking about. How can his own son not be seated at that table?"

"It is a table reserved for those with the most potential," replied Seioh Jennson, "not a table reserved for his biological children. Yes, they have potential, of course, but there are others who show more."

"But what about this girl?" grunted the abrasive voice. "I've never seen her in my lessons. She must be too young. How can she possibly be seated there?"

"She is the only First-year to hold a position on the Colosseum scoreboards," answered a poised Seioh Jennson.

"Fine. I agree Seioh Boulderfell may wish to see her. Why is he seated there?"

"Kian, listen to yourself. You know why he is seated there. He is extremely talented. Not only is he her betrothed, but he is the most improved of last year."

"Of course. Okay. What about these two, then?"

"The only newly betrothed couple to make it into round two of the games. I'm not going to stand here and justify each one to you, Kian. This is Lady Maxhin's floor plan. Her decision is final."

The firm clacking of footsteps marching my way jerked my body into reacting. I stepped around the corner and saw the man responsible for the abrasive tones. He wore an all-black instructor's uniform, but he was not one I recognised. I looked up at him, and he gave me an affronted side glance as we passed each other. Everything about him was thick: a thick, square head and neck; thick grey hair in a faded military cut; a thick nose which looked as though it may have taken a knock or two; and a thick, well-built, solid frame. What the hell did he teach?

Jennson stood in front of a hologram displaying this evening's floor plan. He had his eyes down on his Slate, and I wondered if it were possible for us both to pretend we were invisible to each other for a moment.

"Perhaps next time, Miss Aviary," started Jennson, not looking up from his Slate, "you ought to let your presence be known and not stand eavesdropping on other people's conversations."

"Ah-ah-ah-I-I-I'm sorry, Seioh. I didn't know you were there, and then I did, but it was too late, and then I didn't know what to do, and I really didn't mean—"

"Stop." Jennson held up a flat hand. "Have those two days spent in your room caused you to neglect your brain?"

"No, Seioh."

"Good. Now, use it. Stop clenching your teeth." He gave me a stern look. "Go on—inside. You're on First-table."

"Yes"—I stepped off, taking one long stride—"Seioh."

I entered through fancy panelled doors made of a darkened wood, perhaps walnut. They added to the oval banquet room's outdated feel. Round clothed tables—disappointingly lacking in tabletop screens—were set up, comfortably seating twelve guests each. Being the first to arrive, the hall was empty, but flashing disco lasers spiralled around aimlessly. It was quite creepy, and I felt like I had walked into a post-apocalyptic setting.

Crossing the dance floor to the tables set for Navies, I headed for the table Seioh Jennson referred to as 'First-table'. It was the one placed directly in Seioh Boulderfell's eyeline. He'd be joining all the newly betrothed couples on a long table to the left of the dance floor. And the Musties, not quite old enough to be acknowledged by Boulderfell, were placed behind the long table, completely out of his sight.

On my table, I saw small holographic nametags at each place setting. With a tight backside, I checked to see who my neighbours were, and I let out a sigh when I discovered I had Celeste Antares sitting on my left. Obviously, I had Paxton Fortis on my right, but who cared about that?

Taking my seat, I pushed the silverware back, rested my chin in my hand, and absently watched yesterday's Promises Ceremonies playing in slow motion around the walls. The second-hand embarrassment was real. I almost looked away, when I caught a familiar face. My mouth instantly stretched into an unstoppable smile. It was Silliah and Brindan's ceremony. I watched them reading their lines looking incredibly cute, a little shy, but truly happy.

A parade of Juvies disrupted me, entering the room in single file. All looking uniform in their claret overalls, they circled the room to assume a standing position around the edges and await further instruction. They were followed in by their chaperones, and from then on, the room only got fuller.

"Aurora," sang Silliah. I stood up and was knocked back by the force of her hug. "I've missed you so much. I was so worried for you when you were caught in my room, and then I was told not to make any contact with you. Seriously, Aurora, don't you ever do that to me again. I thought you were going to be discharged for sure."

"Hi, Aurora," cut in Brindan when Silliah came up for air.

"Hey." I smiled at him for being able to get a word in.

He stepped in for a hug. "Hey," he repeated into my ear.

Brindan wore the exact same navy suit to Pax last year. He wasn't as broad as Pax, but it complemented him much the same. The silky navy waistcoat really brought out the blue in his blue-green eyes. Silliah also wore an identical long white dress to mine from last year. It was elegant and floaty and suited her way more than it suited me, hanging gracefully off her curvier hips.

"You look so different without your glasses." I switched to look at her round green eyes. "You look amazing."

"Thank you." She gave a small foot shuffle from underneath her floor-length white dress. "I do not miss my glasses one bit. I've missed you, though. How was your…"

"Solitary confinement?" I helped her out.

"Yeah. How was that?"

"Fine." I shrugged. What I wanted to say was: It was incredible. I had the best time. I miss Tayo already.

"Please take to your seats," Seioh Jennson addressed the bustling room. "Dinner will be served shortly."

"We're on a restricted schedule now," continued Silliah, "for a week. But it's not so bad when there're two of you. Oh, God, I'm sorry—" She reacted to my smile. "I didn't mean to rub it in. I'm so sorry, Aurora."

"It's fine." I nodded subtly. If only she knew. I wished so badly that I could tell her about Tayo.

"We'd best sit down, Silliah." Brindan draped his arm over her shoulder.

"Yeah. Okay," she said, being backed up by Brindan. "See you after dinner, Aurora."

I watched them heading for the long top table, and after they took their seats, I took mine. My bottom had barely touched the chair when somebody whacked me around the back of the head. It wasn't hard, but I tensed up to keep my muscles from lashing out.

"Do that again, Ryker," I spoke without needing to turn around, "and I *will* break your hand."

"I doubt it." He rested against my table, crossing his arms and legs. "A little birdie told me you're on your last warning."

My back slouched. *Of all the people...* "Oh, you would know that, wouldn't you?"

"Actually, I didn't until just then."

"For God's sake, Ryker. Please don't tell anyone."

"I won't, but in future, if you're told to do something, you bloody do it."

"Yeah, alright, Seioh."

"I'm not joking, Aurora. You need to sort it out."

"Ohh, Ryker," I whined, not needing to be reminded of my close call. I already knew I needed to get my act together. "Can you go?"

He stopped leaning against my table and slithered around to my other side. I felt his cheek against my left ear. "I love it when you moan my name," he whispered, slapping me once more and then walking to greet Pipila.

I shuddered at his grossness but started chewing on my fingernail. Ryker knowing I was on my last warning was not good.

Hilly walked in with Calix. She gave me a frantic little wave; he gave me an unfathomable stare. He totally remembered my lie about Seioh Jennson's office. Arriving a fraction behind them were the remainder of the Fanciable Four. Shola and Hyas gave their usual reserved waves. Tyga came in with a boy, touching his arm before jogging over to me, looking like athletes do before a high jump, all straight-armed and straight-legged.

"Missed you, Aurora." He quickly hugged my back before jogging off exactly as he came.

"Alright, Aurora," greeted Nickel, passing by First-table with his friend.

"Alright," I returned to the man whom I'd pushed off the scoreboards last year. The same guy I was punished with and made to keep the Flexon Pro running for four hours straight—projectile vomit guy.

"Have a nice evening," he said, continuing on his way.

"How has she even got a seat at that table?" I heard his friend say in the distance.

"Nah, bro, allow it," said Nickel. "She's alright."

Silliah's old partner joined my table. He sat one away from me, next to Pax's setting. We both flashed empty smiles and then looked opposite ways, ensuring we didn't catch each other's eyes again. But as I looked the other way, I set upon someone else's eyes. They were dark and dangerous, and apparently they didn't appreciate the seating arrangement. Beignley Boulderfell maintained his dauntless stare as he approached. He opened his mouth to speak to me, but after a cursory glance over the top of my head, he turned away. Then Pax placed his hands on my shoulders. Beignley pulled out Romilly Windsor's chair for her to sit down. He kept flicking irritated glances at me before settling down at First-table directly opposite me. I felt like a cobra just reared up to strike but then coaxed back into its basket by the snake charmer. Beignley prised his eyes off me and attended to Romilly.

Pax slid into his seat by my side. "Hey, swe—"

"Stop being nice to me, Pax," I cut him off, starting as I meant to go on.

"Never going to happen."

"Oh, whatever." I shuffled my chair away and swept my cutlery over with me.

"Hello, darlin'." Celeste stroked my hair and sat on my left side.

"Paxton," greeted her betrothed, Thorn, reaching to shake Pax's hand. "Aurora." He patted my shoulder once. These two were betrothed during my Unity last year, and they made it into round two on their very first Parkour Games. I didn't suppose anyone would question their position at First-table.

Bodies moved all around the room, and our table filled up gradually. Beignley's *Coward's Accomplice* joined on with her betrothed. She was the girl who helped Beignley assault me in last year's mid-year rematch of TPG. She looked at me, registering my place at the table and then pulled a face at Beignley. He responded with a sickened eye roll.

Another girl took an empty seat before, finally, Theodred Dorchil and Saulwyn Field were the last to sit down. This picture-perfect pair made the duo *Sovereign Skill*, the many-time winners of TPG. They were also the first-place holders for most, if not all, the machines in the Colosseum. It felt weird being so close to them, especially without a swarming crowd.

A crest of silence broke over the Banquet Hall, and in one sweep everyone stood to attention. Seioh Borgon Boulderfell, the leader of Venair and the adoptive father of everyone enrolled here at the institute, gracefully entered the room. He still had black swept-back hair and a short grey beard.

Walking along the front of top table, he fanned out his cape and regarded every newly betrothed couple in turn. A young brunette woman tailed behind him, and escorting them both in was over a dozen Fell agents. I fidgeted in my seat, putting my hands under the table. The entourage lapped the top table and stood in a long line facing us. Seioh Boulderfell made eye contact with each of us on First-table before finally clearing his throat to speak.

"At ease, my dear children," Boulderfell spoke with exuberance. He waited for us all to be seated before continuing, "Has it been a whole year already? How it has flown by. Time is so precious, and I want you to take a moment to fully appreciate where you are. I want you to take a moment to fully appreciate what you have. You not only have your youth and your whole life ahead of you, but you have the *best* life, a life a civilian could only wish for. This institute was built for you, my children, built for those who had a less fortunate start in life.

"And for those of you at this table"—he gestured to his long top table—"you have just received something exceptional. You have received the rarest perquisite as a Young Enforcer. The person next to you is acutely and scientifically chosen for you. A partnership with such compatibility is difficult to encounter without Unity.

"Now, my lovelies, let us all celebrate together. Without further ado, let us feast. *Serve, Honour, Protect, and Defend!*"

"*Serve, Honour, Protect, and Defend!*" we chanted back with a fist over our hearts. For everyone, repeating that back to Seioh Boulderfell appeared extremely gratifying, and the room's energy was fully charged. I mean, I didn't care for it, but the grit heard in everyone's voices did speckle my neck with goosebumps.

Boulderfell taking his seat prompted the Juvies to turn out of the service doors bordering the room. They returned through one door with a soup bowl in each hand. All Mustards, Navies, and instructors enjoyed tonight's festivities, so each year a maître d' was hired to coordinate the event. This year, they'd found an experienced Juvie for the job. Dressed in her claret overalls, she performed a synchronised service for the top table. As I watched, I spotted a newly betrothed Navy I recognised—Crystal Boulderfell had 'matched' in Unity. I used that term loosely because it was quite probable their match had been orchestrated by her dad. Receiving the Boulderfell seal of approval was a narrow-faced Navy, seemingly a lot older than Crystal. I moved on, still surveying top table, and I paused on the stranger sitting with Boulderfell. I'd never known Seioh Boulderfell to bring a guest, or perhaps I'd never paid attention long enough to notice.

"Who's that woman sitting with Boulderfell?" I asked Celeste about the brunette woman on top table.

"*Seioh* Boulderfell?" Celeste held me with softened brown eyes.

"Yes. Sorry. *Seioh* Boulderfell."

"That's his child bearer," she said, believing she'd answered my question. My expression didn't change, so she continued, "All Seioh Boulderfell's children are conceived using a child bearer."

My forehead pinched, and I opened my mouth but no words came out.

She gave a breathy laugh at my reaction, then lowered her head closer to mine. "Seioh Boulderfell doesn't have a wife. He hires child bearers to carry his children. The women are artificially inseminated, and once they're pregnant, they must stay by his side for the duration of their pregnancy. He only uses a child bearer once, and each of his children has a different biological birth mother." She turned her face closer to my ear to whisper, "All except Ryker and Beignley."

"They have the same mum?" I whispered. She only nodded, so I mouthed, "How come?"

Celeste looked around at the table to check where Beignley's attention was at.

"Sorry you didn't find a match, Roman." Beignley slurped on his soup.

"It's okay," he replied. "I've applied to be enrolled at the *Boulderfell Institute for Fell Agents* when I'm discharged in January."

"Oh, nice."

Satisfied Beignley was preoccupied, Celeste tucked the loose tendril of curly black hair behind her ear and shuffled closer to my side. "You didn't hear this from me, okay?"

I nodded.

"Child bearers sign a contract to say they will emancipate themselves from the children they carry for Seioh Boulderfell, which means they have no right to them and won't acknowledge them as their children. They do it for the Worths because bearing a child for Seioh Boulderfell comes with a lifetime benefit. They'd never have to work again. He only chooses women who haven't had any children, and he binds them into a contract where they can't have children again in exchange for a lifetime of Worths.

"Anyway, Seioh Boulderfell became infatuated with Beignley's bearer. He fell in love with her, and they had Ryker naturally. Ryker is Seioh Boulderfell's only naturally conceived child. Ryker's mother asked to raise him herself and not have him enrolled here. Seioh Boulderfell agreed under the condition she remained at his residence."

"Right, sooo...what's Ryker doing here?"

"His mother passed away."

"Oh. How?"

Celeste held onto a pendant around her neck. "A car accident." She gazed over at Ryker.

"Who wants to enter a wager?" Beignley spoke loudly, addressing the whole table. "Who wants to bet Aurora doesn't last five minutes in the games next week?"

Romilly made a scoffing noise behind her hands.

"Beignley," Pax said, sounding confused but holding a stare.

"I'm joking, Pax. I'm joking. I'm pleased you recovered from your fall last year, Aurora. Nah, that wasn't the wager. Who wants in? The first person to catch the little one"—he looked over at Silliah on top table—"gets a thousand Worths. What do you think, *Smokin' Axe?*"

"Crystal?" I referred to his little sister, who was also sitting at top table and was just as short as Silliah. "Yeah, I'll get in on that one. Should be easy."

Beignley locked onto my eyes with a cutting stare. I held strong, keeping his gaze. It was the mongoose vs. the cobra, and the table wasn't quite sure what to make of the faceoff.

"Who we trying for?" Celeste laughed, squeezing my arm under the table until I looked at her.

"Crystal?" asked Theodred from *Sovereign Skill*, loving nothing more than to wind up his nemesis.

"No. Not Crystal," Beignley said, rattled. "I meant the *other* little one. Never mind."

That's what I thought. Get back into your basket.

The arrival of dessert gave everyone the perfect excuse to continue on with their own conversations. Thorn spoke with Celeste, so I couldn't ask any more about Ryker's mum. Pax didn't speak to anyone; he just picked up his spoon and held it over his bowl of chocolate ice cream. I saw his cheeks flush, and he lifted his eyes my way. I kept myself from meeting his gaze and pushed my bowl away from me, allowing it to melt to nothing…much like our relationship.

A while into dessert, after everyone had their fill, the top table guests were prompted by Lady Liddicott to prepare for the near-touch dance. They collected on the dance floor, and in a well-practised manner, positioned themselves opposite their partners in a long line. The girls faced their handsome fiancés, each holding shy gazes as they waited for the music to begin. We all swivelled round in our chairs to watch. With all eyes on them, the betrothed couples walked towards each other, meeting in the middle and then backing away, all whilst maintaining eye contact. It was a teasing routine, one which was supposed to portray their intimate connection without touching.

Pax kicked his chair back and held his hand out to me. My stomach sucked in at the thought of touching him. It was expected now for every betrothed couple to join in, and I would have no choice but to take his hand. I kept mine twitching together on my lap. I didn't want to feel pain again. Just the thought of dancing with him was already making my chest ache, bringing to mind his softer side, the side that once cared for me, the side that slept up against a wall all night to comfort me.

Unravelling my hands, I wiped them along my combats. His gaze stayed steady on me, and I loosely took his fingers. They were warm and soft, reminding me of everything good about him. He turned, leading me to a clear area, and my eyes prickled, wondering when it went so wrong. We listened for our place to start. Pax's head dropped over to the side when he caught my glistening eyes. I looked through the crowd so I didn't have to see the concern on his face. My swollen heart thumped unpleasantly against my chest. How long was this introduction?

It was time. The swelling in my chest rose to my throat as the tears threatened to break, but I swallowed them down. We held our hands out to each other with our palms facing but not touching. Stepping around in a circle, we switched hands on cue and circled back the other way. Pax's face was pensive, his honey eyes concentrating deeply on mine. His expression gripped me as I tried to decipher it. Finding myself absorbed in his presence, the routine ended. The knot in my stomach began to release. I gave my final curtsy. He blinked slowly as he gave his final bow. Then I turned away.

"I love you, Aurora." His words rushed my veins like burning hot acid, the knot in my stomach wrenching up into my throat.

"What?" I twisted my body but not my feet.

"I'm so sorry."

That could mean one of two things: I'm sorry for everything I've put you through, but I still can't stay, or I'm sorry for everything I've done, and I've changed my mind. My breathing became shallow. I didn't want to know which it was. Before he said anything else, I fled for the exit.

I hadn't made it far down the deserted corridor outside when Pax called after me, "Please talk to me, Aurora. How long are you going to avoid me?"

"What do you *mean*?" I spun on the spot, my white hair whipping onto my shoulder. How long was I going to avoid him? Until he *left*?

"Brindan told me you would make me suffer for a while and to give you space, but this is too hard. I'm so sorry for everything I've put you through." Pax took a step, stopping as if I could be frightened off if he came too close.

"Right…? Apology accepted." My eyes burned, but confusion kept my tears away.

"But you won't forgive me?" He seemed as confused as I was.

"Okay. Yes. Fine. I forgive you. Now what?"

"Let me…make it up to you?"

No. No. No. No. No. No. My eyes burst, soaking my cheeks as Tayo poured into my mind. My chest felt like it was going to implode. "You're not leaving?"

Pax frowned, still looking confused, and he flicked his head as a short no.

CHAPTER TWELVE
IN SHORT, IT'S ALL OUR FAULT

I ran past the elevators and took the emergency stairs down to Khaki Quartz. I heard Pax tailing me, but he didn't follow me into my bedroom. He remained next door in his room. *Because that is what Pax does: he hides in his room.*

Tayo always knew what to do, and right now, he *needed* to know what to do more than anything. A heavy swelling burdened my chest as I waited for the wardrobe door to open.

"Roar." His troubled eyes landed on mine.

Seeing his face made my heart lift into my throat. I was going to hurt him badly with the words trapped in my airways. My breathing became erratic, and then he was a blur.

"Whoa-whoa-whoa. Shh. Hey." He fell on the bed beside me and held on to my head. "I got your message. What's happened?" He leant back for my answer.

"Pax changed his mind." I knotted his T-shirt up in my fist. "He isn't leaving."

"Yes, he fucking is." The T-shirt ripped from my fingers as Tayo bolted straight for Pax's bedroom, punching the access button with his fake picoplant hand.

The adjoining door slid open.

"You fucking coward." Tayo disappeared into Pax's room, leaving the door open. "What—you heard us in the shower and decided you didn't want Aurora to be happy? Or what—you found out we're all Puracordis and thought you could just pick her back up again? You need to *leave*."

I hurried into the room to see Pax on his bed, sitting up on his elbows, temporarily stunned whilst he dealt with Tayo barging into his room.

"Um, okay. No, Tayo." Pax climbed out of bed. "I have no idea what you're talking about, and I think you need to leave."

"You fucked up." Tayo clenched his fists and stepped into Pax's face, red searing up his face and neck. "You dropped Roar when she needed you the most. She was scared shitless, and you cast her away like she was *nothing*."

"Tayo." Pax placed a hand on Tayo's chest and backed him up. "I am well aware of the pain I've caused Aurora, and now I'm trying to make things right *with my betrothed*. Now, I'm going to tell you one more time before I have you arrested. You need to leave." He kept his eyes firmly on Tayo but spoke to me, "Aurora, make him leave before I make him leave."

"Tayo." I quickly recovered from my daze. "Just…maybe you should go for tonight? I'll text you."

Tayo clamped his teeth together, still staring at Pax. They fixated on each other as their breathing grew laboured. My body tensed, but then Tayo peeled away from Pax and came over to me. "I'm not losing you, Roar." His teeth clamping worsened but he kissed the top of my head and turned for the door. "You fucking coward," he spat at Pax before leaving.

I dropped to my knees. They smashed against the solid panels, but I hardly felt it. Pax paced up the room, turned, and paced back. Coming in line with me, an unrecognisable tone came from him, "I know I messed up, Aurora, but *what the hell are you doing?*"

My throat tightened at the harshness in his voice. "You were leaving," I croaked, keeping my eyes down, watching the tears leave dark splashes on my combats.

"Did you think I was leaving, or did you *want* to think I was leaving?"

"No, Pax." I lifted my eyes to his, needing him to believe me. "I loved you so much. More than anything. I would never have…"

"Spent time in the shower?" Pax finished my sentence with an accusatory tone.

I couldn't speak. The word 'yes' got lodged in my throat along with the rest of my innards.

"You need to tell Tayo to leave you alone."

"Uhh…I…" I said breathlessly, my whole body trembling. "I…I can't."

Pax shook his head and walked in a mindless circle. His feet wandered in and out of my periphery. I didn't dare take my eyes off my knees.

Pax's feet stopped, facing me. I knew he watched me, but I couldn't look up at him.

He joined me on the floor. "We are betrothed, Aurora." He took both my hands.

"You wanted to leave me."

"I was an idiot."

I pulled away, taking my hands from him. "When did you change your mind?"

He shrugged. "It just took me a bit of time to get used to the idea. I honestly thought you were giving me time. We've been… good? Until I messed up again, that time you gave the ring back. But I thought you were just mad at me. I asked Brindan for help, told him I wanted to fix things but didn't know how. He said to give the ring back on Unity and see whether you'd put it on. He told me he tried talking to you about it on Monday, but you cut him off and left, and I haven't been able to get a word in edgeways all week."

"I thought you…" I decided to reword my sentence. "You didn't know about Tayo?"

"No, Aurora." His face crumpled harshly. "Why would I know about that?"

"Three showers…?" I said, dropping my eyes but then reading his expression from under my eyelashes.

"*Eww.*" His lips curled, and he looked away, staring at the interconnecting wall. "Oh, God, Aurora, no. I can't even think about that. I literally thought I'd upset you by giving the ring back and you couldn't sleep. I stayed awake so late that night wanting to come in to you, find out if you were okay. I decided to wait until the morning…and you were…*angry*. And you've been angry with me ever since. But you put the ring on. I was so confused. All this time, you…*oh.*" He shuddered, but seeing splashes on my combats, he reached over and wiped the tears falling from my chin. "Do you… love him?"

I only shrugged.

"Do you want me to leave?"

My gut twisted. He was so kind. How could I ask him to leave the institute, leave his friends, his whole life behind, to be dedicated to Boulderfell, unable to have a family of his own?

But Tayo.

I hid my face in both hands, unable to give him the answer he deserved. "I don't know."

"You need to tell me if I'm leaving, Aurora. I can't…I can't stay and watch that."

"What kind of decision is that?" I stopped rubbing my head to look at him. My whole body trembled. "How can I make that decision?"

The pain on Pax's face was unbearable. I knew he was stopping himself from crying. There was a film over his eyes, but he was one blink away from tears. He covered his eyes with one hand and asked, "Have you and Tayo…slept together?"

"No."

He took his hand away from his face. "You're still a—"

"Yes. Not that it matters."

Pax's shoulders dropped. "It matters to me, Aurora. We're betrothed. It was always something I thought we'd share together on our wedding night. Is Tayo Puracordis? Is that how he gets inside the institute?"

"Something like that. Pax, I've got to go to bed." Sleep was out of the question, but I needed space to think. "I can't do this right now. I need to be on my own."

"Aurora, please"—he wiped the tears off my cheeks again—"please don't spend any more time in the shower with him until—"

"I won't."

"I'm not pressuring you into making a choice right away, but you need to let me know if I'm leaving."

"You're not leaving, Pax. I just need time to figure this out."

I left Pax on the floor and turned into my room. I walked in to find Tayo propped up against the display screen. "Tayo, you were supposed to go."

"Not a chance in hell." He got up from the bed as I threw myself down. Storming across to the adjoining door, he looked into Pax's room. "Here, let me make this room a little more familiar to you." He punched the access button, closing the interconnecting door.

I sobbed with my face in the mattress. Tayo came back over and cradled my head. "I know you choose me, Roar." He used his T-shirt to dry my cheek. "I just need to figure out how to get Pax out of the picture without making him a Fell agent."

"Tayo," I warned, pulling out from under him and sitting cross-legged.

"I'm not going to do anything unless you agree."

"Oh, this is too much." I folded in half, pushing my eyes onto Tayo's legs. He rubbed my back, and my muscles began to release. "I don't know what to do, Tayo."

"I know, baby girl." He sighed. "I know."

It didn't take long before we naturally found ourselves in each other's arms. My ear pressed against his T-shirt, and I fought back the overwhelming urge to make contact with his bare skin. My heart still pounded uncomfortably, and I was sure I could physically feel blood being pumped around my body. Tayo's lips rested on my hair. For a while, it felt so safe and familiar. That was until I felt his breath change from his nose to his now parted mouth. I had a feeling he was about to speak.

"Aurora."

"No, not my full name." I squeezed my eyes shut.

"Sit up and look at me."

I didn't move. I didn't want to hear what he was going to say.

"Aurora," he repeated. So much pain hung in my name.

"Don't say whatever you're going to say, Tayo." I looked up to see tears in his round piercing-blue eyes. Mine began to sting. I climbed across his lap and kissed him, preventing any words from leaving his lips.

Tayo pulled my hand off the back of his neck and angled his face away. "Aurora." He exhaled jerkily. "Go and tell Pax you choose him."

"What? No, Tayo. Are you fucking joking right now?"

"You need to go and tell Pax you choose him." He inhaled deeply, fighting back tears. One managed to escape down his beautiful face, but he wiped it away quickly. "You two are *betrothed*. I'm ninety-nine-percent sure there's no way out of it, because if there was, Pax would've done it when he first found out you were Puracordis. You two are going to be married at the end of Thirteenth-year. What else am I supposed to do, Aurora? You need to go and tell him you choose him."

"But I don't want to. I want *you*."

"I know you do." He pulled my hand off his neck again. "But I'm just getting in the way." Tayo tried to stand up, but I wrapped my arms around him. He lifted me up, and I clung on with everything I had. "Baby, there isn't another choice." He leaned forward, lowering my feet to the floor.

"Tayo, don't do this. I don't want this."

"Roar." He dried my face with his T-shirt. "It's not fair to make him a Fell agent. What choice have I got but to leave?"

"Not like this, please?"

Tayo couldn't fight it any longer, and his face was as wet as mine. He opened up the drawer to my bedside table and pulled out my Promises Ring. He took hold of my left hand and slid the plain band on my finger. "I love you so much, Roar." The tremble in his voice broke my heart. "But I don't have a choice."

"Tayo." I wiped my tears, desperately trying to see his face through them.

"I'm so sorry."

"No."

He backed away. "I'm going to let the dust settle for a while."

"No-o-o-o," I cried the word in several syllables between sobs.

"Roar, come on. Be strong, please." The pain made his voice faint and stretched. I could hardly recognise it as Tayo's. "What choice do we have?"

"Let me come with you."

"No way, Aurora. Not a chance," he said, sounding more like Tayo. "That is not a life for you. You're not living in hiding. Now, I'm serious—go."

"Please, Tayo." I tried to reach for his hand.

He avoided me purposefully. "GO."

"NO."

Tayo backed away towards my bedroom door. "If you don't go and tell Pax you choose him, then I am going to walk out of your bedroom and get myself taken to Maximum Security."

"What..." The sound from my mouth sounded more like a whimper. "That's so unfair, Tayo."

"*This whole situation is unfair*," he said severely, tears streaming down his cheeks. "It's unfair you don't get to choose who you marry, it's unfair we don't get to choose each other, and it's unfair to make Pax leave. But that's the institute for you, Aurora. You don't get to choose."

My knees weakened as the uselessness set in. "You said you wouldn't let me hit the ground."

Tayo's mouth dropped as an audible breath escaped. "I—" A crack followed his word, hurt glistening in his tears. "That's not fair." He shook his head. "Baby, you like him. He will catch you. Pax will catch you."

"I want you to catch me."

"How?"

My face contorted as I desperately tried to think of something, *anything*. I couldn't make Pax leave, and I would be married to him at the end of Thirteenth-year. Tayo was the problem solver, and if he couldn't think of anything, what chance did I have?

"Tayo..."

"Go on. Go."

"Will you text me?" I asked, grasping at anything, any tiny bit of him.

"Just give you two a chance to...get back on track." Tayo looked away to hide his face, but I already saw he struggled badly with the sentence.

I couldn't move. This couldn't be it.

"Don't make me walk out of this door, Aurora." He held his hand over the access button.

"*Arrrrrrrrggh.*" The thunderous cry tore through my throat as I clenched every muscle in my body. I wanted to scream the walls down. Constriction in my throat, nails digging in my palms, ringing in my ears, I couldn't take anymore.

Tayo nodded to move me on, and I exhaled an exasperated sigh. He wasn't going to back down. I took a small step towards the adjoining door just to keep him from pressing the access button. This was so unfair. I shook my head at Tayo in one last desperate attempt for him to change his mind, but he motioned for me to go. My throat cramped up. Love fucking hurts.

I turned to face the plain white door and stared at nothing before I found the strength to push the button. I didn't look behind me again. My constant companion, the one person who knew me inside and out, my best friend...I couldn't imagine my life without him.

Pax stopped rubbing his eyes when he heard the adjoining door open. He immediately slid up to lean against the blackened display screen. His face was blurry through my stream of tears, but I could still see his eyes were red and puffy.

I didn't make it far into Pax's room before I found myself face-down on the white leather sofa. I couldn't talk. The crushing around my airways was the only thing holding back my scream. What was I even doing in here?

CHAPTER THIRTEEN
PIP PIP

When the alarm rang in the morning, the smell of leather met me, and I remembered where I was. *'GO'* tore through me as Tayo's words struck my core. I squeezed my eyes tighter, trying to quash everything brewing inside me. My chest hurt from the cracks forming in my heart as I realised I'd never hold his hand again, never hear the deep, soothing hum of his voice through his chest, and never practise conjuring with him again.

During the night, Pax had covered me with a duvet, and I held the sheet to my nose, checking if it was mine. My heart punched me in the chest when the woody aroma of Tayo's aftershave filled my airways. *Yep, definitely my duvet.* I kicked it to the floor.

"How are you feeling this morning?" Pax appeared tentatively in my periphery.

Devastated. Angry. Resentful. Heartbroken. Pick one.

When I ignored his question, he spoke again, "Look. I'm going to leave, okay? I'm going to get an invitation."

"Don't you dare," I growled through gritted teeth, my eyes clamped tightly.

"Aurora, I just want you to be happy."

"Don't. You. Dare," I repeated, less fierce but still sharp.

"Alright, but I'm out of my depths on this one, sweetheart. You just tell me what you need, okay?"

His patience made me open my eyes, and my lip trembled. "It *hurts*, Pax." I almost lost my sentence to the pressure in my throat. My scarcely discernible words etched pain into Pax's sullen face. Those bloodshot eyes were a window to what he, too, contained inside. He managed a half-hearted nod before dropping by the sofa and pulling my head to his chest. He faintly rested his forehead on my shoulder. My tears came heavy, but Pax remained steadfast, occasionally squeezing the back of my neck, allowing me to cry myself empty. Eventually, only our desultory sniffs interrupted my silent tears.

Being Sunday and the last day of Unity, it meant a day of weddings and a pretty clear schedule. Since my solitary confinement was over, I had permission to see everyone, but I really didn't want to see anyone right now except Tayo.

Seeing Tayo's face in my mind, I pulled away from Pax's alleviating stance. I rolled onto my back, hiding my face with my arm. I didn't want to be comforted by him. Pax stood up, touched the top of my head, and got back into bed.

Neither of us left for breakfast.

"We should go to lunch...Aurora." Pax roused me from my sleep.

"I don't want to," I said through a raspy, dry throat.

"Let me take the sofa, then; you get in bed."

"*No.* I'm so mad at you, Pax," I burst along with more tears. "Why couldn't you have just accepted me for who I was, then none of this would've happened. I wanted *you.*" My throat tightened, stretching my voice. "I loved *you.*"

"I'm so sorry." He stood rooted to the spot, rubbing his neck. "It just took me some time, that's all. I didn't know I was against the clock. If Tayo had kept away from you, you would've made me suffer like Brindan said, but then we would've gotten back on track. I just needed some time to get my head round it. Why would I think there was someone else; we are *betrothed*."

I kneaded my eyes until they hurt, distracting myself from the twisting in my gut. "You were *leaving*, Pax."

"Was I?" Pax started to pace. "I'm still here." He turned his face to the ceiling and pushed his hands through his hair. "Yes, I wanted to, back when it happened. But you knew I didn't want to leave." His voice shook, and he stopped pacing. "You heard me say it. I wanted so badly to tell you that I didn't want to leave you, but then you heard it for yourself."

I sat up quickly to defend myself. "That didn't mean you weren't going to leave. I thought you were going regardless because I was breaking the law. You're on the scoreboards."

"So are *you*," he raised his voice, sounding more exasperated than angry.

"What about all the time you're spending in the Colosseum with Pipila?"

"She wants to leave. She begged me to help her get a high score, so I am." Pax stopped pacing, and the room fell silent. My brain tried to make sense of it all. He wasn't trying to leave, he hadn't been trying to leave for months now, and he'd known nothing about Tayo. I lay back down and held my forehead.

"I know I hurt you badly, Aurora. I know I did. I'm so sorry for everything I put you through."

I covered my face with my arm, willing Pax to go away. When I heard him get back in bed, I twisted onto my side, facing my back to him, and I checked my Slate. I had messages from Silliah, Brindan, Ryker, Hilly, and Tyga. Apparently, they weren't checking by my room because they thought Pax and I had worked things out after the near-touch dance. I ignored all the messages and sent one to Tayo.

'*Please, Tayo, don't do this. You're my best friend.*' I put my Slate down and allowed the weight to take my eyes.

Neither of us left for lunch.

⁂

"Swee—Aurora, we have a meeting scheduled with Seioh Jennson in half an hour," said Pax, followed by a clinking sound on the coffee table. When did I stop becoming 'sweetheart'?

My tear-stained eyes peeled open, seeing a steaming bowl of casserole on the table. Closing my eyes again, I turned my back on Pax, having no intention of leaving the room. Instantly, my foot started to judder as thoughts of Jennson trickled in. The progress I'd made with him lately would be lost, and I *was* on my last warning. But did I care?

"Aurora?"

There it was again. "Go away, Pax."

I heard his sigh and then footsteps slinking away. I knew I needed to get up, but I couldn't move. I didn't want to get into trouble, but I needed sleep to take me away. Pax was just making the conflict worse, reminding me I was making the wrong decision.

Help me.

I didn't know who I asked for help, but I knew I needed it.

Get up, I told myself from nowhere. My muscles began to ache knowing I was about to force myself up. I heaved my legs off the sofa before I had the chance to change my mind, and I left for the meeting without changing my creased Navy uniform or bothering to eat.

Last year, Pax's and my time together was usually spent ignoring each other, and nothing had changed there as we made our way to Seioh Jennson's office. Even as we neared the end of the Navy residential corridor, Pax turned one way and I turned the other. It was all too familiar.

"This way, swe—" He coughed.

Stop it, please...

I closed my eyes. My chest was already hurting, and I didn't want to hear him censoring the name he'd called me forever.

"It's in Lady Liddicott's office." Pax waved me in his direction.

It was late, and the corridors were emptying as everyone retired to their rooms for the evening. No one was around when we arrived at Khaki Quartz, so we managed a private transit through to Lady Merla Liddicott's office. Pax reached to press the access button when a deep, abrasive voice made him snatch his hand away.

"I understand it is protocol, Seioh," said Kian irritably, "but surely, there are exceptions."

"Seioh Boulderfell issues the—"

I quickly tapped on the office door, learning my lesson from eavesdropping yesterday and interrupting Jennson's reply.

The same clanking of shoes approached the door. Pax and I stepped to one side. Kian exited as if we were invisible, and Pax allowed me to walk in first. Lady Merla Liddicott perched on the edge of her fuchsia-pink armchair, her hands cupped on her lap. Seioh Jennson stood importantly by her side. Before we could stand to attention, Jennson gestured to the yellow sofa. I flopped down heavily and fought back tears.

"...and though Unity is mandatory," Jennson was saying, "Seioh Boulderfell does not like to see his children unhappy—you seem distracted, Miss Aviary."

I coughed to steady my voice. "I'm fine, Seioh."

He read me for a second, his eyes roving over my face and wrinkled uniform. He switched to assess Pax, but then, as if finding nothing, he carried on talking, "When we are presented with a situation such as yours, we have a set protocol..."

My heavy eyes fell closed for a moment as sadness rippled up my body.

"...if the counselling sessions are ineffective," continued Jennson, "revisiting Unity is usually successful..."

I controlled my breathing, hoping it would help keep my eyes from embarrassing me.

"...after one year, if the problem still persists, then we end the nonsense once and for all." Seioh Jennson walked over to the white desk opposite the seating area. I began to pay attention once he handed Pax and me each a piece of paper. The posh piece of thick paper had golden edges and embossed black writing.

Dear Miss Aurora Aviary,

You are hereby cordially invited by Seioh Borgon Boulderfell to enrol at the Boulderfell Institute for Fell Agents.

When you accept this invitation, you will be received by Seioh Boulderfell to pledge your devotion...

"Now"—Seioh Jennson regarded Pax and me in turn—"here is the decision for you to make. Shortly, Merla and I will leave the office; you will both remain here to make your decisions. Your options are as follows: you take the invitation and wait at the Navy reception to be escorted to the *Boulderfell Institute for Fell Agents* tonight. You will take your vows upon arrival, and the betrothal will be renounced. You will no longer be betrothed to each other and will begin a new life without each other.

"Or you leave the invitations on the coffee table. If you both decide to leave your invitations, you will be choosing to stay betrothed to each other and will retake your Promises tomorrow afternoon. From then on, you work on your relationship. You accept each other, you grow with each other, and you begin a new life together, one with the love and support of each other.

"The decision is yours to make. Merla, if you will." Seioh Jennson held a hand out to Lady Liddicott's lower back, and they left us alone to make our decisions.

We discreetly watched each other from the corner of our eyes. Pax pivoted on his seat, tucking his leg underneath him. If this decision had been presented to us early last year, the result would've been entirely different. I would be begging Pax to stay, and more than likely, he would have left. Time had turned the tables, and now Pax was the one looking at me with a hollow face.

"Oh, just put your invitation on the table, Pax." I put him out of his misery.

"What about yours?"

I held the invitation in both hands. The idea of becoming a Fell agent had never occurred to me. I didn't have much time to make such a life-changing decision, but I knew one thing: Taking a vow of abstinence appealed to me right now. My heart was throbbing, and I wanted to escape the pain. "I hate Unity. I don't want to be betrothed to anyone. In little over a year, I have loved and lost both you and Tayo. I would rather take a vow to Boulderfell than go through this again."

"Being a Fell agent isn't the answer, Aurora."

"I want out. I don't want to feel this again."

"If you love me again, it'll be forever. I promise you, Aurora."

"It fucking *hurts*." I felt the vibration in my throat as the words left my gritted teeth.

Pax ducked his head at my swearing. "I know, I know." He blinked rapidly, leaning over to get his invitation. "Aurora, you don't want to be a Fell agent. Stay and let me go."

"Put your invitation back on the table. If I go, I never have to feel this pain again. I will never be forced to be with anyone again."

"Please, Aurora. Please stay. Let me make this right," Pax's voice shook. "If you never love me again, fine. But do not make yourself a Fell agent." He messed with the invitation in his hands until the edges became tatty. "Stay with your friends, your Nanny Kimly, and allow me to stop you from matching in Unity again. You never have to do it again. You never have to love anyone again."

I looked up from my invitation, seeing water building in Pax's eyes. A blink later and a tear rolled down his cheek.

"What?" I said in a sigh.

"Just leave your invitation on the table. I'll stop you from matching in Unity again." Pax coaxed the invitation out of my fingers. "Please?" He placed it on the table and backed towards the door, waiting for me to move before he walked any farther.

I stared at the fancy paper on the coffee table. "Are you saying we pretend to be united?"

Pax nodded.

I studied his face for deception. "Why?"

"Why?" he asked with a furrowed brow. I had a feeling he wasn't confused but was making sure he gave me the right answer.

"Yes." I banged my heel on the floor. "Why would you do that?"

"This is my fault, Aurora. The pain you're in is my fault. I want to make it right. Let me do this for you."

"And at the end of Thirteenth-year, when we're married and discharged together, then what?"

"Whatever you want: separate bedrooms, separate houses, or separate lives; it's entirely up to you."

"If I leave, you could be matched in Unity again and actually have a good relationship."

"I don't want that, Aurora. I hate Unity. You know that. Let me do this."

I looked at the invitation on the table and then back at Pax.

"Please." His tear-swept amber eyes flinched with the emotional pain hiding behind his voice.

I rubbed the ache in my head. It was all too much.

Pax sat on the coffee table and took my hands away from my face. "I've got this. Please come with me?" He guided me to my feet.

I stood, but my mind wasn't made. Feeling like the decision was being taken from me, I backed away, shaking my head.

"I've got you," Pax said faintly, lowering his eyes in line with mine.

"It just doesn't sound fair."

"On me? If you leave, I could be matched in Unity again. I don't want that. It benefits us both."

For the first time, I heard reason instead of persuasion in his voice. "You better be right about this."

"I am."

"Fine."

I left the office, making sure I turned in the opposite direction of Pax.

Before going to my bedroom for a sleepless night, I sought the Food Hall for a peppermint hot chocolate. I inhaled the empty room like it was fresh air. Only the buzzing from the meal dispenser interrupted the silence, and I found it soothed my mind.

Turning for a tabletop screen, I caught sight of someone slumped over a table. "Ryker?"

The pile of a person didn't respond. Ryker had his head on the table and was cradling it with both arms. I approached warily. His eyes were closed and his cheeks wet.

"Are you…alright?" I lowered down onto the chair next to him.

Again, he didn't respond. So, I squeezed his hand gently before deciding to leave him alone. Ryker held on to my fingers, and I kept my foot from taking another step. He didn't do any more than that, and I regarded the top of his head. Stuck for what to do, I lowered back down onto the seat next to him. I lay my head on the table and joined him in the pool of despair. He looked how I felt anyway.

I wondered what Tayo was doing right now. Was he in pain? I wanted to go back and relive this year all over again: going down to the temple for the first time, seeing his guilty face when he touched the ultraviolet platform, watching our memory wisps, and talking all night about conjuring. My tears resurfaced, but I didn't try to stop them. Ryker wasn't exactly in a position to judge.

The faint ring of a female voice brought me back into the room. It was coming from the corridor over by Claret Quartz. I focused on it. The voice was only vaguely familiar, and the odd grunt from a male meant I couldn't identify the couple. She stopped speaking as they entered the Food Hall. The sight of Ryker and me—holding hands, wallowing with our heads on the table—must have been quite alarming. I wouldn't have known what to make of it, for sure.

"Oh, man up, Ryker. There's plenty more fish in the sea." Along with the venomous notes of Beignley's voice, came an almighty slap across Ryker's head so loud it caused a high-pitched ringing in my ears. Ryker didn't react, but I did.

"*Leave him alone.*" I sprang from my chair before I had time to think. Ryker felt my launch and spun up out of his chair. It was just in time to shield me from Beignley's backhand to the face. Romilly burst for me, but Beignley kept her back. Ryker held his arm out at my waist.

"Touch her…and I'll break your fucking neck." Ryker squared up to his brother, making Beignley take a single tread back.

"She ain't even your girl, bro. What you protecting her for?"

"Touch her and it'll be the last thing you do."

Beignley flicked a look at me from over Ryker's shoulder. He seemed taken aback that I, of all people, could cause Ryker to turn on him. Beignley eyed Ryker and me, but then, after kissing Romilly's head, he led her past us, and they left the Food Hall.

Ryker turned on his heel and shoved me in the chest. "What the hell is wrong with you?" He shoved me again. "He is Beignley *Boulderfell*, you stupid bitch."

"So?" I backed away, seeing Ryker was about to shove me again. I could defend myself, but I felt fragile and tears were surfacing. I didn't want to provoke him into using his training against me. It would escalate the situation and make me look like I cried over it.

Seeing I retreated, he stopped coming for me. "He isn't done with you, Aurora. I could tell by the way he looked at you." Ryker clenched his fists and glanced over at the empty corridor Beignley used to exit. "I swear to God, if he touches you."

"I don't need you to protect me, Ryker."

"You're an idiot, Aurora. What have you done? If he doesn't physically hurt you, at best he'll get you discharged. I've already lost Pipila. I don't want to lose you, too."

"Lost Pipila?" I tried processing my thoughts. She was trying to end the betrothal all last year. Seioh Jennson had to have known. "Were you both offered an invitation, too?"

"Yes. Pipila took it. She's gone. Now sort your fucking life out."

"Well, maybe if you Boulderfell pricks weren't so heavy-handed, Pipila might still be here."

"What the hell are you talking about?"

"You splitting Pipila's lip."

"That wasn't me, you idiot." His black eyes darted around the empty room. "I would never do that to her." Despite being alone, Ryker leant in closer to me. "Her dad split her lip."

"Her dad?"

"Yes. Sir Kian Darlington, the Lethals instructor."

"Kian." I remembered the thick-bodied, thick-headed, thick-everything instructor always arguing with Jennson.

"You wouldn't have had him yet. First-years can't take Lethals. He was partly why she had to go. He bullies her. That and she believes he had something to do with us matching in Unity."

"Really?" According to Tayo, she wasn't far off. "And what do you believe?"

"I don't think my dad would allow a Unity assessment to decide who marries into his family, so yeah, it's probable. Beignley is betrothed to Romilly Windsor, a descendant of Old England royalty. I'm not convinced it's a coincidence. The Darlingtons have been family friends for decades. I love Pipila as a friend, but we don't like each other like that. I don't think we matched in Unity."

"Friends? You two are always arguing."

"Only where you were concerned." He leant on one hand holding the back of a chair. "She wanted me to keep away from you. We were still best friends and have been since Mustard."

Done with the conversation, I turned towards the Navy Quartz corridor. "How can you even be friends with someone like that?" It wasn't a question I needed answering, and I started to walk away.

"Like what? You two are both as bitchy as each other."

"What?" I swivelled back to him. "In what universe am I like her?"

"This one, Aurora." He crossed his legs at the ankles. "Everyone knew how much she liked Pax. Had done since they were kids. Then that day in the Food Hall last year, you rubbed your match in her face."

"She started it." I took a few more steps towards him, returning right back to where I was before.

"Yeah, and you ended it. What was it you said? 'I took the Show of Force Display off you when we were younger, so I thought I'd take your seat at the table, too. You would rather be sitting with Pax, wouldn't you?'"

"Not quite what I said," I mumbled.

"It was close enough." He didn't wait for any excuses and simply pushed off the chair. "Goodnight, Aurora. Oh"—he stopped, turning back to me—"and swear in front of me again and you will see me be heavy-handed."

"Fuck off, Ryker."

He jarred his body towards me, making me flinch and step back. He smirked at my reaction and walked away. "Pax and Pipila kissed, by the way," he called out without so much as a backwards glance. "Thought you ought to know."

Heat fizzled down my face. I opened my mouth to call Ryker a liar, but nothing came out. My teeth clamped together. Pax wouldn't have, would he? Ryker had to be lying.

I didn't walk into my room when I returned to Navy Quartz. I went straight into room 434 instead, but I just stood there lost in my own thoughts. *He wouldn't have kissed her. There's no way. Not* her.

Pax came out from the ensuite, his soggy blond-brown curls clinging to his forehead. He took one look at me and approached warily. "Are you…okay?"

"Did you kiss Pipila?" My stomach turned as I heard the question back.

The sudden drop on his face answered my question, and my hand lashed out, catching him across the cheek. A red blotchy patch instantly rose to the surface of his skin.

He bit down on his lip, controlling his urge to lash out better than I did. "You've been doing far worse with Tayo. Would you like me to slap you across the face now?" The air thickened as he held me with his glare. "Don't *ever* do that again. *She* kissed me."

"Show me."

His eyes crinkled at the sides. "Show you?"

"Yes. Unless you want me to go and take that invitation, you're going to show me right now."

"Aurora—"

"*Now.*" I growled the word from the back of my throat.

"Fine." His body tensed up, raising his broad shoulders. "How?"

"We're all Puracordis, Pax. There's a pollutant in the water supply." I pulled him over to the bed. "Sit down. *Spella Tair.*"

Pax squinted, caught up with the bombardment of information and instruction. He watched the green mist from my hands being absorbed into his skin, and he shook his head at it. He was an Enforcer who obstinately followed the rules, and now he was being forced to break the law.

I grabbed a pen from his desk and drew the symbol of creation on his wrist. Pax's lip hooked when he recognised it as my birthmark.

"Say *Lu-el-ila* with me." I placed my hands underneath his, starting the ko-kree spell. The limp breeze reflected Pax's unwillingness, but I had enough power for the both of us. "You need to focus on the memory from start to finish. Ready?"

Leaking resentment, Pax flicked his head downwards once for a yes.

"Say *Ushine Dadinay.*"

The wind spiralled down into our hands like a cyclone, Pax closed his eyes, and I forced what feeble amount of positive energy I had into the spell. The purple smoky substance circled in Pax's hand, growing thicker at first and then condensing in size. He held the almost inactive memory wisp in one hand and asked, "Now what?"

I knew he wasn't happy, but I didn't care. I took the memory from him. *"Tri-da Dadinay."*

Pipila headed over, so I pulled open the Khakidemy door for her. At the same time, Aurora stepped backwards into view. Seeing her face made my chest clench. I was spending more time with Pipila than I was with her. *Come on, you idiot, talk to her.* Seeing that look on her face made me drop my eyes. She was hurting, and the longer I left it, the more pain she'd be in. I needed to tell her I didn't want to leave anymore. I needed to tell her I was trying to come to terms with it. As long as she was careful, she wouldn't jeopardise my chances of meeting my parents. *It can't be maleficium; it's Aurora. Look at her; she's not dangerous.*

"Hey, Pax," greeted Pipila, swishing her hair and entering the Khakidemy.

"Hey," I replied, glancing back over at Aurora before taking a forced stride into the Khakidemy. "So, erm, what do you want to try today?" I tried distracting myself from the lasting image of Aurora's face.

"I'm thinking the Flexon Pro," said Pipila, checking for my approval. "I still think it's my strongest."

"Alright."

"Was it someone's birthday yesterday? I heard Brindan saying something about wishing someone happy birthday first."

"Yeah, it was Aurora's seventeenth."

"Oh."

"You know, you two would probably get on if you actually spoke to each other."

"She doesn't need any more people trying to talk to her. All she has to do is walk in a room and she has everyone's attention. Besides, she zones out as soon as I start speaking, anyway."

"No, she doesn't. Don't be silly."

Pipila shrugged, and we split up to get changed. Taking my navy jacket off, I saw the pink scar on my wrist from where I had my picoplant replaced. I ran my thumb over the small bump. Aurora had snuck out with Silliah and completed an unauthorised Curfew duty. I could still remember the look on her face when Seioh Jennson confronted us. She was terrified. It was so soon after she…glowed, and she had no idea if I was going to tell on her. The thought crossed my mind for a second. It would've gotten her discharged for sure, and that was my easy get-out of the betrothal. I knew it then, but I couldn't do that to her.

Pipila wasn't in the Colosseum when I arrived, so I jumped up onto the Flexon Pro, completing a round whilst I waited for her. After a while, the game-over drone sounded, and the pads reset back to their starting position.

"One hundred and fifty-nine. A new leaderboard entry. Congratulations, Mr. Fortis."

The room burst with a sea of glittering confetti. Pipila squealed, jumping up onto the Flexon with me and throwing her arms around my neck.

Pipila's lips were on mine. I gently put my hand on the curve in her back. Her familiar natural scent reminded me of the time when I used to rebel, back when I knew I wasn't allowed to kiss her but wanted to be taken to Maximum Security to see my parents. *Wait. Aurora.*

I pulled back.

"Pipila," I spoke quietly. Golden confetti reflected in her beautiful green irises as she met my gaze. "We're not children anymore."

Her eyes landed on the floor. "I know. I'm sorry."

I held her cheeks with both hands and lifted her head. "You're going to be alright, Pipila. I promise you."

She nodded with me, but I could see the uncertainty behind her movement.

"Satisfied?" Pax ignored the purple shockwave bursting from my skin.

"I don't even know why I cared." I got up from the bed.

"Because you still love me, Aurora."

My feet stopped. "No, I don't."

"Yes, you do."

"No, I love Tayo."

"If that's the case, I think you'll find you love us both."

"No. I. Don't." I leant forward with each word, projecting my seriousness onto him so perhaps he'd get the message. Then I carried on for my room.

"Aurora," he called before I passed over the threshold. "Blackmail me into breaking the law again and I'll be the one to take that invitation—"

I shut the interconnecting door behind me.

Collapsing forwards onto my bed, I screamed into the pillow, "*That stupid bitch.*" Then I flung myself onto my back forcefully and threw the pillow at the adjoining wall. After slamming my heels down onto the mattress, the anger dispersed, abandoning me with a tearing pain across my chest.

'*Tayo, I can't do this. Please message me back.*' I put my Slate down over the pain in my heart.

CHAPTER FOURTEEN
A TELLING OFF

*M*onday. My exhale was drawn-out and noisy. *Aurora, you can do this. Monday. Monday. Monday.* I felt the tears swelling beneath my eyelids already. *No, come on. You don't need him.*

"Aurora?"

Again with my real name. I pushed my eyes closed so firmly they had crazy swirly lights in them. "Please, Pax. Please, just get out."

"Are you going to get up?"

"Yes. Yes, I am. Please leave me alone. I will get up."

"Alright." His bare foot turned on the glossy panel.

When I heard the door close, I launched my empty shell of a body out of bed before my brain had a chance to talk me out of it. I'd had enough of feeling broken, and I was determined to return some normality to my life.

This morning, I made it to the Food Hall before everyone else. I spotted a glum group of Pipila's cronies sitting on a long bench, all looking lost and sulky. They watched me as I passed their table and sat on a table of my own.

"Aurora?" someone from Pipila's gang called me. "We're over here."

I glanced over at the crowd of eyes, and without knowing which of them spoke, I addressed them all, "No offence, but I would rather sit here."

They exchanged uncertain looks, and then after a short pause, they all went to stand. The stupid buffoons intended to join my table.

"No, don't." I quickly put an end to the nonsense before it began. "I'll come over there."

"Sad news about Pipila," said a long-nosed girl as I took my seat.

"Not really. She kissed my betrothed. If any of you think her leaving is sad, then you can go sit over there." I used my chin and eyes to point in the direction of Khaki Quartz. The invertebrates fidgeted in their seats but didn't leave, so I double-tapped my tabletop screen to order breakfast.

Pax found his chair next to me and greeted the solemn crowd. Then, once certain their attention was off us, he turned to me. "How are you doing this morning?"

Keeping my head down, I raised my shoulders imperceptibly and continued to browse through the breakfast items with long strokes.

"We need to pretend we're united today. We have our Promises Ceremony later."

I tapped my third finger on the table, showing him I wore my Promises Ring. Then I chose my avocado toast and left for the meal dispenser before he could say any more.

Ryker had positioned himself opposite Pax when I arrived back at the table. He had Silliah wrapped around his neck, and she was pleading in his ear, "Please let me sit there, Ryker."

"Go away, Silliah." Ryker shrugged her off his shoulders.

"Please, Rye. Quickly."

Ryker gave me a dark stare as if asking me to control my friend. I swooped my head back, letting him know I wasn't doing anything about it, and I picked at my toast.

"Fine." Ryker gave a forceful exhale in my direction and pushed his Slate over to the space next to me. "But only because I think you're trying to wind Brindan up."

Silliah triumphantly settled down in Brindan's usual spot opposite Pax. She checked for any overly carefree strands in her messy walnut-brown fringe and waited.

"You alright?" I checked on Ryker when he sat down.

He gave me the same response I gave Pax and simply moved his shoulders.

"They don't know, do they?" I asked him, assuming Silliah had no idea about Pipila, because if she did, I was pretty sure she wouldn't have just done that.

Ryker held a long blink as he shook his head.

"Know what?" Silliah mouthed to me.

I flicked my head subtly to let her know now wasn't the time. She dropped her eyes and attended to her screen.

Brindan arrived for breakfast and wasted no time in picking Silliah up by her legs and taking her to sit on the empty table behind him.

"Brindan!" Silliah hammered her fists on the empty table. "So, being betrothed means nothing to you?"

"It means everything, darling." He took his seat opposite Pax. "But not when you're testing boundaries."

I choked on my toast as my throat cramped. Tayo had once said the same thing to me. Gulping down my last mouthful, I left the Food Hall before anyone noticed the glaze over my eyes. I managed to escape without being stopped, but outside in the corridor, I passed the rest of my friends and their Juvies.

Calix eyed me up yet again, so I decided to address his issue. "Find Seioh Jennson's office in the end, Calix?"

"No thanks to you." He swung his fist, trying to give me a dead arm as he passed.

Effortlessly swerving him, I quipped, "I told you it was in the next corridor along."

"Mmm-hmm."

"What did he want you for, anyway?" I called over my shoulder before he entered the Food Hall.

"Wouldn't you like to know." He disappeared under the archway.

"Oh, I'll live," I mumbled, catching sight of Mimsy Jackson heaving her way to the Food Hall with a weighted trap. Evidently, she ignored my advice to be respectful to Crystal, and she must have acted up. I pursed my lips and flicked my eyebrows at her before I rounded the corner into Navy Quartz.

Reaching my bedroom, I fell forwards into my pillow and released the built-up pressure. I cried into it, allowing the mask to slip before it cracked on its own. It was better to allow it out now before I took my hurt out on someone—most likely Pax. Before I put the mask back on, I scrolled through my messages to Tayo. They were all on the right side. The last message from Tayo was back when I was being punished by Seioh Jennson: '*Yeah. Knowing Jennson, he probably allowed you to punish yourself. I'm thinking about you.*'

I read the message a hundred times, pining for my Juvie back. Anything was better than not having him at all.

'*Are you seriously just shutting me out?*'

⁂

When noon arrived, I made my way to the rooftop garden for my fake Promises Ceremony. I bumped into Pax outside the lift. He sat alone, hunched over, resting his elbows on his knees, his steady hands linked together. I stood away from him and waited for the ridiculous facade to begin.

"Aurora." Pax tipped his head back, wanting me to sit on the bench next to him.

I sighed at the use of my name and looked off to the side. My face felt heavy, and even a fake smile seemed impossible at this point. How was I going to get through this?

Pax didn't allow me another opportunity to ignore him, and he came to me. I pushed up against the wall, turning my face into it. My attempt at putting as much distance between us as possible was falling flat. Pax took me by the waist and guided me to sit on the bench.

"I know you're hurting, sweetheart. You don't have to pretend in front of me, but you do in front of them." Pax used his eyes to show me that Lady Merla Liddicott and Seioh Jennson watched us through the glass.

Clart.

I rested my forehead on Pax's shoulder, hiding my face but also trying to show we were united. Controlling my breathing, I found myself making each inhale longer than the last, just to better catch his clean scent. It was musky and familiar, and somehow seemed to be diluting my pain.

"Paxton. Aurora. You may come through now," Lady Merla Liddicott called to us from down the short corridor. Her head poked around the parted double doors, and despite holding a friendly smile, her tight grey bun and sharp features made her look unforgiving.

Seioh Jennson watched us with intent as we entered. My guts crawled towards my throat. Trying to relax into my role, I pretended to be interested in the garden. It was the mirror image of last year. The layered flower arrangement crowded my view of a snowy Vencen, and hundreds of scattered candles were hidden around like shy fireflies. I was relieved to find that stepping into the garden this time didn't activate any intrusive cameras.

Lady Liddicott reached an arm out to lead me away from Pax. "Are you alright, Aurora?"

"Yes, ma'am." I pulled my lips up. I felt like I was standing in scalding water and was being told not to show the pain. Somehow, Lady Liddicott seemed to know I wasn't being completely honest, and she gave me a steely look telling me to drop the act. After rubbing my face until it was sore, I corrected my answer. "No, ma'am."

"What is it that bothers you?"

"Ma'am, this past year has been really hard. I want to take these Promises, I do, but how am I supposed to act like nothing happened?"

"Aurora, you don't. You don't have to pretend. These Promises are the start to repairing your relationship. You are not expected to suppress your emotions, and you are not expected to do this alone. That is what I am here for. All I need from you is willingness."

"So, are you saying I can still make Pax's life hard?"

Liddicott gave a small hiccup of a laugh. "Oh, yes, Aurora. I highly recommend it."

"And I don't have to pretend I'm okay?"

"Most certainly not."

"Can you tell that to Jenn—*Seioh* Jennson? He's staring at me like he's trying to read my mind."

"Seioh Jennson is only observing the proceedings. From the moment an invitation is offered, he oversees the counselling process. You needn't concern yourself with his attendance. Now, are you ready to retake your Promises?"

"Yes, ma'am." I swallowed back my lie.

She placed her hand on the small of my back and turned me towards the suspended arbour. "I'm pleased you both decided to stay."

"I wasn't the one trying to end the betrothal, ma'am."

"The one who leaves isn't always the one you expect. Some find forgiveness difficult."

Seioh Jennson stood over by the arbour, having a quiet conversation with Pax. They both lifted their heads when they heard the two-tone taps of our footsteps on the dark wood floor.

Lady Liddicott held out a time-worn hand. "May I have your Promises Rings, please?"

Pax and I gave them over, and Liddicott dipped behind the silky white curtains draping down from the square arbour. When she re-emerged, Jennson pulled back the curtain to reveal the set-up inside. It wasn't what I expected. A white chunky-knit blanket had red scatter cushions. There was a single white rose in a glass vase, a pair of parchments, our white marble ring box, and a wicker picnic basket.

"Enjoy your lunch," said Jennson. He nodded to Lady Liddicott, and they both headed for the exit looking pleased with themselves.

"Oh, this is so stupid." I slumped down in a heap, sheltering my head between my knees.

Pax joined me on the blanket and picked up a parchment with our Promises. "And here I was thinking you'd find it romantic."

"Don't, Pax. I'm not in the mood," I said, straight-faced, not returning his smile. "I'm not reading my Promises to you."

"Alright, I'll read it to you." Pax cleared his throat in an animated fashion. "I was made to love—"

"Stop it, Pax." I covered my ears.

He reached over, pulling my hand away from my ear. "I promise to be more than I am, better than I was—"

"Stop." I struggled to get my arm back over to block out his voice.

Pax crawled closer, wrestling with me to remove my arms. He tackled me whilst still trying to hold on to the parchment and read.

"And above what I have been. I PROMISE"—he began to shout after I managed to cup my ears again—"TO BE ALL THAT I AM FOR YOU."

"You're not funny, Pax." I tucked myself up in a ball, shielding my ears.

He cradled my back, pinning me down with his body weight, and he twisted my wrist into an arm lock, freeing up my right ear. He spoke softly into it, "You give me courage, and now we are together, I am braver than ever."

"Shame you couldn't have courage last year."

"No, that's not the line. You're supposed to say, 'and I, you.'"

"I will hurt you."

"Close enough. I promise to protect you, care for you—"

With the hand covering my left ear, I swiped the parchment from him and scrunched it up, throwing it into the flower arrangement.

"Alright, I'll just have to give you some of my own." He held me in place so I couldn't move. "I promise to take the sofa, if you ever need my bed."

"Pax, stop." I didn't like the pain that cut across my chest.

"I promise to be there if you ever get side-tracked chasing black dogs during Curfew."

I almost laughed but held it back. "Pax."

He pushed his lips against my ear. "I promise to eat the ice cream that's already been in your mouth."

A shiver travelled my spine as his silky lips brushed my ear. "Pax," I repeated, shaking it out of my spine. He was talking about our counselling last year when I had to feed him ice cream, back when I wanted so badly for us to work things out.

Feeling my body shiver, Pax held still. When he stopped analysing my body, he leant back down on me fully. *I promise to love you for exactly who you are.*

"Are you finished?" I spoke to the floor, still tucked up in a little ball.

"And I promise to always love you, even if you never love me back." He released me and settled back on the blanket.

"Are you done?" I unfolded myself, brushing sprawled hair off my face.

"So, Aurora," he said, taking no notice of my astringency and picking up the marble box holding our Promises Rings, "will you accept my Promises?"

"No." I reached out to put my own ring on.

"You'd rather I let you chase dogs?"

"That wasn't a dog."

Little did he know, it really wasn't a dog. It was Nanny Kimly's brother using Illusionist magic. Pax got up and disappeared behind me, attending to the flower display. When he returned to the blanket, he removed the white rose from the vase and replaced it with a white tulip.

I crossed my arms, reminded of his laughter that night but not wanting to smile. "You're such an idiot."

"Will you accept my Promises?" He opened the box, removing my ring out of the presentation cushion.

"No, Pax." I stayed grounded, cross-legged, and I reached my flat hand out again. "I'm only going to wear the ring for show, only to convince everyone we're united."

"But even so, why won't you accept my Promises?"

"Because I don't want your love."

"Alright, how about I change that one? What if I promise to never love you any more than you love me?"

I rubbed my forehead to help me think. "Alright, fine. Whatever. I don't love you anymore, Pax."

"Come here, then." Pax patted the blanket in front of his crossed legs.

"No."

Pax shuffled in halfway and then said, "Come here."

My head dropped forward in exasperation. I crept over the rest of the way and held my left hand out for him to place the ring on the tip of my third finger. Then, as a way of accepting his Promises, I slid it the rest of the way.

After putting his own ring on, Pax shuffled back, pulled the picnic basket towards him, and began emptying its contents. He unpacked a khaki-green flask, several plastic containers, a pile of napkins, and two sets of cutlery.

"What do you reckon?" Pax began unscrewing the lid on the insulated flask. "Tea, coffee, or peppermint hot chocolate?"

"Jennson knows I don't like tea or coffee."

"Does he?" Pax gave me an extremely quizzical look.

"Yeah. I…" I thought about whether I wanted to tell Pax about what almost happened to me. "I was almost dishonourably discharged last week. He brought me a peppermint hot chocolate as a final compassionate act before my execution." I fakely curved my lips and picked at the rubber sole on my boots.

"For leaving your bedroom when we were told not to?"

"Yes, Pax. Please save your 'I told you so.'"

Pax shook his head. My stomach twisted.

"I thought he just put you in isolation." He continued to unscrew the lid. "So, how did you manage to get yourself out of that one?"

I felt my cheeks burning, and I jogged my shoulders. Pax poured the contents of the flask into two takeaway cups, and after securing the lids, he held my drink just out of reach. "Well?"

"I begged him to let me stay, said I would prove to him I could keep out of trouble."

"Oh?"

"You could at least try to not sound so happy."

He allowed me my peppermint hot chocolate. "What? I'm just pleased you're going to try and behave, that's all."

I rolled my eyes and reached for my salad. I wasn't hungry, but it was my way of ending the conversation. Pax attended to his own lunch, and I managed to eat most of my food without any small talk.

"Aurora, can I ask you something?" Pax closed the lid on his container, putting his full attention on me.

"No." I threw a red scatter cushion at his chest and stood up. "I'm done talking with you." I dodged the flying cushion coming back my way, and I left the rooftop garden.

I returned to my room alone.

Opening my wardrobe for a set of charcoal pyjamas, I found myself staring down at the closed floor panel. I lifted it up and prayed hopelessly for a pair of piercing-blue eyes to be staring back at me. It was terrible wishful thinking, and I didn't need to dry my eyes to see he wasn't there. I let the panel go, changing into my pyjamas and crawling under the duvet.

"What now?" I responded to a tapping at the interconnecting door.

"Are you honestly trying to sleep?" Pax welcomed himself into my room and sat on the edge of my bed.

"Yes."

"Honestly?"

"No."

I felt Pax get comfy by my side, and I swept the duvet off my head. He also wore his pyjamas, pretending to complete his Mando-sleep.

"You're breaking the rules." I turned on my back to see his face.

"Not really."

"Yes, really. You're supposed to be sleeping."

"I'll go. I just wanted to ask you something."

"If you were such a little shit in Mustard, why are you now so hell-bent on following the rules?"

"Erm…" His eyes fell on his grey pyjama bottoms. "Well"—he looked back at me with a mild grimace—"a threat of being dishonourably discharged can do that to you."

"*You* were almost dishonourably discharged?"

"At the start of Second-year, yeah. I thought it was what I wanted until it almost happened. Crapped myself and had a panic attack in the corridor."

"Shut up." I slid up against the display screen. "The same thing happened to me."

"I thought as much. I could tell by the look on your face earlier."

"So, Jennson wasn't actually going to kick me out? It's all an act?"

"No, he does. I've seen it happen. He does it late at night to make sure no one is around to see, but once, I was wandering the corridors out of hours." Pax's honey eyes glazed for a minute, but soon they focused back on mine. "The dismissal is arranged, and the van is waiting outside to take you, but I think he waits for our reaction first, to see if we are remorseful. But I didn't know that when he threatened me. I thought I was a goner for sure, because I'd seen someone leave."

"Holy shit."

"Will you stop swearing?" Pax backhanded my arm. "I thought it made you want to follow the rules?"

"Yeah, but I ain't going to be like you—annoyingly rigid."

"Aurora, I'm sorry for freaking out on you last year."

"I don't care about that anymore, Pax. What's done is done."

"You do care."

"I wasn't talking about that, anyway. I meant annoyingly rigid by not eating the ice cream during our counselling last year."

"Oh."

"And not letting me stop Ryker when he was beating up a Juvie."

"I was the one who stopped him, Aurora. I broke the rules for you. I also let you come to your room last year after you fell, when we are supposed to stay in the Recovery Centre. And why do you think Seioh Jennson allocated *me* the Davoren Sisters?"

"Great, so you pick and choose which rules you break, but you couldn't do it when I really needed you?"

"I told you, you still cared."

"I don't care. And anyway, everyone is Puracordis, not just me."

"Yeah, that's what I wanted to ask you. What did you mean by that?"

"Boulderfell knows everyone is Puracordis. There's a suppressant in the water supply preventing us from doing magic."

"I'd like to say how could anyone take another person's birthright away like that, but my parents are in prison for having a baby, so I can't really say I'm surprised." Pax reached over and turned over my left wrist. "Are you using magic to hide your birthmark?"

"Yes."

"And is your birthmark magic?"

"Yeah." I pulled my hand away. "It's a magical symbol. I'm weakened by the chemical in the water, but I can still conjure on it because of my birthmark."

"What magic were you doing when we had our first kiss?"

"Oh, Pax." I rubbed my heels together abrasively, crossing them over the other way. "I'm not having this conversation with you."

"Just tell me."

"I wasn't conjuring anything. It—"

Silliah burst into my room. "I know we're supposed to be having our Mando-sleep, but I couldn't wait to see you." She flew onto the mattress knees first and pulled Pax and me into a group hug.

Brindan followed behind. He kicked off his boots, walked on the bed, and held on to all of our heads.

"Congratulations on your Promises Ceremony," Silliah almost sang the sentence. She let go of us and straightened her walnut fringe. It wasn't as long as usual, no longer covering one eye. "I am so happy you two are back on track."

We all shuffled to fit on the bed together.

"Apparently Pax was never leaving," I said, looking at Silliah. "Who told you Pax was leaving last year?"

She tensed up, blinking before hesitantly lifting a finger at Brindan.

"Who told you?" I asked Brindan.

Brindan's blue-green eyes flicked around the room before finally answering, "Ryker."

"Do you know who told Ryker?"

"Pip-il-a," Brindan replied, pausing between each syllable.

My head rotated towards Pax.

He gave a broad-shouldered shrug. "I never told her I was leaving."

"Your *stupid* girlfriend started the rumour that made me give up on you." I allowed the sentence time to sink in before I outed him to Silliah and Brindan. "Did you guys know Pax and Pipila kissed?"

Silliah's mouth fell open. Brindan's freckled cheeks flinched, and he closed an eye.

"At least I didn't kiss a Juvie," Pax fired back.

Silliah gasped and threw a hand over her mouth.

"I didn't kiss a Juvie," I mumbled to the mattress.

"Sorry?" Pax turned his ear to me.

"I didn't kiss a *Juvie*."

"Yes, you did, Aurora."

"Tayo?" Silliah couldn't help herself.

"Don't do that, Aurora." Pax pushed back in.

My lip curled. "Don't do *what*?"

"Don't start being spiteful."

I stared down at my knees.

"Oookay…" Silliah broke the silence. "Not *exactly* back on track, but…going in the right direction?"

Nobody spoke. We all kept our eyes away, ignoring the tension polluting the room. Then all our eyes darted towards my bedroom door when it opened.

"Is this supposed to be your Mando-sleep?" Nanny Kimly regarded everyone but me.

"Yes, ma'am," came the splutter of replies.

"Then what is this?"

Bodies started moving in all directions. "Sorry, ma'am."

"Your *own* bedrooms," she called to Silliah and Brindan who were just about to duck into Pax's room. They changed direction and exited through the main door.

This was the first time I'd seen Nanny Kimly since almost getting dishonourably discharged. Playing with my pyjama shirt cuff, I tried to defuse the bomb before it detonated. "Nanny Ki—"

"Don't you even, Aurora."

I lifted my eyes to check if the steam visibly trailed behind Nanny Kimly as she paced about my room. Her fiery red bun stayed tight to her head despite her rapid strides.

"Why aren't you asleep?" She turned the other way, still pacing.

I swallowed to speak.

"Do you no longer feel like the rules apply to you?"

My mouth opened.

"You were instructed to remain in your bedroom. Were Seioh Jennson's instructions difficult to follow?"

I didn't even bother that time.

"I'm so disappointed in you, Aurora."

Hearing those words from her caused a malfunction in my brain, and my breathing stopped. The lack of oxygen made me whisper. "I'm sorry."

She finally stopped pacing, her eyes coming to mine. "If you want to spend the rest of your life in Maximum Security, you're going the right way about it."

"I don't, Nanny Kimly. I promised Seioh Jennson I'd behave."

"What were you thinking?" Her stare weighed down heavy on my shoulders.

"I just wanted to congratulate Silliah and Brindan."

"Why didn't you ask them *here*?"

"I don't know. Because Tayo was here. I was nervous to have them here."

Nanny Kimly's hazel eyes dropped to the ring on my finger, and then she sat on the bed. "And where is Tayo now?"

"Gone." My eyes prickled.

"Gone?"

"Yes." I felt my insides crumbling. "Gone."

Nanny Kimly immediately cradled my head to her chest. "Oh, Aurora." She didn't hide the concern in her voice well.

My words were almost incoherent. "I love him so much."

"I know. I know you do." She held my trembling body tighter, gently rocking me. "Shh, now. It's okay. You're going to be okay."

"It hurts."

I cried noisily until my head began to throb and my face stuck to the damp patch on Nanny Kimly's black uniform. I just wanted my best friend back. I missed everything about him and would give anything to hear 'my little Roar' again. Peeling myself away, I squinted through my tears at her. "Why does this hurt so much?"

"It will get better with time, I promise. Spending time with Pax will help."

"I don't want to spend time with him."

"You don't? Didn't you renew your Promises?"

"We only pretended to."

Nanny Kimly made a sharp sound as if she touched something hot. "Little Lady."

"Pax knows. It was his idea."

"And at the end of Thirteenth-year when you are married, then what?"

"Separate lives. I don't want anything to do with him."

She held her eyes closed at my answer.

Her reaction made me speak, "It's better than becoming a Fell agent, isn't it?"

With her eyes still shut, she slowly shook her head. "You two are impossible."

"Would you rather I lied to you?"

"No, Aurora. I just wonder when you will both grow up."

Her sentence brought about my culpable silence, and I returned to playing with my cuff button. Maybe I should've just become a Fell agent.

After a while spent in my head thinking about Tayo, I sighed and took my eyes off my button. "Have you ever been in love, Nanny Kimly?"

"Just once." She stopped staring vacantly over at the interconnecting door. "It was a long time ago."

"Who was he?"

"A Navy, back before Seioh Jennson became the head of the institute." Nanny Kimly's cheek reshaped as she held her teeth together. "Obviously it was forbidden. Navies participate in Unity, so our relationship was to stay purely platonic until his honourable discharge and my retirement."

"So, he's waiting for you to retire?"

"No. That was our plan." She looked down at her lap. "It probably wouldn't have worked, anyway."

"Why? What happened?"

"We didn't get to carry out our plan. Our relationship was brought to an end by Iiza Boulderfell, Seioh Boulderfell's eldest daughter. Back when Seioh Boulderfell used to reside here, Iiza was the institute's disciplinarian. If you think Seioh Jennson is strict, you should've met *Iiza-gonna-getcha.*"

I pulled a face. "Who?"

"That's what the Navies used to call her behind her back. They couldn't sneeze out of line without being punished. It was a tough time, but growing up with it meant they didn't know any different. There would be none of this Mando-sleep-meet-up lark."

"They were in *my* room, Nanny Kimly. I *was* completing my Mando-sleep."

"Well, Miss Aurora Aviary doing as she's told for once. I didn't think I'd live to see the day."

I sarcastically danced my head side to side as if it was something to be proud of. Nanny Kimly squeezed my cheeks together, latching on to my eyes with a fake scorn.

I mumbled through my squished cheeks, "So, what did this woman do to ruin your plans?"

Nanny Kimly released my face and sighed. "She suspected we liked each other, but because we weren't doing anything wrong, she couldn't do anything but make up a lie about us."

"Cor, are you sure this woman isn't related to Na-nutta?"

"*Aurora.* How dare you. I may allow the odd 'Seioh' to slip, but don't you for one second believe—"

"I'm-sorry-I'm-sorry-I'm-sorry-I'm-sorry." I held my hands up, palms towards her. "Nanny, I'm sorry. Please continue."

Nanny Kimly's scorn was no longer fake.

"Please?" I tried again, linking my hands on my lap.

Her scorn faded, but her jaw still continued to twitch. "Iiza fabricated a story saying she caught us kissing. We never had. We were not going to jeopardise our chances of being together. But it was our word against hers, and we were given an ultimatum: either I go to Maximum Security, or he pledges himself to Seioh Boulderfell and becomes a Fell agent."

"Whoa, that's so harsh. So…he—"

"He wouldn't let me go."

"He's a Fell agent?"

"He is."

"Do you still love him?"

"It's been many years. It was a struggle in the beginning, but it gets easier."

"But do you *still* love him?"

"Aurora."

"You don't want to tell me because of Tayo."

"Yes, I still love him."

My heart swelled until my chest hurt. "I really hope I…"

"You'll be fine." She patted the leg tucked underneath me.

"Did you know Seioh Boulderfell was in love once?"

"You shouldn't spread rumours, Little Lady." She tapped a finger under my chin and lifted to her feet.

"It's not a rumour. He loved Ryker's mum before she died in a car crash."

Nanny Kimly spun on the spot so fast I thought I was in for it. "Who told you that?"

I shook my head quickly and shrugged.

Then without even moving, she managed to look busy. Thoughts were pouring through her head, and I tried to listen. But Nanny Kimly knew better than that, and she probably intentionally withheld them.

"Clever little girl," Nanny Kimly spoke to the walls. "That clever, clever little girl pretended to have amnesia."

"Wait, Nanny Kimly."

The back of her neat red bun disappeared out the door.

CHAPTER FIFTEEN
ASSHOLY REIGN

"A fury of short yellow lasers?"

"Do you have to do that every time?" I rubbed my eyes, clearing them to see an energetic Pax jogging beside my bed. He was already dressed and wearing our *Smokin' Axe* team badge on his Navy uniform. "Oh, God, take that off."

"I love this video loop." He grinned at the short footage of us together in the booth last year: I kept shrugging his arm off my shoulder until he restrained me in a headlock. I didn't realise it at the time but we were both smiling like idiots.

"It's stupid," I said, watching the loop over and over again, compelled by Pax squeezing my head against his side. I was sure we had just kissed moments before.

"Then why're you smiling?"

"I'm not." I corrected my face.

"Go on—a fury of short yellow lasers—what is it?"

"That's the Bounty your girlfriend fired at me last year."

Pax's head dropped to the left. "Are you going to be like this all day?"

I thought about it for a second. It would not make for a good game if I didn't cheer up. "Lady Liddicott gave me permission to make your life hard."

When an enigmatic look swept his face, my insides squirmed, knowing what was coming. He snatched for my ankle, but I flapped to get my feet on the floor. We stood opposite each other a metre apart, anticipating each other's moves, both jerking our bodies from side to side. He read my body well, moving the same way I did every time, but then I feigned a left and managed to duck into the ensuite.

"It's Cut the Chase," I called to him through the closed ensuite door. "It slows your opponent down."

"Someone's been doing their homework."

"Well, if I don't 'fall' this time, I want to eliminate *Unholy Reign.*"

"Optimistic...but I like it. See you at breakfast, swe—" He broke off, and then his voice grew fainter as he walked away. "And Pipila is not my girlfriend."

"You fancy her, though," I mumbled to myself, getting into the corner shower. "I felt it during your memory wisp."

In the Food Hall, a crowd formed by the meal dispenser, and it became obvious the *Sovereign Skill* duo were present. Saulwyn and Theodred looked immaculate as always. A bucketload of product held every gleaming strand of blond hair neatly behind their ears, and their pristine uniforms hung gracefully over their perfect postures.

"Can those two not go anywhere without attracting a crowd?" I commented on *Sovereign Skill* whilst picking my breakfast apart.

Silliah came behind me, pulled my hairband from my ponytail, and started giving my hair the usual French plait makeover. "They are wearing *your* team badge." She straightened my head forward when it snapped over in their direction.

"No, they're not?" I tried to see them again.

"They are." She guided my head to face forward and held it there until I stopped trying to see.

"Wow. *Sovereign Skill* are wearing *our* team badge." I kept quiet as my words sank in. "But why? They are playing too. I really don't get it."

"I don't know. I guess after your fall last year, everyone is really eager to see you two play."

"No pressure," added Brindan from across the table. "Did you notice how many more *Smokin' Axe* posters are up in the corridors this year?"

"I tried not to look." I frowned at the badge on Brindan's navy-blue jacket.

"The fan base is here to stay." Calix joined in from the table to my right. "So you might as well get used to it."

Hilly sat up taller in her chair. "We will have to come up with a team name for you two now." Her wide blue eyes switched between Silliah and Brindan.

"Oh my God." I looked at Brindan since Silliah was behind my back. "I forgot you two are playing this year."

"I can't wait." Brindan winked over my head at Silliah.

"Me neither," she replied, tugging my plait twice to let me know she'd finished. "Hopefully we can stay alive long enough to see you and Pax in there. I've had my side fringe cut shorter to keep it out of my eyes."

"Oh, nice." I checked Silliah's hair. The sides were freshly shaved, and she had styled the messy brown fringe to flick up to the side. It had a striking resemblance to Ryker's, actually, but her cute feminine features and today's smoky makeup made her look badass.

"Where is Ryker?" I said, noting his absence.

After no immediate answers, Brindan took one for the team. "It's the first game since Pipila left."

"He doesn't get to play anymore," Pax explained. "Not unless he matches in Unity again."

A silence crept over, punctuated only by chinking of forks as food became interesting.

"Well, this just got weird." I stood to leave for the games. "Ready, Pax?"

"Yeah, let's do this." He used the table to push himself up.

"Guys?"

Silliah and Brindan jumped to their feet.

"Good luck," came a merge of voices as we waved everyone goodbye.

I much preferred my entourage this year. We each had our best friends. Silliah almost skipped as she clung on to Brindan's arm with both hands. Every so often she gave a small hop, and the excitement would quite literally burst from her. Pax held open the small white door in the Khakidemy, allowing us all to enter before closing us in a dark corridor. Silliah led the way by brushing her fingertips along both walls as she went.

The noise from us descending the metal staircase stopped a hum of conversation coming from below. But then our arrival into the room encouraged it to start up again. I immediately caught sight of *Unholy Reign* in the centre, being crowded by a group of allies. Beignley was lounging on a black leather sofa, sprawled out, his long arms stretched along the backrest, his foot resting up on his other knee. He followed me with his eyes. Without breaking his stare, he tapped a boy's shoulder, giving a small gesture in my direction, and they both lifted the corner of their lips. I tried to hide my swallow from his unbroken stare and forced myself to keep my eyes on him.

Pax held his head close to mine, interrupting our line of sight. "What are you staring Beignley out for?"

"If you hadn't noticed, he was staring me out, too."

"I did. What's going on with you two?"

"Nothing," I lied. "This is a last-man-standing game. Perhaps he's trying to intimidate me. We are one of the few teams with a fan base; maybe we're a target."

"Yeah, probably. Just watch yourself around him, okay? He is a Boulderfell."

"It's a game, Pax. I don't think it's serious." I lied because I didn't want him to worry. Beignley had been trying to hurt me ever since he accused me of cheating in my first game. There was a real chance he had a plan for me today, but I didn't imagine he'd jump me like the last game. It would be too obvious. Nobody would believe I fell for the second time in a row, but I couldn't fathom what else it could be with all those cameras around. I shoved the thought to the far reaches of my mind, deciding not to think about it again.

Pax stopped at a free booth, waving bye to Brindan and Silliah as they hurried off for their own booth. We placed our hands on the glass together, and once the edges came alive with a golden aura, we stepped through the parted doors. They shut behind us, changing the clear glass to an opaque black, and Pax began unzipping his jacket.

"Can you wait until this partition wall is up." I grounded my boots, refusing to move until Pax stopped undressing.

"Oh, stop it. It's nothing you ain't seen before." He hung his jacket on the hooks and stepped up onto his plinth. "And don't worry; I've got enough self-control for the both of us."

"I have self-control. I just don't want to see—"

"Good morning, Paxton and Aurora," came Soami's untimely greeting. "This is your third game. Would you like an instructional walkthrough on getting suited up?"

"I'm good," Pax said, looking at me. "You good?"

"Yeah."

"We're fine, thank you, Soami."

"Very well," she replied. "Please follow the instructions given on your podiums. *Serve, Honour, Protect, and Defend.*"

"You were saying?" Pax lifted his vest over his head, revealing nicely contoured muscles.

My gaze lingered on his flawless tanned skin before I snapped my eyes away and jumped onto my plinth to initiate the partition wall. "You're such an idiot."

"What's the matter?" he said in a light, playful tone.

"Oh, go and have another sunbed."

"Whatever keeps you happy."

"I hate you, Pax." I fumbled with the zip on my jacket, struggling to unzip it.

"Mmm-hmm," he hummed. "You keep telling yourself that."

"I will. Every day until I leave this place."

"With my surname showing just how much you hate me."

"I swear to God, Pax. I will make myself a Fell—"

"Whoa, shush. Don't say that."

"Then stop winding me up." I yanked the jammed zip down.

The booth fell silent.

I listened out to see if he'd gotten the message, and we changed without speaking another word. Once we were both dressed in our skin-tight picosuits, the partition wall lowered to the floor, and Pax stepped to me with open arms.

"I'm sorry." He gestured me to him. "A *friendly* team hug before we enter the arena? I don't want there to be any animosity whilst my life is in your hands."

"Maybe you should've thought about that before you decided to wind me up." I circled around him, just out of reach.

"Aurora…" he warned in a gravelly tone, quickly working out what I was doing.

"Recording will commence in three, two, one…" I mouthed the sentence along with Soami, keeping my distance from Pax.

"Aurora…" He turned slowly on the spot in front of the camera…alone.

Smiling, I left the booth, meeting up with Brindan and Silliah ready in their picosuits. Brindan slung his arm around me and held his other up for a group hug. We all stepped into the bumbled embrace.

"Even if I have the chance to eliminate you guys," Brindan yelled over the noisy violins, "I'm not doing it."

"Same," Pax and Silliah said together.

"Nah," I replied, pulling out of the hug. "Sod you lot. I'm going in—I'm joking, I'm hmmhmm." The three of them constricted their arms and squeezed me so tight I could hardly breathe.

"I'm sorry, I didn't quite hear that over the music," Brindan said once they freed me.

"Ow." I laughed, rubbing the side of my face which had been squashed against Brindan's armoured chestplate. "*I said* I love you guys, and I wouldn't eliminate you either."

"Oh, I thought that's what you said." Brindan winked.

As he and I were giving each other sour looks, a squeal, matching that of violins, came from behind me, and a pair of arms flung into view, wrapping around Silliah's neck.

"I'm so excited," said the back of Crystal Boulderfell's head. "I cannot wait to play."

"We missed you at breakfast," said Silliah, her voice straining from squeezing Crystal. "Where were you?"

Crystal backed off Silliah and took hold of her hand. "We were too excited to hang around. We ate quickly and came down here to get changed. How good do we look in these suits?" Crystal held out their arms and admired their black picosuits. "I love the gold wire in it. I've never noticed it watching the playbacks before."

"All the better to electrocute you with," I added with a smile.

"Where is Boyd?" Brindan asked about Crystal's betrothed.

"He's over there with Beignley." Crystal's black eyes flicked to me and then back over at her betrothed. "Well, I mean this in the nicest possible way, but I hope I don't see you guys in there."

Crystal ran off to Boyd just in time for the music to stop. We all turned to see Lady Joanne Maxhin at the far end of the room. She stepped onto a sofa and used the smooth black pillar to hold herself up.

"It's time, Youngens—" Lady Maxhin riled the crowd into cheer. She waited for it to cease. "Settle down. Settle down." Unable to be heard, she flapped her hands. "Well, you guys are excited this year." Lady Maxhin laughed at the noise after it started up again. Cheering, whistling, and screaming made her squint, and she waited patiently once more, but when the noise was egged on by a howling, air-punching Beignley, she had no choice but to say, "Alright, alright. Let me cut straight to it. The rules are simple: find your partner, unite, and eliminate other teams to earn Bounty. Good luck and may the best team win. *Serve, Honour, Protect, and Defend!*" She hopped off the sofa and led an overly fuelled mob into the next room.

The pounding of drums timed perfectly with our marching, and it made everyone adopt a puffed-up posture: heads up and chests out. We were soldiers at war, and I gulped at the possibility of returning with some very real wounds. But this year, if I did get hurt by Beignley again, I would make sure I wasn't the only one with injuries. There would be a fist-shaped bruise deforming Beignley's face if I could help it, or better still, a broken rib to requite for the one he broke of mine last year.

Pax leaned into my ear. "Do you want to try climbing up and meeting in the centre again?"

"Oh no, I'm not going up again." I couldn't tell Pax why, but if *Unholy Reign* were attempting another attack, I would be better off sprinting immediately. I needed to reach witnesses as soon as possible. "Let's give the warzone a go."

"Really?" Pax stopped cold. The troops bumped into our bodies as they continued on with their ascent. Pax took my hands and pulled me out of the stampede.

"Yeah, come on." I became distracted by his gentle grasp on my fingers, the warmth spreading through my arms. I took my hands off him and held them behind my back. "I reckon we can do it. It's obviously how *Sovereign Skill* unite so quickly. If they can do it, so can we."

"Yes, they do. I've watched their playback." Pax massaged his forehead with his thumb and index finger. His amber eyes carefully studied mine. "It's going to be chaos. Are you sure?"

"Yeah. Let's try it."

"Alright…"

I could hear he was hesitant, but I couldn't afford for him to back out now. "So, we run immediately?"

Pax moved his head closer and spoke over the rallied troops. "As fast as you possibly can. For us to stand a chance, we need to get to each other before the majority reaches the centre."

"Okay." My muscles started to feel dense, as if trying to warn me against our almost certain death. I ignored that too and forced my legs to move forwards.

We rejoined the crowd, and Pax choked on a laugh as he spoke, "This could be a short game."

"No shorter than my thirty seconds last year."

"True."

Up ahead, Silliah and Brindan reached into the velvety black pouch being held by Lady Maxhin. I watched Silliah pull out a purple token and Brindan the yellow token. They acknowledged each other's selections and parted ways with a smile. Romilly and Crystal both followed in behind Silliah after also taking the purple token. The three girls reached for each other's hands and interlocked their fingers. I didn't know what cage I would rather be in. The purple had my best friend but a grossly affectionate Crystal, but in the yellow cage…was Beignley.

On our turn, Pax didn't take up a token straight away, allowing me to make my choice first:

…a bright-yellow token engraved with 'The Parkour Games, January, 2120.'

Pax tucked me under his arm and whispered into my ear, "As fast as you can, okay?"

I nodded, and Pax turned for the purple cage. Knowing Beignley was somewhere in my cage, I immediately headed for Brindan. He would act as a good deterrent. But crossing over the threshold, Beignley blocked my path. He slung his arm over my shoulder, keeping me at the back of the cage.

"Remove yourself from me, Beignley," I spoke before he had the chance.

He lowered his head to my ear, his waxy brown quiff sticking to my temple. "You better be able to convince everyone you fell again this year," he said with more breath than voice.

"Are you seriously that stupid?"

He merely repeated the same sinister smirk from earlier when he was on the sofa. After pretending to give me a friendly squeeze, he slithered off my shoulder, disappearing amongst the crowd. I spotted him conversing quietly with the boy he'd previously tapped on the shoulder, and I quickly met Brindan.

"Hey, you." Brindan replaced Beignley's arm with his own.

"Hey." I leant against him. "Are you ready for this?"

"You bet." Brindan pulled away slightly and angled himself to see my face. "Do you always shake before the games?"

"Pax and I are doing warzone this time."

"Really?" He gave the exact same response Pax did earlier when I suggested doing warzone. "Whoa, rather you than me."

He rubbed up and down my arm as if I shook because I was cold. I cast a look over at the purple cage, seeing Pax and Silliah holding on to each other too. They faced the front, Pax's arm holding her into his side, her arm holding around his stocky waist. But hot irritation soon smothered the comfort I felt watching them when Crystal ducked under Pax's other arm so that he now held on to both her and Silliah. Crystal was far too touchy-feely with my betrothed for my liking. Silliah, I didn't mind, but Crystal hardly knew Pax. Before she'd moved over to Navy, she couldn't have had many interactions with him. Why was she trying to pretend they were close?

You didn't fall last year, did you?

An icy shiver crackled through my skull. Someone knew I could hear thoughts. I kept my eyes still, gazing blankly, trying to not give away that I'd heard it. Whoever said that must have known I practised magic. Why else would they use that form of communication? After a safe amount of time, I raised my eyes to identify the moron.

The cameras only started to malfunction the year Unholy Reign united. Whenever the cameras are out, someone always ends up hurt.

I heard the vaguely familiar male voice again. This person was not only boldly showing me they knew about Puracordis but that they also knew about me. I maintained my stance and pretended I couldn't hear anything.

The strobe lighting flickered, and I held Brindan tighter. Outlines of people, distorted faces, the blackest of blacks, and the sharpest of whites, all cast themselves before my eyes in a sinister film of flashes. Although I didn't think Beignley would try anything whilst I was with Brindan, last year I was punched in the head when we all entered the archways. So, this year, I was keeping Brindan close.

The stomping of feet aggravated the churning in my stomach, and screeching whistles gave me sharp pains in my ears. A thick smoke filled the room, making it almost impossible to see. Pax and Silliah were completely lost to the haze, and the screaming air raid siren drowned out all voices. Our cage door lifted, and like animals, we bullied our way forwards, entering an archway which veered off to the right. The cloudy yellow spotlights did nothing more than thicken the fog.

"Unity united us,

You and I, unite us.

We will fight and we will fall,

Together we can do it all!

I will fight and I will fall,

I WILL FIGHT,

I WILL FALL,

And for you, I'll do it all!"

Brindan linked our fingers and shouted with the rest, jumping and swinging my arm, encouraging me to join in. His spirit did manage to summon a genuine smile, so I skipped a little and repeated the next verse with him.

"Good luck." Brindan reached his designated capsule, backing up into the dark and taking with him my transient optimism.

"Good luck." I showed my best fake smile and forced myself away, continuing down the pathway alone. I passed black capsule after black capsule, searching the names above each door.

"Here you are, Babyface." Beignley found my pod before me. He leant against the wall and waved me inside. "In you get."

There must have been something wrong with my capsule. Staring into the pitch black, a small part of me wanted to cry and beg for it all to stop, but I slammed that wimp back down into its wet pit. Treading back, I read the names of my neighbours: Beignley

Boulderfell and, a somewhat familiar name, Boyd Livingston. *Crystal's betrothed?*

Sod it. I entered my pitch-black pod, bracing myself. The door closed out Beignley's menacing face. I let out a sigh. Before I'd finished my exhale, a bright-blue glow radiated from my picosuit, freezing my limbs with what seemed like the Bounty *In the Name of the Law.* It was impossible. But yet I was completely frozen, only able to move my face. It seemed Beignley had pre-empted my race for witnesses, keeping me trapped in my pod, out of sight and completely at their mercy.

I desperately tried to think of a way out of this before I ended up in hospital. The chanting from my opponents finding their pods started to fade. I was running out of time. *Think...I need to think.* I could see inside the tight space because of the bright-blue glow emanating from my picosuit. There were ledges and edges, pockets and coves, but nothing else.

Beignley had to have game technicians working for him. Last year, he started the games with Bounty already in his inventory. Bounty was only rewarded after eliminating another team, so he had to have someone on the inside. *Think, Aurora. Think of something.* In a few minutes, I was going to be face to face with Beignley again, but this time, I would be completely paralysed.

Tayo, I shouted his name in my mind. *Help me. Please.* Even though I didn't use my voice, my throat still squeezed as I screamed the words in my head. A tear rolled out my eye, tickling as it trailed my cheek, spreading in the crease of my nose. *Tayo, please, a technician has hold of my picosuit.*

I waited for any signs that he'd heard. The pod remained blue, my limbs still frozen. *Tayo, help me. A technician has hold of my suit. Beignley is going to jump me again.*

Trying to keep calm, I thought about how he would want to help me if he knew I was in trouble. He wasn't ignoring me. He wouldn't ignore me. *Tayo, I need your help. A technician has hold of my suit. Beignley is going to jump me again.* I repeated it over and over and over again.

My suit flickered, and relief leaked from my pores like sweat. I watched my suit with a burning intensity.

But nothing else happened. The blue glow remained vibrant.

With my body still paralysed, the floor started to judder from under my feet. Our descent beneath the institute began.

Having full function of my eyes, I squeezed them shut and watched the dancing lights behind my eyelids. Nausea bubbled up as I anticipated the pain. Another helpless tear slipped from my eye. I contemplated on the flashing blue and black veil, using it to steady my heartbeat until my eyes sprang open.

My suit was switching on and off as if two children were fighting over a remote. Was that Tayo struggling to keep control of my suit? The platform underneath me stopped, and my body rocked unsteadily. I fell against the wall, and a blunt edge of a beam caught me. I bared my teeth, enduring the sharp pain in my shoulder.

The blue glow disappeared, and I propped myself back up.

"Five, four, three, two…one," a male voice counted us in.

I jogged on the spot, preparing to sprint.

The capsule door revolved open. My feet clung to the ground, the technician's blue glow returning. I squinted at the arena, adjusting my eyes to the light. Regaining focus, I held a sharp inhalation.

A bald humanoid robot blocked my corridor. It had an angry red handprint on its off-white fascia and protruding gold wires twisting around its plastic skeleton. My blue light still held me hostage in my pod as it inspected my alley. I kept painfully still, not allowing my eyes to blink nor the breath to seep from my lungs. *Carry on walking.* My eyes stung from the cold air, causing a build-up of water in them. Through the blur, I saw the android's digital red iris rotate, transitioning into a bright green. The creepy thing turned and carried on its way.

Oh. That was too close. I released the air before my chest burst.

A black suit granted me a few steps out of my pod, but then the blue one grounded me to the spot. I used this time to map my route through the maze-like lower levels. Back to black, I made a dash for it, turning right at the end of my short alley. Behind me, Beignley belted my way, closing the gap between us, almost close enough to eat me whole.

The humanoid still prowled the narrow black corridors up ahead, but it was now the easy opponent. I launched myself onto its back, placing my glove on the red handprint. The robot grabbed my arm, but its eliminating touch had no effect. I'd gotten to his handprint in time, and I'd gained an accomplice of my own. I swung the humanoid towards Beignley. He was in trouble; the robot was now under my control.

Beignley's accomplice, Boyd, blocked my route to the warzone. My trainers pressed firmly into the ground as I went for him. The coward held up his hands, backing away and freeing up my left turn. As tempting as it was to break his kneecap, I showed the cretin mercy.

A five-note victory tune filled the arena, the first of the game. It no doubt awarded *Sovereign Skill* for uniting, but I didn't hang around to check the video loops playing on the outskirts. I skidded into the next corridor, almost tripping from friction on the textured black floor. Checking my map, I took a left turn. Another victory tune—and another one—and another. Then a thunder of elimination drones marked the beginning of the massacre.

I was too late.

A constant blend of low drones and musical tones rang out, followed by a dreaded silence. Was Pax okay? I had to unite with him now.

When I reached the warzone, black figures scattered in all directions, narrowly avoiding the colourful Bounty lasers whizzing everywhere. A mass of lifeless bodies littered the arena floor. I stopped, panting for more oxygen and scanning the area for Pax.

My body jerked at *Sovereign Skill* running my way. Theodred gave me a side glance, but my preparation stance proved pointless after they continued past. They clearly kept to a strict game plan: in the warzone—out the warzone.

In the distance, behind duelling teams, I spotted Pax sprinting. I took off, zigzagging, swerving, ducking, and swooping to avoid reaching hands. My pursuers gave up on me, but Pax had a female chasing him. We were almost together. Our hands extended, desperate to unite.

Connecting, a blazing ribbon of light swirled around our joined wrists as the victory tune celebrated our unity. Pax swung me towards his female assassin. She reached for me. An elimination drone sounded. Limbs flailed at the pain. Two bodies hit the floor.

The special wire diamond in my glove touched Pax's pursuer first. The girl convulsed on the floor, marking the pitiful early end to her game. My red Bounty ring spiralled up around my bicep. It rested, evocative of our victims' blood and flaunting as a courageous emblem of power.

My neck whipped from the force of Pax yanking me into him. A girl's finger narrowly missed my shoulder. Pax snagged the girl's passing sleeve. She fell to the ground. Another elimination drone and another red Bounty ring.

Our respite didn't last. I pulled from Pax's embrace, throwing him with a wrist throw. A white oval flew over him. The fall onto his back pushed the air out of him, and he lay panting, grabbing his stomach. He swiped my ankles, knocking me onto my tailbone. A swarm of black and yellow bullets flew overhead.

"I saw them coming. I was going to duck." I dug my elbow into his ribs to push myself up. Our red Bounty ring felt our contact and turned into a golden halo.

"Now you don't have to." He twisted my elbow and hand in opposite directions so I fell and hit my face on his stomach.

I punched his chestplate, but instead of retaliating, Pax extended a flat hand, throwing a black spear. It pierced the heart of a boy, making him stop dead, blinded. Pax pulled my arm out from under me again, collapsing me to the floor, and then he sprang to his feet. He dragged me up by the back of my chestplate, and we ran to eliminate the boy still inflicted by Pax's *Blind Leading the Blind*.

Our third Bounty of the game.

Pax held out his hand.

I eyed it derisively. "I'm not holding your hand."

"I'm not trying to hold your hand, you melt. We have another red Bounty ring. We need to touch for every Bounty we're rewarded." He began to jog, still looking back with an outstretched hand. I swung for it as hard as I could. But Pax made me slap the air. He came to a sudden stop, and after giving me a brief look telling me I was testing his patience, he put his hand out again. "Come on, sweetheart. We've got enough to worry about than trying to get one up on each other."

"Oh, I'm 'sweetheart' now, am I?"

Pax's face dropped as his eyes flicked to our tailing cameras. I didn't understand the expression tainting his face, but it made me stiff, and I knew not to mention it again.

"What did you get?" I placed my hand on top of his to activate our Bounty.

He squeezed my fingers gently. "*Ignorance is Bliss*. It—"

"—disables their computer screen. I know."

Pax stopped attending to his own screen to give me a small smile. I ignored him and broke into a jog.

"What have you got?" he asked, catching up with me.

I checked my inventory and read my Bounty, "*Mere Trifle, In the Name of the Law*, and *The Root of all Evil*." Somehow, I felt like Beignley still taunted me.

"Oh, nice job on activating Neo, by the way. How did you manage that?"

"It was right there when my pod opened. When it wasn't looking, I jumped on its back." I played down the subjugation of Neo and kept Beignley's interference to myself.

"Nice. I wondered what was taking you so long. I could see you hanging around by your pod and wasn't sure if you had changed..." He pursed his lips and gave me a sideways look.

"I'm not a coward, Pax."

"You are *such* a pain in the ass."

"Oh, careful. That's almost a swear word."

We ran together down a wide alley. Both realising it to be a dead end, we completed a wall-run up to the next level. With a clearer view of the arena, I checked for Silliah and Brindan's video loop, wanting to see if they were still in the game. What I noticed almost made me sick in my mouth. A majority of the usually stale video loops were copying our one from last year, all holding each other's heads in headlocks. Unable to express our opinion due to the cameras, Pax and I merely shook our heads. Then he laughed, pulled my neck in, and mussed my hair.

"Here look." Pax pointed up.

Silliah and Brindan were still alive! Their video loop was black and white, meaning they hadn't united, but at least they were still playing. Celeste and Thorn were shining in full colour. They both had matching cornrows in their hair and were looking like a formidable team. Perhaps soon they'd have their own team name from fans, just like *Sovereign Skill* and *Unholy Reign*.

I snorted at our video loop: I'd left Pax standing alone, turning on the spot as he followed me, walking around just out of shot. By far my favourite. Finally, one I wouldn't mind seeing on our *Smokin' Axe* fan material. Pax registered what I snorted at and nudged me off balance.

When a green ball bounced by my side, we checked behind us, seeing a couple quite far back. We jumped down to the lower levels. A victory tune later, we rounded a corner and bumped into Brindan and Silliah. Silliah squealed, and we all held our hands up, sidestepping around each other, being careful not to touch. Even the slightest contact from our picosuit gloves and we would eliminate each other. We giggled at ourselves and continued running in opposite directions.

My heels dug into the ground, hearing Silliah scream. She cried at the pain coming from broken ovals scattered across the floor. A yellow rope came at Pax and me, tethering my right wrist to his left. I ran to Silliah, but Pax held me back.

"What are you doing?" I ripped my arm from Pax.

"The Bounty on us, it's *Give a Monkey Enough Rope*. We need to stay together or we will eliminate ourselves."

Sovereign Skill front-flipped down from the upper levels. Saulwyn landed in front of Brindan; Theodred landed in front of us. He towered over us, perfectly composed, his slick blond hair remaining neatly behind his ears.

Saulwyn ended Brindan and Silliah's game with a single touch, sending them both to the floor writhing.

Theodred stared at me straight in the eyes. *Wait.*

Wait, I automatically repeated to Pax, stopping him from firing Bounty at Theodred. Pax turned his hooded amber eyes on me.

Run. Unholy Reign are that way. Theodred gave a subtle head gesture over to the left.

Without any acknowledgment of Theodred's words, I fired *Mere Trifle* at him and guided Pax away. Theodred's fingers would be like jelly, but I didn't need a Bounty to feel my legs turning the same way: Theodred's brazen use of my telepathy had worked just fine.

Pax, I spoke to him whilst jogging, *Theodred knows I can use magic.*

Are you sure?

Yes. He told me Unholy Reign are this way.

Sure enough, as we reached the next alley, *Unholy Reign* were stalking two unsuspecting victims. They were about to catch their prey, when *Sovereign Skill* swooped down, eliminating the prey first. Beignley and Romilly spun our way. I fired *In the Name of the Law* at Beignley. Spiralling blue triangles made contact with his suit, freezing Romilly and him solid. The blue glow spreading from their suits refined the haunted looks on their faces.

Theodred and Saulwyn disappeared.

"Eliminate me and watch what happens." Beignley sounded desperate.

I stared at him, slowly stepping one foot in front of the other. "I would've wanted to use *Mere Trifle* first for poetry…but *In the Name of the Law* will do just fine. *Unholy Reign* won't be finishing first or second place today or *ever* again for as long as I can help it." What I should have done next was break his ribs like he did mine last year, but I sided with stroking the side of his clenched jaw. The electric shock held their convulsing bodies upright for a few moments before they hit the floor with a thud. I flicked my white plait over my shoulder and turned away. Pax watched me with that small smile and raised eyebrows I'd seen many times before. I smiled, knowing I could enjoy the rest of my game without them.

Our accomplice, Neo, had done a nice job whilst we were busy, and we had an additional five Bounty rings on our arms. I'd only ever seen this many decorating *Sovereign Skill's* biceps. Getting into round two was easy, but before that, I bumped into a lost little Crystal, who still hadn't united with Boyd. Displeasingly to Pax, I ended her pathetic game using *The Root of all Evil*. The black vine grew along the floor, ensnaring her ankles, and tripping her up, giving my foot easy tread on her squirming back.

CHAPTER SIXTEEN

SABOTAGE

The eleventh-place elimination drone echoed around the arena, the lights went out, our cameras hit the floor, and our picosuits held us still with red auras.

What's going on? I asked Pax as my mind's eye threw up an image of Beignley's callous face.

Also prisoner to his suit, Pax held the same stiffened posture and moving eyes. *Don't worry; it must be how round two starts. You don't get to see it on the playback.*

A subtle gust of wind followed loud clanking as the huge access doors opened. Then I heard a mixture of footsteps and moving electronic devices. We were quite high up, but I couldn't move my head to find out what was going on. Distorted shadows were all I could see until a faceless, hooded figure rose into my eyeline. The masked visitor stepped off a hovering device stopped level with our platform. After wrapping an arm around my neck and an arm around my waist, the unwelcomed entity dragged me backwards onto the board, holding me steady against their body as we made our descent back down below.

I'm not sure about this, Pax.

You'll be fine. I'll see you soon. He winked before disappearing from view.

A deep voice invaded my ear, "Beignley sends his regards."

Even though his words sent a crackle down my spine, I retaliated. "How can he send his regards when he is facedown on the floor where I left hi—"

A punch in my back forced an end to my sentence. The splitting pain pulsing through my kidneys kept me quiet as we passed by platform after platform. I could see the shapes of lifeless bodies being hoisted onto stretchers and driven out of the arena. The lower levels were no longer maze-like and few obstacles remained.

My captor took me to the outer edge of the arena, discarding his hover device and dragging me into a dark box room, seemingly official, and not the back of a van or the inside of my coffin. Ice-blue institute logos covered the black walls in various sizes, offering the only source of light in the room.

"Enjoy," said my hooded, masked keeper, stabbing me in the neck with a needle.

It pierced several layers of tissue, the cold metal travelling deep. Three outlines of his body left the room. Once the door closed, the picosuit released my body from its red imprisonment, and I fell onto my knees.

I awoke heaving to a sour stench. Pushing myself up to sit, I held my forehead. The institute logos swirled around the walls as the four corners of the room flashed past me. I followed them with my eyes, trying to slow them down, but they wouldn't cease. I put my eyes down on the black rubber floor, blocking out the nauseating show. The sight of undigested remains of my breakfast induced another heaving attack. With nothing left in me to expel, the unforgiving retching yanked harshly at my stomach.

A door in my room slid open, revealing a capsule. I crawled on my hands and knees. The pod's entrance toyed with me, duplicating and sliding left then right. I reached out to feel the way in, and I sat in the dark rubbing my stinging neck. When the pod rumbled, my training pulled me up to my feet.

Unable to look strong, I rested myself on my elbow, laying my head on my arm. Soon brightness hurt my eyes, and I staggered out into the light. Falling on all fours, my gloves landed on a flat surface. I pushed my forehead onto it, allowing the coolness to sooth my face. The ringing in my ears turned into a buzzing. *A camera?* I hid my face in my hands.

Spella Tair, Aurora. Someone spoke to me. I felt like I rocked in the darkness behind my hands. I swallowed, fighting to keep down the acid sloshing in my stomach. *Aurora? If you can heal, say it in your mind, not out loud. Aurora? I'm going to cleanse your blood.*

A fuzzy sensation coursed my veins, easing the dizziness and disorientation. *Of course!* Conjuring in the mind didn't have any colourful smoke. Theodred from *Sovereign Skill* had managed to cleanse my blood secretly. So, Theodred was a Healer? Or maybe he was branching out. Beginners needed to hold on to the person they were healing, so he wasn't new to magic.

Don't recover too quickly or Beignley will suspect something. Blame your behaviour on the height if anyone asks.

Recovering as he instructed, I sat back on my legs and peered through my fingers, seeing I was in a glass cage in the centre of the arena. Theodred occupied a cage to my right. I wiped my gloves down my sweating face.

Oh... My stomach flipped; we were nauseatingly high. Looking up confirmed we were at the highest point of the arena. Our cages all backed up on a centre pillar, and above my pod, a digital strip of red bars depleted every minute. Assuming it to be a timer of some kind, I checked what Theodred was doing. He had digital numbers covering his glass walls, and he rearranged them with his fingertips.

On the far side of the arena, past what looked like a spinning robot with four laser arms, I saw Pax in a matching glass cage. Resembling a clock's minute hand, a transparent platform connected our starting positions together.

Pax.

No. Don't cheat.

It's not cheating. We can all use magic. A genius is gifted; are they cheating at an exam just because they are using the gifts they were born with? Hmm? Oh look, there's Theodred leaving his cage.

We are supposed to work it out for ourselves.

Alright, whatever, you deadhead. I stood up and left him to his own devices.

It didn't take me long to realise what we had to do. The eight empty cells on the glass walls were waiting to hold eight digital numbers jumbled around my cage walls. At first, I slid in '31072102' thinking it would be my birthday, but when this proved fruitless, I searched for numbers '30062100'—being Pax's birthday. The newly filled cells accepted my answer and flashed green, leaving me tapping my foot, waiting for Pax to solve his puzzle, and also half pretending I was still affected by Beignley's *Snakey Sabotage*.

Oh my God, Pax, will you figure it out already? How many eight-figure combinations do you know? Shortly after my admonishment, the glass door to my prison dropped down. Pax had finally entered my birthday, and we could move on to the next section.

Why do you have to be like that? Pax sprinted towards me.

"Oh, hi," I called over the spinning robot separating us. "I was starting to forget what you looked like."

"Give me time and I'll make sure you never forget."

"You always say things that make no sense. What are you even saying?"

He didn't bother to reply and busied himself with the objective of this next task. We each had a neck-high barrier blocking our way into a robot's confines. We were being shielded from its passing lasers by the clear plastic surroundings. To my right, appealing to the child in me, was a big red button.

"I'm assuming we press this?" I hammered it with a fist.

Nothing happened.

"Together, but hold on," Pax said like a sensible grown-up, assessing the spinning robot. "Once we are inside with the robot, I think we will be locked in." He ran his finger along his lip as he focused on the task. "We need to time it so the lasers don't get us as soon as the barrier drops. Wait until they are at one o'clock and four o'clock. Then we slip in and walk around the circle with the lasers."

"Zero one hundred hours and zero four hundred hours?"

"Yes."

"Why not just say that, then?"

"O'clock too difficult for you?"

"Oh, shut up. We don't even use o'clock." I held a long dismissive blink. "And then what do we do?"

"I'm not sure. During round one, there's a robot like this called Nomax. To activate him, you need to jump over the lasers until he overheats and turns off. Then, you can touch the handprint on his head and make it yours."

"Try that, then?"

"Okay." Pax watched the lasers carefully. "On three, we press our buttons. One, two, three."

My inner child rejoiced at slamming the big red button. A nice clunky click later, the four-note victory tune played, and the barriers dropped down flush with the floor. This gave us access to the robot's circular confines, so we swooped in and carefully followed between two lasers in a clockwise direction. Pax was right about the barriers returning, and now we were trapped inside the plastic cage, slave to the rotating lasers.

"Alright," said Pax, walking at a constant pace in the quarter opposite. "I'm not sure how we are supposed to jump over—Oh." The red beams dropped down to ankle height. "I see." He checked back at me. "Okay, we've got to jump over them until the robot overheats, but be careful, he will get really quick."

I lightly hopped over the passing beam. Four seconds later, I hopped again. And again. And again. My mind oscillated between being bored and being alert. Two feet together, I hopped again. In one, two, three, four, I hopped again. Each beam glided swiftly under my black trainers. I resisted a lazy stretch, but my yawn began surfacing—

"Aurora!" yelled Pax.

I snapped my jaw shut, every cell in my body awakening. I gave the cage an urgent sweep and dropped to the floor, belly down, weight on the points of my toes and sprawled fingers. The laser swiped over the top of my back. It maintained its regular speed but without me noticing, had risen to waist height.

"This is stupid. Are you sure this is what we're supposed to be doing?" I asked, unable to make eye contact. My cheeks were sure to be tinged, and I didn't want him to notice. Jumping to my feet, I ran up the entrance barrier, clinging on the top and hanging there, holding my legs out of the laser's reach.

"I think that's cheating, Aurora." Pax still lay on his belly, letting the red beams pass over him.

"I'm utilising the facilities given to us. This thing isn't getting any quicker."

"I dunno." Pax jumped to his feet when the lasers dropped back down to ankle height. "He doesn't have a red handprint either."

"Come here," I said, still crouched on the door. "Walk around with the lasers and try uniting with me."

"The victory tune has already played. I think by entering this cage, we already united."

"It only sang four notes, though. Just try it."

Pax stopped hopping and began walking around with the lasers. He reached his hand out for a high-five. On contact, a high-pitched beep sounded completing the five-note victory tune. Whirling lights rose all around us like smoke from smouldering ashes, dancing higher and higher, twisting and twirling in a boastful display. Nomax's lasers disappeared.

I jumped down from my safe place and flicked an eyebrow at Pax.

"Well done." He humoured me with a returning smile. "But now what? The barriers haven't dropped."

"Hmm." I pivoted in a full circle. We were extremely high up, surrounded by a transparent barrier and co-existing with a corrupted version of Nomax. "There." I nodded at a deactivated Nomax. "Is that a button on its head?"

Pax honed in on the red globe and pounded it. Nomax's red interior light shone gold. Without warning, the see-through ground beneath our feet shifted. Catching our balance, Pax and I locked on to each other's eyes, both adopting a stance similar to that of surfing. Pax backed up towards me, assessing the cage for any signs of joining danger. I did the same, keeping guard of my side. The ground jolted again. Pax's hand automatically grabbed my forearm to steady me.

"I'm fine." I took my arm back.

"We're going down."

Our platform dislodged from its dock and took us down into a clear tube. We passed through a clear section of the arena. The view up here gave us a great advantage, and we could see everything. From a quick glance at the video loops, we were the only other couple (besides *Sovereign Skill*) to have escaped Nomax.

The lower levels were significantly more spaced out than normal, calling for a more skilful gameplay. It reminded me of a Bricks-'n-Mortar Man city skyline during a power cut, scaled down and blacked out. Tall skyscraper-like platforms had holes in them redolent of windows. Connecting the blocky obstacles together, long rails looked like washing lines or those old wires they had hanging everywhere. There were balconies and ledges and a whole array of climbing apparatus.

Plunging deeper down into the arena, shadows were setting in, and then the clear tube transitioned into solid black. We were cast into complete darkness, and a chilly breeze washed over my body. The eliminations were about to begin, and, boy, did my insides know it.

"Erm, Pax, do we have a game plan?"

"You're not nervous, are you?" Pax's voice came out of the infinite darkness.

"No"—I coughed—"of course not. I just want to win."

"We've done well to get this far. You achieved what you said you wanted to and eliminated *Unholy Reign*, but round two is full of the best."

"*We're* good, Pax. *We* are in round two. Why do you still not believe we are good enough for this?"

"Alright." Pax gave a small half-hearted laugh. "With you on my team, we might stand a chance."

"Without you, I would've hung us with *Give a Monkey Enough Rope*. I'm a monkey"—a smile stretched my lips—"and without you, I'd be nothing." My lips dropped when I heard my sentence back. I covered my slip with a change of tone, a direct, bossy one. "Now come on… game plan? We are running out of time."

"I'd say"—Pax hesitated, clearly still thinking of one—"keep at the edge of the arena for a bit, and let the others get the numbers down. What do you think?"

"Yeah, that could work."

"There're a lot more traps and tripwires in round two, so be careful."

The platform came to a swift stop, sending my stomach swooping in a circle. Unable to see where the exit was, I waited for the doors to open. The arena was deathly silent. My gut clenched as sharp prickles kept me alert. The black doors parted, exposing a flood of light. Pax gave me a small nod before we stepped into the blinding rays.

Sorry. Theodred's silken voice infiltrated my head.

My body began convulsing. A merciless current grabbed my insides and shook the consciousness out of me. *You're our main competition now.* Theodred's distant words passed through my mind before the emptiness devoured me.

CHAPTER SEVENTEEN
PRETENDING

Back in my bedroom after the games, I picked up my Slate to leave for dinner, and my heart took a sudden slap. My full name...ouch.

'*Hey, Aurora. I just wanted to check you were okay?*' Tayo's name on screen didn't feel as comforting as I had imagined. It only reminded me that he'd left, and the excitement I once used to feel seeing his notification had been replaced by a pain in my chest.

'*What do you care?*'

'*I care, Roar. Did they get to you?*'

Detecting a small trace of Tayo in that message, my eyes turned the whole chat into a blur. Huge silent tears fell from my cheeks, splashing my thumbs poised over my screen. All I wanted to do was ask for him to come back and be my best friend again. But I knew he wouldn't. It would be a waste of breath, and I was done letting him drag my heart around. I wiped my wet thumbs across my navy combats, shut off my Slate, and left for dinner.

"Aurora, wait up," a call followed me down the Navy residential corridor. I knew whose voice it belonged to, but I didn't turn to acknowledge the owner. "You are a piece of work, you know that?" Pax advanced by my side, breathing heavy.

"I'm not pretending to be united with you, Pax." I kept my eyes trained forward.

"I think you'll find you are."

"Only when people are around."

"And here I was, thinking we would skip and hold hands."

"Hm, well, I thought I'd give being the disappointment a go for a change."

"Phohh." Pax blew his lips outwards. "You could always sneak out the institute with Silliah; you know, get me a new picoplant again; this one's getting a little old."

I rubbed the back of my neck and checked the corridor to see if anyone around had heard. The foot traffic was heavier today as everyone eagerly sought out the Food Hall in time for *Sovereign Skill's* arrival. I met with countless eyes, and my stomach clenched. Unbeknownst to Pax, it was actually Tayo—not Silliah—who left the institute with me last year. It was stupid and reckless, and it was a rumour I couldn't afford to get back to Silliah, so I hoped these passing ears were too interested in the events of the games and not our topic of conversation.

"*Smokin' Axe*," called Brindan behind us, appearing hand in hand with Silliah.

Silliah squealed and tried pulling Brindan down the corridor towards us. But Brindan had other ideas, and with no intention of joining Silliah in the excited jog, he playfully leant back, digging his heels into the ground and preventing Silliah from running any farther. She looked like a puppy on a lead, hungrily pulling at Brindan's wrist as he used her momentum to swerve her from left to right like a pendulum. Her smile could be seen from here, and the same was true for the sparkle behind Brindan's blue-green eyes. For a while, they were entirely devoted to each other, the rest of us not there.

A spell of something cast over me, making my gaze slip to Pax. That was us last year. It wasn't fair. Why did our betrothal have to go so wrong?

Feeling my gaze on him, Pax opened his arm out to me and held it there, giving time to read my face, trying to decipher my thoughts. We kept still on each other's eyes as he waited to see whether I was going to seek comfort in his arms or not. He wasn't Tayo. But I needed to pretend to be united with him. I could stand in his arms. I wouldn't be doing anything wrong, right? I *had* to do it.

Turning into him, I leant up against his familiar frame, inhaling him and breathing in soapy notes with his natural aroma. There was something fresh and masculine about it, embodying the strength of the ocean. It fulfilled a longing I didn't realise lingered under my skin. The tightness of his arms around my back made me push my face harder into his chest. Their bodies were so different and their hugs completely unalike. He was encompassing. My spine stiffened, aware I compared them, and I twisted around to face Silliah.

She smiled at Pax's arms around my neck, and it stopped me from pulling away.

"Sorry about him." Silliah excused Brindan, giving him a dig in the side.

Brindan pulled her in tightly, preventing her from using her elbow again. With his other hand, he guided me and Pax to face the other way, resting his arm over my shoulder. I hooked my arm around his waist, and we all walked towards the Food Hall in a row.

"Good game today, guys," said Brindan, looking down the line at Pax. "You two were incredible, as per."

"I had so much fun," added Silliah. "Seeing you two in there was the best. But-oh-my-God," she said without a breath. "Nothing prepares you for that electric shock. I'm surprised I'm still alive. I literally felt like I was dying."

Pax snorted in a burst of air.

"Oh, I know," I said, turning away from Pax. "The worst pain I've ever felt, and you literally can't avoid it unless you win. It's traumatising."

"It ain't that bad," Pax said. "Try being awake whilst they take your picoplant out." He nudged the whole group sideways as a way of implying Silliah and I were to blame.

Tension rushed to my skin like magnets. Not this topic of conversation. Silliah didn't know I left the institute last year, and she definitely didn't know Pax thought she was with me.

Brindan doesn't know, I said to Pax privately, making up a reason as to why we couldn't talk about it.

Okay. He gave me a nod.

"Shut up," said Silliah, curving the group round so she could see Pax at the end of our line. "They numb the area, don't they?"

"Yeah, but they let you watch, and *ergh*"—Pax shook his picoplant arm like he was expelling the memories—"I just felt everything."

We entered the Food Hall and disbanded. Pax walked up to a table in Navy Quartz and used the tabletop screen to expand it into a long bench. Silliah and Brindan sat side-by-side opposite Pax and me. The room was busy already, and an awful lot of *Smokin' Axe* memorabilia played under the press of eyes.

Pax leant over into my ear. "Ever feel like you're being watched?"

I leaned towards him, resting my chin on my hand to cover my mouth. "It's a bit intense."

"*Smokin' Axe,*" said Ryker behind us, holding Pax's and my head together in a sort of Ryker hug. "Brindan. Silliah," he greeted them, still keeping us in his arms.

I zoned out of his conversation with Silliah and Brindan and became fully engrossed in Pax's hot jaw on my cheek. I turned my forehead on it and allowed him to take the weight of my head. When he stroked his knuckle along my jaw, a tingling kindled in places it shouldn't. Ryker let go, and I lifted my head like I awoke from sleep, a little tired and a little dazed. *Pretending, Aurora. Pretending.*

"Teaming up with *Sovereign Skill*, you dirty dogs," Ryker said, pushing me into Pax's shoulder. "They done the dirty on you, though. How d'you feel?"

"It's every man for themselves in round two," replied Pax.

"I don't see my dear old brother winning for a while, not with you four working with each other. Rumour has it, you're favourites to win. Everyone loves *Sovereign Skill*, but there hasn't been a new winner for ye—"

Ryker's last words were drowned out by the outburst of applause. *Sovereign Skill* made their graceful entrance into the room. An entourage followed them, and they led the crowd straight up to our table. Saulwyn and Theodred looked immaculate, every shining strand of blond hair still in place. Their cheeks were softly blushed, perhaps from a recent shower, and their Navy uniforms looked fresh out the packet.

"Good game today, *Smokin' Axe*," said Theodred, reaching to shake Pax's hand. "Sorry to have to turn traitor on you." He reached out for mine and cupped it with both hands.

"It's all part of the games." I shrugged, trying to ignore the fact that they were basically the institute's celebrities and had walked straight over to us. Also trying to ignore the fact we knew each other were Puracordis. "No hard feelings. There's only room for one winner."

"Of course. Of course." He patted my hand.

"Better watch your back next time, though," I added, giving them both a smile.

"We're looking forward to it."

"*Move*," said a scathing voice near the back of the crowd. A few yelps came from a kerfuffle in the middle. "*Move*." It was a forceful, arrogant demand likely to be heard from an older brother. "Get out the way." Beignley appeared from the disturbance, pushing two flustered fans aside. "They are *using* you to eliminate their strongest competition, you infants." He came abreast of *Sovereign Skill* and switched to look between Pax and me. "You're not good enough on your own, so you have to team up in a survival-of-the-fittest game."

"Works well for me." I shrugged one shoulder. "As long as I never see you crowned victors again."

"You wanna watch yourself around me, or I'll give you something more than heights to be scared of."

"Beignley, I think you should leave." Pax rose from his chair. Beignley rounded on him, pushing his chest out and standing taller than all of us.

"Careful, Brother," said Ryker, also standing up. "You're starting to look like you're scared you'll never win again."

"Go get another girlfriend, Ryker. Or didn't you notice, this one"—he nodded at me—"is already taken."

"Leave, Beignley," repeated Pax calmly but keeping his eyes locked on him.

"Waste of breath, all of ya. Not worth my time. I could get the lot of you booted like that." Beignley clicked his fingers.

"The lot of us?" I laughed, standing up between Ryker and Pax, not wanting to be sitting whilst I added fuel to the fire.

Ryker angled his body in front of mine. "The lot of us?" he repeated my question, staring Beignley dead in the eyes.

"The lot of us?" Theodred joined in, also coming to stand in front of me.

"Oh, look at you, you pathetic pieces of shit not worthy of my boot." Beignley backed away. "You look pathetic." He looked at us like we were a bad smell, all the while edging farther and farther away.

"Yep, just keep walking away, you bean." Ryker stepped out from blocking me.

With Beignley out of sight, the gang dispersed, all exchanging looks of bewilderment.

"You alright?" Pax turned to check on me.

"Yeah."

He nodded and turned back to *Sovereign Skill.* "Sorry about that, guys."

"Poor showmanship," said Theodred. "People who can't stand to lose, shouldn't play games. You alright, Aurora?"

"Yeah, I'm fine," I said, feeling like I hadn't been convincing in my first answer to Pax. "I can handle a Boulderfell. I've had to put up with this one for a year." I nudged Ryker lightly with my shoulder.

"Don't act like you ain't scared of me." Ryker walked into me, backing me up. "Hm?" He still stared at me intensely. "Don't act like you ain't scared of me." He raised his fists and feigned a few jabs to my face. It was mildly irritating until his punches got closer and closer, forcing me to keep backing up between the crowd. They separated, and we reached a clear area in Claret Quartz.

I put my arm up to block a very real right hook coming for my face. "Stop it. I'm not playing this game with you, Ryker." I blocked another of his punches, this one coming for my chin. My arm clashed against his forearm, bone on bone, and I was this far away from deliberately breaking his wrist.

"Say sorry," he said, still using real punches to force my pull-back between the tables.

"Stop it, Ryker." I trod back, blocking another real punch.

"Say sorry for acting like you ain't scared of me."

"I'm not scared of you. Don't make me kick your ass."

"That's enough, Ryker." I heard Pax from over in Navy.

Ryker came at me harder, polluting the air around him. I could sense the 'fun' had turned into a toxic battle of egos. Behind him, a field of eyes all watched us. I realised Ryker couldn't afford to lose face and back down in front of everyone, especially not his brother. I was creating a dour situation, one I couldn't get out of without surrendering.

"Alright." My arm collided painfully against one of his harder swings. "Alright. Stop. I'm sorry." I held my hands up to him instead of blocking him.

He grabbed my wrist and twisted it a way it shouldn't bend. He lowered his head and spoke quietly into my ear, "Don't ever make me look stupid again."

"Ow, alright, Ryker." I controlled a flush blazing down my face, making me want to retaliate. I knew the counter move out of his lock, but I also knew not to detonate the bomb I'd just defused. "You've made your point. Stop."

Feeling like he'd proven himself, Ryker finally listened and released my wrist. I rubbed it and let out an agitated breath, eyeing the back of his head as he walked away. We arrived to a huge bench spanning nearly the whole length of Navy Quartz. It was full of everyone I knew and some. *Sovereign Skill* had expanded our table and sat with a few of their friends. Celeste and Thorn had done the same too. My place next to Pax was saved, so I took my seat. Ryker tapped some Tenth-year on the shoulder, sending him way down the end of the bench, allowing Ryker to sit next to me.

Our table was loud and lively this evening, with Ryker re-enacting parts from the Parkour Games and playing the role of jester. Pax and Brindan ordered more food than usual and placed it in the centre of the table for everyone to share. This touch of amity spread like a smile, and nobody seemed to be eating off their own plates.

"No, this is ridiculous," said Seioh Jennson from behind me. "How many queens do you need sitting on one table? Split up, now."

Nobody moved besides turning to look at each other. He tolerated it for a few seconds before helping us out. "Aurora, Saulwyn, Celeste, split up. Look at the size of this table. It's ridiculous."

"Yes, Seioh," answered Saulwyn and Celeste.

I didn't speak or move. Since when was I a 'queen'? But to Seioh Jennson, I would probably be considered the guilty party in everything. I usually was, so why would tonight be any different? A lot of jumbling later, plates were divided, goodbyes were said, and our gathering thinned to its usual amount.

Less than impressed with how close Crystal was near me now, my mood took a slight dip. Pax passed behind me and placed a takeaway cup in front of my setting. "Goodnight, sweetheart." He kissed the top of my head.

Sweetheart? I pressed my lips together to stop my smile. "I'll come with you," I said, grabbing the cup.

"Aurora, book on to Lethals tomorrow, okay?" Silliah said quickly.

"Lethals?"

"Pax will tell you. We have a lesson slot together."

Pax and I cleared a few empty plates before wishing everyone goodnight. Heading off, he held his hand out to me. His fingers were bigger than Tayo's, but there was something about Tayo's veins that I liked. My back stiffened, realising I had done it again, and I took his hand before anyone noticed I hesitated.

On our way back to our room, Pax explained the plan for our Lethals lesson tomorrow morning, and then his thoughts turned on today.

"Have you had a good day?" he asked, his wide fingers twitching between mine.

"Yeah. It was good," I replied, knowing the small talk was just a lead-up to what he really wanted to say.

"I think Beignley's taken it a bit far this time."

"Don't worry about him." I took a sip of my hot chocolate to keep my sentences short.

"I don't like the way he looks at you, and I don't like the way he speaks to you either."

"I can handle him, okay? He is all bark and no bite."

"Does Ryker hurt you?"

"You can let go of my hand now, Pax." I turned into our empty residential corridor. I pressed my bedroom's access button, and Pax followed me inside. "I don't need you to protect me, Pax, okay? We are *pretending* to be united. I don't want anything from you."

Pax inhaled deeply and obviously. "Alright, Aurora," he said, leaving through the interconnecting door and closing it behind him.

I copied his deep and obvious inhale to help the twisting pain in my throat. I knew it was harsh, but I needed him to know. The guilt was becoming too much to bear, and I didn't want it to feel nice spending time with him.

"Pretending?" Tayo appeared around the ensuite archway.

CHAPTER EIGHTEEN
UNTAMABLE

"No," I uttered, the pain in my throat splitting through my chest. My shattered heart couldn't take the impact, the shock, the *audacity*. How dare he just appear in my room after walking out on me, blackmailing me to walk into Pax's room, ignoring my messages, and leaving me alone to deal with all this pain. "*No,*" I growled fiercely, charging his way, my peppermint hot chocolate slipping from my fingers. "You do not get to just walk back in here." I swung to hammer his chest. "You *do not* get to do that."

"Whoa. Oh. Calm down." Tayo hopped backwards, avoiding my swings.

"*You do not get to just walk back in here.*"

"Okay. Whoa." He dodged me again. "Okay-okay-okay. Please, Roar."

"You do not get to just walk back in here after leaving me like that." My nails dug into my palms as balled fists sought the source of all my pain.

Tayo stood still and allowed my fist to hammer his chest. "Okay," he said mildly, taking my punishment.

"You don't…" My arms dropped uselessly by my sides.

Tayo pulled my head to his chest and cradled it.

His crisp aftershave travelled my airways, spicy but touched by a smooth vanilla. I thought I would never smell him again. I thought I would never press my head to his chest again, feel his breath against my hair, hear the bassy tones of his voice.

"How could you leave me so easily?" I mumbled into his arm, pressure building in my throat.

"It wasn't easy, Roar." He kissed the top of my head, squeezing me tighter. "It wasn't easy."

"Why didn't you message me back?"

He freed my head and wiped my tears with his black T-shirt. "I just couldn't."

Couldn't? Why *couldn't* he put me out of my misery? Why *couldn't* he take some of my pain away? I wanted him more than anything. "*Why?*" I asked, forcefully. "You have no idea how hard it's been."

"No, Aurora, *you* have no idea how hard it's been. *You* have no idea what's been going on in my head. You're the girl I care about more than anything in the entire world, and I'm having to imagine you playing happy families with another guy. I can't bear it."

My eyes dropped to the floor. I hadn't really thought of it like that. I was so caught up on how I felt; I didn't, for one second, consider how he must've been feeling. I stared at his black trainers, dealing with the new type of hurt, a hurt for what Tayo had been going through.

Tayo walked over to my spilled hot chocolate and collected the takeaway cup. The lid hadn't popped off, and he swirled it, feeling the contents in the bottom before handing it to me. "Your heart wasn't the only one that broke that day, Roar."

"You didn't need to leave me, Tayo."

"I thought..." He held his fingers and picked his tidy nails. "I thought I was making things easier for you by getting out of the way." More attention was placed on his hands than necessary, and I could tell from his jerky inhales that he battled with something internally. "I...I've never felt this way about anyone before. You've been my whole life since I was six, and you being in my head is

252

all I've ever known. I shouldn't have left. But I thought it was for the best. I thought it was only a matter of time before you'd fall for him again. I know you never really got over him, and with him staying…" Tayo winced at his own sentence, turning away before he thought I'd seen. "You'll be leaving with his surname."

My chest ached for him. There was a time when I thought nothing really fazed him. I'd seen beneath the surface for the first time, and I felt like I was just starting to understand him.

Feeling lightheaded, I backed up to the bed. He joined me, adopting my stance and resting with his feet on the platform steps. His gaunt face made him almost unrecognisable. I could tell it was him, but he looked like a soldier who'd seen combat. What it was exactly, I couldn't put my finger on it. His defined cheeks told half the story.

"You look ill," I said, feeling numb and still processing.

"I haven't been eating much. I've been fasting all day so I can conjure. I eat last thing at night."

"Have you been going to the temple?" I realised I'd neglected that part of myself the moment he made me walk into Pax's room.

"Yeah, every day."

If I'd remembered to practise magic, I could have seen him sooner.

Although my mind felt foggy, I placed my hand on his arm to fully cleanse his blood. "*Spella Tair.*"

"Thanks." He observed his spread fingers, flexing them like I had released his chains.

"You need to eat, Tayo."

"I know. It's just whilst I'm growing my own food. I've just started, and it's nowhere near ready yet."

"Do you want me to get you something from the meal dispenser?"

"No, it's okay. I was just coming to check you were alright."

A moment ago, I would have believed him, but now I wasn't so sure. "You knew I was okay."

He held still, looking at me from the corner of his eye. Then he faced the display screen to answer, "No, I didn't."

"You would've seen by my picoplant that they didn't reach me."

He pursed his lips, still not looking at me. "I was too busy trying to keep control of your suit."

"You're lying. Just be honest with me."

He sighed and rubbed his forehead. "I had to see you."

I knew it. He struggled not seeing me just as much as I struggled not seeing him. "So you heard my message earlier?"

He stopped rubbing his head to look at me, his fingers still cupping above his eye. "Heard? What message?"

"During the Parkour Games, I tried to call to you in my mind."

"No." He scratched his neck under his jacket collar. "I knew it was the Parkour Games today, and I was keeping an eye on you at work. I saw your suit had been breached, so I disabled the hackers and locked them out. That idiot has game technicians working for him."

"I thought so. Thank you…for stopping them. They would've gotten to me if it weren't for you."

"*Fuck.*" Tayo stood up, ripping off his black leather jacket. "I can't *stand* them."

"Hey. Tayo, I'm fine. Look." I shot up, showing him under my vest. "You stopped them from hurting me."

"You need to learn magic, Roar." He ran both hands down the length of my body and then lowered my vest. "I mean it. What if I hadn't been watching your suit today?"

I nodded quickly, distracted by the afterglow of his hands gliding across my skin.

"I mean it. You need to practise. You *need* to be able to protect yourself from them if I'm not around."

"Okay, I will." I tried closing the distance between us.

He stepped away. "What if I wasn't watching over you today, Roar?"

A sudden lurch in my chest reminded me how much it could hurt, and I dropped down on the mattress. "Okay."

Tayo huffed through his nostrils. "Okay," he repeated, sitting back on the platform steps. "I'm going to teach you magic so you can protect yourself. Beignley will know you have someone on the inside now after he speaks to the hackers. So, any abnormal activity from your suit can be blamed on me. Well, my fake picoplant me. You'll be able to defend yourself next time."

I nodded, still thinking about his hands on my skin and wondering why he stepped away.

"I've learnt a lot this week. I can show now, look." He pivoted towards me and watched his skin *not* shining like a beacon. "Okay. I really have learned how to do it. It's one of the easiest things to do. Mine doesn't shine as white as yours, but I really can do it. I must be too unsettled. Magic is powered by emotion. The better you feel, the more powerful you are."

"There're two Enforcers here who know about Puracordis. They used it to talk with me today."

"Really? Do you trust them?"

I gave a small shrug, staring down at the floor. "I don't know. I don't really know them."

"Get them to show. It will let you know if you can trust them."

"I think I want to tell Silliah first. She's my best friend, and she doesn't even know about any of this."

"Alright. Do you know how you'll tell her?"

I shook my head, chewing on my lip.

He lifted a hand to my cheek, running a thumb over to stop me from biting my lip. "I've missed you so much, Roar."

His gentle touch weakened me, making my heart throb. I forced myself to lean away and pushed his hand off my face.

"What?" He held still, his hand floating in mid-air.

"No, Tayo." I just shook my head.

"Pretending?" He repeated what I'd said to Pax before I knew he was hiding in the ensuite.

"Yes, Tayo. But that doesn't mean we go back to the way we were. I don't want a relationship with either of you."

Tayo's lips curved subtly. It was a smile I'd only seen from him in the early days of Juvie duty. "You don't want a relationship with me?"

"No, Tayo, and it's not 'challenge accepted'. I mean it. I will use my *enforcery* stuff on you."

Confusion wrinkled his eyes, but his smile strengthened. "Okay."

"I'm serious."

"You realise I'm an Intuitionist, right?"

"It's time for you to leave. I'm tired."

"Alright. I'm going. But you know I know, right?"

"Leave."

Tayo's annoying smile returned. It was thin and subtle and accentuated a burning look behind his crinkled piercing-blue eyes. "Goodnight, Aurora."

CHAPTER NINETEEN

A CLOSE ENCOUNTER

My wardrobe slipped open without a touch, and my Navy uniform floated on its invisible hook. I made it dance in the air, taking the jacket off the hanger, separating the navy-blue vest from the combats, and making all three items swirl around me as I jumped in a circle. I was going to be sharing my magical side with my best friend today. I hadn't quite worked out how, and several different scenarios played in my head. Sometimes my mind took me down a darkened path, imagining her reacting badly, so I decided it was best to stop thinking about it and just do what felt right in the moment.

Breakfast saw the return of Juvie duty for Silliah and Brindan, both chaperoning children under the age of twelve. This was her first Juvie since Natashly left last year, who she grew close to and, like the rest of us with our Juvies, was saddened to see her go. So, this time Silliah said she wasn't even going to learn her Juvie's first name. Ryker and Crystal's blonde friend, Maylene, had been paired up together as partners, sharing every duty together from here on out, unless either of them united. And Mimsy Jackson, Crystal's Juvie, still hauled her way to the Food Hall with a weighted trap.

Quite a few of us had a lesson slot first thing, and we all arranged to book on to Lethals together. Both Ryker and Pax said they'd done the lesson before, but they liked Sir Darlington's lessons, so they decided to join us.

"I've been waiting so long to book on to Lethals," said Silliah, leaning up against Brindan outside the classroom. "It's not fair they stop First-years from taking it."

"You say that now," said Brindan, "but you haven't had the lesson yet. There's a reason First-years can't take Lethals."

"Can't say I even knew about it," I added, pretending to be united with Pax and leaning against him too. "I didn't even know there was a lesson I couldn't take."

"Did you ever read your welcome pack?" Silliah shook her head at me. "It was in there."

"Some of it." I shrugged.

"*Serve, Honour, Protect, and Defend,*" greeted Sir Darlington, appearing out of his classroom.

"*Serve, Honour, Protect, and Defend,*" we all chanted with a closed fist over our hearts. Silliah and I got off our betrotheds and queued up.

"Okay. Line up, please. Nice to see some new faces. Very good. Come forward, Eighth-year, Geosar Weaver." Sir Darlington shook Geosar by the hand and welcomed him into his classroom. It was a strange welcome but none of my friends caught my side glance. Apparently, they were used to it. "Good to see you, too, Eleventh-year, Victori June." He shook her hand, inviting her in. He reached his hand out to Hilly. "A new face, welcome to your first Lethals class, Second-year, Hilly Lafern. You, too, Second-year, Calix Bane. I've had my eye on you since your very first Show of Force Display." He waved them inside. One by one he received his pupils by the hand and welcomed them into his class. "Fourth-year, Brindan Haywards, good to see you again. Hello, Second-year, Silliah Van de Waal, nice to meet you. Ah, Fourth-year, Paxton Fortis, great to see you." After patting Pax on the arm and waving him inside, Kian held his hand out for me. "Introduce yourself," he said flatly, giving my hand an overly firm shake.

"Erm"—I felt my palms beginning to sweat—"Second-year, Aurora Aviary."

"*Sir*," he prompted me to say.

"Sorry. Second-year, Aurora Aviary, sir."

"Right. In you get." He waved me inside. "Ah, my boy, Ryker. Come in, come in. Great to see you."

I entered his classroom stiffly, feeling uncomfortable in my own skin, as if it had grown and stretched and hung off my bones heavily. Pax, Silliah, and Brindan were choosing seats in a huge classroom rivalled only by the size of the Auditorium. It was circular with curved rows of tiered seating and a huge staging area. The salon-esque chairs all faced the wall towards the door. I trod on the silver bar step and climbed onto my chair, getting comfy between Pax and Ryker. It swivelled to face the stage, and my legs slid under a desk attached to the arm. I rested my elbows on it and waited with a twist in my gut.

Sir Kian Darlington took up position behind a curved control station on centre stage. He brushed down his black instructor's uniform and stroked the sides of his fresh military haircut. I couldn't see any resemblance to Pipila and wouldn't have known they were related if I hadn't been told. He had a wide, strong jawline, a square head, and a thick, solid build. Pipila was slender like me. She clearly took after her mum, but perhaps, she got her height from her dad. Maybe they even shared the same green eyes, too, but I couldn't say I paid that much attention to Pipila's eye colour.

Sir Darlington's hologram appeared, flickering at first, on all of our special desks. Then his deep voice came from our headrests. "This lesson is not for the fainthearted," he began in a low, gruff voice sounding like he needed to cough, "but then neither is being a Young Enforcer. If I find you are not cut-out for my class, then, unfortunately, a dishonourable discharge is the only way for you.

"My lesson's hands-on learning style classifies Lethals as high risk. So, it is crucial you follow my instructions immediately and exactly. Failure to listen to my orders will have severe consequences. It's a dangerous class, and I need to keep you all safe.

"Right, with that said, are we ready to play a game? Everyone raise their hands like this." Sir Darlington extended his right arm as if waiting to ask a question. We cautiously obeyed whilst he put a small device on the control station. He lifted a parabolic dish out of the device and turned it towards us. "I want you to put your hands down if you can feel this." Sir Darlington attended to his control station, and the show of hands snatched back in a flash. He laughed at the crowd's response. I didn't feel anything, but the collective response made me act out of impulse, and I pulled back my hand. Sir Darlington gave me a side-on glance, noticing I was the last to retract my hand. The classroom quickly became noisy as everyone expressed their surprise and laughed at themselves. From what I could gather, the device made everyone feel like they were hot.

"Okay, quieten down," said Sir Darlington, still chuckling at the audience's reaction. "This is a directed-energy weapon, DEW for short. It has been around since the twentieth century and has been known to make people jump from buildings. We use it for perimeter security and crowd control. Electromagnetism has the ability to disrupt the molecular bonds of matter and can turn buildings into dust. This particular weapon uses electromagnetism to make the target feel like they are cooking from the inside out.

"Okay, shall we see who can bear it the longest? Let's see who the last man standing will be. Everyone raise their hands. There are no windows to jump out of in this room, but as a precaution, no one is permitted to leave their seats."

I raised my hand ready for the DEW to be activated. The immediate snatch of hands thinned the competition considerably. Even though I could just about feel a warmth flicking underneath my skin, I removed myself from the game regardless. I did not want to bring attention to the fact I could hardly feel a weapon that made people jump to their deaths.

The class squirmed in their seats, groaning and trying to curl up. Ryker and Pax were fighting the pain, beads of sweat trailing their faces. Although I was sure Pax could have held on, he took one sweep around at everyone and lowered his hand, crowning Ryker as champion. Everyone gave an audible sigh when the machine was switched off. Sir Darlington commended Ryker by coming up the tiered seating to shake his hand. I couldn't help but feel every time Kian laid eyes on me, he was full of contempt, proving that the apple didn't fall far from the tree—distaste for me was something Pipila and Kian shared in common.

Sir Darlington returned to his control station and talked us through the appliance. Then he invited us all up on stage and made us use the machine on each other in turn. We were allowed to run out of the ray as soon as we felt heat. I was lucky I could feel a slight tickle, because otherwise I wouldn't have known when to run. After firing at Pax and then Ryker firing at me, I slumped back into my seat and waited for the queue to dwindle down.

Sir Darlington told us a few 'funny' stories about the DEW before moving on to his next weapon. "For those who haven't taken this lesson before"—he held up a glass canister filled with a glowing red liquid—"can anyone tell me what this is?"

Nobody spoke; a few jogged their shoulders.

"Okay, can anybody tell me where they may have seen it before?"

Silliah raised her hand.

"Yes, Silliah?" Sir Darlington turned his ear to her.

"I've seen it in the underside of the black Fell agent guns."

"Correct, Silliah." He flicked the four-pronged pointy end towards her. "Can you tell me what it is?"

"No, sir."

"Paxton, could you tell us?"

Pax removed his hand away from his mouth to speak. "It's a ransom dart, sir."

"Very good. And, Ryker, could you tell us what it does?"

"Yes, sir. It injects a slow poison which is fatal unless you have the antidote."

"Excellent, Ryker. Now, Aurora, can you come and join me on stage?"

My eyes widened at the sudden use of my name. "Yuh-yes, sir."

"No"—Ryker held a flat hand out towards me—"I'll do it."

"No, no, Ryker," said Sir Darlington. "Seioh Boulderfell would not stand for it. Aurora, come and join me on stage."

My chair swivelled to face the right wall, and I leant forward to get up.

"No"—Ryker kept his hand out to block me—"I said I'll do it." He swivelled his chair round and stepped down from it.

"Mr. Boulderfell—"

"Sit back down," said Ryker, standing by my chair. "Sir, I said I'll do it."

"Okay, if you insist, then you can both do it together. Ryker and Aurora, come and join me on stage."

Ryker shook his head but had no choice but to accept the compromise. I left my chair with the tightest double knot in my abdomen. Eyes watched me closely as I passed row after row of Navies. My arms felt like they'd grown, and I couldn't figure out how to hold them. I clenched my fists and shoved them into my combat pockets.

Once on stage, Ryker lowered my zip down from my small straight collar and rolled up my sleeves. "Pipila said it helps," he said quietly, finishing with my sleeve and taking off his own navy jacket.

"Right then," started Sir Darlington, coming to stand behind me. "This weapon, although potentially fatal, is considered a less-lethal weapon." He placed one hand on the right side of my neck and injected the ransom dart into my left side. Leaving a small sting, he walked over to Ryker. "We use it to encourage fugitives to hand themselves in." He injected Ryker with the glowing red chemical.

I couldn't feel the poison. Why couldn't I feel the poison? The other weapon, the DEW, had little effect on me too, and I was dangerously close to giving away my secret. The sea of eyes all pressed on me whilst they waited for my reaction to the dart. I watched Ryker closely. I was going to have to imitate him, maybe milk it a little more since he showed he was very good at fighting pain. Black travelled the veins in Ryker's neck. I checked my chest. I, too, had the black poison coursing my veins. Ryker stood unaffected, so I maintained my poker face.

"Okay," began Sir Darlington. "So, as you can see, the subjects show no adverse effects to the poison. This is because it is slow-acting and takes twelve hours before the afflicted are bereft of life. We don't have that long, so I'm going to use an accelerant to speed up the process." Sir Darlington jabbed us both in the neck with another needle, this one clear. He used the control station to place a holographic timer on everyone's desks reading 11:59. "Then we can all see the full effects of the ransom dart in its entirety. It is important you all remain where you are. These two subjects have a fatal chemical injected into their system with an accelerant speeding up the process. They will die in less than twelve minutes if they do not receive the antidote." Sir Darlington stood behind me and turned my head to the right, showing the audience my neck. "The subject has a visual sign of the poison, but nothing else. This is to alert the fugitive and others that they have been poisoned."

Kian's fingers held the sides of my face firmly, my head tipped slightly back and over to the right. I caught Ryker's eye. He rubbed his lips together abrasively. The veins in his cheeks were black. It was extremely unnerving and would be enough for any civilian to keep their distance. The fugitive wouldn't be able to hide in plain sight, that was for sure. After shaking his head, Ryker faced the other way. When Kian released me, I dropped my gaze to the floor, avoiding the onslaught of eyes. I caught a glimpse of my birthmark appearing on my wrist and quickly turned it onto my combats. The ransom dart appeared to be interfering with my invisibility spell. *Lis-Vuluta*, I ran the spell through my mind. *Lis-Vuluta*. I tried the invisibility incantation again, but it wasn't working.

"For the first six hours," Sir Darlington was still speaking, "the sole purpose is to alert the fugitive that they've been struck with the poison, so the chemical travels the whole body, turning the veins black. At some point they will notice and will know to turn themselves in. Now"—Sir Darlington waited for the timer to read 06:00—"this is where it gets interesting. After the first six hours, the chemical starts to encourage the fugitive to seek medical help."

Before Kian finished his sentence, I felt an intense burning under my skin. Every tiny vein was infected with a hot black poison, and my face was on fire. I wiped the sweat on my sleeve. Ryker was bearing it with clenched teeth. *Fight it, Aurora*. I tried to remain composed like him. *Oh*. I couldn't. I couldn't fight it. *The heat*. I couldn't pretend. My feet danced on the spot, and I wiped my face uselessly.

"Stay where you are, Miss Aviary." Sir Darlington sensed I was becoming overwhelmed. He injected Ryker with the antidote. "You can return to your seat. A round of applause for Mr. Boulderfell. Thank you, Ryker."

Ryker nodded towards the audience with a pursed mouth. I waited for my antidote, my weight switching from foot to foot, helping to keep my attention on anything other than the heat. Sir Darlington walked to the control station. I fought against my body's instinct to move away from the source. There wasn't a source, but the intense urge to move was powerful, the need to move, move anywhere, run, escape from this heat.

"Stay where you are, Miss Aviary," Sir Darlington repeated. "So, this takes place over the course of five hours. After this, the chemical starts to affect the mobility of the fugitive. A person who can't run is easier to catch. If, by this stage, the fugitive hasn't turned themselves in, the likelihood is they aren't going to. They may think they have a solution or a cure. So, it is the purpose of this final hour to incapacitate the felon. By the end of this hour, they will die without the antidote. It is better to have one less criminal in the world than a criminal on the loose."

When the time turned to 00:59, my body felt like it was giving up. It couldn't cope and neither could I. Feeling weaker with every passing second, my legs gave way, and I collapsed to my knees. I tried to stay silent; I desperately wanted to stay silent, but a cavernous groaning expelled from somewhere deep down inside me. Every tiny vein in my body carried burning hot tar, and I pushed my forehead into the stage floor. The cooling plastic didn't help, but the crushing of my nose was a better pain to concentrate on than the fire roaring through my veins. Growing weaker and weaker, my head wouldn't lift. I couldn't hold my body weight, and I fell onto my side. Through watery eyes, I saw a hazy 00:05 on the timer. Silence drowned me as panic-stricken faces told me he was leaving me for dead.

❧

Distant murmuring, clicking, and footsteps brought me round. A line of concerned faces all passed me at eye level: Hilly, Calix, Silliah, Brindan, and then Pax.

Are you alright, sweetheart? Pax came to the edge of the stage.

"Hmm," I mustered, trying to sit. Ryker passed behind Pax, observing me but not stopping.

"Stay where you are, Miss Aviary," came the same order from Sir Darlington. He was over by the control station on centre stage, tidying away remnants of the lesson past. "Mr. Fortis, you can continue with the rest of your day. You won't be seeing Miss Aviary for a portion of it. Check your schedule."

"Yes, sir." Pax studied my body like it was an alien.

"There are no lasting effects," reassured Kian. "You can continue on with your day."

I sat cross-legged on the stage with my face in my hands. Sir Darlington dimmed the lights, ready to leave, and I regarded him for instruction. The door to my left opened.

"Miss Aviary, come with me," said Seioh Jennson with one step in the door. I picked myself up, and he disappeared from the room. When I left the classroom, he'd already made it halfway down the corridor. I jogged to catch up and followed him all the way to Navy Quartz.

"Seioh." I twisted my knuckles together. "Am I in trouble?"

Jennson didn't speak or acknowledge me until we reached his office. "In," he said after pushing the access button.

"Seioh—"

"Be quiet, Miss Aviary."

"Seioh, am I in trouble?"

Seioh Jennson put his hand to his face, pinching the bridge of his nose. "*Be. Quiet. Miss. Aviary.*"

I shut my mouth tight, holding in my 'sorry, Seioh.' He turned my shoulders towards the black sofa and pushed me towards it.

"Correct your uniform," he said, sitting behind his desk and pulling up his touchscreen monitor. "Just sit there and be quiet."

I rolled my sleeves down and zipped up my jacket. What had I done wrong? I was on my last warning and couldn't get into trouble again, but this was exactly what happened the last time I was almost dishonourably discharged: Jennson had me waiting on his sofa whilst he arranged for Fell agents to take me away. I needed so badly to ask what I'd done wrong. But to stop me from putting myself in Maximum Security, I kept my nails in my mouth.

For a good two hours, I sat there biting my fingers in an uneasy silence. Seioh Jennson brought me a salad at lunch, and I found reassurance in the fact it wasn't Juvie crap. At least I wasn't having an *exact* repeat of last time.

Jennson was eating his own salad when he said, "Aren't you on your last warning, Miss Aviary?"

I gulped down a half-chewed tomato and answered, "Yes, Seioh."

"Hmm."

I discarded my food, pushing it away on the coffee table. "Am I in trouble, Seioh?"

"Disobeying a direct order, Aurora," he said, without taking his eyes off his lunch.

"A direct order? Whose?"

"Sir Darlington had to ask you to the stage three times."

"But, Seioh—"

"I have spoken to Paxton. He relayed the story. Mr. Boulderfell prevented you from following the order. I understand, but it doesn't take away from the fact you should've followed Sir Darlington's instructions immediately. Lethals is an extremely dangerous class. You've shown previously your inability to follow instructions. What am I to do with a Young Enforcer who can't follow a direct order?"

My mouth was already open whilst I listened to Jennson. I opened it further, but a sound didn't come out.

"You show potential, Aurora," he continued, setting aside his empty container, leaning back in his chair, and placing his hands behind his head. "A Navy who has sat on First-table during Unity seldom finds themselves in Maximum Security."

At this point, my eyebrows were furrowed and my head forward. I was in a state of shock, on tenterhooks, and unsure about my imminent future. Seioh Jennson waited for my reply, but when it didn't arrive, he shook his head, leant forward, and continued his work.

"Seioh, am I being discharged?"

"No, Miss Aviary. Just sit there and be quiet. You're prohibited from taking any further Lethals lessons until you're a Third-year."

The relief! "I had a ransom dart demonstrated on me until I nearly died. I think I'll live."

"Would you like me to place you as the subject for every Lethals class instead?"

"No, Seioh."

"Shut up, then."

CHAPTER TWENTY

SHARING SECRETS

"Good luck, my little Roar." Tayo gently cupped my cheek.

I slapped his hand away. "Stop it."

"Stop what?"

"You know what." I roughly rubbed the pleasant echo his touch left behind. "I'm not telling you again. Now leave." I twisted him to the wardrobe, nudging him towards the hatch.

"I hope you're right about this."

"I am. She's my best friend. It'll be fine." Hearing the access button being pressed, I pulled up the panel. "Go."

Tayo pretended to lean in for a kiss. My gaze skimmed over his perfect lips before I turned my head and pushed him into the wardrobe, closing him in. I could hear him laughing as he climbed down the tunnel. On his way down, he unlocked my bedroom door, and I tried to act naturally.

"You locked the door?" Silliah came into my room, looking at me sideways.

"Yeah. Sorry. Punishing Pax."

"You still don't forgive him?"

"He made me think he was leaving for almost a year. I think I'll punish him for at least half of that."

"Fair enough." She jumped on my bed and checked that her walnut-brown fringe kept in place. It was still short like Ryker's, with a longish top flicking up, but she had freshly shaved lines drawn into her sides. "So, what is it you wanted to tell me?"

"I wanted to show you something." I grabbed a pen from my desk and joined Silliah on the bed. We sat opposite each other with our legs crossed. Silliah's big green eyes switched between the pen in my hand and my face. I took in a long breath for encouragement. "You remember that book I got you for your birthday?"

She nodded quickly.

"Well, what would you say if I told you your letter got lost in the post? Or, more accurately, was torn up by Seioh Boulderfell?"

Silliah smiled crookedly and swooped her head back. "Are you accusing me of being Puracordis?"

"No, of course not."

"Okay, good, because if I was, you know I would've told you."

Ignoring a small nick of guilt for not telling her sooner, I asked again, "So, what would you say…?"

"If you told me my letter got lost in the post? I'd have to say prove it. Why?"

"Do you trust me?"

She giggled and rocked on her seat, holding her knees into her chest. "You're weirding me out at the moment, but yes, of course I do. You're my best friend."

"Close your eyes."

Silliah dropped her knees and closed her eyes tightly. I took her hand, drawing the symbol of creation in her palm. I closed her slender fingers around it and rolled up her jacket sleeves.

"You're going to feel a little pins and needles feeling but keep your eyes closed, okay?"

Spella Tair.

"What have you given me?" Silliah still smiled but a trace of worry hid within the creases of her eyes. "I can feel that throughout my entire body. Can I open my eyes yet?"

"No, not just yet. Has the feeling stopped?"

"Yeah, it's stopped."

"Can I trust you?"

Before Silliah even spoke, her skin blinked with an orangey light. "Of course you can."

I asked her again, "Can I trust you?"

"Yes!" Silliah laughed, bouncing her knees into the mattress. She showed again, but this time it stayed, shining brighter and fuller, engulfing her whole body.

"Open your eyes."

"Whoa. Aurora." She jolted back as if trying to flee her own skin. Her show vanished, and she slowly lifted her eyes to mine, shaking her head apologetically.

I showed to her instantly so she knew she wasn't alone.

"I—I…What the hell is this?" she said, swallowing loudly.

"Your letter got lost in the post?" I lifted my lip, holding half a smile.

"What?" Silliah held her head in her hands, no longer caring about the perfection of her hair. "What does this mean?" She checked her palm and yanked my wrist towards her. "Your birthmark?"

I nodded. "It's magic."

"You're Puracordis?"

"We all are."

"Wait…what?" Silliah rubbed her frowned forehead. "Magic actually exists?"

"Yes."

"And you think Seioh Boulderfell knows?"

"Yes. I'll explain everything to you later, but I've something else I want to show you first. Will you come with me?"

Creases deepened between her eyebrows, but she gave a subtle nod. I opened my bedside table for a jewellery box and held open a golden woven rope bracelet exactly like mine. I had already slid on a black hematite stone for her. "This is for you." I walked over to my wardrobe, ready to show her the hatch. "I didn't make this. It was already here." And then I pulled up the panel.

Silliah dashed to my wardrobe and looked down the tunnel. "You have got to be kidding me. This is just like another book I've read. Don't tell me there's a whole new world down there."

"Not quite. Come on. I've got someone I need you to meet." I waved Silliah into the wardrobe and closed us both in.

"Meet?" asked Silliah, climbing down the ladder underneath me. "Are you sure this isn't maleficium, Aurora?"

"I am positive. I promise you."

"Whoa." Something startled Silliah at the bottom of the ladder. "*Tayo*?"

"Silliah meet Tayo. Tayo meet Silliah." I officially introduced the two under the dingy light of the tunnel.

"Hey, Silliah." Tayo held still, waiting for her reaction. It wasn't common for a civilian to meet an Enforcer.

"I'm so confused. You two aren't..." She waggled a finger between us.

"No," I answered.

"Yes," said Tayo.

"No." I gave Tayo a firm look. "No, Silliah, we aren't."

"We were," added Tayo, flicking his eyebrows at me.

"I'll explain everything to you later when we are back in my room"—I took Silliah by the hand—"and away from this idiot." I pushed Tayo aside.

"I'll fill you in," he said, walking backwards down the tunnel in front of us. "So, she used to come into my cell and force me to do all these things to her—"

"No, I didn't. Shut up, Tayo. Silliah, he's lying."

"In the end, I couldn't help but develop Stockholm Syndrome," Tayo said to a giggling Silliah. "And here I am, still afflicted."

"Seriously?" I kicked my leg out at him. "Say you have Stockholm Syndrome one more time."

He jumped back, avoiding another of my kicks. "See how mean she is to me? This is what she used to do when I was a Juvie. All these threats, I had no choice."

Silliah still giggled, so I stopped defending myself. It was only encouraging him. We walked through the transportation barrier, and I cut through Tayo's rambling to explain the magic to Silliah. I also told her about the walls being concrete and the blue mosaic tiles being an illusion I could somehow see through. When we arrived at the temple door, Silliah ran her fingers down the trunk of the golden tree.

"*Oh,*" she gasped, touching a carving. "There's your birthmark."

"It's how I knew she was Puracordis," said Tayo.

"You knew?" She turned to him.

"We had an encounter when we were kids. I saw it on her wrist."

"I told you Tayo was there the night my parents died," I said. "This temple is beneath my old family home, and he saw my dad come up through a trapdoor in the woods." I pointed over to the staircase at the other end of the pipe.

"That's how I get in," said Tayo. "It's a short way from my family home."

"This is so amazing"—Silliah panted, pretending to be out of breath—"but a little overwhelming."

"We can sit down and talk about it all. I'll tell you everything you want to know."

"*Mandus Erdullian.*" Tayo placed his hand on the door and gave it a push.

"Whoooa." Silliah walked in with her head up. She spun in a circle following the golden balcony with her eyes. "What is this place?"

"It's the ancient Puracordis Temple," answered Tayo, following behind her.

Silliah ran across the entrance hall, leaping up a few steps at the end. "It's so beautiful." She jumped down the stairs and ran back to us. "What's over here?" She skipped between two white columns, heading over to the grimoire room.

"It's got a massive book explaining conjuring in detail," said Tayo, "and a lot of musical instruments around the room. Upstairs on the balcony, there are loads of artefacts and storage cabinets with random objects from the past. And over here"—he began heading to the octagonal tree room—"is the Tree of Conjuring."

Silliah ran to catch up with Tayo. "Oooh, what does this do?" She looked around at the tree carved into the floor, paying extra attention to the six exquisitely detailed ornaments on each branch.

"There are six branches of magic, and we are all born with one. This tree tells you which one you're born with."

"What are you?" she asked Tayo.

"I'm an Intuitionist."

"What are you?" She turned to me as I entered under the carved archway.

"I think I'm an Illusionist, but the tree didn't do anything when I tried. Have a go. See if it works for you."

Silliah observed the ultraviolet platform before gingerly stepping a toe through the mist as if she were stepping onto thin ice. Then, feeling a secure bottom, she placed both feet on the glass panel. The mist swirled around her boots, lifting around her combat trousers. A bright-orange light raced up the trunk and down the fifth branch.

Silliah's eyes widened when the golden device started to unfold. It opened up in small intricate sections. The ornament spun like the last one, but the pierced-metal pieces revealed silhouettes of animals. Smoke started streaming through the holes. It twisted into shapes until the room was full of parading ghostly animals, all with an orangey hue. They hopped and galloped and weaved around one another. As the animals let loose, bouncy trumpets played an up-tempo song for them to dance to. It was in stark contrast to the emotional violins that played when Tayo stepped on the panel. This tune was one I couldn't help but tap my foot to.

Whilst the party was in full swing, a few affectionate animals circled around our bodies. Two or three took turns landing on Silliah's shoulders. I tried to touch a fox, but, like the Intuitionists' orbs, it swerved my touch. Tayo and Silliah had better luck with their magical buddies, being allowed to brush through their smoke.

"Silliah's a Summoner," Tayo said, flashing his beautiful smile. "Should we go see what you can do?"

"Yes!" Silliah sprang off the platform and headed for the other room. The animals vanished in thin air.

Before I followed after Silliah and Tayo, I tried the Tree of Conjuring again. I waited hopelessly for nothing and gave up. "Tayo, why doesn't that thing work for me?"

"I don't know, darling." He wrapped an arm around my shoulder and rubbed my arm. I leaned against him, but when we entered the bigger octagonal room, he let go and went to search through the grimoire with Silliah.

"Okay, you little Summoner." Tayo ran his finger down a page in the book. "Go upstairs and grab something from one of the cabinets. We'll give this a go."

Silliah ran off, leaving Tayo and me alone together. I turned to him, but he carried on reading through the grimoire as if I wasn't in the room. I pouted and played with my thumbnail.

Soon Silliah returned with a multi-coloured cube. "What is this?"

"It's a toy from the 1980s." Tayo leaned against the lectern, crossing his legs at the ankles. "You're supposed to get all six faces the same colour."

Silliah began twisting and turning the puzzle for a bit before giving up. "This isn't possible."

"It is." Tayo reached out a hand. "You want me to show you?"

Tayo completed the puzzle in under a minute and tossed it back over to Silliah.

"What is your magic again?" she asked, giving me an astounded look.

"That wasn't magic," Tayo said. "I've been able to do it since I was a kid."

"Bloody hell. What were you doing as a Juvie?"

"I got caught on purpose to meet Aurora."

"He was also going to match me in Unity if I didn't match with Pax." I inserted some balance into the getting-to-know-you brag.

"Oh." Silliah leaned away from Tayo.

He came and circled my body so close it made my breathing stop. "Play nice," he said into my ear on his way round.

"So, what am I doing with this?" Silliah held up the completed colourful cube.

"Give it to Aurora and sit opposite each other, about here and here." Tayo tapped his foot in two places either side of the white quartz walkway. He re-read the grimoire and came back over. "So, Roar, you just put it on the floor in front of you, and, Silliah, you're going to try and get it from her. Magic is powered by positive emotion, but it says you can do whatever you want to stir and move the energy. It's different for everyone. Some people close their eyes. Some people hold their temples. Some even fan the air. Play with it, and see what feels right for you. The incantation is *Nayoachon*."

Silliah repeated the incantation a few times at the cube, and then she shook her head at Tayo. Nothing happened to the cube, and she held her shoulders up to her ears. He nodded reassuringly, and she tried again, this time closing her eyes.

"Relax," said Tayo, after the cube stayed in front of my legs. "You're thinking about it and not feeling it. Leave the room and try without us watching."

Silliah left, and I stayed on the floor, resting my cheek in my palm, staring at my own reflection in the glassy quartz floor. Tayo wandered around, looking at the instruments.

"So, when are you going to play the piano for me?" I asked Tayo, reminding him of the last time I asked.

"When you're my girlfriend," he said, without turning to look at me.

"So never, then."

"Sure."

I rolled my eyes and decided sitting in silence was better than engaging with him.

"Much been going on with you since I left?" Tayo's voice was distant, so I knew he didn't even bother to look at me when he spoke.

"No."

Tayo's footsteps continued around the room.

"Actually," I said, sure I would grab his attention, "did you know Pipila's dad is an instructor here?"

"Is he?" His footsteps came closer. "That doesn't surprise me. He is obsessed with you guys. What does he teach?"

"Lethals." I kept my eyes on the white quartz and traced my finger along the golden trim. "He teaches us all about our advanced weapon technology. He used me as one of his subjects and demonstrated a ransom dart on me."

Tayo came level with me, standing in my eyeline, trying to get me to look up. "What's a ransom dart? That thing that turns veins black?"

"Yeah. It's a Fell agent weapon used to get fugitives to hand themselves in." I winced at the memory, the burning hot tar, the sludge in my veins. "It's a slow-acting poison, but it really hurts. It affected my magic."

"Affected it how?" He knelt down now.

I continued my inspection of the floor. "Stopped it from working. It made my birthmark reappear, and I couldn't make it invisible again."

Tayo reached to stop my fingers from touching the golden trim. "It must be full of a concentrated dose of Cryxstalide."

I lifted my head, landing on his deep blue eyes, and I gave a solemn shrug.

Tayo's shoulders dropped with his small huff, and he looked at me with soft, sympathetic eyes. Taking hold of my hand, he ran a thumb over my knuckles. It warmed my cheeks, and I felt like a hunger had been satisfied.

Silliah came running back into the room with a big grin. "Okay, I think I've got…" Her smile fell, catching Tayo holding my hand. Her eyes flicked between us both, and Tayo stood up. Silliah's feet shuffled forwards a few steps. Her eyes were on the ground and her movement sluggish. I took the cube from her, and she reengaged, sitting back in her place with a concentrated expression.

"Go on, then," prompted Tayo.

Silliah began circling her right hand over her left in big sweeps. "*Nayoachon*," she said with a foreign inflection. A hazy orange mist swirled between her hands, and the cube in front of me flickered. Silliah clapped a hand over her mouth. "Did you see that? There's no way *I* actually did that."

"You did it," said Tayo with amusement in his tone. "Well done." He headed back to the grimoire. "Keep trying."

Silliah squinted and focused on the cube with immense determination. Whilst she didn't need my assistance, I left her on the floor practising, and I gravitated towards Tayo. Silliah watched me leave, but I ignored her.

"What else can Illusionists do?" I asked Tayo, turning my back on Silliah so I couldn't see her.

"You can branch out already, can't you?" Tayo heaved the heavy pages over to a new section. "Want to try a healing spell?"

"What can I heal?"

"One sec." Tayo disappeared from the room and returned with a pen knife. I tried to snatch it from him before he grabbed the blade, but he already sliced a nasty gash in his palm.

"This is my wan—"

"Ergh, shut up." I backhanded his arm.

"—so you better be able to heal it."

"I should leave it and make you suffer."

"Now, we both know I wouldn't suffer."

My stomach tightened thinking he meant other girls would help him. "Tayo." My face twisted, unable to hide the hurt.

He turned his back to Silliah and made our arms touch. "Sorry," he said quietly.

I pressed against him, craving for more than our arms to touch. Seeing blood dripping from his fist, I yanked it towards me. "What's the incantation?"

"It's *Tepior*, but I guarantee you don't need it."

I closed my eyes and ran the incantation through my mind. Tayo's bleeding wound immediately underwent the healing process, first scabbing and then scarring.

"The more you practise, the better it heals." Tayo stroked his new scar. "Advanced conjurers will heal the scar also."

"Hold on." I took back his hand. "*Tepior.*" The green mist usually accompanying the blood cleansing spell pushed its way into Tayo's scar, taking the blemish with it.

"Thank you." Tayo pushed his thumb across his clean palm. "You're pretty impressive, you know that?"

Before my heart burst, I diverted his attention. "Have you learnt to do anything yet?"

"Nah, I've just been reading a lot. I know my intuition is naturally better just by having my blood cleansed. I can read people well and get a sense for what they're feeling, and I make better decisions too, but I'll start looking at more things soon. It's getting late. Don't you think you should head back? You want to speak to Silliah still, don't you?"

"Yeah, you're right. Do you wanna head back, Silliah?" I called over to her still trying to summon a flickering cube.

"Ohh." She got up off the glossy red floor. "I'm getting better, but I think it's going to take me a while before I actually materialise anything."

"You guys go ahead," Tayo said, holding his hand out for the cube. "I'm going to stay here for a bit. The Kalmayans were out in the woods earlier. I don't want them to see me coming up through the trapdoor."

Even though I knew I needed to speak to Silliah, I looked back at him before I left the temple. My feet didn't want to step out of the door. After hearing Silliah's small cough, I forced myself to leave.

We lay side-by-side on my bed, and Silliah hugged a pillow, twisting onto her side to speak. "Besides Unity, this has got to be the best night of my life. How did you know about all this?"

"I guess the answer is Tayo. He saw my birthmark the night I was enlisted here, and he spent his whole life planning to meet me again."

"I like Tayo. He is funny...and smart...and good looking..." She pursed her lips, dipping her head forward.

I tried to prevent pain from showing on my face, but Silliah knew me too well. "I...okay, truthfully"—I exhaled through a lack of words—"I...ohh." I vigorously rubbed my face. "I don't know what to do, Silliah."

Silliah's eyes watered at the sight of my pain, and she wrapped her arms around me.

"You're going to make me cry. I don't want to cry." I pulled from the hug. "I'm okay."

"Want to change the subject?" She pulled the pillow back into her chest. "Tell me whenever you're ready?"

"I'm not in a relationship with either of them."

"But you and Tayo have been...like...dating?"

"For a little while." I turned on my back, staring at the ceiling.

"Have you...done bits?"

I kept my eyes on the purple mood lighting, unable to look at her. I nodded and then checked her reaction out of the corner of my eye.

"Oh." She bit on her manicured fingernails. "Have you and Pax done bits?"

I sighed at the opinion she must've been forming of me. "We've only made out."

"What—and now you don't want to choose because you like them both?"

"I'm betrothed, Silliah." I twisted back on my side to face her.

"So you'd choose Tayo?"

"No. I don't know. I *can't* choose. I can't hurt either of them. I'm better off being a Fell agent, but that would mean leaving you and my Nanny Kimly."

"Firstly, the reason you can't hurt either of them is because you like them both, and secondly, don't ever say that again; not just because I don't want you to leave, but because you don't want to be a Fell agent. You just about tolerate being a Young Enforcer. You've never been happy here."

"Pax didn't want me to leave either. He offered to stay united with me and then go our separate ways after we're discharged."

Silliah grimaced and glanced over her shoulder at the interconnecting door. "You want my advice?" She looked back at me, her face full of concern. "Choose one of them. All three of you are hurt. Put them out of their misery?"

"I can't, Silliah." I held a long blink. "I can't choose. If I choose Tayo, Pax is stuck here forced to watch. And if I choose Pax"—I tutted at how just thinking of Tayo made my chest hurt—"just Tayo."

She bit her lip. "Does Pax know about Puracordis?"

"Yeah." I slid up the display screen, rubbing my chest. "He freaked out. It's the real reason he wanted to leave me. He doesn't want anything to do with it."

"Oh." Her bright-green eyes dulled as she entered her thoughts. "How did you tell him?"

"I didn't tell him. I had no idea I was Puracordis, and I showed to him by accident. He tried ending the betrothal the next day."

"But he's obviously come to terms with it now, right?"

"Yeah. He won't practise, though."

"Do you think we can tell Brindan?"

"Don't tell him about me and Tayo, or Pax and me pretending to be united."

"No, I won't. I just want to tell him about Puracordis. But I can imagine him having a similar reaction to Pax."

A tapping on the interconnecting door made us both look over. Brindan walked in shortly followed by Pax. A horrible feeling trickled through me, tugging at my abdomen. I didn't want to tell Brindan now.

"You girls had a nice catch-up?" Brindan asked, coming up to the bed.

We both nodded.

"We're gonna be out of hours soon if we don't head back." Brindan hugged me and climbed across the bed for Silliah. He pulled her to sit between his legs and enveloped her.

Pax stroked the top of Silliah's head and sat in the middle besides Brindan and me. Not receiving any affection off Pax made me stiff, but I lowered my shoulders before anyone noticed.

"Did you boys have a nice evening?" asked Silliah.

Pax pulled his Slate out from his pyjama pocket. "We were going through old archives of the Parkour Games footage to see if we could find my parents." He unfolded the device into a tablet. "We didn't find any of my parents, but look what we found."

Silliah sat up between Brindan's legs to get a better look at what Pax was playing. "Nooooo way." She grabbed the tablet off him.

"Whoa." I leaned over Pax, not quite believing my eyes.

"Mad, innit?" said Brindan.

"Seioh Jennson was united," said Pax, nodding.

"They were really good, as good as *Sovereign Skill*," added Brindan. "But he only played fifteen games. We think his betrothed must've become a Fell agent."

"Explains why he's such a miserable bastard."

"AURORA," came the bombardment at my swearing.

CHAPTER TWENTY-ONE

OVERWHELMENT

Turns out, Ryker and Seioh Jennson weren't the only ones left by their partners to become Fell agents. Whilst watching Jennson's playback, we spotted a fitter-looking Nunetta, the Navy receptionist, playing two games of TPG with her partner. It left me wondering if rejection made people assholes, and it gave me even more reason not to make the decision between Pax and Tayo. The outcome may only make one of them as heartless as the others.

Silliah and I couldn't decide the best way of telling Brindan about Puracordis. I decided I would ask my Nanny Kimly, and one evening at dinner, I spotted her over in Mustard, supervising a group of children.

"I'm so sorry I haven't come to see you recently, Little Lady," Nanny Kimly called out, seeing me on my way over. She carried two trays back from the meal dispenser and placed them in front of her toddlers. "I have been so busy with my new Mustards." She placed her hands on her babies' heads.

"It's okay, Nanny Kimly," I said, feeling the weight of all the curious young eyes staring up at me. "Come see me soon, okay? I need to ask you something." I backed away, leaving for my table.

"Who's that, Nanny Kimly?" squeaked a toddler.

"Are you her nanny, too, ma'am?" asked another.

"No, no. Navies don't have nannies." I heard her say. "But I will never stop caring for you all, no matter how old you get."

I slumped back down in my chair next to Pax and pulled out my Slate after feeling it vibrate. I held it under the table, obscuring it from Pax's eyes. A text from Tayo read: '*The Kalmayans are out tonight. I'm running late.*'

"Come on, Maylene," said Ryker, standing up. "Let's get these goons back to their cells. We have Curfew duty."

Ryker chaperoned a teenage Kalmayan girl with a shaved head and tattooed face. I checked my birthmark was still invisible, remembering the trouble I got in with a Kalmayan Juvie last year. Hilly slid over into Ryker's empty chair and pulled my birthmark-free wrist towards her.

"I *knew* that wasn't a birthmark," she squawked, her big blue eyes switching from me to my clear wrist.

"Yeah, funny trying to convince you, though."

"All this time I thought you were mad at me for asking."

"Yet, here you are, still sitting on my table."

"I know. I don't know why I thought I made you mad. That was a good one."

I nodded with the best fake smile I could muster and sipped on my peppermint hot chocolate.

"Hey, Aurora," said Tyga, moving over onto Hilly's chair. "I got ninety-two on the Flexon Pro earlier. A year late, but I did it. Whereabouts are you on the scoreboards now?"

"Thirteenth, with one hundred and ninety-two. I'm one behind Pax. Show me tomorrow during practice?"

"Yeah, alright," he replied, nodding, his recently dyed black hair reflecting the light as he moved. "There's something I wanted to ask you." He glanced over his shoulder, but as if not seeing what he expected, he searched the hall over his other shoulder. Turning back at me, he shook his head. "Never mind. It's fine."

"Sure?" I studied him, really curious and unable to fathom what it could've been.

"Sure." He gave a small smile.

"Alright." Controlling the impulse to insist, I slid to my feet. "Night, everyone."

"Goodnight," Tyga said whilst pulling out his Slate.

"Are you coming, Pax?" I butted in his conversation with Brindan.

"Yeah. Night, everyone." He put his arm around my shoulder. "Do you want another one of those?" He gestured to the peppermint hot chocolate in my hand.

I swirled the liquid in the bottom. "Are you going to have one?"

"I am."

"Alright, go on, then." I grinned cheekily, knowing two hot chocolates weren't exactly doing me any good.

Pax collected our drinks and tucked me under his arm as we walked back to our room. We passed Mimsy, stuck in the main corridor with an excessively weighted trap. She had sweat dripping from her nose and her usually curly hair stuck to her wet cheeks. *Help me,* I heard her say in her head. Her foot could hardly move an inch. I shrugged at her and passed with guilt weighing on my own legs.

"Mimsy," I said, finishing a sip of my hot chocolate. "Do you think she's being a little mistreated? I haven't seen her walking once without a weighted ankle trap."

"There's nothing you can do about it, sweetheart."

"I feel bad for her."

"Didn't you say she had a really bad attitude?"

"Yeah, she did. I tried to warn her; I told her to rein it in."

"Maybe she deserves it, then. At least it's only a weighted trap." He brushed his knuckles up my cheek and rested his hand back on my shoulder. "Try not to worry."

We entered my room, and Pax left through the interconnecting door. He kept it open, so I popped my head in. He was over by the laundry chute, ready to throw his navy jacket down the hatch.

"Pax." I wandered into his room. "Can I…ask you something?"

Pax threw his jacket down the chute and slid his fingers under his navy-blue vest. "Do you mind if I…?" He lifted his vest half way.

I shook my head, put my cup on the floating bedside table, and fell forwards onto his bed. I kept my face in the Pax-scented pillow until I heard him finish changing into his pyjamas.

"What's up, sweetheart?" He sat down beside me.

I rolled on my side to see him. "You know Silliah wants to tell Brindan about Puracordis?" I waited for his nod to continue. "Do you know how we can tell him without him freaking out?"

Pax's light-amber eyes crinkled. He inhaled, and on his exhale, he lay down on his side to meet my eyes. "You want me to be honest with you?"

"Obviously."

He reached for the fist I had over my mouth. "Don't tell him."

"Pax."

"He is an Enforcer, Aurora. Maleficium or not, it is still illegal; that's the dangerous part."

I rolled onto his hand, lying on my front and squashing my face into the mattress. "Hmmmm," I groaned, almost agreeably. "But Silliah wants to tell him. She can't come with me to practise as much as she'd like, and she also doesn't want to keep lying to him."

"I get it; I do." He squeezed my fingers being crushed between myself and the mattress. "I don't know what to say, sweetheart."

"Do you not want to practise?" I tilted back to see his face. "Please come with me to see what branch you are."

"No. I'm sorry."

I just nodded and lay still for a while, thinking. "What if Brindan was coming to the temple with us, would you come then?"

"Nope. I'm assuming 'us' means Tayo as well."

My chest twisted. "Is that why you don't want to come?"

"No. No, it's not that. I want to keep you out of trouble, not encourage it. I can't bear the thought of you going to Maximum Security."

"That's the least of my worries. It's a noose around my neck I'm scared of."

"That's not funny."

I sat up and pulled him by the pyjama sleeve. "Come on. I'll cancel on Tayo tonight. Come with me instead." I leaned back, tugging at his buttoned cuff.

"No. You're going to hurt yourself. Give up."

"*Spella Tair.*" I cleansed his blood and shook his stubborn arm like a thick rope. "Come on, Pax, *pleeeeease*? Your blood is cleansed now; it'll be rude not—" My body stiffened as a long cold inhale rattled down my throat. Pax reacted, catching my rigid body before it hit the floor.

A figure watches me sleep from beneath the shadows of their hood. They pull a twisted black dagger out from under their cloak. With two hands around the handle, they thrust it downwards, impaling my chest. Starting from the roots, my hair turns a deep auburn.

A bright flash. Pax's forehead touches mine as we hold each other's eyes. He meets my lips. I'm sitting astride him when he lifts my vest over my head. A scar blemishes my chest.

Another bright flash. Tayo collapses in my arms. The dagger slips from his fingers. Gulping, he claws at my clothes. He grows weaker as the life drains from his eyes. I scream for him to come back.

A strong raspy inhale rattled my throat, and Nanny Kimly's relaxed hazel eyes gradually came into focus.

"You're alright, Little Lady. You're alright. Don't get up." She pushed up the pillows behind my back and stopped me from sitting. "Just rest."

Behind her, Tayo and Pax watched me anxiously from over Nanny Kimly's shoulder. My breathing stopped, seeing them both in the same room together. But a moment of reasoning put my mind at ease. Tayo was no longer a secret. I rested my head back on the pillow and closed my eyes.

"Aurora is going to be fine," said Nanny Kimly. "Just a bit tired, if anything."

I forced my eyes open, seeing Pax and Tayo both nodding. Nanny Kimly pivoted back towards me. "I take it you've been practising a lot lately, Little Lady?"

"Every day." I swallowed thick saliva as images still played in my mind, the cloaked figure, the twisted dagger, Tayo... "I...I saw things, Nanny Kimly."

"What were you practising?"

"I wasn't practising. I was playing. I cleansed Pax's blood but accidentally cleansed mine. Then I saw..." I glanced over at the boys intently hanging on to my every word.

"Give us a moment, please, boys." When they left the room, closing the interconnecting door behind them, Nanny Kimly turned to me. "What did you see?"

"Someone in my room with a dagger. They stabbed me." I touched the spot on my solar plexus. "Then Tayo, he..." I couldn't finish my sentence. My eyes prickled, still seeing him lifeless in my arms. "What *was* that, Nanny Kimly? Was that the future?"

"You were overwhelmed by magic, Little Lady. Conjuring is stronger during the current moon phase; tonight is a full moon. Overwhelment is not too common because beginners need to use incantations, but you've been able to bypass that stage and practise advanced magic. Just take it easy for a few weeks."

"Did I see the future?" I had to ask again, feeling like Nanny Kimly deliberately avoided my question.

"Not necessarily. Precognitions are subjective. The future cannot be predicted because it doesn't account for people's freewill. It is best not to dwell on what you saw."

"But it is a possibility? If I keep doing what I'm doing?"

"What isn't a possibility, Little Lady? Accidents happen. Nothing is certain. Minds are changed. An Astralist's precognitions are best kept private. They are intended for you and only bring burden to others. Don't worry, okay?" She held a hand to my head to check my temperature. "I see you worked things out with the boys?"

"I'm not with either of them. Tayo just helps us practise magic. He is very good."

"Us?" She took her hand away from my forehead, resting it on my thigh. "Paxton has come around to the idea?"

"No, not Pax... Silliah. She doesn't know about you, though, Nanny Kimly."

"Okay. Good. Tell Paxton to keep it to himself, won't you? Tayo told him to come fetch me. I suspect he's put two and two together."

"Yes, of course. I'll talk to him."

"So, you and Silliah are conjuring? What branch is she?"

"She's a Summoner," I replied with a smile. "She glows a little bit orange when she shows."

Nanny Kimly jerked her body away. "You're certain? Her glow isn't white, like this?" She showed to me, a flash of pure brilliant-white light blazing from her skin.

"No, Nanny Kimly. It's definitely orange. Why?"

Nanny Kimly covered her mouth. She glanced around at nothing and smiled vacantly beneath her hand. "Your friend is a Primary." She put her dancing hazel eyes back on me. "She holds the magic of the original Summoner. When a Primary dies, their magic merges into the atmosphere for a while before passing onto someone suitable. Primary magic is strong, and even stronger when collaborating with the Guidal. The six Primaries and the Guidal together can conjure extremely rare, extremely powerful spells. There are no incantations to the advanced magic you can perform with each other. It comes from within, and with mutual intention."

My mouth didn't close the entire time Nanny Kimly spoke. My best friend was special, and together we were powerful. It was the best thing I'd ever heard. "Wait until I tell her this." My goose pimples prickled me all over at the thought of what we could do together. "I wanted to ask you something, Nanny Kimly. Silliah wants to tell Brindan about Puracordis but doesn't know how to say it without him freaking out like Pax did."

"It is a delicate subject for an Enforcer. It goes against everything they've been taught. The best way is for his blood to be cleansed covertly; otherwise, they think you are the one making them do the magic. The symbol of creation can be placed anywhere and still work. Get Silliah to place it in his pocket, cleanse his blood without him knowing, and then get him to show. He will realise he is Puracordis and instantly seek reassurance that you are the one not about to freak out on him. Then he will be susceptible to the explanation and accept it readily."

"Whoa. How many times have you had to do that?"

"My family has a long history of Puracordis. Grimoires are passed down through generations and with it, diaries and notes. We all learn from each other."

"Is this my parents' old room, Nanny Kimly? How did they know about the temple?"

"The tunnel is the work of a well-practised Illusionist. I suspect your parents learned the whereabouts from a friend. Which reminds me, Celeste Antares, she may know about your extracurricular activities. She was involved in the car accident that killed Ryker's birthmother. Celeste's family and Ryker's mother were practitioners of Puracordis. They were caught by Kalmayans.

"Ryker's birthmother lived at Seioh Boulderfell's residence in Avalon of Second City. She wasn't allowed to travel with Ryker, and she'd been on a shopping trip with Celeste's family. Instead of a public execution, their self-driven vehicle was tampered with and the incident covered up to prevent shame being brought upon the Boulderfell family. An official story of terminal illness was released.

"Only one person witnessed the accident: a little girl they pulled from the vehicle alive, not a scratch on her. Only one little girl knew about the accident, but the clever girl pretended to have amnesia."

"Celeste?"

Nanny Kimly nodded with a raised forehead. "She would've been executed if she hadn't. They needed to make sure nobody knew Ryker's mother was in that car. Celeste's decision to pretend she couldn't remember kept her alive, and it's the only reason she was allowed to enrol into Mustard.

"It is so, so important Ryker never finds out about this, Little Lady. It will put Celeste—and anyone she associates with—in terrible danger if Seioh Boulderfell ever finds out. It'll only take a whisper of the real event, and Celeste's ruse will be known."

"I won't say a word, Nanny Kimly. You know who else is Puracordis here?"

"Everyone, but I'm going to assume you mean practising Puracordis."

"Yes, practising. Although, I'm not sure how much they know, but yeah, *Sovereign Skill* conjure. Theodred knew the incantation *Spella Tair.*"

"That's interesting." Nanny Kimly scratched her eyebrow from underneath her red fringe. "How did they know they could trust you?"

"I have no idea. I'm assuming by my birthmark before I used to hide it." I shrugged. "We're thinking of showing them the temple if they can show to us."

"Just always be cautious, okay? I don't like you all breaking the law. It is extremely dangerous."

"The better practised we are, the better we can protect ourselves."

Nanny Kimly nodded subtly. "Where is Silliah tonight?"

"It's Valentine's Day. She's spending the evening with Brindan."

"Ah, that's lovely. I will get my brother to bring you a few hematite stones. You must all wear them down in the Puracordis Temple. Your picoplant detected down there could get you all caught. Be very careful, Aurora."

"I will, Nanny. Thank you."

"Ikegan will be down by the temple tomorrow night. Let Tayo know." She brushed off her black tunic, making for the door. "I'll leave you three alone to enjoy your Valentine's Day together."

"*Ergh*, Nanny Kimly."

"Goodnight, Little Lady. Oh, and tell Silliah to show to the Tree of Conjuring. 'Show the tree the six and thus the tree will show the six. The temple has a secret of its own hidden within its bricks.'" After reciting the prophecy, she left the room with a wink.

I jumped to my feet, and the whole room swayed in front of my eyes. Lowering back down, I waited for the room to stop moving before walking—slowly—to the adjoining door.

A static silence stuck to my ears. Tayo had commandeered my super-sized bed, lying feet-crossed, hands behind his head, staring up at the ceiling. Pax was on the sofa, feet-crossed, hands on his lap, staring at his fingers. They both welcomed my entrance into the room like I was a doctor in a hospital waiting room, standing up and expecting my news.

"I'm alright." I quickly put their minds at rest. "Just been overdoing it a bit. I'll be back to normal in a week or two. Long story short, I experienced overwhelment, Silliah is a Primary, and Celeste may be Puracordis."

"I'll let you two talk," said Pax, sensing the magical nature of my explanation. "I'll catch up with you in the morning, sweetheart." Pax kissed the side of my head and closed the door behind him.

Tayo came and hugged me tightly with both arms. "You scared me, Roar."

"I'm alright," I repeated into his expanding chest.

"Your eyes were ice white, and you were hardly breathing. I've never seen anything like it. I came out the wardrobe, hearing this demonic rattling noise. When I looked in, Pax was laying you down on the bed. I told him to run and get Nanny K." Tayo let me go and looked into my eyes, assessing them, checking I really was okay. "That noise should not come out of a human."

A dizzy spell swayed my body, and Tayo wrapped an arm around my shoulders. He walked me to the bed, propped the pillows up against the display screen, and helped me into them. Seeing I was comfortable, he settled down by my side.

"Did you know the full moon makes conjuring more powerful?" I asked, leaning into the pillows and resting my head against the wall.

"No. I haven't come across that yet. That grimoire is huge."

"Well, I've been overdoing it a bit. I used magic accidentally tonight." I glanced at his soft hands but pulled my attention back quickly. "It was so powerful, it overwhelmed me."

"What did you see?" Tayo turned his hand up, placing it between us. "Earlier you said you saw something."

I watched his hand whilst feeling my own fingertips buzz. "Nanny Kimly called it a precognition." I put my hand on the bed beside his. "It's nothing. It doesn't mean it's going to happen."

"I'm going to look into it." He tilted his wrist so that our index fingers touched. "What did you see?"

Knowing I shouldn't be encouraging our contact made it harder to stop, and I hooked my finger under his. "I don't want to say."

"No, Nanny K told you not to say. Since when do you keep things from me?"

"I saw someone in here. They had a black dagger, and they stabbed me." I decided to end my precognition there and keep the part of him dying to myself.

"The only way in here is through the trapdoor, and I'm the only person who knows about it. I'll never be caught using it, I promise."

My eyes kept landing on our hands. The subtle touch sparked a desire in me. Not so long ago, it would've been normal for me to satisfy it, for me to press my lips to his, and for us to get skin on skin. The inability to relieve myself was making it louder until I had to look at him.

He met my eyes, and a familiar smile lifted the corner of his lips. "I can feel that," he whispered, his eyebrows slowly lifting.

"Which means you didn't eat lunch." I took my hand away and slid down the display screen, staring at the ceiling and dealing with myself.

"I can help you with that."

I groaned and crossed my legs, holding a pillow over my face.

"Happy Valentine's Day, my little Roar."

CHAPTER TWENTY-TWO

WILL HE? WON'T HE?

A few days later, Silliah built up the courage to finally tell Brindan our secret, so on our way back from dinner, I initiated our plan by cleansing his blood discreetly. He frowned at his arms and shook his hands out as though trying to expel pins and needles. He scrunched his knuckles together, and then he hugged Pax and me goodnight. We pretended to walk into my room but waited on the threshold for Silliah and Brindan to turn into 442. When they disappeared, Pax and I tiptoed to Silliah's room, letting ourselves in. We sat still on the sofa, trying to listen. The interconnecting door was closed, and I was beginning to realise how soundproofed the rooms actually were; I couldn't hear a word.

When I heard the humming from the shower being switched on next door, I pushed backwards into the corner of the sofa, kicked off my boots, and settled in for the wait. "Thank you for doing this with us, Pax," I said, bringing my feet onto the sofa. "I think he will feel better about it when he knows you know. I hated hiding it from Silliah."

Pax sank down, after realising he couldn't hear anything either, and he rested his feet up on the coffee table. "It's alright. I still can't believe Nanny Kimly is Puracordis."

"We are *all* Puracordis, Pax."

"I know." He held onto my white sock, pulling my foot onto his lap. "I just meant…"

He rubbed the ball of my foot and squeezed my toes. After a long day spent on my feet, an appreciative smile developed as I indulged myself in the massage. "You should come down to the temple with us when we take Brindan."

Pax blinked, gazed over at the adjoining door, and then shook his head.

I huffed, kicked his hands off my foot, and lay with my feet on the other side of the corner sofa, facing the bed.

"Don't brat out." Pax reached out a leg to nudge me. "I'm doing this with you, aren't I? I'm going to show to Brindan with you."

I folded my arms.

"So, Celeste and Thorn are Puracordis?"

"We are *all* Puracordis, Pax," I repeated for the millionth time, turning back to face him. "Celeste knows about magic, but I don't know if she's practising or not. I'm not sure how much you can do without incantations. She might remember some things from her childhood before she was enrolled here." I sat up, sliding closer to cleanse his blood.

Pax flexed his fingers, also sitting up. "I do *not* like that feeling."

I rolled my eyes. *Can I trust you?*

He nodded as a brilliant-white light radiated from his body. His light-amber eyes concentrated on mine, and splinters from my shattered heart cut at my chest.

"Showing to you was the first magic I ever used."

"I am so sorry, Aurora." He cupped my hands. "I'm so, *so* sorry," he repeated, his eyes penetrating deep into mine. Seeing him glimpse my lips, my broken heart swooped, but I stayed still, staring back into his remorseful amber eyes. Thinking about his gentle lips touching mine sent a brilliant-white light pouring from my skin. Pax's skin continued to glow, and both our bodies expressed our feelings in a radiant aura of white light. He ran a thumb over my lip.

"Don't," I said, my white hue extinguishing with the drop in my stomach.

"I'm sorry." He pulled back, his show vanishing.

"Don't do that again," I said, images from my precognition fresh in my mind: Pax's kiss leading to Tayo's death.

"Alright." He faced away, feet going back on the coffee table. "I'm sorry. And I'm sorry for reacting the way I did when you showed to me last year. It hurts knowing what it really means, the feeling you have when you show, how you must've been feeling in that moment, and then my reaction to it. I'm so sorry."

"What's done is done," I said, not wanting to think about it.

We both returned to staring at the interconnecting door. I hugged my knees into my chest, hoping Brindan was taking it better than Pax did that night.

"How do you think it's going in there?" I asked, wishing I was a fly on the wall in the other room.

"Well," he said, "Silliah's not running in here crying. That's got to be a good sign."

Soon after, Silliah appeared at the adjoining door with a hesitant smile. Pax and I shot up. Brindan was on the bed, pale as a sheet. Simultaneously, Pax and I showed to Brindan. He nodded like he was only just beginning to accept the truth. Then his nodding transitioned into a head shake as he dropped his forehead onto his fingertips. "I don't know about this, guys."

"It's something we all are," said Pax, completing his part like a true gentleman.

We wandered over to join Brindan on the bed. Nobody spoke. We all allowed Brindan time to adjust. He now had his head in both hands, elbows resting on his knees.

"So," Brindan finally spoke, lifting his head, "there's something in the water supply that prevents us from being Puracordis?"

We all nodded.

"*Why?*" Brindan said, his blue-green eyes flicking between us all. Pax and Silliah turned to me.

"Last year, did you hear that little Kalmayan boy refer to himself as Taheke?" The nodding from everyone prompted me to continue. "Well, Taheke are people who can't conjure, even if they haven't any Cryxstalide in their system. Conjuring is powered by positive emotion, and some people don't practise enough positive emotion to be able to do it. A traumatising experience, persistent dark thoughts, or habitual negative thinking can cause blockages. These people can't conjure until they work through their blockages and work on activating a better vibration, a better state of mind.

"So basically"—I took a deep breath—"we think Boulderfell's circle are Taheke. We think that's the reason why they don't want people using magic, because they can't use it. And if everyone can conjure, there's no reason to have them in positions of power, there's no reason for the new-world leaders to rule their cities, there's no reason for anyone to earn Worths, and there's no reason for civilians to work. We would basically be free: free to raise our own children, free to educate ourselves, and free to live our own way. What would be Boulderfell's purpose?"

"I love it here," said Silliah, "but that life sounds amazing. Who wouldn't want to be a civilian?"

"Civilians don't raise their own children?" questioned Brindan sceptically.

"Well, no. They're too busy earning Worths. Their children are sent to school and are raised by teachers. These teachers instil the beliefs and values into the children that Boulderfell has determined. The system was created to stop civilians thinking for themselves. It imposes on them duty, discipline, obedience, and respect for authority."

"Wouldn't they just be unruly without it...and without us?"

"Crimes only come through feeling the lack of something," I repeated what Tayo had once explained to me. "Feeling the need of something, and thinking you would feel better if you had it. We have everything we need here; that's why we don't steal from each other. In a fulfilling world of abundance, where time is spent doing the things they love the most and having everything they need to keep themselves and their families safe, civilians would live a harmonious existence. Why would they need us?"

Brindan's nodding grew stronger, and he started to regain colour in his freckled face. "Alright. It makes sense. So, you're *one-hundred-percent* certain it's not maleficium?"

"One-hundred-percent," I returned confidently.

"When do we see this temple, then?" he said with a grin.

CHAPTER TWENTY-THREE

TEMPLE SECRETS

I don't think any of us slept well that night. We all agreed it was too late to go down to the temple and decided we would go straight after dinner the next day. Finally, after an apprehensive, yawn-filled day, Pax and I left the table first, heading straight to my bedroom.

"Pax, *please* come with us. You don't have to do any magic. Just come see what branch you are."

"Sweetheart, the last time you tried to convince me to go, you hurt yourself. Take that as a sign."

"That was overwhelment because of the full moon. It had nothing to do with you."

Seeing I was about to take hold of his hand, he backed away to the interconnecting door, preventing my play fight. "You can't win. Don't even try it."

Spella Tair. I cleansed his blood as he crossed the threshold to his room. "Maybe not at being an Enforcer..." I watched him flex his hands and knuckles.

"Stop doing that," he warned before disappearing out of sight.

I didn't pursue him. It was probably better to wait until the others got here. Maybe they could help persuade him. They were having a shower and getting changed into their charcoal pyjamas. We agreed it was better to be caught in our sleepwear if we stayed at the temple out of hours. Although Brindan and Silliah only had to get to their room a few doors down, it was probably better to be caught in their pyjamas than their Navy uniforms.

I got myself ready and waited for them to arrive. Earlier, Tayo had dropped off the hematite stones Ikegan gave to him, and I put a few spare in my top pocket just in case.

"How exciting is this?" Silliah dashed through my door, dropping her boots and propelling herself onto my bed. She jumped around me, making my body wobble along with her bounces. Her walnut-brown hair was dry but not styled for a change, and it danced around with the enthusiasm of every bounce.

"Where's Pax?" asked Brindan, his freckly face still holding a rosy glow from his shower. Specks of water beaded his hair.

Still smiling at Silliah's bed jumping, I flicked my head at the interconnecting door. Brindan headed straight in. Silliah and I gave each other a quick glance before she launched herself off the bed, landing firmly on her bare feet. Together, we raced in after him.

"Are you coming, bro?" Brindan asked Pax.

Pax's blond-brown curls held the weight of his recent shower, and his amber eyes passed between Brindan, then Silliah...then me. They narrowed on me as his mouth quirked at the corner. *This is exactly what you hoped would happen, isn't it?*

I didn't stop my smile. *Yep!*

Pax swung his legs off the bed, heaving himself up. "I will come just this once."

"Yes!" we all burst out.

"But I'm not using magic," he added to balance things out.

"You don't need to use any magic." I grabbed his black boots, shoving them in his arms. Once he slid them on, we all turned into my bedroom. I opened my wardrobe door and lifted the white panel.

Brindan stepped forward to take a look down the hatch. "This is mental."

"I know," I said, looking back up at Pax. "I'm just glad I'm finally sharing it with you guys."

"Mental." Brindan sat down to place his boot on the first rung of the ladder. "It's mad to think this has been here the whole time."

"Do you have your bracelets?" I held up my golden rope bracelet with my black hematite stone.

Silliah jumped up from putting her socks and boots on, and then she showed me her matching bracelet. Brindan felt around in his pocket and pulled out a fourth golden rope bracelet for Pax. I slid on a stone from my top pocket, and I held it open for Pax. He offered a steady hand and watched me secure it around his wrist over his picoplant-replacement scar. A knowing smile showed on his face, and he shook his head at me teasingly. He had realised two things: one, how I managed to sneak 'Silliah' (actually Tayo) out of the institute undetected last year, and two, why he had to have his picoplant replaced. I felt the heat leaving my cheeks and broke eye contact with him. I still felt bad for him, and even worse that it was Tayo, not Silliah, whom I'd snuck out of the institute with. I closed the clasp without looking back up at him.

Four pairs of shiny black boots reached the concrete, and we all made our way down the tunnel together. Brindan hooked Silliah into him, and they took the lead. I tailed at the back, watching them sharing this moment together. Brindan was whispering into her ear, and she giggled, looking up at him adoringly. I felt like I was on a family outing, and I switched to see Pax. He sensed my eyes on him and offered out his arm. I tucked under it, being pulled in tight and kissed on the head.

"This isn't real," chirped Silliah, pointing around at the blue mosaic on the tunnel walls. "Is it, Aurora? It's an illusion Aurora can see through."

Brindan's head tilted backwards, looking all around the dingy tunnel walls; Pax's turned towards me.

"No, it's not real," I said. "I can see what it really looks like if I want to. The first time I came down here, I saw what it really looked like before the tiles covered it. Now I see the mosaic unless I *want* to see through the illusion."

"Oh." Brindan's head continued rotating left to right—Pax just continued to stare at me.

"See?" said Silliah. "It's actually just a concrete tunnel with these lights. And there's magic here, too, somewhere." She reached her hand out as if she walked blindfolded. "Can you feel that?"

"I can," answered Brindan. "What is that?"

"It's transportation magic," Silliah said, bouncing on her toes and hugging Brindan's waist. "It should take us ages to get to the temple, but we're almost there."

"Who built this tunnel?"

"No idea," I answered, still feeling the press of Pax's eyes. I turned his jaw to face forwards. He licked his teeth, fighting a smile. "You know my parents were ex-Enforcers? Well, they were practising Puracordis, and my room is their old room. My family home isn't far from the temple."

"There it is!" burst Silliah, pointing at the temple entrance.

We all walked towards it in a line, arm in arm, staring up at the beautifully carved door.

"*Mandus Erdullian.*" I cast the spell to open it. The golden tree trunk split in half, and Silliah heaved open the right-hand door.

"Whoa," said Brindan, walking inside and spinning in a complete circle. "It's huge in here." He walked in farther, taking everything in. "And so much *gold*."

"I love it," said Silliah. "The red, the gold, the carvings, all of it. Come on, Brindan." She tugged at his arm, pulling him towards the Tree of Conjuring. "So, you know I told you there are six branches of magic? Well, this tree will tell you which one you are."

Pax and I caught up with them. "*Spella Tair.*" I cleansed their blood. The bright green smoke spread from both my hands and washed over their bodies. Despite using the beginners' incantation, I wobbled on my feet, still suffering from overwhelment, and Pax grabbed my arm. "I'm fine." But he kept close, pressing up against my back. I leaned into him, curling my spine and feeling his sturdiness.

"You've done that to me before, haven't you?" Brindan said quickly, staring at his arms. "Yesterday before I glowed in front of Silliah."

"Yeah, sorry. I thought Silliah told you."

"I've told him as much as I can. There's just so much to remember: six branches of magic; Cryxstalide calcifies your pineal gland; your birthmark decalcifies it; there's a spell to cleanse your blood; beginners need to use incantations which have a colourful smoke, but spells in the mind don't; and you're the Guidal. Is that everything?"

"Almost everything," I replied with a smile. "I've got something else to tell you, but should we find out what the boys are first?"

"After you, Paxton," said Brindan, waving him onto the misty glass panel.

"After you," Pax replied, hooking an arm around my neck and keeping me close.

"No." Brindan waved an arm again. "In case you get scared off by whatever happens when I step on it."

"I'm not going to be scared off. After...*you.*"

"Do you trust him, Aurora? Will he get on it after?"

I turned my head to see Pax. "Promise me?"

"I promise." He pulled me closer until my body was in front of him. "I promise I will see what branch I am."

"Alright," said Brindan, waving a boot through the ultraviolet mist. "Here goes nothing."

Brindan stepped through onto the panel, standing boots together, facing the tree. The purply mist spiralled up around his pyjama bottoms. Then a beam of red light raced up the tree trunk and veered off down the sixth branch. It met with the golden ornament on the branch, and the room began to change. As the pierced-metal ornament opened, the temperature of the room dipped, and the lights dimmed as if a red storm cloud covered the sun. The bassy pound from a drum vibrated through my core. Then another. Then another. Then another deep penetrating boom. A flash of red light followed the next drum, and just as if it conveyed the birth of a storm, the ground rumbled, the drum's beat quickened, and bolts of red lightning shot down from the ceiling. They forked and struck the ground with a lacerating crack.

We all stood transfixed by the rainless, electrical storm until Silliah yelped at a bolt cracking right by her feet. She hopped back, making us all laugh, but then we continued watching the room. I could watch it forever, the jagged red forks climbing from the sky, the drums sending waves through my skin, and the cold chill in the air. The tiny hairs on my neck stood up, feeling around like sensory receptors.

Brindan stepped off the panel, returning the room back to normal. "Apart from the red reminding me of Juvies…I like it. So, what am I?"

"You're an Elementalist," I said, rubbing the charged energy from my neck.

"Cool." Brindan nodded at Silliah. "Do you think I'll be able to create fire?"

"I reckon you'll be able to do more than just create it," said Silliah, hooking on to Brindan's arm. "I bet you can manipulate it. Elementalist really suits you. I shoulda guessed that was your branch."

"Summoner really suits you," Brindan returned, tipping her head back and pecking her lightly.

I crammed my hands into my pyjama bottom pockets and turned away. Pax still held around my shoulders, and he put both hands on the back of my neck, pulling me in until his mouth pressed against my forehead.

I closed my eyes, breathing him in.

"Go on," I said, pulling away. "It's your turn."

I felt his deep breath before he let go. Hands held into fists, he stepped onto the panel. A green light burst up the tree trunk and off down the third branch.

High ethereal notes instantly touched my soul. It suited Pax's kind, gentle nature, and the strings overwhelmed me in a completely different way to the brooding violins I'd heard previously. This song was played from the heart and on the instrument of an angel. The harp's crisp, clear sound deeply moved me, and I couldn't take my eyes off Pax. His face had softened at the beautiful music, his hands now relaxed by his sides.

As the metal ornament spun, a mild breeze rushed the room, and long green wisps lightly stroked our bodies, swirling and twirling around us. They gave me a warm feeling inside my chest, filling my thoughts with my Nanny Kimly. I remembered when I'd just arrived here, I was missing my mum and dad and desperately wanting to go back home. Nanny Kimly hugged me until I cried myself empty. She sang lullabies and rocked me. I was only a baby, but I remembered it vividly. I heard her soft voice and felt her loving essence passing through my soul.

We all stood, faces to the sky, hair tousling gently, tears in our eyes, fully immersing ourselves in our senses. When the music stopped, Silliah threw her arms around me, her face as wet as mine. "I don't know what it was about that music," she said, squeezing me tight, "but I couldn't help thinking about you. You're my best friend, Aurora. I don't know what I'd do without you."

"Hey," said Brindan, pulling Silliah into him. "That music made me think of you."

I smiled at them in each other's arms before Pax wrapped his arms around my shoulders. He squeezed me so much tighter than Silliah, and it was a real embrace, like he hadn't seen me in years.

"Well, that was nice," said Brindan, as if a film had just finished and the credits were rolling.

"Why are we all crying?" Silliah laughed, wiping her face dry.

"Did everyone have thoughts about someone they love?"

Silliah spun on Brindan. "You love me?"

"Er…" He shrugged, his freckly face turning pink. "Erm, nah. Nah, I just care about you a lot. That's all."

"You *so* love me." Silliah covered her mouth with both hands. "This definitely counts as you saying it first."

Brindan hooked her in and held her face into his chest so she couldn't speak anymore. She wriggled around laughing and attempting to gain her freedom. He ignored her and asked us again, "Did you guys get that, too?"

"My Nanny Kimly," I answered.

Pax just nodded.

"Well, that was nice," said Brindan again, releasing a quiet Silliah. "So, what branch is Pax?"

"He's a Healer," I said, blinking at Pax, heaviness in my chest. Something about him being able to heal made my eyes well up, reminding me of his kind heart and soft nature.

Then Brindan said what I was thinking. "Suits you."

"Alright," said Pax like he woke up from a daydream. He put his arm around me and led me into the entrance hall. "I've done what I said I'd do. I'm gonna go back up. Could you open the door for me, please, Aurora?"

"Bro, wait." Brindan came jogging over. "Stay with us a bit longer."

"Nah, bro. I said I'd find out what branch I am. That's it. I'm not doing magic."

"If we get caught, we're all gonna die whether you're down here with us or not. What's it matter?"

"I'm not encouraging it. I want Aurora to stay safe. I'm not about to start participating in it."

"Cor, your parents have done a right number on you."

He shrugged one shoulder and turned to the door, still keeping me under his arm. "Please, Aurora." He gestured at the door.

"*Mandus Erdullian.*" I opened the door, knowing when the fight was lost.

"We're both on our final warning," Pax said to me, stepping out of the door.

Brindan shouted from over my shoulder, "This is a death sentence, Pax, not a trip to Maximum Security."

Pax carried on out the door, turning away. "Tayo," he said, nodding as the door closed him out in the tunnel.

"*Mandus Erdullian.*" I yanked the door open.

"The Juvie?" I heard Brindan say to Silliah.

Tayo was alone in the tunnel, sitting on the bottom step. He wore his normal all-black leather jacket and baggy trousers, blending in quite well with the staircase. I was surprised Pax had even seen him. On my way to Tayo, I checked up the tunnel, seeing Pax heading back to the institute alone.

"Hey." My feet shuffled as I held my hands behind my back, restraining myself. "How long have you been waiting out here?"

"Not long." He noticed my feet and held out his arm. "Was just waiting for you guys to finish in there."

I stepped into him, relieved I didn't have to control myself. I inhaled him deeply. "Have you eaten since I cleansed your blood at lunch?" I kept my arms securely around his waist, hoping he wouldn't pull away too soon.

"Nah."

"I wish you would eat more, Tayo. It's not good for you to keep missing meals."

"I didn't know I was going to see you tonight, and I needed my blood clear to practise. I've got food in my bag for when I finish."

I leant back from his hug to see his face. "Eat now, please, and I'll cleanse you again."

Tayo pressed our foreheads together. "Or we could skip training and go to your ensuite. Kiss me and I'll carry you up there."

I squeezed my legs together, feeling pulses reaching around my body. My show was surfacing, and I concentrated extremely hard on stunting it. It would only encourage him if I did. Because I smiled, Tayo guided me to the wall, holding his lips temptingly close to mine. It felt unnatural not kissing him, and controlling the urge caused me actual pain. *No, Aurora. No. No. No.*

Just one kiss? I looked at his perfect lips remembering what it was like to have him completely, to relish in his kisses, to have his hands on my skin. Why wasn't I kissing him, again? *It's Tayo...my Tayo.*

My smile slipped away, and the tear rolling from my eye made Tayo stand up straight. "Oh, hey. I'm sorry." He wiped his sleeve across my cheek, drying my tear. "Why are you upset?"

"I'm not upset. I'm fine."

"Yep, you're always fine and never upset, I know." He pulled me in close and exhaled on my head. "I've been with you almost every day from the moment we met. I know when you're not okay."

"I'm fine. C'mon let's go inside. I'll introduce you to Brindan."

"Isn't that Ryker's friend?"

"Pax's best friend."

"Hm. I remember."

Making sure my face was completely dry, I opened the door. "*Mandus Erdullian.*"

"Tayo!" Silliah ran out of the grimoire room. She closed her eyes tight, squeezed her fists to her stomach and showed to him. A bright orange light burst from her body. It faded when she opened her eyes again, and she turned to wave Brindan into the entrance hall.

"Silliah," Tayo returned, showing back to her.

"Wait," I said, twisting Tayo towards me. "Do that again."

"Do what again?" he asked, leaning away and studying my face.

"Show to me."

Tayo closed his eyes and opened them again. Nothing had happened, and he looked down at his hands, confused. "I can't."

"What? What do you mean you can't?"

Tayo clearly tried again, but nothing happened. "I don't know." He spun to see Silliah. A bright yellow aura shone from his skin. He pivoted to me, hesitancy clear in his turn. Neither of us knew what it meant, but it didn't feel good.

"Why can't you show to me, Tayo?"

"I..." He scratched his reddening neck. "I have no idea."

I thought back, realising I'd never seen him show. "You've never been able to show to me."

Silence rolled over the room. My chest hardened as the wall ascended around my heart. A foot shuffle from Silliah reminded me they were still in the room.

"Can I trust you, Tayo?"

"Yes," he said earnestly.

"*Show* me, then."

Again, nothing happened, so I side-stepped to see Silliah. "Ask him if you can trust him."

She grimaced at first because I think we all knew where this was going, but she obliged. "Tayo...can I trust you?"

"Yes," he answered weakly, a ray of light pouring from his skin.

"So it's just me who can't trust you."

"Of course you can trust me, Aurora." He turned back to me and held on to my eyes with a desperate intensity. "You *know* you can." *After everything we've been through together. How can you think that? You're my whole life, Roar. I love you more than you'll ever know.* "Of course you can trust me."

"Fine," I said, just to end it. It wasn't fine. I didn't know what exactly about it wasn't fine, but I knew it was *not* fine. This barricade over my heart was hurting, and I needed off the subject. "Well," I said, heading to the Tree of Conjuring, "you're going to need to do some homework because you and Silliah are both Primaries."

"What?" they both blurted, coming after me.

"Brindan meet Tayo. Tayo meet Brindan."

"Alright, mate," Tayo said with a flash of yellow light.

"Alright." Brindan didn't show back to Tayo. I didn't blame him.

"I know you said Silliah's a Primary"—Tayo held my arm to slow me down—"but how'd you know I am?"

"The colour when you show isn't white. A Primary's show is the colour of their branch. Yours is yellow."

"What's a Primary?" asked Silliah, following us into the Tree of Conjuring.

"You and Tayo both hold the magic from the original conjurers, the first ever Puracordis when everyone was human. You have the magic of the original Summoner, and Tayo has the magic of the original Intuitionist. When a Primary dies, their magic passes onto someone suitable. You are both powerful, and together with me and the other Primaries, we can conjure really complex stuff without incantations."

"Okay," said Silliah, holding her head as if it hurt. "A little overwhelming."

"There's something else," I carried on. "The prophecy tells you to show to the Tree of Conjuring. The temple has a secret of its own apparently."

"You want me to show to the tree?"

Tayo walked to the panel. "I think we'll need to be standing on this. Wanna give it a go first, Silliah?"

"Can you go first?" She hid behind Brindan's arm.

Tayo took a long step onto the ultraviolet panel. Just like it had done the first time, a yellow light raced down the fourth branch, making the golden ornament open up and the room fill with yellow translucent orbs.

Tayo showed to the Tree of Conjuring.

His radiant yellow glow exploded outwards brighter than ever. I shied away as the whole room flooded with his light, devouring him, us, and the orbs, until I couldn't see anything. Tayo extinguished his mighty show and looked around.

Silliah gasped and pointed to an archway appearing in the wall behind the fourth branch. A thick white mist poured from it, washing out over the floor. Without saying anything, we all advanced on the new enticing archway. It was another highly decorated room, small, though, with a continuous flow of white mist engulfing our feet. Set into the rear wall, in a highly carved archway of its own, was a large golden statue of a sitting man, his hands cupped into a bowl, a soft smile on his face, and seven gems positioned in a line down his body. They were all clear except the one inset into his solar plexus, which was shining yellow.

As if detecting Tayo's presence, the statue's hands began releasing a yellow smoke like it had used an incantation. The smoke reached out towards Tayo, encircling around his entire body. Before he was consumed by it, Tayo's face lost all expression, and his eyes closed. Silliah, Brindan, and I exchanged concerned glances. But before we could see if Tayo was okay, he disappeared with a *pop*.

"Oh," said Brindan, almost casually.

I held back every swear word, trying to work out what to do, how to bring him back. "Maybe you shouldn't show to the tree tonight," I said to Silliah.

"No, thank you," she said, anchoring herself to Brindan.

CHAPTER TWENTY-FOUR

THE CONFESSION

A strong gust of wind from above made us look up. Along with it came a small whirring, getting louder and louder until an audible, "Wooooooooo," came from a reappearing Tayo. "*Wow,*" said Tayo, catching his balance, his eyes shining with tears from the fall. "You're still here?"

"Obviously," I said. "You were only gone for a minute."

"Was I?"

"Yes. Where did you go?"

Tayo pulled up his sleeve. The veins under his tattoo were infected with bright yellow from his wrist to elbow. He held out his fist, peeling open his fingers and showing us a wide gold ring with a single yellow crystal carved into it. "I just spent the day with Tullosh, the discoverer of Puracordis." He nodded, his smile turning into a laugh. "Wow."

"What is that?" Silliah gestured at Tayo's new ring.

"It's a gift from Tullosh." He slid it onto his middle finger. "I watched everything as if I were there that day. Puracordis has always existed. He discovered it through meditation and learned how to harness it from the universe. He gifted it onto the six Primaries, and from then on, it became genetic, each of their children born with abilities. This ring is a gift which will return to him when I die. It gives me the ability to tell if someone is lying."

"Well, I've always been honest with you," I said, making my way back into the Tree of Conjuring. "So, I don't have anything to worry about. Shame I can't say the same about you."

"Oh, okay, I'm-Fine," he mocked in a goofy voice. "I don't know why I can't show to you, Roar, but I will figure it out, okay? I promise." He caught up with me and touched my arm. *I love you, Roar.*

"Whatever."

Silliah skipped into the room and jumped two feet onto the misty panel. Her animals appeared, and she watched them gallivanting to the bouncy trumpets. Tayo's Primary archway disappeared back to white stone.

Silliah showed to the Tree of Conjuring, her bright orange glow flooding the room and consuming us all. Then an identical archway appeared behind the fifth branch. "I need to see this." She ran into the white mist.

"Silliah," I called for her to wait.

But she didn't wait, and her eagerness led her to being engulfed by her statue's smoky spell until...*POP.*

"Oh, Silliah." I walked into her empty Primary room. It was identical to Tayo's, but the statue's seven gems were all clear except the orange one in his stomach.

"What's the issue?" Tayo followed me into the room. Brindan came in, fixing on my eyes with a furrowed brow.

Silliah's high-pitched squealing accompanied a strong gust of wind. "Whooooooooooa," she yelled as she came in for landing. "Oh *wow.* That was *amazing.* Was I only gone for a minute, too?"

"Yeah." Brindan pulled her in as if she'd been gone longer.

"So," said Tayo, "what did you get?"

Silliah swivelled around in Brindan's arms and yanked up her sleeve. Bright orange fluid coursed the veins in her forearm. She opened a matching golden ring, this one with an orange crystal inside. "I watched it, too. The old man unlocked our abilities and gave them to the original Primaries when they were teenagers. And I found out something else. Summoners can summon a spirit animal called a remilliar. They come from the place we go to when we sleep, but they can only be in this world for a limited time. This ring"—she slipped it on her finger and held it up for us all to see—"stops it from despawning. I can have my remilliar with me forever."

"I'm so proud of you, Silliah," Brindan said softly into her hair.

"I didn't do anything." She giggled.

"I know. But I'm just proud of you. My Silliah is a Primary." He turned his head to me. "And you too, Aurora. This couldn't have been easy for you. I can't imagine what you've been through holding onto a secret like this. But thank you so much for sharing it with us. Our lives are never going to be the same again."

Silliah held her arm out for me to join them in their hug.

I stepped in and after a quick squeeze, I let go and said, "Actually, Tayo did all the hard work. Most of this is because of him."

"Thanks, Tayo," said Silliah. She looked up at Brindan. "Tayo was there the night Aurora's parents died. Her dad pushed up through a trapdoor right under Tayo's feet. That's how he found this place."

"Oh, right. Regularly break Curfew, then?" He raised an eyebrow at Tayo.

They stared at each other, and I tried to hear what they were thinking. Tayo wasn't too fond of Enforcers, but he was putting his differences aside for the sake of Puracordis. It didn't really seem like Brindan was making the same allowances for Tayo.

"Look, mate," Tayo spoke before the staring got too awkward. "I know we've gotten off on the wrong foot, but I promise I only have Aurora's best interests at heart. I'll always keep her safe."

"That's Pax's job, *mate*. Remember that and we won't have a problem." Brindan kept Silliah under his chin the whole time, and she didn't know where to look.

Tayo's jaw tightened, clearly holding back his words, harnessing the years of self-control he developed to become Band A. "We're not going to have a problem."

Silliah, who was keeping her eyes anywhere but on Tayo, suddenly gasped.

"Penny drop?" I said, pursing my lips at her.

"How am I going to hide this?" She whipped her head up at Brindan and then back over at me. Bright orange liquid flowed through her veins.

"Welcome to my world," I replied, showing her my birthmark. I hadn't been able to make it invisible for as long as I used to after suffering with overwhelment. Despite feeling weak, I held my hand over Silliah's veins. "*Lis-Vuluta.*" I cast the invisibility spell. Energy quite literally drained from my body with the dark-blue smoke. I wobbled to keep on my feet.

"Are you alright?" Silliah asked, grabbing my arm.

"I'm fine," I lied, letting go of her wrist and slipping it through her grasp.

Tayo tutted behind me.

"I'll hide your veins every day, okay? When I'm back to normal, I should be able to keep them invisible for longer."

"I'm sorry, Aurora. I didn't think."

"It's fine. I get to see you every evening." I smiled, but my body rocked unsteadily. "I'm a bit tired. Do you mind if I go back up? You can stay if you want."

"It is getting late," Brindan said, turning his back on Tayo. "Maybe we should call it a night and start afresh tomorrow?"

Tension still beaded my skin from their confrontation, and a new day sounded like the best idea. Edging out of the room, Tayo twisted his Primary ring around his finger. "Aurora, can I come up and talk to you?"

"I'm not sure there's much to talk about, Tayo." I put my hand on the temple door.

Tayo removed my hand, placing his own on the tree trunk. "*Mandus Erdullian.* Please?"

"Alright. Fine. I don't care."

We all walked up the tunnel in silence. I don't think I'd ever seen Silliah so quiet. Having Tayo with us definitely polluted the air, but to be honest, I felt sorry for him. This was his thing, his life, his discovery, and he had more right to the temple than we did. I had hijacked it and brought my friends into the equation, outnumbering him Enforcer three to civilian one.

"Goodnight, guys." Silliah waved to us as Brindan led her out of my room.

"Brindan doesn't like me very much, does he?" Tayo walked over to the adjoining door, looking into Pax's room and then pressing the access button. "He's asleep."

"It'll be better next time. He's never interacted with civilians unless they're Juvies. Just give him time." I kicked off my boots and threw myself face down into the mattress.

Tayo sat on my left-hand side. "So what branches are they?"

"Pax is a Healer. Brindan is an Elementalist." I turned on my side to see him. "Why can't you show to me, Tayo?"

Tayo opened his mouth but then closed it, putting his attention on his ring.

"Just say it, Tayo. I can see you know."

"I don't know. Well…" He rubbed his neck, still not meeting my eyes.

"What do you *think* it is?"

He sighed and twisted his ring around and around on his finger.

"Oh my God, Tayo. Just tell me." I sat up, facing him.

"I'm so sorry."

My voice hitched as I said, "I'm getting *sick* of you telling me you're sorry all the time. What have you done?"

"But I don't think you're ever going to want to see me again."

"*What have you done?*" I ducked my head, trying to get in his eyeline.

"You lied on your Unity test about your sexual orientation."

"Yeah…I thought it would stop me from uniting."

"It would have. I changed it back to straight." He covered his eyes with his palm.

I pulled his hand away. "Right?" I asked, not understanding his reaction. I already knew he was going to match me with a stranger, and I had gotten over it. "I still matched with Pax?"

"Yes. But"—he swallowed—"you would never have united for as long as you lied on your test. It was detected as a lie but anyone who says they're gay would never be matched in a heterosexual relationship."

"So it's actually your fault Pax and I are united?"

Tayo nodded, his watery eyes staying on his linked hands.

"So you realise this situation is your fault, me being betrothed is your fault, the reason we can't be together is *your* fault."

Tayo's face filled with the immeasurable pain we both felt under the surface. He rubbed his forehead. "I know. I should've just left your test alone. I didn't know I was going to fall in love with you, Roar. I just wanted to give you this room."

The hurt in his voice made my chest ache. "Look, I couldn't care less about that anymore, Tayo. What's done is done. If you hadn't, I wouldn't have this room. And I really like having this room. Do you think that was it? Can you show to me now?"

Tayo finally lifted his eyes to mine. He shook his head. "No. There's something else. There's a shard of china hidden in my old cell. I cut myself on purpose."

"*Why?*" I slapped him on the hand.

He smiled and leaned away. "I needed to be able to spend more time with you, see if I could trust you, and just get a general feel about you. I needed to see how forceful you were going to get if I tested your boundaries, find out if you would report me for anything. Ultimately, I needed to see how likely convincing you to sneak out of the institute with me would be."

"You are such a dick."

"I know."

"Anything else?"

"The first time Ryker's tray dropped to the floor...it was me. I let it go on purpose. That's why he beat me up." Tayo laughed, guarding himself from me.

"Oh my God, Tayo, you are *insane.*" I shifted onto my knees, slapping his legs, his arms, his head.

"I needed that shard of china." He laughed some more, flinching and trying to grab my hands. "The rest of the time it was him, but then I couldn't get him to stop. Until I did that time you saw me knock it out of his hands." Tayo managed to get hold of my wrists, and he lifted onto his knees. His skin blazed with a yellow glow.

"You are crazy," I said, blinking, mesmerised by his magical complexion. His eyes were always bright, but now they were radiant.

"It was for you." He pushed me over onto my back, holding my hands by my ears. He stared into my eyes. I only stared back, bewitched by his deep blue. They held steady on mine, and a crease formed between his eyebrows. "Will you punch me in the mouth?"

I shook my head, and he brought his lips down to mine. Our skin glowed together, reflecting the fire which just ignited inside us. I wanted all of him. He was my Tayo.

CHAPTER TWENTY-FIVE
GUILTY CONSCIENCE

Tayo stayed the night, and I woke up in his arms the next morning. I lay there in the dark, my eyes wide open. Did this mean I'd chosen Tayo? The thought of seeing Pax in a little while made me feel dense. What if Tayo assumed I'd made my choice?

Tayo hovered a hand in front of my eyes, checking if I was asleep. I turned my face into his bare chest.

"It was just a kiss," he said, guessing why I lay immobilised in the dark. "Don't overthink it." It was more than a kiss, but somehow, he knew I was lying awake with my brain in overdrive. I exhaled slowly, trying to dissipate the prickling in my core. At least I hadn't led Tayo into believing I'd chosen him.

But I had to see Pax soon.

Oh, he tried to kiss me the other day too. Whatever.

It wasn't helping. I still felt bad.

Tayo clearly didn't, though. He pushed me over onto my back and kissed me, licking my lips before getting out of bed. "Lights on, Soami."

Rubbing my eyes, I brought his slim silhouette into focus. His ribs were too prominent, and I shook my head. "Tayo, please eat properly now. You can come and get your blood cleansed whenever you want. Just let me know when you're coming."

"Alright, I will." He slipped his black T-shirt over his head. "I didn't get a chance to tell you yesterday because tensions were high, but I looked in what I thought was a cupboard in the temple. It's not a cupboard. It's another tunnel…and it…leads directly into your old family home."

I was not expecting that, and I felt like Tayo had just stabbed me in the heart.

"I just wanted to let you know," Tayo said to my lack of reaction. "I don't want to keep anything from you again."

"How do you know it's my family home?"

"Erm…" He put one leg in his black baggy trousers and stood there frozen. "It's almost untouched, a bit of a mess in the main room, but the rest of the rooms are untouched." He put his other leg in and stood up straight. "There're photos on the walls."

Tayo twisted the knife already in my heart. There were photos of me with my parents?

"Sorry, Roar, I didn't mean to drop a bombshell on you."

"I'm fine."

Tayo's head dropped at the same time as his expression did.

"I'll *be* fine," I corrected myself.

"Better." He took my hand and pulled me up to stand. "I know it's a lot, but if you ever want to go up there, I'll come with you if you want me to."

"Thank you."

The alarm rang, giving us both a start.

"I'll come see you at lunch?" he asked quickly.

"Eat!"

"I will." Tayo opened up the wardrobe. "Fill me in with any gossip."

"I will."

And he disappeared down the tunnel. I stared over at the interconnecting door. My conscience pricked at the thought of seeing his face. I wandered over to it. Taking a breath, I gradually depressed the access button.

Pax was still in bed, sitting up using his Slate.

"Morning, sweetheart." He glanced over at me quickly before going back to his Slate.

I threw myself onto his sofa, lying on my front and angling my head his way.

"Brindan's raging about Tayo." Pax laughed at his Slate. "Should I tell him we're only pretending to be united?"

Tayo must've left that knife in my chest, because it twisted again. Something about hearing Pax say we were pretending felt wrong. The idea of everybody knowing made it feel too real. My life was a complete mess, and I just closed my eyes.

"Sweetheart? Are you okay?"

"Yeah, I'm fine." I opened my eyes and sat up, putting my feet on the coffee table. "It's up to you."

His eyebrows furrowed as he tried to read my face. "Yes? No?"

"I guess so. It'll make it easier."

"I'll talk to him later." He took his earpiece out and put it on the floating bedside table along with his Slate. "Are you sure you're alright?"

Pax followed the tears trailing my cheek, and he took the duvet off his legs, coming to sit by my side. Our arms touched, and I put my head on his shoulder.

"Just life?" he asked, resting his cheek on my head.

"Hmm," I hummed flatly.

"Do you want to talk about it?"

I only shook my head. How could I? How could I say what was on my mind? *I love you, and I really wish I'd never fallen in love with Tayo, but I have.* What I'd give to go back to the start of First-year, for my life to be normal, to be happy like Brindan and Silliah—how being united should be.

He pressed his mouth on my hair. "I think this is something only you can work through." When I nodded, he put his feet up on the coffee table next to mine. "Did you sort your differences out with Tayo? Brindan said you got into a fight."

"Yeah, we sorted it." My belly tensed at just how much we 'sorted' it. I could still smell him on my skin. "He couldn't show to me, but he can now."

"What was stopping him?"

"Something was bothering him, something he thought I wouldn't forgive him for."

Pax's feet flexed, arching forward and back until he crossed his legs. "Nothing too serious, I hope."

"Nah. I'm over it." I put my feet back on the floor, leaning forward to get ready for my day.

Pax took his cue from me and stood. "So, are you all back down there tonight?"

"Yeah, are you coming?"

"No, sweetheart."

"It was worth a try." I shrugged and backed up into my room.

After a shower, Pax and I left for the Food Hall together. We were the last to arrive, but our seats were saved opposite Brindan and Ryker. Silliah was on Brindan's other side, talking to Crystal.

I sat down and Brindan jogged his eyebrows at me.

"What have I done?" I asked, my voice fluctuating.

"What haven't you done," Ryker answered, spooning porridge into his mouth and staring at me.

"Shut up, Ryker," I said with a quick side-glance, looking back at Brindan. "Oi, what have I done?"

"Nothing," said Brindan. "As long as you make sure it's nothing."

Ears were starting to prick in my direction, so I dropped my eyes, choosing my avocado toast and leaving for the meal dispenser before the timer ended. When I returned, everyone seemed to be back into their own conversations.

"Aurora," Hilly called from my right. "Are we booking on to Lethals later? Pax said you have a lesson block too."

"You guys go ahead. I'm banned from taking Lethals again this year."

"Why?" She put down her spoon.

"Ryker got me into trouble. I didn't follow Sir Darlington's instructions right away."

"Being banned is probably for the best," chimed in Ryker, still shovelling in his breakfast. "Pipila used to be his subject in all his lessons. With her gone, it seems he's switched his attention onto you. I don't think you'll ever have a lesson without being put in pain in one way or another. You have to complete fifty-two Lethals lessons a year. That's a lot of pain. I'm pleased I got you banned."

"And what did you come out of it with?" I asked Ryker, folding my arms. "What punishment did you get for getting me banned and also not following Sir Darlington's instructions?"

"Pfft. I'm a Boulderfell. What do you think?"

I shook my head and ate some more toast. "Why me?" I said with a sigh.

"I don't know if you've realised, Aurora," said Ryker, "but you're good. You're good at everything, way above your year group. You're better than Pipila…that's why."

"He hates me because I'm better than Pipila?"

"It's nothing to do with hate. Pipila was his subject, and he loves her. But yeah, he chose you because you're better than his daughter. That and nobody likes a show off."

Saying 'I'm not a show off' would only make me look bothered, so I tried something else. "At least it's one more lesson without you near me."

I failed. Ryker gave me a smug look. He knew I was bothered. I think anyone listening did.

"Do you want me to book on to a different lesson with you?" Hilly pushed her bowl aside, her half-eaten porridge remaining untouched.

"Nah, it's fine." I pulled my toast apart, not knowing what to do with my hands. "I'll see if I can get on to an advanced mixed martial arts class."

"I can do that with you if you want," offered Calix. "That's what Seioh Jennson wanted me for last month; he wondered why I wasn't taking advanced classes."

"It's up to you."

"Ohh," whined Hilly, putting her chin in her hand. "I want to do that with you two."

"Practise then, babe." Calix knocked her elbow off the table so that her head fell.

She checked for imperfections in her sun-kissed-blonde hair and then dug him in the ribs. I left them to whatever 'that' was and ate some more toast. Crystal's incessant giggling made me look over. She was whispering with Maylene, Roebeka, and Silliah, but I noticed Silliah looked uncomfortable.

"Come on, Silliah. You should come watch," Crystal said, sliding to her feet. The other two followed suit.

"No, thank you," Silliah answered with a different type of smile, not one I often saw on her. "I'm going to stay with Brindan."

"Okay"—Crystal gestured to Roebeka to take all their trays— "maybe next time. Cute ring by the way." She touched the orange crystal in Silliah's golden Primary ring. "We'll see you in the Khakidemy later."

Roebeka stacked their trays and followed behind Maylene and Crystal. They all still had matching blue ribbons in their ponytails.

Hey. I gave Silliah a moment to register my voice in her head.

Silliah's bright-green eyes widened, and she looked over at me quickly. *Hey?*

Are you okay?

You can hear me?

I can. I couldn't help a small smile lifting my lips. *Are you okay?*

Yeah. It's just...Mimsy. Her eyes flicked to Crystal's Juvie standing at the chute.

I looked over at Mimsy and nearly choked on my toast. The teenage girl's face was unrecognisable, covered in nasty scratches and fresh bruises, but most unrecognisable of all was her bedraggled shag of hair. The young girl no longer had shoulder-length tight curls. It was now all different lengths, some short around her chin, some sticking up a few inches, none of it blending together.

They held her down and cut her hair. Silliah looked like she could cry.

I dropped my toast as my undigested food churned over in my stomach. *They?*

Crystal, Maylene, and Roebeka.

No. I stood up, my food soon turning to acid as a burning soared through my organs. I squeezed my fists together.

"Sweetheart?" Pax touched my arm.

All eyes were on me.

"Are we going now?" said Hilly, ready to stand.

Before I battered that stupid Boulderfell bitch and her friends, I unclenched my fists, loosened my jaw, and said, "I'll be back in a minute."

I left my tray on the table and took the exit between Khaki Quartz and Navy Quartz. I turned into the second from last corridor and knocked on the door.

"Come in."

Seioh Jennson was eating toast at his desk. He put his piece down on the plate and dropped his head forward. "What is it now, Aurora?" he asked, without easing my stand to attention.

I sucked on my teeth and moved nothing around my mouth. Panting, I stared at Jennson straight on but couldn't see anything. It was just pure molten lava bubbling inside my head.

"Sit down on the sofa, Miss Aviary." He huffed. "Why didn't you calm yourself down before you walked into my office, Aurora?" After shaking his head, he picked up his toast. I dropped down onto the black leather sofa, and Jennson continued working on his computer as if I hadn't arrived.

Sitting there, I couldn't get the picture of Mimsy out of my head, and I couldn't help but feel responsible. She'd asked me for help in her mind, and I just ignored her desperate cry. I needed to do something about it.

"Seioh."

"Calmed down now?" He placed his napkin on the empty plate and leant back in his chair.

I nodded.

"What can I do for you, Miss Aviary? And please think very carefully before you speak."

"Seioh, I know..." I was trying to figure out the best way of wording it. "I know I can't interfere with an Enforcer doing their job—"

"Correct." He sat up, giving me a firm look.

"But"—I swallowed, my mouth becoming dry—"I think a Juvie is being mistreated."

"A Juvie is a Juvie, Miss Aviary. There is no mistreating them. Who are you to question a Young Enforcer's correctional protocol? Think carefully about what you are doing before you commit gross misconduct yourself and interfere with an Enforcer carrying out their duty."

"There's no protection for Juvies at all?"

"What are you suggesting a Juvie needs protecting from?"

"Arsehole Enforcers."

Seioh Jennson's forehead hit his fingertips. With his eyes closed, he took a second to say, "Aurora, get out."

I wanted to back up, but I forced myself to stay put. I knew I was in a lot of trouble for swearing in front of Seioh Jennson, but I wasn't about to pretend that this situation wasn't fucked up. Boulderfells were pricks, Mimsy was in danger, and she needed protecting.

"I would listen to my order *immediately*. I'm not going to give you another chance to walk out of my office without two Fell agents by your side. I suggest you get out right now."

"Mimsy needs protecting," I said bluntly as I walked out the room. What more could I do? I tried. So, I took my lifeline and returned back to my seat in the Food Hall.

※

That lunchtime, during Mando-sleep, Tayo had just left after getting his blood cleansed, when Pax walked in through the interconnecting door, yawning and stretching his arms.

"Sorry," I said. "Did we wake you?"

"No. I wasn't sleeping." He got in my bed, pulling the duvet over him. "How was advanced mixed martial arts?"

"It was alright." I climbed under the duvet also, holding it under my chin and turning on my side. "It was fun being partnered with Calix. I haven't been his Uke since Mustard. We were acting like children again. Sir Hiroki almost sent us out."

"Did he get you back for lying to him? He said you sent him on a wild goose chase looking for Seioh Jennson's office."

The day I lied to Calix was the morning I woke up with an ankle trap on my leg. I sent Calix in the opposite direction so he wouldn't walk with me and find out I couldn't walk properly. It was when Tayo and I were together, and I was having the best time of my life. I almost told Pax the real story but then decided against it.

"He tried getting me back, but he failed miserably." I decided that was the better response. "I've had you as an Uke; he was nothing in comparison."

Just then, Nanny Kimly stormed into my room, red-faced, hands clenched by her sides. "*You swore in front of Seioh Jennson?*" she growled, coming at me and slapping the duvet where my legs were. She suddenly turned on Pax. "Get out!" She slapped him. It wasn't hard, but he knew to do as he was told. Pax jumped out of bed, laughing. She swatted after him, and he just about swerved her kick to the butt. "*Out.*" She flapped her hands, trying to hit him. "You miscreant. Go and complete your Mando-sleep." He ducked into his bedroom, and without another breath, Nanny Kimly turned back to me, her hands still on the attack. "*You swore in front of Seioh Jennson.*" She slapped me around the head.

"Ow." I laughed, rubbing my head. It didn't hurt, but she had never hit me before. "You two love talking about me, don't you?" I shuffled away, avoiding her second swipe for my head.

"You *swore* in front of Seioh Jennson."

She was clearly deranged, and I saw no way out, so I scrambled to the other side of the bed, jumping to my feet. She charged over, but I anticipated her movements, skilfully dodging her relentless attack. I escaped into Pax's room, closing the door behind me. Nanny Kimly gave the interconnecting door one resounding bang. Then there was silence.

Phew.

"You swore in front of Seioh Jennson?"

"Oh, shut up, Pax."

CHAPTER TWENTY-SIX

ONE, TWO, SKIP A FEW

I was tired the next morning because Tayo, Silliah, Brindan, and I stayed out too late practising in the temple. I was still experiencing dizziness from overwhelment, so I mostly watched the others. Tayo had discovered he could harness Chi, and he was trying to form a material energy in the palm of his hands. Silliah was trying to summon a remilliar but nothing showed. All whilst Brindan tried to blow a feather across the room...and nothing moved. It was amazing I didn't fall asleep right there on the floor.

I woke up in the morning alone in my bed after Tayo stayed in the temple long after I'd left, and I thought I was going to have a better morning until Soami decided she had other ideas. "Good morning, Miss Aviary. You have a last-minute alteration to your schedule today."

Oh, clart. The lights turned on, and I pushed my face into the pillow, waiting for him.

"Not again." Pax burst through my door. "If we are on a restricted schedule again because you swore in front of Seioh Jennson, I am going to make your life miserable today."

"You already make my life miserable," I mumbled into the pillow.

"Such a cow," he said in an airy laugh, taking a seat on my back. He must have weighed over fourteen stone, and I had to take strong breaths just to get some air in my lungs. "I mean it." He lifted his weight and fell back down, forcing a grunting noise from me.

"Alright." I laughed, trying to prepare for the worst and eyeing the ensuite archway.

Pax's weight lifted off me, and the duvet was swiped from my body. Now was my chance to run. Pax grabbed my ankle, using a leg control technique to turn me on my back. "Right." He dragged me down the mattress, threw the duvet back over me so that only my head showed, and then climbed to sit on me. My brain tried to figure out my next move, but I was completely defenceless, my arms locked in tight by the duvet. "You better hope we're not on a restricted schedule." Then he held a pillow up over my face, ready to plough down if the news was bad. He gave me a frightening side glance before checking his Slate.

"Well…?" I asked after his eyebrows pulled together.

"You're lucky." He hammered the pillow over my face anyway. "But for some reason"—he hit me with the pillow again—"I'm still affected when you misbehave."

With my head turned as far to the right as possible, I tried to speak through the pillow jabs and my giggling. "I will hurt you, Pax." I took in a gulp of air.

"I'd like to see you try."

Before I had wriggled my arms free, Pax threw the duvet on the floor and grabbed my foot. I used my legs to get him into an arm lock, but he knew how to counteract it, and he tried to get his own lock on me. We were both good at keeping ourselves free from each other's holds, and we continued to grapple. Pax's only advantage was his weight. He had his whole body keeping me down. Our hands slipped through failed attempts, and I realised my only option was to flee. There was no way I was securing him in an immobilising lock like I'd done to Tayo.

"I'm still waiting for you to hurt me," Pax said. But he actually wasn't; without me realising, he'd been planning two steps ahead.

I thought we were in an equal battle, but it turned out, during the wrestling, Pax was actually positioning my body exactly how he wanted me. Then, in one swoop, he twisted my wrist behind my back, scooped me in-between his thighs, and wrapped his legs around my waist. He rolled up against the display screen so I was between his legs, my hand pinned behind my back, and his legs wrapped securely around me, keeping my feet from doing any harm. For a brief moment, I had one free right hand, but Pax quickly grabbed my wrist.

"Go on," he said into my ear, squeezing me tighter. "Hurt me, then."

I was completely out of ideas and didn't know my way out of it. "You can't hurt me either; you're as locked up as I am."

Pax laughed, and squeezed his legs together, constricting my whole body unbearably. Then he pulled the arm behind my back up an inch, causing me more pain.

"Ow." I laughed, realising how wrong I was. "I mean it. I will get you back."

"Say I win."

"I will headbutt you."

"Headbutt me and I'll bite you. Now, say I win."

I assessed my body again. There had to be some way out of this. Maybe using magic?

Pax sensed I wasn't yielding, and he took my thoughts away from an escape plan. He pressed his mouth into the side of my neck. "Say I win."

His soft lips and warm breath made me quiver. The want for freedom was replaced with an overwhelming urge to feel his lips on mine. My fingers ran up through his hair, and I kept his mouth pressed to my neck, inviting him to kiss me. He obliged, kissing me behind my ear, his lips grazing my earlobe.

"Mm." A light moan slipped from me, and I pursed my lips, feeling my cheeks turning pink. I panted to prevent any more noise.

Revelling in his tenderness, I turned my head to push my cheek against his. His grip loosened on my body. Feeling his legs slacken around my waist, I turned to face him, sitting on my knees between his legs. I guided his head up from kissing my chest and held his lips to mine. "I win," I said, leaping off the bed, and running into the ensuite. I composed myself behind the closed door, crossing my legs and holding onto my ear to stop the tingling. Then I gave myself a cold shower.

By the time I came out of the ensuite, Pax was already showered and dressed. He had that familiar soft smile and raised eyebrows whilst handing me a clean Navy uniform. "You took your time."

I just narrowed my eyes at him and tried to stop myself from smiling. I turned back into the ensuite to get dressed. Keeping the door open, I called out to him, "So, what's the last-minute alteration to our schedule?"

Pax came to stand in the walkway. "It seems Seioh Jennson has realised a restricted schedule doesn't work on you, and he has filled our day up with duties—no lessons, no training, just a whole day of duties."

"Ah, man, that sucks. I would've rather had the restricted schedule. I could've spent the whole day down in the temple practising."

"Well, you're lucky you're not in Maximum Security. I don't know how you do it, but I think you've probably expended your nine lives by now. And why I have to do it with you, I have no idea. It's like he's punishing me for not keeping you out of trouble."

I passed him in the walkway with a sly smile. "Better try harder next time."

"Trust me, you wouldn't want that. I wouldn't let you out of my sight." He waited for me to put on my boots and followed me out of the room.

"So what's first?" I asked, entering the main corridor, red tube lighting one side, navy on the other. "Do we have time to go to breakfast?"

"Yeah, but we're Juvie chaperones again." Using his body, he guided me to turn left towards Claret Quartz.

"Oh. The return of Juvie duty. I haven't had a Juvie since Tayo."

"Just try not to kiss this one."

My feet stopped moving.

"Sorry, I meant to say don't fall in love with this one," he said over his shoulder at me. It wasn't any better, and he tried with another suggestion, "Don't grow attached?"

I gave him a dirty look and stormed past him.

"Don't take showers together?" he called out one final time before the door to Claret Quartz closed on him.

Realising I didn't know where I was going, I waited for Pax to catch up. He led me through to our Juvies' cells and looked into his observer window. "Oh." He pulled out his Slate and double-checked his Juvie's cell allocation. "That's Boyd Livingston's Juvie." He looked back at me. "That's weird."

"Boyd?" Like I was supposed to know who that was.

"Crystal's betrothed." He moved over to my Juvie's window. "Seems you've been assigned her Juvie too."

"Mimsy?" I said quickly, my eyes sharpening on him.

Pax nodded. "Weird. I've never heard of a Juvie being reallocated before."

I kept my voice low and said, "That's what I went to see Seioh Jennson about yesterday. I told him Crystal was mistreating Mimsy."

"You can't do that, Aurora." He lowered his eyes to admonish me.

"It worked." I shrugged, backing away.

"No. There's no way it worked. Seioh wouldn't swap Juvies like that, not without a reason."

"Like...she's abusing her position as a Young Enforcer?"

"Correctional protocol is correctional protocol. There is no abusing it."

"God, you sound just like him." I looked into Mimsy's cell. She was in the middle of the cell, her head bowed and holding her shaking wrist out ready for Crystal.

"What the hell is this, then?" I hissed at Pax.

"You're lucky you're still here." He shook his head, pressing the access button to cell J-229.

I opened my cell door, stepping in tentatively, still dealing with the state of her. Mimsy didn't move. She stood trembling, her bedraggled hair covering her downward stare. "Mimsy," I said, after she didn't look up. "It's okay. You're my Juvie now."

Her bruised eyes lifted off the floor before her knees buckled.

Seeing her go, I grabbed her claret overalls with both hands, but I collapsed trying to catch her. Our knees crashed to the floor as a weak "Thank you" broke through her sobs.

I helped Mimsy onto the bed and went into the ensuite to get her some tissue. Tufts of her dark-brown hair lay atop the bin. A flame ignited in my belly, and I smothered it before I became consumed with thoughts of strangling Crystal. It didn't matter; Mimsy was safe now.

Giving the tissue to a despondent Mimsy, I rested against the counter. She blew her nose, and I allowed her time to recover.

Pax opened the cell door. "Ready?"

"Yeah. Can I have your wrist, Mimsy?"

She held up her trembling wrist.

Pax chaperoned a teenage girl. She was mark-free and eyed us curiously. As she walked ahead with Mimsy, I could see her talking out the side of her mouth. The girl pulled open the Claret Quartz doors and allowed Mimsy to walk through, rubbing Mimsy's back as she passed. When Pax opened the door for me, my fists clenched.

"Thank you for taking our Juvies," Crystal said, swinging her arms as she took light steps.

"It's alright." I shrugged, looking past her whilst trying to keep my fists by my sides.

"Seioh Jennson wants us out in the city on special patrols." Crystal carried on despite me not stopping. "Apparently, there're reports of a man frequently breaking Curfew, and Seioh aims to increase our presence in the city as a deterrent."

I turned back. "There's someone breaking Curfew?"

"Apparently." She shrugged. "We couldn't have done it with Juvie duty. Lucky you two were free to take them." She skipped through the Claret Quartz door being held open by Boyd.

"*Shit,*" I said under my breath.

Pax tutted at my swearing. "That doesn't bode well for Tayo."

"I know. I'm going to message him."

Sitting down in the Food Hall, I hid my Slate beneath the tabletop.

"Good morning, then." Ryker kicked my shin from under the table.

"Ow!" My leg lashed out, kicking him straight back with the same weighty boot.

"*Ow,*" he hissed with an edge to his voice. He reached over, pulling my arm towards him and bending my wrist the wrong way. "Say sorry to me right now."

"You kicked me first!"

"Say sorry right *now.*" He twisted my wrist harder, sending shooting pains through my bone.

I knew my way out of it, but did I dare try? Ryker had been so unpredictable since Pipila left, and I was getting away with less and less.

"I'm sorry," I said with a shrug and head flick.

He let go, throwing my arm towards me. I rubbed the sharp pain out of my wrist and then picked up my Slate.

'*Tayo, there are reports of a man frequently breaking Curfew.*'

His response was prompt. '*I have an untraceable picoplant, access to your schedules, a thermal-radiation contact lens, and a picoplant tracker. I'm safe, darling.*'

It wasn't what I was expecting, but then again, Tayo never really was fazed by much. Before ordering my food, I spoke to Silliah from across the table:

Mimsy is my Juvie now. Do you think you could help me with her hair?

She threw her eyes on me. *I don't think I'm ever going to get used to you doing that.*

My grin broke out. *Sorry.*

No, I love it. It's amazing. I'm so pleased Mimsy is away from Crystal. I'll go grab my hair bag after and see what I can do.

We exchanged small nods and then carried on with breakfast.

When we got back to J-227, Silliah managed to braid Mimsy's hair in small rows. She cut a few long straggly bits and made it look presentable considering what she had to work with. Mimsy smiled for the first time in a long time, and although I was dreading my punishment, I was glad I swore in front of Jennson. The swap of Crystal's duties was too coincidental. It had to be because I went to see him. Perhaps I'd know for sure via my punishment. If it wasn't too bad, then my question would be answered.

When Silliah finished, Pax and I took our Juvies to complete phase one of my punishment. Our first duty was taking the Juvies to clean Mustard bedrooms. We were sitting in the corridor, playing on our Slates, when Seioh Jennson's voice followed up the corridor, "Stand up, Miss Aviary."

I reacted at once, feet together, hands behind my back. *Please don't leave me standing up all day. Please.* I feared my punishment was about to get a whole lot worse. A day standing on my feet, whilst Juvies completed their duties, was going to get tiring fast.

"Paxton, take the Juvies back to their cells to rest. Leave the trolley; Aurora is going to need it to clean the rest of the rooms. I want you back here to check them. Make sure they are completed to a high Juvie standard."

"Yes, Seioh."

Jennson said no more and walked away. I decided for myself I wasn't going to stand up all day, and I slumped down on my plastic chair. "He has got to be kidding me."

"Miss Aviary, come here."

I said that way louder than I thought. The walk to him felt endless. I lifted my eyes off the floor to read his expression. It was impassive but still made my gut clench. *I wasn't talking about you. No. That wasn't me; I didn't say anything. No, that wouldn't work either. I didn't mean to say it out loud? I love my punishment, thank you; here, let me clean some more rooms for you.* Of course I hated it. What did he expect?

I reached him and left a gap, hoping it was large enough to prevent my face from giving my emotions away.

"How old are you, Miss Aviary?"

"Seventeen, Seioh."

"How old do you think you should be before you start thinking before you speak?"

"Sorry, Seioh."

"Take a guess."

I held back a groan. I knew whatever answer I gave, it wasn't going to be the right one, and I couldn't help but sigh before I answered, "Eight?" I shrugged dismally.

"Hm. Now tell me, what's eight multiply seventeen."

"I don't know, Seioh," I answered, clamping my teeth. I knew whatever he was doing I was going to find myself even more wound up. *Just get to your point.*

"Work it out," he said bluntly.

I stood there for a minute, quietly working it out in my head. The pressure was making me crumble, and I couldn't come up with an answer straight away. Seioh Jennson kept painfully still, barren blue eyes concentrated on me. He really was waiting until I had figured it out.

"One hundred and thirty-six, Seioh."

"Now, that is how many times you are going to run up and down this corridor before you start cleaning your Mustard rooms."

"Seioh," I moaned, looking up at him.

"Now."

Arguing was pointless, so I swivelled on my heel and broke out into a jog. Pax hadn't hung around. He was already turning the corner, taking the Juvies back to their cells. I reached the end of the corridor and doubled back.

"One," said Jennson when I arrived back to him.

"*That's not two?*" I almost squawked.

"One," he repeated.

I held in my 'for fuck's sake' and ran back up the corridor, a curse word bonanza blethering through my head.

Stupid useless punishment wasting my time. Go and buy another suit, you pointless human being. That was the tame version.

"Two," said Jennson.

I'll give you flipping two. I swear to God, I don't care how much trouble I get into, I will—oh you will what, Aurora? Shut up.

On one of my runs back up the corridor, Pax turned in, giving me a puzzled look. "What are you doing?" He looked around trying to figure it out. "Ah." He answered his own question, seeing Jennson over my shoulder.

I reached the end and turned back. Pax continued walking towards our housekeeping trolley.

"Mr. Fortis," Jennson called to Pax. "I want you to count Aurora's laps. She is to run one hundred and thirty-six times. There and back. She is on eight."

"Uhh," Pax croaked, the sheer amount of laps registering in his brain. "Yes, Seioh."

Jennson disappeared, and I ran back to the start, speaking quietly, "You're not going to count properly, are you?"

"Yes, Aurora. I am. I'm not breaking the rules. Eight."

I ran back up and down before speaking between gentle pants, "Come on, Pax. Don't be a dickhead."

"Nine."

"For God's sake." Another lap, I returned. "Come on, Pax. For once in your life stop being such a melt."

"Ten."

"*Ugh!* You have got to be kidding me." Back the other way, I reached the end and doubled back. My breathing heavier, I stopped at Pax's feet this time. "Come on, Pax. Please. Just one, two, miss a few, for me, please?"

"Fifteen." Pax skipped five laps but gave a subtle eye roll.

"Thank you." The words came out in a relieved pant. "Thank you, Pax."

He only nodded, and I turned on my heel. I felt the need to say "Thank you" every time I returned back to him. Keeping a steady pace, I stopped only to take my navy jacket off, throwing it at Pax's feet. I wasn't going to say it was easy because it wasn't, but I knew I could do it. It was a matter for the mind, and it remained focused until: "One hundred and thirty-six."

With a long groan, I slumped down on the corridor floor in a messy, sweating heap.

"You should stand up to catch your breath." Pax picked up my jacket.

"Shut up." I leant against the wall, panting, hands on my stomach as if it helped the air fill my lungs.

"Not exactly the way you should talk to the person who's about to check your rooms."

"OHHH." I collapsed on my side, pushing my forehead on the cold panels.

Quite some time later, after I had dragged myself up off the corridor floor, I was in a Mustard bedroom, hot, flustered, and tangled up in a mustard duvet cover.

"This is so unfair," I said to Pax, shaking a single duvet into the case. "And what am I supposed to do with these." I kicked an army action figure towards him. "Since when do Musties have *toys*?"

Pax bent down to pick up the incoming attack. "He must have an older sibling in Navy earning Worths." He slid open the desk drawer. "And you put things away in the nearest drawer." He laid the action figure down and pushed the drawer closed.

"You want to stop smiling at me." I threw a dirty pillowcase at him. "I'm not in the mood, and I will hurt you."

He caught it and put it down the laundry chute. "I think we already established this morning that you can't hurt me. Now get to work."

"*Argh.*" I threw the first thing I found.

Pax dodged the flying toy gun.

Later that day, after I'd completed uniform delivery, I was in the Food Hall waiting for the Juvie team to finish cleaning the room.

"Stand up, Miss Aviary," Jennson's voice came from behind me.

I stood up and huffed loudly. Pax shot me a look, but I faced the other way.

"Everyone, please take your Juvies back to their cells. You are no longer needed." The crowd dispersed and Jennson put a housekeeping caddy in my hand. "Finish the room."

"Please, not by myself." I dropped in my chair, discarding the caddy on the table.

"Yes, Miss Aviary, by yourself. And I want you to do the same after dinner. After which, I want you to deliver the Juvies their dinner, and then I want you up early in the morning to bring them their breakfasts."

Juvies ate before the alarm and were expected to be ready for collection at any time. This meant I would be up at zero four hundred hours. It also meant no temple time for me and an early night, which I was grateful for when I collapsed into bed later that evening. I closed my eyes and prayed for it all to be over after breakfast duty in the morning.

But this schedule remained for an entire week, and I, for absolute certain, would be sure never to swear in front of Seioh Jennson ever again.

CHAPTER TWENTY-SEVEN

I'M ALL WHAT?

Sitting cross-legged on the temple's cold stone floor, I kept my eyes closed and tried to concentrate.

"Stay in your happy place, Aurora," said Silliah, throwing a hollow white ball at me. This one hit me on the cheek, and I tried to tune out the clicking sound as it bounced away.

I knew from the absence of a clacking noise that the colourful cube I held in mid-air with my mind still hovered there. *Stay in your happy place*, I repeated to myself.

"Ooh, well done." Silliah threw another ball at me. It clicked off in the same way as the others.

"Stay in your happy place, Aurora," said Brindan, firing a pellet gun. The bullet hit my arm, leaving a sharp sting. "Stay in your happy place."

I ignored the pain and focused on keeping the cube floating. My thoughts were switching between every positive thing I could imagine, my Nanny Kimly's face, the taste of peppermint hot chocolate, the angelic white bouquets of flowers, Tayo; I meant Pax. Pax and Tayo? The cube crashed to the ground, sending an annoying clattering noise through my nerves.

"Well done, Aurora," said Silliah. "That was pretty good. Ten balls this time. Ready to go again?"

"Fire that gun every three?" I asked Brindan, flinching and rubbing my arm. "It really hurts."

"That's the whole point." He closed one blue-green eye, aiming the gun at me. "Now go again."

Happy place, Aurora. I lifted the cube with my mind.

See, a few months ago, Tayo had figured out why our magical practice was so slow. Knowing conjuring was powered by positive thoughts, he realised the distraction of using magic and the full focus on it working was hindering the magic itself. We were putting pressure on ourselves and not harnessing positive emotions. He called it "getting into our happy place", and he set up this exercise for us, providing us with an array of distracting objects. Brindan's favourite? The pellet gun.

"Are you in your happy place?" asked Brindan, firing the gun.

A ball bounced off the top of my head, but nothing stopped the colourful cube from floating...until the sound of his voice.

"Well done, Roar."

My eyes flew open, and the cube clattered to the ground. He slid his backpack off his shoulder, leaving it against a stone column. Looking healthier than ever, he proffered his hand and helped me up onto my feet.

"If you don't mind," he said to the other two, "I just want to borrow Aurora for a minute."

"Hi, Tayo." Silliah high-fived him and headed for the grimoire room, grabbing Brindan by the arm and dragging him away.

Tayo kept hold of my fingertips and led me to the wide staircase, walking me up to the balcony. The swirling in my tummy was mild until Tayo checked over his shoulder to make sure we were out of sight and then bear-hugged me from behind, walking me up the last few steps.

With a shiver, I easily cast the spell to cleanse his blood. *"Spella Tair."*

He turned me around and eased me against the wall, bringing his lips to my ear. "Are you going to kiss me yet?"

I smiled and interlaced our fingers, pulling him closer.

"So, I've been thinking about you," he said, kissing the side of my face.

I closed my eyes, rolling my head back so he would move down to my neck. "Mm?"

"Yeah, and you remember when I used to come into your bedroom and do all those naughty things to you?" He unbuttoned the top button of my pyjama shirt, kissing me lower.

"Well"—he double-checked behind him over the balcony—"it made me realise something." He pushed his thigh between my legs, pressing for my body to grind against. Totally immersed in it, I hid my face in his chest. What I would give to be in my bedroom right now.

Tayo lifted my jaw, steering my lips to his. "Kiss me, and I'll lay you down right here."

Oh.

Luckily for me, Brindan and Silliah were way too close for that to happen, and it made my answer easier. "Never going to happen, Tayo."

He took his leg away and smiled. "Oh, it will."

With his leg gone, my mind fizzled back to me, and I pressed my fingers on my warm cheeks. "So, did you really realise something or were you just being a jackass?"

"I realised something." He backed away, busy searching around the balcony. His eyes were bright, and he was looking the fittest I'd seen him in a while. He was clearly eating properly again. "I think you're going to like it."

Up here there were tons of old wooden storage cabinets, some with glass-fronted doors, some with shelves, and some with drawers with fancy metal handles. From the cabinets, Tayo took an old chunky candle, a small electronic device, and a golden figurine.

Tayo placed the objects on the floor. "So…" He guided me to lay on the floor behind them. "Are you sure you don't want me to take you first?"

I laughed in surprise. "Tayo." I grabbed the collar of his T-shirt and pulled his face close to mine, waiting for his eyes to drop to my lips before I pushed him away. "Have you realised something or not? You've got five seconds before I go downstairs."

"I've realised something." He rubbed his lips together. "I've realised something." Standing up straight, he skimmed over me one final time as his head turned but his eyes lingered. He cupped his hands together as if holding an insect. *"Day Alanjay,"* he said, pulling his hands apart. In the space between them, a pale-yellow energy pulsed. The outer edge shone brighter than the middle, which was almost completely white. He fired it across the balcony, hitting a cabinet and knocking the contents behind a glass door over. This was his newly discovered ability of harnessing Chi, and he was getting pretty good at it. "So"—he joined me on the floor, sitting opposite, behind the random pile of objects—"you're an Illusionist, right? And Illusionists can branch out to both Astralist and Healer."

I nodded for him to continue, my gaze slipping to his lips.

"Do you remember when I was cleaning your bathroom that time, and I came out to warn you Jennson was on his way round? You told me that you thought of Jennson, too, and that it was normal. But it wasn't—I was using magic."

"Right?" I said, forcing my attention to stay on his eyes.

"Say *Day Alanjay.*"

"What's the point? That's an Intuitionist's incantation. I can't use your branch."

"Say it."

I crinkled my forehead. "*Day Alanjay.*" I shrugged and held back a yawn.

"Do this"—he pushed my hands together as if I now held the insect—"and *try* this time."

"*Day Alanjay.*" I humoured him, pulling my hands apart. I gasped, clapping my hands together and snuffing out the yellow energy in my palms. "That's not possible."

His beautiful smile touched his piercing-blue eyes. "Yet true."

"What does that mean?"

"It means I know why the Tree of Conjuring doesn't work for you." Tayo held up the chunky, decorative candle. "Say *Lasil Buna.*"

That was the incantation Brindan was practising the day before. It was the Elementalist spell for fire.

I stared at him with my mouth open. One side of me really didn't want it to work, whilst the other didn't even want to try. I didn't want to know if I could use yet another branch that I shouldn't. It would make me undeniably different and placed a scary amount of emphasis on being 'the Guidal'.

"Don't be nervous. It's alright." Tayo's smile lessened as concern for me filled his eyes.

"But that's too much power. I don't want to be more than one branch."

"You've got this, Roar." He discarded the candle to hold my hands. "You were born special, and you've handled your powers this far. Knowing you're more than one branch isn't going to change anything. You've got control." He then patted my knees and said, "Now, go on."

I sat quietly, his words sinking in. Maybe I did have control. Or perhaps maybe it just wouldn't work. Tayo held the candle steady in both hands. *Don't work. Don't work. Don't work.*

"*Lasil Buna,*" I said the incantation, my eyes drifting down to the flame. My belly rolled. That was five out of the six branches.

"Want to summon a remilliar?" Tayo was definitely enjoying this more than me.

I shook my head. "Not before Silliah has. She's been trying for months to summon hers."

"That's just an excuse, but fine. *Nayoachon*, then?" He held up the golden statue of a meditating man. "Take this from me?"

I put my hand to my head and stared at my reflection in the glossy stone floor. Could I really be all six branches? That was way too much power for one person, but before the doubts set in too deep, I rolled back my hunched shoulders and looked at the golden figurine. "*Nayoachon*," I said, followed by a swallow.

It only flickered in Tayo's hand.

"You're nervous," he said. "Happy place, Aurora."

I closed my eyes and thought of Nanny Kimly. Her reaction finding out I was all six played before my eyelids.

"*Nayoachon*." I cast the spell again. The figurine vanished from Tayo's hand and instantly appeared in mine.

"You're all six." Tayo held out a low five. I put my hand on top of his, waiting for him to feel what I wanted. When I checked his eyes, he tilted his head back, but I tugged on his fingers until he lifted onto his knees and cuddled my head. I breathed in his confidence, filling my airways with his essence.

"Are you guys done yet?" called Silliah, the sound of her boots hurrying up the balcony stairs.

I ripped from Tayo's embrace, trying to remember how to hold my face so I looked normal.

"What are you doing?" Silliah's head appeared over the golden hand rail. "You've been ages. Can you come downstairs now?"

Brindan appeared behind Silliah, his eyes glancing over the scene, the items on the floor, the closeness of Tayo and me, the look on my face.

"Erm." I stood up, needing to escape Brindan's dissecting. "Come on, let's go downstairs, and I'll show you."

"Top button, Aurora," said Brindan, his hardened eyes landing on Tayo.

"Oh." I grabbed my pyjama top closed. When Brindan turned around, I checked on how much he saw. I wasn't particularly full-chested, but you could still see too much. Tayo winked at me, but I shook my head at him, my stomach still clenching. He tapped my backside as I walked past, and I held my index finger up at him, warning him silently.

He ignored my scolding and nuzzled my neck.

He knew to be quick, and I didn't need to push him off. We followed Brindan and Silliah downstairs, and Tayo jumped down the last few steps into the entrance hall. "Aurora is all six branches."

They both twisted to look back at me. "What?"

"I'm all six."

"You're all six branches?" Silliah asked again.

I nodded. "*Day Alanjay.*" I cupped my hands, creating a ball of Chi, and I fired it at Tayo. He fell onto the stone floor, sliding back until friction stopped him.

"How did you know that wasn't going to hurt me?" he asked, his voice high.

"Intuition?" I smiled smugly and shrugged.

"You little bitch." He patted himself down, checking he really was okay.

Brindan gave Tayo a long side glance before focusing back on me. "So, you can do all our magic?" The lines disappeared between his eyebrows.

"*Lasil Buna.*" I used his incantation, creating fire in the palm of my hand. It flickered and swayed, leaving a gentle touch of heat on my skin. Closing my eyes, I focused on my happy place. When I opened them again, a roaring ball of flames spiralled towards the ceiling. The panic at losing control sent a wave of anxiety crashing over me. Every positive vibration washed away, and with it, the fire ball extinguished. "Whoa." I let out a relieved sigh. "It's actually really scary. I'm not sure I like it."

"Aurora." Brindan's dilated blue-green eyes held mine. "That was *mental*."

"It's amazing." Silliah jumped in my arms and spun us around. "You are incredible, Aurora. You really are the Guidal." Silliah's response drew a smile from me. I hugged her, and she hopped back. "Can you summon a remilliar?"

"I didn't want to try it without you having summoned one first."

"Do it." She bounced on the spot. "I've waited months to see mine. I want to know what the hell it is. It can't just be orange smoke. Something else must happen."

"What's the incantation?"

"*Weppomil*."

As soon as I repeated the spell, an orange smoke wrapped around my body, the only part Silliah had conjured. The smoke grew erratic, speeding up, darting this way and that way, growing thicker and faster. After finding momentum, it began to fade. Silliah and I looked at each other, ready to speak, but before we did, a wispy cloud appeared on the floor between Silliah, Brindan, Tayo and me. As the active white cloud thickened, the motion of the smoke began drawing an outline.

Getting denser with every swirl, the gas formed a solid, leaving a bundle of white curled up in the comfort of its own bushy tail. It was cartoon-like but already changing. The longer it stayed in the real world, the more realistic it became.

The big ball of white fur cracked open an eye. They were a sapphire-blue just like mine. The remilliar sleepily uncurled itself, standing up and stretching its long, agile limbs. A bushy tail sprang up behind...her. It had to be a 'her' because it was so beautiful.

Standing from her cat stretch, she took the shape of a majestic, fox-like creature standing as tall as my shoulder.

As the remilliar woke fully from its slumber, I felt my own body becoming fatigued, and within seconds, it faded out of sight.

The boys and I looked at each other incredulously whilst Silliah jumped in the air turning in a full circle. "That was incredible. Oh my God. I really, *really* want to summon mine."

"They are unique to the individual, too," said Tayo. "So yours will look totally different." He walked over to Silliah. "And with this"—he held up her hand with the Primary ring—"you'll be able to keep it here for as long as you like."

"I have the best branch," said Silliah, grinning at Tayo.

"I don't think so." Brindan stepped in, spreading his arms, hands, and fingers wide, pushing Silliah back with a strong gust of wind. He walked with her, pushing her all the way until her back touched the temple wall. She tried to hold her hair flat but left her charcoal pyjamas whipping furiously from the strength of Brindan's magic. He ended the spell and held her cheek, tipping her head back to kiss her.

As usual, I didn't know where to look, and my eyes fell on a pair of narrowed piercing-blue ones.

No. I gave Tayo a strong look, stepping back. *No.*

He came at me, a disobedient glint in his eye.

No. I tried to not return his contagious smile, all the while stepping away from a defiant Tayo. *I mean it. You will be going down on this floor.*

Even better.

My toothy smile broke out, but I still tried to sound convincing. *I will use my enforcery stuff on you.*

He jogged his eyebrows, all whilst perfectly anticipating my moves and backing me into a corner. *Remember when you used to try and get me to sleep with you, and I would say 'no' but you wouldn't listen? It's hard, isn't it? Having to make someone stop something you really don't want them to stop.*

My eyes darted to the other two and back.

When my heels touched the wall, Tayo cupped my cheek. "Just kiss me," he whispered softly.

He always managed to make my heart race, and I kept glancing at his perfect lips. After checking on Brindan and Silliah again, I tucked my hand under his black T-shirt, grasping the hot skin above his waistband.

"Just kiss me," he whispered again, persuading me with his eyes.

I licked my lips. *It's just a kiss.*

My Slate vibrated in my pocket, snapping me out of my infatuated trance. Tayo heard the buzz and backed off, knowing it could be a notification warning me of someone entering my room. The game had to stop.

I checked what it was, reading a message from Pax.

'Want to come up and watch TPG with me? I'm so bored.'

My heart clenched at his message. We were down in the temple every night, and Pax spent every evening on his own. My heavy heart persuaded my message back: *'Of course. I'll just finish up down here.'*

"It's only Pax," I said to a silently questioning Tayo. "I'm gonna call it a night. He spends every evening on his own."

"He has you all day."

"We're working during the day. It's different."

"Not really. But you do what you need to. I'll see you tomorrow during Mando-sleep?"

"Yeah." I turned to the still-kissing couple in the far corner. "Guys, I'm gonna go back up. Pax wants to hang out."

"Tell him to come down here," said Brindan, barely taking his lips off Silliah.

"You know he's not going to." I wasted my breath because they were back on each other's mouths. "Are you staying here?" I asked Tayo, fighting with a smile.

He looked over at Brindan and Silliah and rolled his eyes. "I'm used to it. Those two need to hurry up and shag already."

"They aren't allowed."

"They will."

"They won't," I said deeper, placing my hand on the door.

"Watch this." Tayo took my hand off the door and called out to the other two. "You know I could get you guys some contraception if you wanted?"

Brindan and Silliah instantly stopped kissing to look into each other's eyes. "No," they said together breathlessly. "No?" they said again, but this time it was a question to each other. They both looked over at Tayo.

Tayo jogged his eyebrows at me, an arrogant smile on his lips.

"*Guys,*" I shouted out, disappointed by their reaction. "No!"

They both laughed and said, "No," to each other again. Then after another laugh, they were back to making out.

"They will," Tayo repeated.

No longer convinced they wouldn't, I put my hand on the door. "*Mandus Erdullian.*"

Tayo walked me into the tunnel and cuddled me goodnight. We kept each other's hands, separating gradually as we backed away, our fingertips slowly losing connection. I kept peering over my shoulder at him whilst I headed up the tunnel alone.

Crawling back through my wardrobe, I kicked off my boots and went straight into Pax's room. In the time it took me to get back to the institute, Pax had gotten us both a peppermint hot chocolate.

"You're the best," I said, taking the delectable drink from his hands. He put the last playback of TPG on the display screen, and I settled into the duvet pile facing it.

"I hope I didn't pull you away from anything," he said, stretching out.

"It's fine. I was getting tired anyway." This was the truth. I wasn't feeling recovered from summoning the remilliar, and I was pleased to be on his comfy bed, holding onto my peppermint hot chocolate. I took a sip, making an effort to really relax into the duvet pile.

Pax lifted his Slate which had already been unfolded into a tablet, and he pulled up the platform to watch the games, using it to start *Sovereign Skill's* playback on the display screen. We watched quietly and comfortably, both enjoying our drinks.

"See how they're in and out of the warzone?" Pax watched the display screen.

"Yeah, I noticed that during the last game. Look, I'm there." I pointed at me preparing to act, thinking *Sovereign Skill* was about to eliminate me. "They just run straight past me."

"They ignore all the possible eliminations and just get the hell outta there. Might be something to bear in mind if we go warzone again."

I nodded; then quiet ensued. We were content and sipping on our silky hot chocolates.

"That's a new Bounty." Pax rewound the playback to Saulwyn sending out a green fog. Their opponents were completely shrouded by a thick green haze. Saulwyn reached in and simply eliminated the disorientated couple. "It's called *The Grass Isn't Greener*. It only follows the victim for a minute before fading. The danger is that the person who used it is probably going to be on the other side by the time it fades." Pax leant forward, discarding his empty takeaway cup on the bedside table. I held mine out to him, and he put it down, settling back into the duvet, on his side, slightly closer to me than before.

"I found out something today," I said, ignoring a burning itch to lean into Pax. I tried to concentrate on *Sovereign Skill*. They were sticking close to the warzone, thinning the competition by targeting the recently united couples fleeing the centre. A favourable display of Bounty collected on their arms.

"Hmm?" He peeled his eyes off the playback slowly, genuinely more interested in the games than how close our bodies were.

I met his warm gaze. "I found out I'm all six branches."

He leant up higher on his elbow to see me better. "You're supposed to only be born with one, right?"

"Yeah. I always thought I was an Illusionist."

"You really are the Guidal." He brushed a knuckle over my cheek. "So, what does that mean for you?"

I shrugged and touched my face, my gaze briefly slipping to his lips. "I wish I knew. I'm supposed to return balance, return magic, but I could really do without the monumental responsibility."

"You amaze me, Aurora. Everything about you. It kinda scares me how much you amaze me."

I looked at him with a confused smile. "Stop gushing." I snatched a pillow and threw it in his face.

CHAPTER TWENTY-EIGHT

LOSING CONTROL

A gentle cough roused me from my sleep. Realising where I was, my limbs stiffened like water turning to ice. I peered through the darkness at Pax lying on his side facing my way, still fast asleep. If I was quiet enough, I could sneak back into my bedroom, and he would never know I stayed the night in his bed. Slipping my toe out the duvet, I held my breath and slid towards the edge of the mattress. A driving force in my hip pushed me until I rolled down the platform steps.

"Ow." I sat up on the floor, sweeping the hair from my face.

"You've outstayed your welcome," Pax said in a playful tone.

"Oh, as if. I could take your virginity right now if I wanted to."

"Y-you're a little too sure of yourself, Miss Aviary."

"Hmm." I licked my lips. I heard him falter, and in that moment, I knew I could if I wanted to. If the lights were on, I would see his cheeks turning pink. He was the strictest, most annoying Enforcer I knew, but yet, he would allow me. I smiled at my newly realised power. Then I left the room without saying anything else. I didn't need to say any more. He knew I knew.

Stealing a few moments of peace before my day started, I waited for Pax in Mimsy's cell, sitting on the counter using my Slate. Mimsy perched on her bed, glancing at me occasionally.

"Do I unsettle you, Mimsy?" I asked, not taking my eyes off my Slate.

"Erm…no, ma'am."

"Sit back, then. What're you doing?"

"Yes, ma'am. Sorry, ma'am."

She pushed herself against the wall, legs outstretched, looking like a china doll. Her face had healed, no more scratches or bruises, and her hair had grown out a bit. Silliah braided it a few times, but I think it was long enough to be left alone now.

Mimsy didn't speak much. I didn't blame her after the treatment she'd received from Crystal, but I did try to show her we weren't all psychopaths. Undeniably, it was nice having a Juvie who respected me and actually called me ma'am—it just would've been better if it wasn't induced by fear.

"Do you like being a Young Enforcer, ma'am?" asked Mimsy.

My eyebrows lifted, hearing her speak. *Do I lie?* "It's alright," I half-lied. "I'd rather be…" *How do I put this?* "…free."

"Everyone wants to be an Enforcer." She looked down at her claret overalls. "All my friends, I mean. I thought by getting in here, I would be able to become one."

"Is that why you're a Juvie?"

She nodded, brown eyes still trained downwards. "I broke Curfew on purpose."

"Cor, what's with all you Juvies getting in here on purpose? I can't count the number of times I've heard that. Are you looking forward to going home on Saturday?"

Her eyes emptied, and it took her a minute to say, "Yes, ma'am."

"Do you still want to be an Enforcer?"

"No." She looked at me instantly. "Not anymore."

"Good." I returned back to my Slate, feet up on the shelf, waiting for Pax.

Breakfast was uneventful and so was most of the morning. With our new extracurricular activities in the temple, Brindan, Silliah, and I couldn't talk freely, and we struggled with censoring our conversations. Puracordis was the single biggest thing in our lives, and it was hard to talk about much else. I could tell Silliah was distancing herself from Crystal, but that didn't stop Crystal from forcing her into conversation. I just tried to keep myself to myself, consciously avoiding any interaction with Ryker. He was still being unpredictable, and I felt on edge whenever he was around.

We had training in the Khakidemy for the first half of the day, and Pax was using the Flexon Pro whilst I waited for my turn. Hilly and Calix were queued up behind me, playing some weird game of tread-on-each-other's-feet. Tyga and I were on either side of them, just trying to keep out of their way. Tyga acknowledged what we were both thinking, and he took a wide berth around them to stand with me.

He didn't mention their strange antics, but instead dismissed it with a headshake, turning the way I was facing, and saying, "Ready for the Parkour Games next week?"

"More than I've ever been."

"Beignley didn't take losing too well last time. Beat them again this time, won't you?"

"Yes." I took my eyes off watching Pax to smile at Tyga.

He brushed up his shiny black quiff and winked at me. "Good. I didn't like his attitude towards you after the last game. He may've tried to scare you by saying he could get you discharged, but Seioh Boulderfell—and anyone with eyes, for that matter—will know it's only because you're his competition. I really wouldn't worry about that. He can't get you discharged."

"Thanks, Tyga," I said with a tiny smile. "I think I needed that."

He nodded before his eyes followed a tall boy passing behind the Flexon. I opened my mouth to ask about him, when a sudden confetti explosion sparkled above our heads. Someone had broken a new scoreboard record, and we turned to the boards bordering the room. The pixels broke down, gathering together and circling around the arena, passing through every board in turn. The swarm wrote 'Paxton Fortis' in the tenth position for the Flexon Pro. I could hardly hear Soami's voice through the spirited applause. "Two hundred and two. A new leaderboard entry. Congratulations, Mr. Fortis."

He was only twenty-eight points off first place, almost beating Saulwyn Field with two hundred and thirty.

Wiping his forehead on the back of his fingerless glove, Pax jumped off the black foam pads. I held my arms open, and he pulled me in, resting his sweaty cheek against my head. My body rocked along to his heavy breathing. He let go, getting his high-fives off everyone, and I stepped onto the pads.

"Age before beauty." Ryker barged onto the Flexon with me.

"There's a queue, Ryker. Get off."

"Are you going to fight me for it?" He squared up to me, pushing his chest against my chest.

Why did I even bother? I stepped backwards off the pads, leaving with my palms facing him.

Recently, where there was Ryker, there was also his new shadow, Maylene, which inevitably meant Crystal and Roebeka, so I left the Flexon with Pax and joined him on another machine, this one called Cityline.

Pax pressed a button, activating a long conveyor belt. It whirred as it engaged, and Pax timed his step carefully onto the moving black belt. The machine's components instantly began transforming. They assembled themselves into obstacles ready for Pax to overcome. The machine initialised the same set of obstacles each time, so you could rely on memory alone to advance on, but the speed and intensity would increase, meaning higher obstacles, closer together. The top twenty longest times spent on this machine were recorded on the scoreboards, and Saulwyn Field held the first-place position on this machine also.

Pax was pretty good at it, too. He looked as though he knew the sequence really well. He jogged on the spot as the belt bombarded him with obstacles. I could see when he struggled to keep up, and finally, nine minutes and thirty seconds later, an eight-foot wall dragged him to the start before he could get over it.

"*Argh,*" he growled, shaking his head at me. "I can never get over that bloody wall."

"Oh no, is Mr. Fortis crap at something?" I teased him with my eyes.

"I'd like to see you get over it."

"Easy."

"Pfft. I'll give you till the end of this session, and I bet you still won't be over it."

I'd been on the machine a few times before, but I wasn't well practised. Maybe if I had a few goes in a row I could quickly improve my score. I took one go, but for some reason our attendance at the Cityline attracted visitors all suddenly wanting to try their luck at beating their scores. But soon enough, everyone lost interest, and I was left to my own devices trying to get over that wall.

My competitiveness got the better of me. For a while, I managed around my usual time of six minutes, but about an hour later, I caught right up to Pax. I made it over the succession of three-foot walls, up the steps leading to a balance beam, back down to the ground, and across the stretch towards the undefeated eight-foot wall. I ran and planted my foot on the wall, driving myself up. But my fingers only snagged the edge, and I was dragged all the way off the conveyor belt.

"Give up," said Beignley Boulderfell, passing with his clique. "You look pathetic." They all sneered and sniggered; it wasn't behind their hands but done intentionally to make me feel uncomfortable. I got back onto my feet and glanced around for Pax.

"Start again," said a calm, almost angelic voice. A quick look behind me and my eyes landed on *Sovereign Skill*. The picture-perfect pair must've also been watching me fail time and time again. "The trick is to run all the way to the end of the belt whilst the obstacles are small," Saulwyn said, blocking Beignley out of my sight and starting the machine up for me. "Then you can catch your breath so you'll have enough speed to reach the eight-foot wall."

"Thank you," I said, a little relieved to not be mouthing off at Beignley, but also a little overwhelmed at being helped by *Sovereign Skill*. They were the most (genuinely) popular people in the institute, and a crowd was already forming around them. Before my limbs seized up with stage fright, I jumped on the Cityline and began to jog at a steady pace.

"You're going to have to run a lot faster than that." Saulwyn ran alongside me. "That's it, as fast as you can. Over these easy obstacles and right to the end." She stayed adjacent to me as I jumped the easy obstacles: the short walls, up the stairs, and over the beam. "You've got a chance now to catch your breath before the eight-foot wall comes."

I stood still, panting and being pulled back towards the start. Just before I was pushed off the end, my wall arrived and Saulwyn gave her order: "Now sprint at it. If you don't hit the wall fast, you won't get the drive you need to reach the top."

I pushed my trainers forcefully into the flexible plastic, ready to attack the wall. I planted a foot on the vertical surface and propelled my body up for the catch. My fingers latched on. Feeling my grip slipping, I used my feet to crawl up. The end of the belt was fast approaching as I hung on to the wall. Throwing my leg over, I pulled myself on top, jumping to the other side.

I'd done it.

But landing badly, I tripped up and was thrown off the end.

"Well done, Aurora." Saulwyn helped me up.

My face burned under the press of eyes, but the applause soon made my flushed cheeks return back to the assumed workout rosy red. My fingers felt cool against them as I laughed it off.

"Try again." Theodred patted me on the back. I say 'patted' but it was more of a guided shove towards the machine.

Saulwyn kept by my side, giving me tips and tricks as I tried again. They didn't leave my side until I successfully scaled the wall and then some…

The confetti had cleared when Pax bumped my shoulder. "Mentored onto the scoreboards by *Sovereign Skill*, eh?"

"I know." I felt my cheeks flush. "I'm on two scoreboards now."

"Eleven minutes, eleven seconds," he read my score off the board. "You're not that far off getting nineteenth place."

"Yeah…but now I have a *nine*-foot wall to get ov—" The colliding of Silliah's body threw the breath out of my sentence.

"I cannot believe you got trained onto the scoreboards by *Sovereign Skill*."

※

"Come on, Roar. We've got to do this," said Tayo, trying to coax me into the grimoire room.

"Ten more minutes?" I groaned, looking back at Silliah. My orange remilliar smoke vanished into thin air along with hers.

"No, come on. If you summon your remilliar, you won't have enough energy to practise."

"Look, man, if she doesn't want to, just leave her." Brindan stopped playing with his mini tornado to stare at Tayo. He was cross-legged on the glassy stone floor, spinning a tiny vortex in his palm. Like our magic, the tornado disappeared with the drop in Brindan's mood.

Aurora, come on! Tayo threw me an exasperated look. *Unless you want me to tell Brindan why we really have to practise. The Parkour Games are in a week. You need to be ready for when Beignley comes for you.*

"It's alright, Brindan," I said, backing away to meet Tayo. "I should practise."

"Only if you want to, but it sounds to me like Tayo just got into your head." He eyed Tayo instead of me.

"I asked Tayo to help me. I want to."

"Just mind your own business, Brindan, yeah?" Tayo gave him a curt nod.

"Yeah?" Brindan got to his feet.

"Yeah." Tayo took one step towards Brindan.

No-no-no, Tayo, stop. I put myself between them.

But Brindan took the bait, striding over fast. "You think you could win against me, do ya?"

"Guys, no." I held my hands out at both their chests.

"Get out the way, Aurora." Brindan used his forearm to sweep me aside. "I'll have this over within a second."

"Don't fucking touch her." Tayo pushed harder to get to Brindan.

Now the boys' foreheads were touching, and Silliah was running to my aid. They were similar builds, and head-to-head, they were similar heights, but I didn't like either of their odds.

"Brindan, stop it." Silliah grabbed the back of Brindan's pyjama top.

Tayo's fists spat yellow sparks. He was getting into his happy place and summoning Chi. Brindan was an Enforcer and would have usually won this fight hands-down, but Tayo was *very* good at magic. Fearing this situation was about to get a whole lot worse, I got into my own happy place.

Sending my palms out towards them, I imagined holding them still. A shockwave of energy blasted from my hands, throwing the three of them off their feet. Tayo flew through the air and smashed against the carved archway. Brindan and Silliah soared in the other direction. I caught Silliah with magic and placed her gently on the ground. Brindan plummeted to the floor, sliding until he hit the far wall. Silliah immediately ran to him. I ran to Tayo.

"Fuck me, Roar." Tayo winced, holding the back of his head.

"Sorry. I lost control. Are you okay?"

Tayo removed his hand, red splashing the stone floor.

I pulled his head forward to see the wound. "What's the healing incantation?"

"*Tepior*," he mumbled.

I repeated the incantation out loud and held my hands over drenched clumps of his hair. Fresh blood trailed the nape of his neck. I separated the clumps to see Tayo's scalp. There was no wound and no scar.

"I'm sorry, Tayo."

He moaned and slid down the wall onto his back. He lay there with his eyes closed, recovering from his fall. I went to check on Brindan.

"I'm fine," Brindan said, still sitting against the wall where he landed. "How's the dickhead?"

"I'm fine, you prick," Tayo called out, still on his back, eyes closed.

Brindan nodded, so I knelt back down to see Tayo. "You hit the wall pretty hard, eh?" I huddled over him, stroking the hair off his forehead.

Tayo groaned. "I am going to ache in the morning." He blinked his eyes open. "That was pretty incredible, though, Roar." His lips curved into a tiny smile. "Like…seriously impressive. What branch of magic was that?"

"I have no idea. I just meant to hold you two still."

"Your intuition can't tell what magic that was?" Tayo dragged himself up to sit, flexing his back as he did so.

"I don't really know how to tell."

"It's a strong feeling, like a gut feeling you just can't shake."

Unsure what he meant, I just shook my head.

"Come on." Tayo stood up unsteadily, holding out a hand. "Let's go practise."

I glanced at his hand and pulled my own back into my stomach. "I don't really want to practise anymore."

Tayo stepped towards me, holding two hands out. "Come on. Don't be scared. You have to get straight back to it, otherwise it'll only get worse."

"Can't you just stop Beignley and control his suit for me?" I mumbled quietly, checking over my shoulder to make sure the others weren't listening. On the far side of the entrance hall, Silliah was straddled over Brindan, and they were locked on to each other's mouths.

"What if I can't, Roar? What if they lock me out? You need to learn to protect yourself."

I stared at his hands, thinking whether to take them. He crouched and held my hands, brushing his thumbs over my knuckles. "You've got this." He pulled me up to stand and led me into the grimoire room.

He hopped onto the octagonal plinth, reaching the leather book. "So, I did have some Illusionist magic ready for us to practise"—he slapped the open page—"but I think you need to work on something else first. I want you to hold me still."

"No, Tayo—"

"Shush, Roar. You have to practise. If you hurt me, it's my own fault, okay?"

"I don't want to hurt you."

"But I might like it." He pulled a face. "Now come on—no *enforcery* stuff—I'm going to kiss you unless you hold me still."

Butterflies picked up in my stomach. It was a good feeling to conjure with, but Tayo probably already knew that. He didn't give me a chance to argue, and he stepped off the octagonal plinth, approaching me slowly, giving me time to think.

I returned his smile but reacted by backing away, passing the archway to check on Brindan and Silliah. They were still on top of each other.

"I don't want to hurt you, Tayo."

He kept moving at a steady pace. "I'm not stopping until you hold me still. Now do it."

"I'm scared of hurting you." I trod back again and again, only checking behind to make sure I didn't bump into any musical instruments.

"You put Silliah down nicely when you threw us all, so you *can* do it."

I held my hand up hesitantly, facing my palm towards Tayo. *I only want to hold him still. I only want to hold him* still. I imagined holding him mid-step, picturing him in his black T-shirt and drop-crotch trousers, seeing his cheeky piercing-blue eyes and beautiful face. Drawing power from the light fluttering in my belly, I sent out my intention.

Tayo's jet-black fringe tousled as if touched by wind, but his feet welded to the red stone floor. I stopped backing away and clapped my hand over my mouth.

"Nice one, Roar." Tayo winked, only having movement of his face. I let him go, and my stomach lurched at Tayo's determined strides towards me. "Now do it again."

"*Ahh.*" I began backing away again. "One sec."

He came at me, committed and steady, long stride after long stride. Holding my palm out, I drew upon the power of my squirming belly.

I held him still again, this time without any surge of energy ruffling his hair.

"That's it," he said with an encouraging nod. "And again."

We circled around the grimoire room as I held him still time and time again. My confidence grew with each successful hold. The lack of control had been a moment of panic, jumping into my happy place without time to think. Tayo showed me I could control it.

I stopped him once more.

When I let go, he said, "Again."

But he was too close. He took one step towards me, gently holding the back of my neck. He leaned in and pressed his cheek against mine. I closed my eyes, letting myself be enveloped by his presence, feeling the tension between us as his lips only grazed the edge of my parted mouth. Filling with gratitude for all that he was, I turned for him.

He pulled away just as our lips were about to meet.

I clamped on my bottom lip, savouring the remnants of his taste, and then I pretended like I hadn't attempted to kiss him. "So, what now?"

Tayo took my hand and softly kissed my palm before turning his attention to the grimoire. "Come on. Now you can hold me still, all you need to do is make the picosuit look like it's glowing ice blue. This type of Illusionist magic relies heavily on your imagination. If you can picture it clearly, you can conjure it. You have one week to perfect it."

CHAPTER TWENTY-NINE

RISK

It was still dark in my room when I woke up for the millionth time. I'd lost count how many times I'd opened my eyes tonight trying to get a sense for the time. It had to be early now, but the alarm still hadn't rung. All night, my mind oscillated between playing the games and then using magic against Beignley. The shifting feeling upsetting my stomach kept my brain from switching off, relentlessly bringing me back to consciousness like a lightbulb.

"Lights on, Soami," I heard Pax say from the open interconnecting door.

Yes! If it was early enough for him to be awake, it meant I didn't have to force myself to remain inactive any longer. Usually, on the morning of TPG, Pax would be up before me, dressed, and running into my bedroom, assaulting my mind with a Bounty-related question. This morning, I grabbed the chance with my whole body, throwing it out of bed and bolting for Pax's room. My flitting bare feet hardly made a sound as only the balls pumped the smooth panels.

"A dirty green fog?" I threw myself on top of the duvet where his body rested.

"*Arh.*" He recoiled as I landed on top of him. "Ow, girl. You gotta be careful where your knees land."

I pressed the shield of cupped hands holding between his legs, giving a strong pulse downwards, before turning over and jumping to bring my full weight down on him again.

Pax laughed in pain, air being forced out of his chest. Using the duvet like a wing, he swiped me off him. I lay on my back, legs resting on him, duvet over my face. "A dirty green fog?" I asked again, fighting to get back up.

He kept his arm over me, holding me down on my back and answering, "That's that new one."

"It is. But what's it called?"

"Ah, sugar." He stopped to think.

I took the opportunity to assume a better position, sitting on my legs, pillow on my lap. "Too late." I smacked his sleepy face with the pillow. Before he could snag my charcoal pyjamas, I ran from the room, shouting the answer behind me, "It's *The Grass Isn't Greener.*"

Surprisingly, Pax didn't pursue me, and I got ready for breakfast. As I was making my birthmark invisible, a pillow hit me square in the face. I stumbled backwards and caught a glimpse of Pax fleeing from the interconnecting door. Chasing him down the Navy residential corridors, I skidded to a stop when I saw our *Smokin' Axe* posters standing over us.

Now, this was a video loop I wouldn't mind recreating. In this one, I walked around barely in shot, leaving Pax on his own in front of the camera with a brooding look on his face. He was trying to warn me without actually being able to say a word to me, otherwise that would have been recorded too.

I let the pillow to the face go and quit chasing him; the hall of solo-Pax posters was punishment enough. Although I had seen our fan memorabilia on the walls before, it was the sheer amount which overwhelmed me to the point of appreciation this time. Navies had gone to the trouble of making the posters, whilst others had sought them out to display on the walls. Every single couple housed in these Unity rooms were playing the games themselves, yet they rooted for us. Standing there, taking it all in, my mind returned when Pax stood by my side, staring up at the same poster as me.

"Mad, ain't it?" He turned to take in the whole corridor.

"What did we do to attract so much attention?"

"Probably teaming up with *Sovereign Skill* in the last game. After seeing the same two teams win for the last nine years, I think I would be rooting for the new people too."

"We ain't even close to winning." I left the *Hall of Paxton* and continued on to the Food Hall.

"Accomplishments are made by people who have hope despite having no reason to."

"Alright, Eckhart." I scoffed in my throat.

"How do you even know who Eckhart is?"

I shrugged. "Silliah. She loves all that old clart."

"Anyway, I didn't quote anybody, but if I did, it wasn't Eckhart. He teaches the power of living in the moment, not about having hope."

"So what? He's still a philosopher, isn't he?"

"No."

"Alright, Eckhart." I moved on, leaving him to argue with himself.

"Gah, you are impossible."

Eyes followed us as we entered the hall. A few Musties were crowding our table when we arrived, and I tried to work out what was going on. The white-blond moppy-haired boy immediately stopped talking to Calix when he saw Pax and me.

"Hi, *Smokin' Axe*," he said quickly, hiding something behind his back. It was either that or he was pushing his chest out to show us his *Smokin' Axe* badge pinned to his mustard jumper.

"Hi," I returned. Pax just gave him a nod.

"Their names are Pax and Aurora, you dope." Calix slapped the young boy around the head. "Now, go and take that back to your room. I'm not going to tell you again."

"I just wanted to show it to you," the boy answered, keeping his eyes on us sideways and still holding whatever 'it' was behind his back.

"I've told you, Tan, you're not allowed to bring toys out of your bedroom. I won't buy you any more if you keep breaking the rules."

The boy's arms twitched behind his back. "I-I-I don't play with toys anymore." He trod backwards. All his friends retreated with him. Tan flipped around, whipping his hands in front of him, still trying to hide the item. But I saw it. He was holding an army action figure similar to the one I kicked at Pax when cleaning that Mustard room.

"Can I play with it now?" asked a friend, clinging on to Tan's elbow as they walked away.

Another Musty butted in, "No, it's my turn. Tan, you said it was my turn."

"*Stop it,*" hissed Tan, checking over at us. "Not now."

In a big huddled bundle, the crowd disappeared into the Mustard residential corridors.

"Who was that?" I asked Calix, finally sitting down.

"My little brother."

"I didn't know you had a brother."

"You've never paid attention to anything other than yourself."

My head swerved back as if avoiding a sudden attack. "That was a bit harsh."

"But true," he said, keeping his relaxed blue eyes on mine.

"Yeah," I agreed with a laugh. Up until I was a Navy, I didn't talk to anyone except Silliah. The only time I interacted with Calix was during martial arts training…not exactly the time to bring up siblings. "How old was he when you were enrolled?"

"Newborn. I was seven."

I really wanted to ask what happened, but we weren't allowed to talk about our pasts. He could see I dithered by the way I stared at him nodding constantly.

"My birthmother left when Tan was born," Calix explained, answering the question he knew I wanted to ask. "Turns out my father was terminally ill, so he didn't live long. With no biological parents around to look after us, we were enrolled here. She did us a favour. Could you imagine being a civilian? Erh."

"I couldn't think of anything worse." Hilly joined in. "She could've done that on purpose? You know, so you had a good upbringing."

Calix's blond fringe fell over his eyes as his head declined. "Who cares."

Something told me he cared. I agreed he'd rather be an Enforcer, but nobody forgot a mother's love—he remembered her. I remembered my mum, even after all this time. Feeling a little bad for being the one who brought it up, I changed the subject to TPG.

The mood changed around the table, and we all enjoyed a lively breakfast. Ryker gave survival tips to Brindan, standing up, ducking and swerving as if he avoided Bounty. Crystal did what she did best and grated on my nerves, continually squealing in excitement and not keeping to her seat. Tyga and Calix sat arguing about the best Bounty to leave till last, whilst, obviously, Hilly added in her two cents. Everyone else was overshadowed by the rest of us. Shola and Hyas were always there but barely noticed, whilst Roebeka, Maylene, and Pipila's old gang all had nothing interesting enough to say for anyone to pay them attention.

After Silliah finished putting my hair in a French plait, Brindan, Silliah, Pax, and I left to get ready for the games. We didn't fail to notice the pointless crowd of *Smokin' Axe* badges following us. Fortunately, they couldn't tag along with us any longer and their pursuit ended when we reached the plain white door in the Khakidemy.

"Good luck, *Smokin' Axe*," several voices called out as we slipped through the door.

"You're popular today," said Brindan, leading the way down the dark, narrow corridor, Silliah tucked under his arm. "Teaming up with *Sovereign Skill* last time was a smart move."

"I'm feeling the pressure today, though," I said. "What if we don't even get into round two?"

"You've put in a lot of work since the last match," said Pax. "You're more prepared for a TPG than you've ever been."

"Thanks to you." I knocked him sideways into the wall.

He hooked me in and kissed the side of my head. "And besides," he said, "what is it you said to me in the last match? '*We* are good.' Remember?"

"I remember."

We all separated to walk down the metal staircase at the end of the corridor. Downstairs, we once again attracted more eyes in our direction. I spotted an undesirable pair of beetle-black ones, but I didn't bother staring him out this time. Today, I had to be in a good mood to conjure, so I joined Pax into a booth and began to change with only the occasional thought of Beignley.

Not wanting to see Pax bare-chested, I jumped onto my podium straight away, initiating the partition wall between us. I heard Pax laugh to himself, but I told myself to ignore it. The games were more important, and I didn't want to be distracted by him. With our full attention on the upcoming round, we stood a better chance of survival. My nerves were no longer about the incapacitating electric shock as it used to be. Now my belly rolled at the first few moments of the games when Beignley was hell bent on hurting me and I had to use magic in plain sight. It was dangerous and risky and just plain stupid.

Out of the booth in our jet-black picosuits, Pax and I met up with Brindan and Silliah. Our flushed cheeks didn't go unnoticed by Brindan's observant eye.

"What the hell were you two doing in there?" he said, still assessing our faces.

I looked at Pax and smiled. He shook his head, tongue in his cheek. I backed away from him before an arm could cuff me into a headlock.

Silliah reached up to tidy my hair. "Let me guess"—she tucked loose strands behind my ears—"we have another unconventional video loop from you both."

I burst out laughing, and Pax walked away. He wasn't upset; he was just not entertaining the conversation any longer. We all jogged to catch up with him.

"Me and Silliah were thinking of doing warzone with you," Brindan said to Pax. "Go-hard-or-go-home style."

"*Really*?" Pax's high tone was barely heard over the newly beating drums.

"Yeah." Silliah put her knee up on the black sofa, hugging the pillar with one arm. "I really struggled finding my way on the blueprint during the last game, and I think it'll be easier uniting with Brindan on the ground."

"And…go to the warzone instead?" Pax's eyes switched between Brindan and Silliah.

"Maybe we can meet you two there?" Brindan gave a small shrug. "You can help us get out?"

"I like it," I added, joining Silliah on the sofa. "It sounds like fun. Go hard or go home."

Brindan put a hand in the centre of us. "Go hard or go home."

We all placed our hands on top of each other. "Go hard or go home," we echoed, lifting our hands out the middle, and then laughing at ourselves.

The music dipped, and we faced in the direction of Lady Joanne Maxhin. She was standing on a black sofa, facing the forming crowd. Pax's fingers slipped into mine. I stood frozen, concentrating on his warm, gentle touch, his wide knuckles filling mine.

"*Are we ready, Youngens?*" A real grit distorted Lady Maxhin's voice. Equal responses were given as fists pumped the air, animal sounds were hollered, and my ear drums split from people who could whistle on their fingers. "We're in for an interesting game," she said, her eyes briefly falling on Pax and me. Under the weight of her expectant gaze, my stomach knotted up, and I felt like I'd grown taller than the crowd. "On this game," she continued, "I want to see more of you tackling the warzone; I want less of you around the edges; I want less walking and more running; and I especially want to see more tricks, more front flips, and more daring moves. This is the Parkour Games, guys. Give 'em something to talk about."

With the noise of the mob transcending the sound of her voice, Lady Maxhin front-flipped off the sofa. "*Serve, Honour, Protect, and Defend.*" She held a fist over her heart and jogged the crowd into the next room.

Pax's fingers squeezed mine as we marched along with the crowd. The music didn't help the feeling that I was heading to my death. It built up tempo, screeching with violins and thundering with drums until I was almost expecting the climax to unfold before my eyes. But the climax was us; the battle was us; my opponents were them.

I slid my fingers out of Pax's to reach into the velvety black pouch being held open by Lady Maxhin. Pax joined me, and we pulled out our tokens together.

My original purple token engraved with: The Parkour Games, June, 2120.

I dropped the token back in the bag. Pax gave me a strong nod with a determined smile. I headed for my cage, a mixture of nerves and excitement clashing around inside me. Silliah pulled out a purple token, and I rushed to the door to greet her. She hurried down the illuminated runway into my cage and caught my high-five. Then we waited, facing the back of the cage, watching to see who else was coming in to join us.

Things only got better when Crystal pulled out a yellow. They got slightly worse when she linked arms with Pax and Brindan, but then they got better again when Romilly pulled out a purple, leaving Beignley in the other cage. I didn't underestimate Romilly; she could hurt me just as much if I was immobilised. But that being said, it was nice not being tormented the whole way into my capsule. I enjoyed my respite, arm in arm with Silliah, watching the last few tokens being drawn. A muttering started once we were all divided.

Do you want to eliminate Unholy Reign again? Saulwyn's calming voice infiltrated my mind.

I smiled down at my black trainers. *Hell yeah!*

We will see what we can do. See you in there.

The music drowned everything out.

Strobe lighting made the air raid siren dizzying, the rise and fall in pitch fragmenting my brain. The prolonged whining high tones stretched my nerve endings like they were hung on strings. I held out, feeling myself squinting through the sinister flashes, the cruel repetition, and the persistent vibration until the noise built to a crescendo. It was psychologically demanding and enough to send anyone over the edge. But I assumed that was what they wanted; they wanted us riled up like animals, unable to think for ourselves, our minds on the hunt.

Smoke poured from the archways before the cage doors burst open with a loud, resounding clang. Silliah jumped on the spot. She held my hand, and my arm swung like a rope. Despite only being a reach in front of me, she disappeared around the dense fog. The crowd spaced out as everyone pressed on into the archway to find their pods.

"I will fight. I will fall," Silliah was chanting. "I WILL FIGHT. I WILL FALL. AND FOR YOU I'LL DO IT ALL." She sprang in the air with every sentence, turning to engage with me whilst beaming from ear to ear.

I smiled and began chanting the second verse with her, but my energy was not in the song. It was spent searching the names above our pods. Silliah released my hand and hugged me. "See you in there," she said, stopping outside my pod. I was surprised to see my neighbours did not belong to Romilly Windsor, Laucey Astor, Boyd Livingston, or any of Beignley's accomplices. Just maybe they'd given up? They had to have figured out by now it was pointless trying to attack me, pointless now they knew I had someone on the inside, too.

"You must be up ahead," I said to Silliah, "which means you'll be coming into the warzone on my left. Pax will be on your right, and Brindan will be on my right. Run to whoever is nearest when you enter, okay?"

"Okay," Silliah replied, her face dropping. "You on my right; Pax on my left. Got it." She looked as if she'd reassured herself, and her naturally cheerful demeanour returned. "Good luck." She jumped to reach my high-five.

I readied myself in my pitch-black pod, feeling the ground move beneath my feet and listening to the whirring of the lift as I waited to see if my suit would emit any unusual light. The lack of activity could mean Tayo was keeping the hackers out or quite possibly that Beignley really had given up. My belly lifted at the pod coming to a swift stop.

A male voice counted us into the arena. "Five, four, three, two, one."

With my suit still black, my entrance into the arena was easy. *Run*, I reminded myself. But then I hopped to a stop mid-way up my corridor, my trainers gaining friction on the textured rubber floor. My camera hadn't followed me out of my pod. Theodred said the cameras only started malfunctioning when *Unholy Reign* united, which meant they used the absence of cameras to cheat in some way. What were they up to now? Not wanting to hang around to find out, I sprang off again. Silliah and Brindan depended on me being quick to the warzone.

Checking my blueprint to plan my route, I saw Pax's dot making a healthy advance on the warzone. He was rapid, wasting no time at all. I sped up, squeezing through narrow corridors with towering black walls, and passing, left and right, through confusing short ones, all the while, checking my blueprint, making sure I didn't take a wrong turn.

A five-note victory tune sounded, but I knew I wasn't far behind *Sovereign Skill*. I'd made a great start this time, only wasting seconds when my camera didn't follow me out of my pod. I hit the warzone and saw Pax across the clearing. We were second to arrive after *Sovereign Skill*, who were making their swift exit as practised. They belted in my direction, and I braced, fists clenched. Theodred held out a high-five, but I backed away from it. He was united, so touching his hand would mean an embarrassing early end to my game. Giving a chuckle, he pulled back his hand, running behind Saulwyn and using my alley to exit.

Pax pointed to his right, indicating for us to meet where Silliah would be entering the warzone. She was likely to be later than Brindan, since she couldn't navigate the arena well, and it meant Brindan could start making his way in our direction as we protected Silliah.

People were bursting through the warzone as we ran to meet each other. These opponents hadn't united yet, so we didn't pose a threat to each other, but they still reacted as if the sight of me gave them an electric shock. One guy entered directly in front of me, and even though I couldn't eliminate him because I hadn't united, I pretended to anyway, and it sent him tripping over his own feet, skidding across the floor.

A melody of victory tunes turned into a wave of elimination drones. Instantly, Bounty discharged in all directions. Some clever person let off *The Red Queen* in the middle of the warzone, and the drones sang out in an endless note. The red laser closed in on me diagonally. I came away from the wall to clear it, but now it went for Pax at an even worse angle. He knew to come away from the wall, too, giving him space. Hurdling over the laser and dropping into a forward roll, he finished in a crouched position as a second beam passed over his head. As it came at me, I copied his forward roll, standing up after it cleared my head.

Everyone who stayed alive anticipated the second laser, but now we were all in grave danger. This second beam was moments away from turning into an impossible grid swarming the entire warzone, annihilating anyone left.

"Sweetheart," Pax greeted me, panting, but had a radiant glow on his face. "We gotta go." He snatched my hand, sending a swirling golden ribbon around our wrists. Our victory tune played, and he led me out of the warzone. "It shouldn't get us here." Pax checked towards the warzone. "With the angle it was at, it should end there. We're safe here."

"It's not looking good for Brindan and Silliah."

"No." Pax's cheeks flinched. "They won't know about *The Red Queen*. It's bound to get one of them."

I touched Pax's chest to stop him speaking. Footsteps were thundering down the joining corridor, and they were close to passing ours. If I timed it right, I could get our first Bounty reward. I pressed my back to the wall, guiding Pax to do the same. The guy saw me out of the corner of his eye and swung his hand up. But I touched him first. The drone marked the end of their game, and a red Bounty ring travelled our biceps.

"Well done, sweetheart." Pax reached for my hand, turning our red rings into golden halos.

"Oh, nice," I said after checking my inventory. "I got the new one: *The Grass Isn't Greener.*"

"We should get an easy elimination with that. I've got *The Root of all Evil.*"

I laughed. "Save that one for Crystal, yeah?"

"Oh yeah," he said, remembering the Bounty I'd used to eliminate Crystal in the last game. "Maybe you can at least wait for her to unite with Boyd this time."

"Not a chance. It's survival of the fittest. If I see her, she's taking a nap."

Pax rolled his eyes, but he knew I was right. He checked back up towards the warzone, watching the red grid swarm our corridor, narrowly missing our safe place. "Come on." He headed back to the centre. "Let's go check for the others."

When we re-entered the warzone, *The Red Queen* was gone, but she had left devastation in her wake. Lifeless bodies littered the glossy black floor, the most I'd ever seen at once. Silently scanning the scene, we dealt with the disturbing remnants of battle. We stepped over limbs, between body parts, and around bodies, looking for the outlines of Silliah and Brindan.

After no sign of Silliah, we crossed the warzone to where Brindan was likely to be. We soon spotted his freckled face, unconscious and pale. He'd managed to make it halfway across the warzone but (odds suggested) he was met in the back by *The Red Queen*. Poor Silliah would've met the same fate as soon as Brindan was hit.

I checked their video loop playing in red on the arena outskirts. They stood in each other's arms, smiles brightening their eyes, not really doing anything to show off in their loop, just standing still as if waiting for a photo to be taken. It was able to bring a small smile to my lips even though I felt sad for them. They hadn't even managed to unite this time.

Pax snorting in his throat pulled me from my thoughts. He was shaking his head at our video loop. Many of the loops once again copied ours from the last game and most had only the boys in front of the cameras as the girls circled around them, but ours was different this time. I'd like to see people copy this one. As we filmed ours, Pax took my proffered hand, and I threw him with a wrist throw so he was no longer in the shot; it was just me standing there…until I was yanked to the floor by Pax's reaching hand. The rest of our loop was empty. I *loved* it.

Thanks to the clever person who let off *The Red Queen* in the warzone, round one was easy and uneventful. I found the spinning robot, Nomax, on our journey, and with hardly anyone in the arena to interrupt us, Pax dared me to reprogram it. Naturally, I took on the challenge, and I jumped over the robot's laser arms with ease, until it overheated and turned off. After I touched his handprint, Nomax began rebooting, switching on with golden lasers. Pax and I made a safe exit in case its lasers could still eliminate us. But just when we passed out of Nomax's reach, the room descended into total darkness. Chills rushed my neck.

CHAPTER THIRTY

THE RAT RACE

A black-sleeved arm reached through the darkness and cuffed my throat, dragging my frozen suit onto a hover device.

"Hello, again." The hooded keeper breathed into my ear.

"Oh, let me guess, Beignley can't win without cheating, so he's ordered you to sabotage me again."

"Those electric shocks have clearly killed what little brain cells you had left. You are *defenceless*. How can you think you're in a position to speak? Are you stupid or do you just enjoy pain?"

"Are you completely spineless or do you just enjoy hurting people when they can't fight back?"

The masked figure held my shoulder, coming to stand in front of me. "Know when to shut up." He drove his fist into my stomach. A grunt forced its way out as my diaphragm threw all the air from my lungs. I couldn't double over even though every muscle in my belly collapsed into itself. Before I could catch my breath, his fist impaled my stomach again. The same grunt pushed up from its depths. I felt saliva hit the roof of my mouth, and I spat it at his feet. His gloved knuckles struck the side of my face. I tasted blood from my smooth, metallic lip. Clamping my teeth on it, I panted, trying to control my reaction.

"So you're not stupid." He held around my neck again as the board took us through the clearing arena. "You do know when to shut up."

"I dare you to try that when I'm not restrained."

"Oh, I was wrong. You really are that stupid." He dragged me off the board into a small box room. The ice-blue glow from the institute logos highlighted his featureless mask. I stood, held hostage by my suit's red prison, glaring at the mask. He removed a needle from inside his hooded jacket. Holding it upright, he squirted clear liquid before bringing it to my neck. The icy metal pierced my burning flesh, and wooziness rippled in from the neck up.

The shadowy figure took something from his back pocket, using it to remove my suit's imprisonment. My body swayed, and I trod back to keep my balance.

"Come on, then." He advanced on my unsteady body. "You dared me to try again once you were free." Four of his masks floated past my face. "I'll let you take the first hit."

I tried to focus on one of them.

"HIT ME THEN." He shoved me into the back wall, swinging his foot round with speed. Pain exploded in my jaw.

꧁꧂

When I regained consciousness, my jaw throbbed to the rhythm of the pulsing room. Blue institute logos rode invisible waves backwards and forwards, sending my breakfast swashing. Vomit burst through my lips until chewed-up lumps turned into froth and nothing but violent retching ripped at my insides.

Happy place, Aurora, my mind told me through the static in my head. *Happy place, now.* Hazy thoughts of Tayo filtered into my mind. Water dripped from his fringe whilst the shower poured around us. His soaked lips glistened under the stream. "Will you punch me in the mouth?" I heard his deep voice carrying under the downpour. The beautiful smile on his face told me everything was okay.

Now he was in his cell, sitting on the spare chair, drawing a sketch at the counter. My mind focused on his capable hands. They were strong and masculine with subtle veins and neatly trimmed nails. I couldn't help but admire the way they moved with precision, clearly skilled at what he was doing. He lifted to his feet, placing a gentle hand on my cheek and pressing his forehead to mine. "I'm waiting for you here," he whispered. "You've got this." I felt his spirit transcending his core, merging in harmony with my soul. Calmness lifted my chest, and I could sense my power rising. *Spella Tair.*

The spell targeted my mind first, clearing the disorientation and stopping the tormenting parade of institute logos. They set back on the walls, no longer pulsing and floating on psychedelic waves. With my head clear, immense pain filled my entire face, and I felt like a weight hung off my chin. I cradled my jaw. Despite the sharpness, I cupped it, feeling it but not recognising its shape. My jaw was unmistakably broken.

Unable to say the incantation out loud, I willed my hand to take away the pain. I closed my eyes and repeated *Tepior* in my mind. I held my chin tighter, closing my eyes harder. *Please heal. Please heal,* I asked the sacred power inside me. I imagined the magic working, my jaw mending, the pain gone, everything back to normal. I envisioned it fully. *Come on, please.*

As I closed my eyes, I could see Pax standing on the panel in the temple. The image of him was so vivid that it was as though I watched a film. The sweet music filled my being, soothing my heart. I saw the look on Pax's face as he listened, face to the sky, feeling love branded on his soul. This feeling travelled down my arm, and my mind transported me to the Banquet Hall. I stared into Pax's eyes as he held out his hand, inviting me to dance. The room around us faded away, and it was as if nothing else existed but the two of us, moving together in the darkness.

I gasped as if surfacing above water. The pain vanished, and my chin felt familiar again, but I hadn't noticed the healing or the magic. Before I could fully appreciate the relief from the immense throbbing, the door to my box opened, giving me access to my pod. I rushed for it, tripping over and crawling the rest of the way. Falling was probably for the best in case cameras caught me, alerting Beignley's accomplices that I recovered too quickly.

I braced in my pod, preparing for what was to come, waiting as an anxious jogging claimed my foot. *You got this. You got this. You got this. Just be quick, whatever it is.*

My enclosure rumbled, lifting me through the arena until light flooded my pod. I raised my hand to shadow my eyes, stepping into the light. My senses sharpened on the scene. All my purple token opponents were in a row, showcased in transparent boxes, pacing in their confines like tigers coming out to feed. We swapped glances, summing up our competition. I had Saulwyn a few pods down on my right, and Thorn a few down to my left. My direct neighbour— Romilly, Beignley's betrothed.

Saulwyn and Romilly had the advantage of reaching this round consecutive years. They'd figured out its secrets many times and knew what to expect. I ignored Romilly pacing in my periphery and focused my energy on figuring out this round. In front of me, I had a long, enclosed platform leading to another transparent box. That was all we had—nothing more, nothing less.

Beep, beep, beep. A commanding noise counted us in.

Our cage doors lifted. Everyone set off racing down their platforms. The material under my feet was springy and familiar. I drove my toes down forcefully, concentrating on reaching the box at the end. Thorn was faster than us all, taking a clear lead. I tailed shortly behind Saulwyn. Everyone pelted for their boxes. With no room for sabotage or cheating, and no skill required, we had only our own speed.

Beep, beep, beep.

"Ouch!" I hopped from stinging in my feet. Jagged ovals scattered my platform. The cries from everyone experiencing the same torture as me made my stomach turn. We were running over sharp splinters, trapped in an enclosure with nowhere to go, no safe place, no escape from the cutting pain.

A mechanical noise shook the ground beneath us. The platform began revolving to the start. We were on conveyor belts, and I instantly recognised its adjustable components. It was the Cityline, the machine Saulwyn coached me on a little while ago. No sooner had the familiarity been noted than a knee-high hurdle came at me.

Thorn, being closer to the finish, was caught off-guard, tripping over the hurdle and hitting the belt face first. He was dragged back, way behind Saulwyn and me. Being nimble, Romilly scaled the hurdle expertly. Opponents were screaming and failing and running and tripping and falling all over this stretch of the arena. It was disturbing chaos.

Beep, beep, beep. I anticipated a new Bounty just like the white ovals, but nothing appeared. Instead, the ovals vanished, and the conveyor belt reset to being completely flat. Panting and tired, I raced for the end, realising we were all best to have just remained in our pods until the fiasco passed. At which point, I noticed Saulwyn had stopped, allowing the belt to drag her to the start. Was she giving up? Surely not.

She was catching her breath, and I couldn't help but trust her judgement. I stopped with her. *What am I doing?* All eight opponents were racing ahead of me, Romilly in the lead. *Should I run? Why am I just standing here?* Coming level with Saulwyn, I heard her voice in my mind, cutting in and out like receiving a phone call with poor signal. She wasn't communicating with me.

Theodred, it's—let it—

I listened harder, concentrating with intent.

—and they will all fail. We will be the first over it.

The first over it? The first over what?

—I think Aurora knows. She's stopped too. She must've remembered the sequence from Cityline.

She was talking about the machine in the Khakidemy, the one she trained me on. Before I'd figured it out, Saulwyn began racing up her platform. She ran with might and determination. Then I saw it.

A nine-foot wall assembled out of the conveyor belt. The barricade blocked the exit for the eight sprinting opponents. None of them had enough room to run up it, and they were being dragged back to the start, hopping and reaching desperately for the top. Not even Thorn could reach.

Thanks to Saulwyn, I had my breath back, I had the space, and now I had the speed. My fingers latched onto the top, and I jumped over it. Saulwyn and I entered our finishing boxes. The door dropped down, trapping us in our transparent confines.

Nothing else happened, so I watched Saulwyn. She was also trying to work out what we were supposed to do. I touched the walls. Three were clear, but the one at the back, the one I assumed backed onto Pax's finishing box, had a gold film. It had to be that one. The floor was solid black, the walls were clear, nothing showed on them, and the ceiling was out of reach. It had to be the gold wall.

"Aurora, are you in there?" My heart skipped hearing Pax's distant voice. "Aurora?"

I searched the walls for the direction of the muffled sound. "Pax?"

"Good, you're there."

Seeing a circle of tiny pin-prick holes in the golden wall. I placed my hands on the glass and held my ear over the holes. "You got over the wall?"

"Yeah." I heard him better now. "I copied Theodred. He stopped running—" Before Pax finished, the golden film dissolved, and the bottom dropped out of our confines. We began free-falling through the arena. The edge of a clear funnel caught us, sending us soaring towards the centre. Wind rushed our hair, and Pax snatched my hand. As our victory tune sang its little five-note song, we fell through the centre of the funnel, falling through the air again. His fingers squeezed tighter as the ground drew nearer.

"Lift your legs up," Pax shouted over the rush of wind.

I copied him, lifting my legs into my chest, bracing for impact. We struck the ground together, vaulting back into the air.

"Now, break your fall." Pax sent his feet down to land.

We bounced together again and again before we slowly bobbed to a stop.

"We're the first out," I said, wrapping my arms around his neck.

"Well done, sweetheart. They're too busy...you know"—Pax touched my head—"to figure out what to do."

I pulled back, nodding. He was talking about Saulwyn and Theodred. They were too busy talking in their minds to notice the holes in the wall. If I hadn't heard Pax's voice, I wouldn't have put my ear to the wall, accidentally placing both hands on the glass. "It's like the booth door?" I asked.

"Yeah," said Pax, looking up the funnel where we just arrived. "It was waiting for both our hands to make contact on the—watch out!" He pulled me out the way of two falling bodies. *Sovereign Skill* had finally figured out the boxes and were second to fall into the arena. "Aurora, just before they hit the ground, jump, okay?"

"Okay." I prepared myself, bending my knees.

"We can send them back in the air if we jump, and we will have a better chance of eliminating them. Stay away from their hands."

"Wait," yelled Theodred, plummeting towards us, his neat blond hair being mussed by the breeze. "We can help you eliminate *Unholy Reign.*"

I looked at Pax, waiting for him to make the decision. Just before the duo hit the elastic ground, we jumped together, sending the pair straight back up. I re-positioned myself as they scrambled in the air, turning to protect themselves. They fell out of sync, so a double-bounce wouldn't work again.

It was now or never.

"I don't think so," said Pax, slapping Theodred's ankle before he hit the floor. "Every man for themselves in round two."

The formidable pair instantly rigidified and shuddered in a painful display. I watched their bodies wriggle and writhe until they bounced lifelessly. Then I jumped on the bouncy platform and landed on Pax, sending him to the ground. "*We did it*," I shouted, shaking Pax by the shoulders. "We actually did it. Well, *you* did it."

Pax laughed. "*We* did it." He grabbed me by the wrists and stared purposefully into my eyes, allowing his words to convey. "Now, come on." He let go of my wrists and patted my leg. "Let's move their bodies out of the way and try that again. We won't have long."

When we climbed to our feet, I noticed the room. It wasn't set up as I was expecting and was pretty flat, considering it was the Parkour Games. A grid of square stepping stones, all different sizes and heights, bordered the large bouncy platform. Down below, the ground flashed red. I didn't want to find out what happened if we fell down there, but Pax didn't mind finding out what'd happen to *Sovereign Skill*. He instructed me to let go as he lowered them down between the square pillars.

"Safer for them down there." He dropped Theodred down feet first. "They could be trampled up here." Two bodies safely off the obstacles, Pax headed back to the centre. "What Bounty did you get?"

"*Slightsaber*," I answered. "That's the laser bar one, isn't it?"

"Yeah. It's not bad, but it only has a limited reach. I've got *Don't Count your Chickens*. Not the best again but good for round two when every Bounty counts. Okay." He bounced in preparation, gearing himself up for another victory. "Let's see who's next."

Eliminating the second team was as easy as the first, and we sent them back up into the air with a double-bounce. I had a clear pass to the girl's leg, even though she tried kicking me in the face. The second elimination drone rocked the arena, and another Bounty ring celebrated around our biceps. "Nice work." Pax high-fived me, turning the second ring golden. Before we had a chance to check our inventory, another couple were on their way down the funnel. I readied myself for our third elimination, only for a drone to sound. The falling pair were already unconscious, sliding down the funnel with another team who stole our kill.

"Oh, clart," said Pax, containing the swear word within. "Come on, I don't like our odds." He pulled me away.

It was *Unholy Reign*, and they had Bounty. And it wasn't just them we had to be cautious of. Everyone had obviously copied each other to escape their boxes, and they were dropping through the funnel in a swarm. Victory tunes and drones relayed bloodshed as bodies fell out of the sky en masse. Romilly landed graciously, bouncing and back-flipping away from the massacre. Beignley managed a similar stunt, and now they were away, preferring their odds of avoiding the centre, too.

Just four teams remaining, we watched from the outskirts, considering our next move. Celeste and Thorn fought in a head-to-head battle with another team. Celeste used the bouncy surface to jump way above their heads. Thorn gave her a double-bounce, and she front-flipped over her opponents, landing with an eliminating strike. A drone rang out.

Beep, beep, beep. The springy ground beneath our feet started flashing red like *Sovereign Skill's* resting place. Only three couples left in the competition, we all ran for the square stepping stones. "Quickly." Pax helped me to safety.

The stone under my feet immediately flashed red. I jumped over the short gap to another. It, too, flashed red. The triggered stepping stones kept us jumping from platform to platform, not allowing us time to think.

A drone made me flinch.

Looking back, I saw Celeste and Thorn lying on the platform after not making it off in time for the red floor to consume them. Pax changed direction so fast that adrenaline told me we were close to being executed. I checked around, seeing no one. Only when my fight or flight settled did I see it. Pax ran for two Bounty rings bobbing idly above Celeste and Thorn's bodies. He dashed towards them with all he had…but he wasn't the only one.

Unholy Reign had changed direction, too. We were running from opposite sides, charging recklessly towards the reward. Pax reached the platform, launching into a forward roll and firing *Don't Count Your Chickens* at Romilly. Her Bounty ring pinged off her bicep, breaking up and dissolving. Pax finished his roll, snagging the two idle Bounty rings.

Beignley changed direction, coming for me.

He was low, sprinting fast, his black eyes shadowed with hatred. Pax fired his last activated Bounty at Beignley. It was a red knife, the Bounty which cut the victims sight and sound. Beignley would be cocooned in emptiness, hearing nothing and seeing no one. It would be an easy win for me.

But before he was struck in the back, Beignley fired *Throwzone* on the ground. This Bounty caused the ground to be slick like ice, making the victim fall over, but Beignley wasn't using it on me. He used it to slick the ground *beside* me. Beignley was quick, and before I worked out his move, he threw himself down on the slippery surface, skidding on his side towards my legs. He reached for my ankle. I threw my legs up over my head in a no-handed cartwheel. Upside down in mid-air, I withdrew my Bounty. The laser bar extended out into Beignley's path. He couldn't stop sliding towards it. He extended up to touch my head. His fingers skimmed my hair. My Bounty sliced through his body. A drone boomed.

I landed back on my feet.

Starting from my hands, my black picosuit evolved into golden armour. Like a shockwave, the gold snuffed out the black until my entire suit sparkled. A wordless music rang out in the arena louder than my ears were prepared for. Seeing the convulsing body of Beignley, I realised I'd actually done it.

Stood frozen, I found Pax's shining amber eyes. He tilted his head, beckoning me. Finding my legs, I ran to him, jumping on the springy surface to wrap my legs around him. He caught me and spun me around as our lips met. An image of him in a navy-blue suit burst through the darkness behind my eyelids. He had a short beard and fine wrinkles around his almond-shaped eyes. They were concentrated on mine, and I felt myself falling deeper and deeper into their depths until I returned to the darkness. I pulled back, smiling timidly and dropping my feet to the floor. "We did it," I said through the golden confetti party raining down on us.

"You did it," he said, adoration gleaming in his eyes.

I broke his gaze to take one last look at *Unholy Reign*. "*We* did it."

The cameras from everyone's befallen bodies rose up and circled around us. Pax wrapped his arm around my shoulder. The outskirts of the arena replayed our victory, our current live recording, and a montage of all clips from our Promises Ceremony to our in-game footage. From a hundred to two, we were the winners of the Parkour Games 2120.

CHAPTER THIRTY-ONE

STOP RUNNING

Putting on my socks, I thought about seeing *Sovereign Skill* for the first time since Pax eliminated them. I hoped they would understand. They eliminated us in the last game and said it was every man for themselves in round two. *It'll be fine.*

Pax was next door having a shower before we met up for our celebratory dinner. The shock still hadn't worn off. We had won the Parkour Games—*Pax and I.* It felt so surreal. Nobody other than *Sovereign Skill* and *Unholy Reign* had won in the last nine years.

A noise by the wardrobe made me turn. I discarded the sock in my hand to greet him.

"We won, Tayo. We actually won." I threw him a high-five. "Can you believe it?"

He took my fingers and gave them a weak squeeze. "Well done, baby girl."

"What's the matter?" I asked, noticing a withdrawn tone to his voice.

"Nothing." He walked past me.

"What? What is it?" Every muscle in his face told me something was wrong. The tone of his voice, his mannerism, this wasn't *my* Tayo. He was being the boy I'd seen once before, the boy who walked out on me and told me to tell Pax I chose him. The familiarity made a nervous energy flitter in my heart. "Tayo?"

"Nothing, Roar." He exhaled, standing in the middle of the room.

"Tayo," I said, feeling everything tightening.

"You kissed him, Roar." He swallowed and lifted his eyes off the floor.

My voice got caught in my subtle gasp. The flitter in my heart grew in waves throughout my entire chest. "It didn't mean anything, Tayo."

Tayo didn't speak. He kept his eyes on mine, but they were impenetrable.

"I promise you. I haven't chosen him. I haven't chosen anyone."

"That's the problem, Aurora. I just can't help but feel that if I left you alone, you would choose him."

My heart pounded painfully. This was all way too familiar. I couldn't go through it again. "You're wrong, Tayo. I'm not choosing either of you, and I don't want to lose either of you. Don't do this to me again. You don't want to be without me just as much as I don't want to be without you."

He nodded, his sad eyes softening. I felt safer to touch him without him backing off. "I don't choose him, okay?" I took his hand and squeezed it under my chin.

"Okay." He pulled his hand away, but he hooked it around my shoulder, easing me into him.

Relief washed over my heart. I wasn't losing him again. "Look"—I rubbed my face across his chest, soaking him up before stepping back—"I've got to go to dinner now, but come back after, please?"

A tiny smile lifted his lips. It wasn't smirky or arrogant, just genuine and relieved.

"Will you come back?" I asked again, wanting to know I'd see him again tonight.

"Alright."

"Alright," I repeated, ready to leave and backing away to Pax's door.

"Roar," he called before I pressed the access button. "If Pax wasn't in the picture, would you choose me?"

I narrowed my eyes at him, unsure of what he was thinking.

"I'm not planning anything. I just want to know."

I pressed the access button. "I did once, didn't I?"

Tayo smiled and nodded.

Pax gave me a perplexed look when I entered his room. He turned his palm up to the ceiling and gestured at my feet.

"Oh." I laughed, looking at my single sockless foot.

"Get distracted, did you?"

I ran back into my bedroom for my sock, and then we left for dinner. Leaving his room, I couldn't see a step in front of me. People were everywhere. Our arrival triggered the chanting of 'Smokin' Axe', and Pax and I both struggled to navigate our way through the swarm. Poor Juvies were caught up in the celebration, and they nervously tried to keep out of the way, cautious not to bump any Enforcers' shoulders or step on any toes.

Hands were being thrown in our faces for high-fives, and I tried to meet as many as I could, whilst flinching and shying away from elbows and arms. Pax's fingers slipped in mine, and I felt slightly better about the jostling of my body. Pax's personal space was being invaded, too; I wasn't in this alone. How did *Sovereign Skill* put up with this?

"—Congratulations, *Smokin' A*—"

"—*Smokin' Axe. Smokin' Axe. Smokin' Axe*—"

"—Good game, *Smokin' Axe*—"

"—Aurora, you were awe—"

"—You've always been my favourite, *Smok*—"

"—Paxton, can we have a pho—"

"—Aviary. No—"

Everyone spoke over each other, and I couldn't make sense of anything. My body was being pushed and shoved by the excited crowd. I lost my footing and ripped my hand from Pax's to break my fall. A Kalmayan Juvie fell on top of me, and boots trod on my fingers as more bodies fell on top of us. I struggled to breathe under the weight of them.

"GIVE US SOME SPACE," yelled Pax, causing the crowd around us to stop chanting. He held the crowd back, giving us all a chance to untangle ourselves and get back on our feet.

The Kalmayan Juvie offered her hand to help me.

"Do *not* touch her," Pax ordered the Juvie, helping me to my feet instead. "You're lucky I don't extend your sentence. Get out of here." He blocked the Juvie out of his sight and turned to me. "Are you alright?"

"Yeah." I held my pink fingers up to him.

He wiped the blood from a graze on my knuckle and stroked the folds of skin back the right way. Putting his arm around me, he guarded me from all the nudges and bumps.

Our entrance into the hall was met with cheering and applause. Everyone was there to greet us, and my eyes passed over the sea of eyes: Nanny Kimly, Seioh Jennson, Lady Maxhin, Celeste, Thorn, Saulwyn, Theodred, Ryker, Shola, Hyas, Tyga, Hilly, and Calix. They all cheered as they stared devotedly at us. The greeting made Pax and me smile. There was a time in my life when I didn't want any friends, and I thought I wanted to go through life alone. But now I was standing there, seeing their proud faces and feeling emotional. I wouldn't be without them now.

The clapping didn't cease, and Pax and I shared a laugh before smiling back round at everyone.

"Congratulations, guys." Lady Joanne Maxhin came to shake our hands. "You deserve this moment. Enjoy it."

"Okay, Navies." Seioh Jennson silenced the crowd. "Enjoy tonight's celebration, but leave the victors to dine in peace. Remember lights-out at twenty-three hundred hours. I don't want to see anyone wandering the corridors after lights out. We still have our responsibilities and duties. Congratulations, Mr. Fortis, Miss Aviary. You played well. *Serve, Honour, Protect, and Defend.*"

"*Serve, Honour, Protect, and Defend,*" everyone repeated, holding a fist to their hearts.

Seioh Jennson waited for the crowd to disperse, ensuring we were left to eat in peace, and then he headed to his office.

We had a bombardment of praise from our friends when we reached our table. It was pleasant, though, and not like the commotion in the corridor. We hugged in a bundle, Pax and me in the centre, all reaching our arms around each other whilst our heads burrowed into one another's shoulders.

Celeste, Thorn, Saulwyn, and Theodred joined our table despite being separated last time.

"Are we sharing?" asked Saulwyn, checking Seioh Jennson couldn't be seen down the corridor. "Does anyone want nachos?"

I shrugged, not entirely sure what nachos were, but Pax nodded. It was nice to see *Sovereign Skill* hadn't taken the loss badly. But as soon as Pax and I answered, we exchanged puzzled looks. "Where's Brindan and Silliah?" Pax asked the table, both of us diving into our pockets for our Slates.

I had a message from Silliah: '*I'm so sorry. I don't want to ruin your celebration. Come see me after dinner.*'

Yeah, right. As if that was going to happen. Now I was worried, and there was no way I could eat.

"They told us not to tell you," Ryker answered Pax. "They didn't want to ruin the evening."

"What's up with them?" I asked, getting ready to stand.

"Wait, wait, wait." Pax put his hand up to stop Ryker speaking. He also put his arm across me to stop me from getting up. "Don't say anything," he said to Ryker. "Aurora, sit down and eat first. We will see them after, okay? If they've asked these guys to keep quiet, then they're fine. You need to eat."

I glanced at all the still faces fascinated by our discussion.

Pax, I can't. Let me go.

"Please eat?"

Again, I sat silenced by the interested ears. "Fine." I huffed, choosing food I could share with everyone.

The table understood why we had to leave the celebration early, and they didn't make a fuss. Pax arranged for two lattes and two peppermint hot chocolates to take with us, and we headed straight to 440.

"I'm so sorry." Silliah burst into tears when we walked into her room.

"Hey." I immediately dumped our drinks on the bedside table and wrapped my arms around her. "What's happened?"

Silliah sobbed in my arms as the boys stood on the outskirts. Her body trembled in my arms, and I tucked her head tightly under my chin. Brindan nodded to Pax, and they left the room, closing the interconnecting door behind them. My eyes began to well up for my best friend.

"What's happened, Silliah?" I asked again, needing to know.

Silliah pulled back and gingerly leant against her pillow. She winced and held onto her stomach. *Oh my God, no. Was she pregnant?*

"I don't know what I did," she spoke through her sobs. "I don't know what I did to them."

Okay, not pregnant.

I'd never seen Silliah like this. She was my little ray of light. Even if she had no reason to, she would still look for the good in every situation. But now her face was almost purple with agony. I crawled up beside her and held on to her head, allowing her to cry. Her body still trembled even after the sobbing settled.

"What happened, Silliah?"

"They beat me up"—she snivelled, her breathing ragged—"and I don't know why."

My brain instantly drew an image in my head. "No, they fucking didn't."

"I don't know what I did, Aurora." Silliah hid her red face in her hands, more sobs consuming her.

Not Silliah. My eyes filled with tears. *Not Silliah.* She was the sweetest person I knew, always so kind and friends with everyone. This was my fault. *Unholy Reign* were after me.

"You didn't do anything, Silliah."

"All they said was 'stop running'. I don't understand."

"It's me they want, Silliah. They are telling me to stop running. That message is for me."

Silliah lifted her blotchy face from her hands. She sniffed as she settled her tears. "For you?"

"They want me. They've been trying to get me since my very first game. Beignley doesn't like me. They couldn't get me, so they went for you. I'm so sorry."

"They want you? What did you do?"

"Nothing. I knew he had *The Red Queen*, and he accused me of cheating."

"This is not your fault, Aurora. Don't apologise for them. I've been so scared because I didn't do anything to them." Silliah's watery green eyes unfocused. I tried not to listen to her thoughts. "What does that mean for the next game?"

I pinched the pain between my eyes. My head hurt, and I had some thinking to do. I just shook my head. If I ran, Silliah would get beaten up again. If I didn't run, I would get beaten up.

"They broke my pelvis," Silliah added after I didn't speak. "You can't let them get you. I think we need to tell somebody."

"Without any proof, the whole Boulderfell family will turn on us. Seioh Boulderfell won't put up with an accusation slandering his family."

"We are all his family."

"Silliah"—I tipped my head to one side—"we are here to serve him. He couldn't care less about us. He cares about his bloodline, his power, and his protection. We're just bodyguards. Why are Musties sat facing the back of his head during Unity, whilst he faces the grownups who are old enough to protect him? If we're all his children, why are the young ones *ignored*?"

Silliah's puffy red eyes dropped to the duvet.

"They have no toys, no time outside, no love or attention. The only time we can buy our own toys is when we're too old to have them, the only time we go outside is when we're old enough to protect him, and the only time we have the opportunity to feel love is when he forces us into an arranged marriage to populate his city. What about the people who don't match in Unity? When do they get to feel love? They don't. They are encouraged to pledge their devotion to him, take a vow of celibacy and become Fell agents. We are *not* his children."

Her expression grew despondent. "I've never thought of it like that."

"I know you just go with the flow, and I didn't mean to offload on you; I just hate that they've done this to you."

"I'll be fine in a week. Well—I'm on a restricted schedule for a week; it won't actually heal for about twelve weeks. But I'm fine. I was scared because I didn't know what I did."

"You didn't do anything. Does Brindan know you didn't fall?"

"Yes, of course."

I bared my teeth as I grimaced. "Pax doesn't know about me. I didn't want him to worry about me during every game. He's going to be so annoyed that I've lied to him."

Silliah bared her teeth with me, giving a slight inhale. "Are you going to tell him?"

"Not yet. I will. I just need to find the right time."

CHAPTER THIRTY-TWO
A LIE TOO MANY

Tayo and I stayed up till late in the temple. It was nice being just us two. With Silliah being bedbound for a week and Brindan not wanting to leave her, they weren't coming to the temple to practise. Silliah asked if we could practise little things in her room tonight, and that was why Tayo was loitering in my room this morning.

"Tayo, you know you should be gone before the alarm." He followed me into the ensuite walkway. "Nuh-ah." I extended my arm, palm on his bare chest. "You're not watching me shower." Using my body to block him from coming in the ensuite, I slowly unbuttoned my pyjama shirt.

Tayo's eyes didn't lift from my buttons. "It's nothing I ain't seen before."

"You're not watching." I stepped back, undoing my buttons so he could see skin.

"I know what you're doing." He trod a foot in the doorway, stopping the ensuite door from closing. Almost in a trance, he continued to follow my fingers along my buttons.

"Mm." I bit my lip. His intuition must've been going crazy. Turning away, I swept the shirt to the floor. Tayo stepped in the door and brushed my hair off my bare shoulders. I closed my eyes, enjoying the sensation of his lips on my neck and his hot breath on my skin. But as his hand crept towards my waistband, I felt myself

411

losing control. "Go home," I mustered, finally pushing him out and shutting the door.

When I finished in the ensuite, I walked into my room to find him on my bed. "Tayo." I laughed, pleased with myself. "What are you still doing here?"

"Your hair looks nice like that. It's like when we first met."

He was talking about it being mostly white. Although I listened, I didn't respond. I'd slipped on my navy jacket from yesterday and pulled scrunched-up paper from my pocket. We didn't use paper here often, so it must've been Tayo's.

"What is this?" I held it up to him, showing him a symbol which looked like it belonged in the grimoire.

He shrugged and shook his head gently. His beautiful face held me still. Sometimes I'd forget we weren't together anymore, and I'd get an overwhelming urge to show him how I felt. The urge was pleasant, but the reminder I shouldn't touch him was painful. It was like a sharp ache in my chest, reminding me of what I'd lost.

Tayo gave a small sigh with pursed lips. "You can kiss me, you know? I wouldn't tell anybody."

I ran my tongue over my lips at the thought. "Can I kiss you without it meaning I chose you?"

Tayo just nodded once slowly.

"No." The thought of Pax crept in my mind, the guilt I would feel, how hurt he would be. "I can't."

I finished getting ready, pondering whether I could do it and manage my guilt. Unable to contrive a reason why it would be okay, I left giving him a long hug.

That day, Pax didn't come to dinner, so I stopped by Silliah's to find him. I walked into an empty room and turned to check through the interconnecting door.

"She just has everything," Silliah spoke loudly over the shower. "I'm allowed to be a little jealous, aren't I?"

"You've got everything, baby." Brindan's voice had less of an echo, which I took to mean he wasn't in the shower with Silliah. "We are all Enforcers. We are all equal. You're united; she's united. You both have big rooms. You don't need to be jealous of anyone."

"She's just so good at everything."

"It's magic, Lil. She uses magic to be good."

"But even that, she gets to be all six."

Oh, clart. They were talking about me. I turned left and right, deliberating which door I should leave through. Silliah was jealous of *me?*

"And she gets to have Pax and Tayo."

"Silliah, she's *united*; she does *not* get to have Tayo. Stop saying that."

I left through Brindan's bedroom door. *Oh, wow.* How was I supposed to pretend I didn't hear that? I would give Silliah my powers in a heartbeat. I would give anything to go back and be normal, to kiss Pax for the first time all over again and not show. I wished I had what she had: no heartache and a normal relationship. *I'm jealous of* her. She was friends with everyone, she loved the man she was betrothed to, and she didn't have the monumental responsibility of being 'the Guidal'. Silliah didn't realise how lucky she was. Being a Primary was the best of both worlds, still powerful but with no expectations.

I wandered back to my bedroom, wanting to see Pax. He'd know what to say to make me feel better. I pressed the access button and paused at the pitch-black room. The mood lighting from my bedroom cast a dim purple light across the doorway. I almost thought Pax was asleep until I saw him sitting on the sofa.

"Are you okay?" I asked, remembering he didn't come to dinner. I heard a chilling huff.

"Mood lights on, Soami," I told the digital assistant, needing to see him, needing to interpret his face.

Clamping on his lip, he locked eyes with me.

"Pax?" I said, anxiety clawing at my stomach.

He licked his lips before saying, "Who did you sneak out of the institute with last year?"

Oh...

"Who did you sneak out of the institute with?" he asked again, getting to his feet. "Huh? Because it wasn't Silliah."

"Pax—"

"WHO WAS IT?"

I trod backwards, blinking fast. "It was...Tayo."

Pax made a sound as if he held back the f word. Clenching his fists, he turned towards the sofa and then back to me. "I'm done, Aurora. I am *done*. It might be fine for you and him to lie to each other all the time, but it is not fine with me. I am *done*. Go and be happy with Tayo, and just leave me alone."

"I'm so sorry—"

"I don't want to hear it, Aurora." He threw his hand up like he batted away my apology. "Get out. You two are made for each—"

"Pax, stop it," I said through a crack in my voice.

"No. I mean it. I am done with it all. Separate lives, separate houses; I'm good with all that. I'm not playing this game anymore. You're a liar, you deserve each other, and I am DONE. Now, *get out.*"

CHAPTER THIRTY-THREE
NIGHT TERRORS

I found it hard to breathe, my chest crushing my heart after being yelled at by Pax. Pulling out my Slate, I sent two messages. The first to Silliah telling her I was getting an early night and not seeing her to practise tonight, and the second to Tayo: *'I'm not seeing Silliah tonight. Can I see you?'*

'I'm in the temple, gorgeous. Come down.'

'Can we'—I hesitated, thinking how to word my message— *'hang up here? I'm not really in the mood to practise.'*

'I'll be up soon.'

I dried my eyes thoroughly, trying to hide that I'd been crying. Pax's words still cut deep. I'd seen that side of him once before, and I hated it. He was stubborn when his mind was set, so rigid and harsh, completely bereft of his gentle charm. I felt bad for lying to him. But if anything, I could understand now why Tayo kept his secrets from me. You can never find the right time for them to be mad at you, so you just keep it to yourself.

I kept the wardrobe open to wait for Tayo, and I changed into my charcoal pyjamas. Finding that piece of paper in my pocket again, I chucked it in the bin whilst throwing my dirty uniform down the chute. He took longer than I was hoping, and I settled into bed, obsessing over my Slate. My fingers hovered over Tayo's chat, ready to message him again. I couldn't care less about coming on too strong right now. But before I pressed 'send', the panel lifted up, and Tayo's blue eyes filled the space between. I held my arms open for him.

Climbing onto the bed, he crawled over me and nuzzled into my neck. Warmth flooded my heart. Disregarding any guilt for Pax, I immersed myself fully in his attentiveness. I missed my Tayo.

"You've been crying?" he said, taking one look at my face.

"We fell out."

His head anchored towards the adjoining wall, musing at it. Then his eyes drifted back to mine, staring deeply into them. "Do you want to talk about it?"

"No. I want distracting."

He slowly lifted his eyebrows as I allowed him time to feel what I wanted. When he smiled, I knew he knew.

He got to his feet, pulling me up to sit. "I'm an Intuitionist," he said, walking behind me, lowering down, and placing me between his legs. "And a Primary."

I leant against him, but my forehead wrinkled, wondering if he'd gotten the right idea or not.

"I know what you want," he spoke softly into my ear. "Just relax."

My forehead smoothed out, and I watched him readjusting my hands. He placed his hands on top of mine, palms facing the ceiling.

"Say *Lu-el-ila* with me."

"Are you sure you know what I want?" I slanted over so I could see him better.

"I know what you want." He cupped my jaw, rolling my head back and kissing my neck, leaving a trail of delicate kisses to my ear. "Relax." He tightened his legs around me and put his hands back on top of mine. "Ko-kree with me."

I leaned fully against him and held the back of his hands, waiting for his instruction.

"So, we're going to say the ko-kree spell together, and then all I want you to do is conjure the image I have in my head."

"What's the incantation?"

"It's Illusionist magic like you use for your birthmark, but I don't want you focusing on an incantation. Let me do the work, and just allow me to transmit through you. Ready?"

"I guess."

"*Lu-el-ila.*" We cast the ko-kree spell together.

A breeze rushed the room, coming from all angles. It blew my hair around, and I laughed, feeling it whipping in Tayo's face. My laughter made the wind stronger, which in turn made my hair crazier and my laughing more uncontrollable. He tapped my leg with his foot, ducking behind my shoulder to avoid my wayward hair. An image flashed before my eyes. As I concentrated on it, the wind organised itself into a compact vortex and started pushing into our hands. Eventually the room became calm, but our bodies rocked as it turned up and down inside us.

Tayo held me tighter, leaning his chin on my shoulder. "I love that feeling."

"Me too." Feeling a deeper connection to Tayo, I saw the image in his mind clearer. I focused on projecting it, and our bodies stopped rocking as a mini ocean appeared in my palm.

"That's it. Now make it bigger."

My magic usually worked with intent, so I imagined it swarming the entire room. The mini ocean expanded suddenly, making me flinch away from a shoal of yellow fish swimming in front of my face. "Wow." I covered my mouth, watching the extremely detailed illusion. "How do you...?" A turtle appeared from behind me, its spotted legs gliding smoothly through the crystal clear water as it swam over to the door. "How are you giving it so much detail?"

"I have an eidetic memory."

"Wow." I reminded myself to breathe. The light reflected off the back of a dolphin, silvery and bright, barely creating a ripple as it came over. A baby dolphin swam out from under it, catching me with its kind eye. It rested on its mum's back, and I had to blink to stop my eyes from blurring. Tayo was a sweetheart.

The fish dissolved, and we lifted above the water. The ocean became a lake with mountains towering in the distance, their white necklaces glistening in the morning light. A lush, verdant valley stretched out at their feet, and I watched as the rising sun began washing over the peaks.

We kept ascending towards the sky until we were above the clouds, blue turned into black, and wavering crowns of green light danced over the earth's surface.

"It's called Aurora," Tayo whispered. "Aurora borealis."

My chest swelled, and my eyes grew misty from the angel's view of earth. "It's beautiful." Wiping my eyes, I sank deeper into Tayo and pulled his hands under my chin, kissing his fingers. I gazed at the curtain of flickering rays, feeling as though they wrapped around my own heart.

Tayo slid my collar aside and kissed my shoulder. Aurora borealis faded, and a hazy image of my face filled the room. More of my naked body started to appear, so I stopped conjuring his thoughts and turned around between his legs.

※○※

My dreams were filled with the night I shared with Tayo. He was gentle and showed me the tenderness of a perfect man. So deeply enamoured of him, I fell asleep protected in his arms.

Roar, wake up.

I woke to him gently patting my hand.

Roar, make me invisible. Someone's in your room.

My eyes sprang open to the endlessly black room. *Lis Vuluta.* I did as Tayo said and instantly made him disappear. With my skin crawling, I sat up on my elbow.

"Lights on, Soami." I squinted through the sudden rays.

My room was empty. I hopped out of bed to check the ensuite.

"Tayo, you were dreaming." I made him visible again.

"Sorry, Roar. I thought I heard movement." He rubbed his messy bedhead. "That's so weird. I listened before I woke you up, you know, to be sure. I could've sworn I heard clothes rustling."

Alarm widened my eyes. "My clothes? In my wardrobe?" I jumped up to look under the panel.

"Let me look." Tayo leapt to his feet. "If they've come through the tunnel, then they already know more than they should." Tayo grabbed his trousers and climbed down the ladder.

I waited, peering into the dingy hole. When Tayo didn't return, I took a few steps down the ladder, seeing him coming back, shaking his head. "Nothing. Sorry, Roar."

I laughed. "Don't worry, you nutter."

Closing the wardrobe door, he followed me back to bed. Before I could let him go back to sleep, I stole a long, slow kiss. Until it was a new day, it didn't count.

In the morning, Tayo's gentle strokes up and down my forearm woke me up. The mood lights were already on, but the alarm hadn't rung yet. Remembering my night, I hid my smile in my pillow.

Tayo adjusted onto his elbow and hugged my head, whispering against it, "You'll remember that for the rest of your life."

"I will." My insides felt like they were glowing, and I smooshed my face harder into the fluffy pillow. He swept the hair away and left tiny kisses on my temple. If only I could go back and relive the entire evening all over again.

Tayo climbed out of bed, and I already wanted to pull him back on. Watching him get dressed, heaviness set in my chest. Our night was really over. I dragged my body up and looked at my new self in the mirror. I didn't know what changes I expected. Nothing had changed, but I felt different. Doing a double take, I gasped at my reflection. "*Tayo*, my neck."

"Oh shit, sorry, Roar." He came over and stroked the nasty purple mark on my skin. "I really...I honestly don't remember doing that."

"What am I going to do?"

"Don't you have makeup to cover it?"

"No. Silliah does. I'll go see her before breakfast." Reminded of my night with Tayo, I smiled and held onto my neck. "Go on, you should go. I've gotta get going."

He came and kissed my neck, brushing my hair behind my shoulder. "I love you, Roar. More than you'll ever know."

"I love you, too."

Tayo's forehead lifted. "You...you've never said that to me before."

I shuffled on the spot, unsure where to put my hands. "I...we can't do that again, though. I wanted it to be you, but I still can't be with either of you."

"I know. This place has fucked everything up. I know you love him, too. I know you can't choose. But I can't leave you alone either."

"I don't want you to leave me alone. But you know we can't do that again, right?"

"I couldn't care less about him and what he thinks, but yeah, for you, fine." He ran a thumb over my love bite. "Kiss me one last time before I have to go back to controlling myself?"

Before we found ourselves in the ensuite, Tayo left, and I went to see Silliah. Still recovering from a broken pelvis, she was in bed when I arrived.

"How you feeling?" I asked, hugging her gently, making her Primary veins invisible, and then sitting at her feet.

"Thank you." She checked the veins in her wrist. "A lot better. You should see my stomach, though."

"I remember what mine—"

Brindan came out of the ensuite. Only Silliah knew I was beaten up by Beignley, and I had asked her to keep it to herself.

"What are you doing, Aurora?" Brindan's impolite greeting stunned me into silence. "He is not *done*. Why can't you see what you're doing to him?"

I opened my mouth to speak but then realised he wasn't done.

"If you had any decency, you would get rid of that f'in loser and choose your fiancé. You're his whole world. I wish I could tell him to walk away, tell him you're not worth it, but he physically *can't* walk away—"

"Brindan," Silliah cut him off.

"No, Silliah. Somebody has to say it. You're being so selfish, Aurora. I don't know what you did to upset him last night, but I've never seen my best friend cry. Imagine if I was doing to Silliah what you're doing to Pax. You'd be saying the same thing to me. Stop being so selfish, and be faithful to your betrothed."

All I could do was nod as this great balloon swelled in my stomach. If he was treating Silliah like I was treating Pax, then I would definitely be having the same conversation with him.

"I'm not choosing either of them, Brindan."

"Really? Because that mark on your neck is telling me differently. You are *betrothed*. It's disgusting, Aurora."

Tears rolled down my cheeks.

"Brindan, that's enough," Silliah said, bringing her legs out the duvet.

"Lil." Brindan reacted to his injured partner getting up. "I'm going. Stay in bed." He kissed her head and tucked her under the duvet. "Aurora, I love you. You know I do. But seriously, sort yourself out. You are an Enforcer. The institute chooses our partners. Whether you like it or not, that's just the way it is. Now, get rid of the loser and be with your fiancé. You don't get to *choose*; you are betrothed." He edged closer and closer to his room until he shut the door behind him.

The tears came heavy, and I covered my face.

"Aurora, don't cry." Silliah got out of bed and cradled my head. "Let me get some makeup for you." She turned into the ensuite, returning with her makeup bag, and starting to dab foundation on my neck. "You and Tayo did…" She nodded as the last word in her sentence.

I nodded, eyes on my lap.

"Oh."

My stomach turned at her lack of response. What had I done?

I stayed with Silliah for a little while before her breakfast arrived and Brindan came back into the room. I'd had time to talk to her about my excursion to the temple with Tayo last year, and I apologised for pretending it was with her.

When I left her room, my Slate vibrated, and Tayo's name showed on screen: '*Gorgeous…you're all six. Hide the mark, numpty.*'

It was kind of coded, but I understood. Why didn't I think of that? I smiled, holding the love bite and thinking of my evening.

"Aurora."

My smile dropped, and I turned around. Pax tipped his head back to beckon me. I couldn't look at him after what I'd done, but I forced my feet to go to him. He pulled me to one side, allowing Navies to pass us in the corridor.

"I'm sorry, okay?" he said quietly. "I don't want things to be awkward between us. I didn't mean to talk to you like that."

I only nodded, stuck for words and staring into his dull amber eyes.

"I forget I can't just—"

It was tears coming to his eyes that made him break his sentence. I continued nodding, not exactly sure what his sentence was going to be but knowing even the thought was hard for him.

"Sometimes"—he inhaled sharply—"I forget I can't just...not see you again, block your number, you know, what normal people would do after they...break up." He shrugged, not feeling like he was choosing the right words. "I forget I have to see you again in the morning, and I don't want things to be awkward for the rest of our time here. You already said separate lives and separate houses; I shouldn't have acted like we were anything more."

I nodded more until Pax laughed. "Yeah?" He nodded with me. I wasn't giving him much to gauge my feelings. "Do you forgive me?"

Remembering what I'd done with Tayo last night and feeling I'd gone too far to ever turn back, I pushed my fingers onto my eyes, uselessly blocking my tears. The guilt was severe, making me feel physically sick. I now had another secret to keep from him, one which was easier to keep when he hated me.

"Hey, sweetheart, stop." Pax led me round to our bedrooms, stepping in and turning to me. "Look"—he wiped my tears with his wrists—"I'm not saying this so you pick me, okay? I know you don't. I just want us to get along whilst we can't go our separate ways."

"I don't choose either of you."

"Aurora, it's fine. Just be with him, okay?"

I shook my head. "If I choose him, I lose you. And I can't lose you."

"Sweetheart, I couldn't be here without you either. That's why I asked you to put your invitation down." He broke eye contact and gazed towards the floor, shaking his head. "Look, I'm keeping my promise, and I'm stopping you from being united again so you can still be with your friends and Nanny Kimly. Then, after we're discharged, I'm going to move to another city. I know it's not what you want to hear, but you'll be happy. But right now, just please hide it from me. Please? I can't see it."

"Pax, I'm not being with either of you. I'm not lying when I say that. I'm not choosing to be with either of you."

"Brindan told me."

My heart punched me in the chest.

"Pax—"

"It's okay. You're free to do whatever you want. I'm just saying I'm out, please do what makes you happy, and *please*, hide it whilst we're here together."

"It's not going to happen again, I promise you. When I'm with you, I want you, and when I am with him, I want him. It's not fair, and from now on it stops. When I leave here, I want a friendship with you both. You can be my friend, can't you?"

Pax's face showed discomfort.

"If I was single, could you be my friend?" I rephrased my question.

"Yes."

"We control ourselves. That's it. That's all we have to do. Please don't move cities."

After Pax nodded, a silence crept between us. Although I felt empty, I weirdly felt less pain. I could have them both, without having them both.

"Come here." Pax pulled me under his chin. "I love you, Aurora."

"I love you, too."

✹✿✹

Hmm, yes, control…that word. So…Tayo had been staying over for a while, but tonight I'd told him not to. Tonight, I told him he had to go home after we were done practising in the temple. We'd been purely platonic, though. I wouldn't kiss him again, that much I was sure. No matter how hard it was. If I kissed one, I would hurt the other, and I wasn't doing it.

"You know what?" said Tayo, creating a ball of yellow-white Chi in his palms and making it disappear. "I'm pleased I'm going home tonight."

"Oh, really?" I closed the grimoire with a hefty thump, turning to face him.

"Yeah, I've been waking up in the middle of the night with the weirdest feeling, and I think I just need my own bed."

"You probably feel weird because we're not supposed to be doing it anymore."

"Pfft. Yeah, that's why I feel weird." He laughed, forming another ball of Chi without an incantation and snuffing it out. "I can do whatever I want, Roar."

"Okay, well *I'm* not supposed to be doing it."

"Hmm. I'd like to see you try and stop me."

"Tayo, I'm stopping you tonight."

"That's cute you think that."

"Oh…" I shook my head speechlessly.

"Ohhh…" Tayo shook his head, mocking me.

I fired my own ball of Chi at his chest. He knew it was coming, though, and he casually stepped aside.

"Nice try, but I'm an Intuitionist."

"Good night, loser." I walked out of the grimoire room. "I'm going to bed."

Tayo jogged after me. "Friends still hug, right?"

"Fine, but as long as you *are* moving on, Tayo."

"Oh, I'm on, way, way on. I'm beyond on."

"You're a twat." I placed my hand on the door. "You'll always be a twat."

"You'd hate it if I hooked up with someone else," he said quietly into my ear. He spun me to face him. "So stop telling me to move on."

I glanced at his silky lips but quickly switched to his eyes. "I just don't want to cause you any pain or string you along. I'm never choosing. You're free to go."

"I'm not going anywhere." He playfully bit my neck, latching on until I wriggled free. I smiled and held the tingling in my neck. He stepped back and waved me down my tunnel, knowing he wasn't allowed to come with me. I pretty much walked backwards, keeping my eyes on him, all the way to the transportation barrier. It felt weird walking back to my bedroom alone. When I climbed the ladder, I stood there, staring around the empty room. Sighing heavily, I touched my Slate in my pocket. Could I ask him to come back?

Distracting myself from sending the message, I went to say goodnight to Pax.

He put his Slate down on his lap. "Tayo not with you tonight?"

"No. I told him to go home."

Pax nodded. "You can stay in here if you want."

"Nope. I've gotta do this. I'm feeling weird, and I've got to learn to sleep on my own again."

"Alright." Pax laughed. "But you've slept on your own your whole life; I'm sure you've got this."

"I'm even going to shut the door, look." I closed the interconnecting door, shutting me off alone in my huge, dark room. "Okay"—I reopened the door—"no, I'm not. That's too adult for me."

"You *can* stay in here."

I glanced over his bed, at the space next to him where I could snuggle in. "Next time."

Pax gave a slow nod, a slight pensive look in his eyes. "Goodnight, then."

"Goodnight."

I cosied up in my bed, stretching out and trying to convince myself I liked the space. Forcing my limbs to remain idle for about thirty seconds, I opened my eyes to see if Pax's light was still on. His room was pitch black. *Get a grip.* I pushed my face into the pillow. Pax was right; I'd spent most of my life in my own bed. Tonight was no different. But a horrible drawing in my gut told me it was.

Feeling around for my Slate, I clutched it, thinking about Tayo. I was so used to hearing his voice before I drifted off to sleep. A sinking feeling travelled to my stomach. *Would it be wrong to call him?* Each finger pressed to my thumb repetitively as I wondered whether I could ask him to come back. I lifted my Slate to check the home screen, hoping to see a message from him.

It was clear.

I huffed, twisting onto my side, blocking the Slate out of my sight.

Pax and Tayo were at two ends of the room. Fell agents restrained them, stopping them from coming to me. Poison blackened the veins in their necks. I held one antidote. I had to choose. They both dropped to their knees, the poison passing through into its final stage. They would both die if I didn't choose. I turned from one to the other as they crushed their faces into the ground. Who do I choose? *Who do I choose?*

My body twisted side to side restlessly. Waking up was a mercy. I felt the sheets damp beneath my cold body. Sliding from Tayo's side of the bed, I grabbed his pillow and switched to my side.

A figure watches me sleep from beneath the shadows of their hood. They pull a twisted black dagger out from their cloak. With two hands around the handle, they thrust it downwards, impaling my stomach.

Excruciating pain burst under my rib cage. A shadowy figure moved beside my bed. I grabbed their wrist, spinning them into a chokehold and strangling the life from them. They wriggled and thrashed, flapping desperately with their cloak. Then, as if by magic, they evaporated in my arms, something metal clanging to the ground.

"PAX," I screamed, clutching onto my dripping wet stomach.

"Aurora?" I heard scuffling. "Lights on, Soami."

I met his eyes and watched his face disfigure. I fell to my knees, blood soaking through my fingers.

"I've got you." He caught my depleted body. "I've got you," he said again, pushing down on my wound. He removed one hand, horrified by the amount of blood dripping from his fingers. "Aurora, can you—can you heal it?"

I couldn't see.

"No. Stay with me, Aurora."

Darkness devoured me as his words slowly registered. "*Tepior,*" I mumbled the spell.

Numbness set in my toes, travelling up my body.

"No, no, no, no. You're not dying. Come on, Aurora, *heal yourself.*" His trembling voice sounded in the distance. "No, Aurora. Open your eyes. Please stay with me. *Please.*"

Sleep consumed me. I felt nothing.

CHAPTER THIRTY-FOUR

WHO IS SHE?

"She is breathing, but she's not responding. I tried healing her as much as I could, but I don't know what I'm doing. It won't heal. You have to help her, Tayo."

"Mmm," I groaned at the pain in my stomach.

"Baby girl." Tayo touched my face. "Can you hear me?"

"Mmmm-guh-gug." Liquid felt like it gurgled up my throat. I coughed, feeling water spray through my fingers. Blood spotted Tayo's face. I choked again, drenching myself in red.

Tayo could see I started to panic, and he held a towel up to my mouth. "You're okay, Roar. You're okay. You're going to be fine." He nodded jerkily, wiping blood from around my neck. "Pax, you need to heal her *now*."

"I don't know how."

"Come here." Tayo kept his hand behind my head and attended to me as I coughed up more blood. After wiping my hands clean again, he turned to Pax. "It's a full moon. You *can* do it. You need to relax, more than you've ever relaxed in your whole life. You think of this one, you think of her and everything she means to you. It's the strongest emotion and the most powerful for magic. You have the full moon to help you. *Tepior* is the incantation, but you don't need to say it like me. You say it however feels right to you. Do not think about magic. Think about her. Now, use your hands." Tayo placed Pax's hands over my wound above my stomach.

Pax closed his eyes and breathed himself calm. He was following Tayo's instructions exactly. I could see by his face he had completely disassociated himself from the present moment. He looked peaceful, almost angelic. "*Tepior*," Pax said with a hearty vibration in his throat.

He opened his eyes, watching the smoky green mist swirling in strands. My body soaked it up. When the magic stopped, the drowning sensation faded, and I reached my hand out to Pax. He took it with both of his, coming to sit by my side.

"Thank you, Pax."

He gave a slow bow of the head, cupping my cheek and giving a relieved exhale. "You scared me, sweetheart."

I looked over at Tayo. "Somebody tried to kill me, Tayo."

"Who was it?"

"I don't know. I didn't see them."

Tayo came to undo the bloody pyjama shirt tied around my torso. The pressure released, but I winced at a sharp sting. "Shh. I know," Tayo spoke gently. "I know. Just let me see." He undid the bottom buttons on my pyjama shirt. "Oooh-kay." Tayo immediately covered the wound with Pax's bloody shirt. "We're going to need another shirt."

Pax fetched a fresh one, and they both fixed up my wound. After one more attempt, Pax managed to heal my cut, leaving a bumpy pink scar on my solar plexus. Tayo helped me out of my bloody clothes and began throwing all the stained items down into the tunnel to be disposed of later. I felt so abnormal and empty, and I think still in shock from being stabbed in the dead of night. Neither of them wanted to leave me alone, and we sat on the bed, recovering from the evening's events.

"What's happened to your hair?" Pax asked with a mild frown.

I ran my hair between my fingers, recognising it by touch but not by colour. Deep auburn covered every trace of white. "I have no idea." I now had auburn hair to explain to everyone at breakfast.

Coming out of my thoughts, my eyes focused on something shiny by the bed. "What's that?"

Pax followed my eyeline, leaning over to get the item beside the platform steps. He turned it over in his fingers and gave it to me. "It's not yours?"

"No." I examined the foreign object. It was a gold cuff bangle with a hinge, covered in familiar symbols and patterns.

"Show me that." Tayo narrowed his eyes on it. "I've seen that before."

He took it from me and gave it a sudden perplexed look like it had just done something abnormal. It hadn't done anything visibly, but he looked back up at me. "Can't you feel that?" He held the bangle out like he was weighing it.

"What? Can I feel what?"

"I don't know what it is. It feels like…" He looked at me, his face muscles taut. "I know whose this is—but it has magic."

Nanny Kimly burst through my bedroom door. "Lock the door, please, Tayo," she said, her eyes small and serious. "Why isn't it locked? That is very careless of you."

Tayo's eye pinched, not appreciating being told off, but he listened anyway, locking the door with his Slate. "Sorry, Nanny K, I was too busy saving Aurora's life."

"Well, that's no use if you're found in her room, now, is it?" Nanny Kimly had no intention of listening to his reply, and she stepped closer to me. "What happened, Little Lady?"

I explained every detail I could remember, after which Pax and Tayo explained the aftermath.

"How did you know, Nanny Kimly?" I asked, still startled by her sudden arrival.

"I'm an Astralist. I saw you fighting with her."

"Her?"

"Yes, the Kalmayan Queen."

Tayo gave Nanny Kimly the bangle. "This is hers. But I can feel it has magic."

"Is it just a bangle, Aurora? Can you see through an illusion?" She held it out in her palm for me to see.

"No. It's just a bangle. How did she get into my room?"

"Magic." Nanny Kimly answered simply. "She used a sepuldel."

"A sepuldel?"

"Yes. You can only traverse into a place you have physically been to before. *Unless* you have a sepuldel in the room. It's a Puracordis symbol, similar to your birthmark."

I widened my eyes at Tayo. "The piece of paper I showed you a while back. The one I thought was yours."

"Where is it now?" asked Nanny Kimly.

"It's gone. I threw it in the bin."

"That'll be destroyed now, but she already has access. I don't know what arrangement you have here"—she gestured between Tayo and Pax—"but you're not to sleep on your own until this room is protected, do you understand?"

"I can protect myself," I said, curling my lip.

Tayo, Pax, and Nanny Kimly exchanged uncertain looks.

"Aurora." Pax tried with a small frown. "I think it's for the best."

"Pffft. Aww, Paxton." My mouth twisted into a sardonic smile. "Do you want me to sleep in your bed?"

Pax took an obvious intake of air, paused with a bewildered look, and glanced at the other two. He let go of his breath. "It doesn't have to be my bed; you can have Tayo stay with you."

"No, really, I'm good."

Tayo scratched his eyebrow but didn't say a word.

"We need a protection spell on this room." Nanny Kimly stared blankly at the wardrobe. "Do it with Tayo and Silliah." She turned back to me. "Two Primaries and the Guidal together will make it last longer." She paused in thought again, chewing on her lip. "One thing I don't understand is why somebody who practises Puracordis would want the Guidal dead. But it does make me think she's acting alone. If she is acting alone, it means she hasn't informed Seioh Boulderfell of the magic being practised under his roof.

"Now, I'm not certain, but I think you have the source of her power"—she handed the bangle to Tayo—"which means she's not coming back anytime soon. Somebody with her intentions would be Taheke for absolute certain, so she doesn't have access to her own powers. But she will be back for that. Can you put it somewhere safe, Tayo?"

"Of course."

"We'll want some Illusionist magic on that, too, but for now, you must all carry on as normal. You have duties, and you're expected at breakfast soon. Tayo, I'm sure you have work to attend."

He gave me a glance out the side of his eye. Tayo was a law unto himself. "No, Nanny K. I'm going to sleep, and then I'm reading through the grimoire to find out more about this." He opened and closed the golden bangle.

"Of course. Well, I'm going to have to use a bit of magic myself and find out what I can see. Aurora, I'll come back later, okay?"

"Okay." I shrugged.

She ran my auburn hair between her fingers, gave me a small touch on the head, and made for the door.

"Are you...okay, Roar?" Tayo observed my face carefully.

"I'm fine. Why?"

"You just"—he looked at Pax to finish his sentence—"seem a bit off?" He gave Pax a nod for his agreement.

"I've just been stabbed, you doofus. I think you'd be a little bit off, too." I swung my legs off the bed. "I'm having a shower."

Pax and Tayo stayed behind, sitting still and rigid. I could still hear them from the ensuite.

"Do you think she's a bit…off?" Tayo said quietly.

"Maybe she's in shock."

"Yeah." Tayo didn't sound convinced.

There was a small pause before Pax spoke, "Tayo, could you… could you teach me how to protect her?"

"Yeah—yeah, of course."

"I *can* hear you, you know?" I shouted out.

"Aurora, come here," Tayo called me by my full name.

"*Ugh. What?*" I leant against the archway.

"Can I trust you?" Tayo asked me to show.

I rolled my eyes, expecting my skin to respond in kind. Only my skin didn't react, and I actually smiled down at my ivory paleness. "Hm. Well, maybe you can't." I shrugged, turning back to the ensuite. I was about to close the door for the second time, when I heard Tayo whispering. I tiptoed into the walkway to hear.

"—isn't just negative thinking; it can be caused by a traumatic experience. She couldn't feel the magic in the bangle, she can't show, and there's something about her that's completely off. I think being stabbed has made her Taheke."

Not convinced, I checked down at my birthmark to see if my magic still covered it. My skin was clear. Everything seemed fine. Just to double check, I went back into the ensuite and made a ball of Chi.

My stomach dropped at the empty space between my palms.

I tried again, not feeling anything in my body, no emotion, no power, no magic.

"*Day Alanjay.*" I tried the beginner's spell for Chi.

Nothing, no flicker, no flash, no yellow and white light.

"*Spella Tair.*" It had to be my blood. "*Spella Tair.*"

Nothing.

I looked down to see through the illusion on my birthmark.

My birthmark was no longer on my wrist. I rubbed the spot as if to uncover it. Tayo was right. My magic really was…gone.

9 798890 069986